DATE DUE			

Reaper

Also by Larissa Ione

Reaper
A Demonica Novel
By Larissa Ione

EVIL EYE
CONCEPTS

Reaper
A Demonica Novel
By Larissa Ione

Copyright 2019 Larissa Ione
ISBN: 978-1-970077-44-5

Published by Evil Eye Concepts, Incorporated

This is a work of fiction. Names, places, characters and incidents are the product of the author's imagination and are fictitious. Any resemblance to actual persons, living or dead, events or establishments is solely coincidental.

Acknowledgments from the Author

Hey, everyone!

Okay, grab yourself a mug of coffee, or a glass of wine, or a bottle of beer (yay, beer!), because I want to have a chat.

See, I love writing. I love being an author. I love the characters who live in my head and demand to get out so readers can get to know them.

But sometimes life gets in the way, and creativity gets sidelined. Thanks to an incredibly busy few years, I had to slow down as we built a new house, sent our son off to college and then moved him back home, moved my mom from Oregon to Wisconsin, adopted a crazy dog, and...the list goes on.

All the while, the voices in my head still demanded stories. I couldn't indulge them as much as I'd have liked, but thankfully I had incredible support from everyone around me. I owe so many people so much, starting with Liz Berry and M.J. Rose, who allowed me to keep my head in the Demonica world while maintaining a schedule I could handle.

Now we're at the end of the series they let me write for Evil Eye, and we're ending on a big note.

REAPER is a book I've wanted to write for years – a book of pure action, of dark twists, and of lasting consequences. What happens today will have repercussions decades from now...as you'll soon find out.

But before we turn the page, I want to send some gratitude out into the world.

To my friends and family who have put up with my deadlines and crazy schedules, thank you for your support and patience. Bryan and Brennan, you have been especially supportive, and I love you more than I can say.

To Liz Berry and M.J. Rose, I truly can't thank you enough – not just because of what you've done for me, but what you've done for so many women. Your respect for authors, readers, and the genre, is obvious in everything you do.

To Kim Guidroz...damn, girl, you have saved my ass a million times, and I'm so grateful to you! You're a treasure and I adore you, and I'm so happy that you're in my life. You are truly one of my favorite people ever.

Speaking of treasures, Chelle Olson, thank you for all your hard work making sure REAPER is polished to perfection. I'm going to smother in you in hugs when I see you next!

I also have to send out oodles of hugs and thanks and Jell-O shots to a group of ladies who have become the people I count on for my sanity. Once a year, you Babes set the tone for the rest of my year, and I always look forward to our time together. Lara Adrian, Shayla Black, Lexi Blake, Lorelei James, Suzanne Johnson, Julie Kenner, and Jillian Stein and, of course, the already mentioned Kim and Liz. And special thanks to Steve Berry for putting up with us! (OMG, Steve Berry washed my dishes!!!!)

And Judie Bouldry! I'm not even sure what to say to the woman who has had my back for years now. I love you and appreciate everything you do, and I wish we could spend more time together…in Europe would be ideal!

Kat Daugherty, thank you for the last-minute read and the fabulous advice. You're just what I needed when I needed it. Let's keep doing this, k?

And last but not least, to my readers who have followed my journey, thank you for being there and for trusting me to give you tales with happy endings…even if the journey to get there was rough as hell.

As we dive into REAPER, I'm going to ask that you trust me one more time.

But you really might want to refill that wine glass first…

Glossary

Fallen Angel—Believed to be evil by most humans, fallen angels can be grouped into two categories: True Fallen and Unfallen. Unfallen angels have been cast from Heaven and are earthbound, living a life in which they are neither truly good nor truly evil. In this state, they can, rarely, earn their way back into Heaven. Or they can choose to enter Sheoul, the demon realm, in order to complete their fall and become True Fallens, taking their places as demons at Satan's side.

Harrowgate—Vertical portals, invisible to humans, which demons use to travel between locations on Earth and Sheoul. Very few beings own, or can summon, their own personal Harrowgates.

Inner Sanctum—A realm within Sheoul-gra that consists of six Rings, each housing the souls of demons categorized by their level of evil as defined by the Ufelskala. The Inner Sanctum is run by the fallen angel Hades and his staff of wardens, all fallen angels. Access to the Inner Sanctum is strictly limited, as the demons imprisoned within can take advantage of any outside object or living person in order to escape.

Memitim—Earthbound angels assigned to protect important humans called Primori. Memitim remain earthbound until they complete their duties, at which time they Ascend, earning their wings and entry into Heaven. See: Primori

Primori—Humans and demons whose lives are fated to affect the world in some crucial way.

Radiant—The most powerful class of Heavenly angel in existence, save Metatron. Unlike other angels, Radiants can wield unlimited power in all realms and can travel freely through Sheoul, with very few exceptions. The designation is awarded to only one angel at a time. Two can never exist simultaneously, and they cannot be destroyed except by God, Satan, or the Heavenly Council of Orders. The fallen angel equivalent is called a Shadow Angel. See: Shadow Angel

Shadow Angel—The most powerful class of fallen angel in

existence, save Satan. Unlike other fallen angels, Shadow Angels can wield unlimited power in all realms, and they possess the ability to gain entrance into Heaven. The designation is awarded to only one angel at a time, and they can never exist without their equivalent, a Radiant. Shadow Angels cannot be destroyed except by God, Satan, or the Heavenly Council of Orders. The Heavenly angel equivalent is called a Radiant. See: Radiant.

Sheoul—Demon realm. Located on its own plane deep in the bowels of the Earth, accessible to most only by Harrowgates and hellmouths.

Sheoul-gra—A holding tank for demon souls. A realm that exists independently of Sheoul, it is overseen by Azagoth, also known as the Grim Reaper. Within Sheoul-gra is the Inner Sanctum, where demon souls go to be kept in torturous limbo until they can be reborn.

Sheoulic—Universal demon language spoken by all, although many species also speak their own language.

Ter'taceo—Demons who can pass as human, either because their species is naturally human in appearance, or because they can shapeshift into human form.

Ufelskala—A scoring system for demons, based on their degree of evil. All supernatural creatures and evil humans can be categorized into the five Tiers, with the Fifth Tier comprised of the worst of the wicked.

Watchers—Individuals assigned to keep an eye on the Four Horsemen. As part of the agreement forged during the original negotiations between angels and demons that led to Ares, Reseph, Limos, and Thanatos being cursed to spearhead the Apocalypse, one Watcher is an angel, the other is a fallen angel. Neither Watcher may directly assist any Horseman's efforts to either start or stop Armageddon, but they can lend a hand behind the scenes. Doing so, however, may have them walking a fine line that, to cross, could prove worse than fatal.

Prologue

Somewhere in the Arabian Peninsula, thousands of years earlier...

Gabriel stared at the hut built of sticks, stones, and animal hides and wondered how a fellow angel could possibly live there. Willingly. It wasn't as if Asrael had lost his wings and had to live in the human realm as a powerless, pathetic Unfallen, after all.

He'd just done something stupid.

And really, who hadn't? Stupidity wasn't a reason to isolate yourself for centuries from all living things and live in squalor.

The full desert sun scorched everything it touched as Gabriel approached the dwelling, but he barely noticed. Nothing else stirred, not even in the shade cast by the rocky outcroppings surrounding Asrael's hut. Which was probably why he'd chosen to live here. No one but thieves and demons would venture into this desolate region, and he was well equipped to handle both.

"Asrael?" he called out. "I know you're in there."

There was a pause, and then a gruff, "Why can't I sense you?"

"Because I'm controlling my emotions." Gabriel turned his face into a hot breeze, letting it blow his blond hair out of his eyes. "Also, I drank some plum wine with a nip of *flittablume*. I'm so numb, you could punch me in the throat, and I wouldn't care."

The door creaked open on wobbly hinges, and Asrael filled the doorway. "I'm not passing up an opportunity to throat punch an archangel."

Gabriel laughed. Asrael's humor was still intact. And he looked the same as he had the last time Gabriel saw him, except his once short black hair was now down to his shoulders. And instead of plush, colorful robes, he now wore a pale-beige, coarsely woven tunic.

That thing had to itch.

"I knew that would bring you out of your hovel."

"Hovel?" Asrael stepped out, his sandaled feet slapping on a mat woven of reeds. "I built this with my own two hands."

Gabriel eyed the rickety hut and wondered how it was even standing. "I can see that."

"Jackass."

"See how well the *flittablume* is working? I'm not annoyed in the least by your insult."

"Well, maybe you should share the flying flower juice with me, because I'm annoyed by your presence." Asrael folded his arms across his chest. "Why are you here?"

"Why are *you*?"

"I live here."

"You don't have to."

A shadow dulled the emerald glints in Asrael's eyes. "I do, and you know it."

"Asrael, you could just as easily isolate yourself in the vastness of Heaven. There are corners of our realm no one will ever step foot in. You need to punish yourself this way."

"I'm responsible for Jaguriel losing his wings, which makes me responsible for his death. My arrogance got him killed. I should have lost my own wings for that, but for some reason, the Council of Angels chose not to punish me."

"You accused Jaguriel of murder," Gabriel said, "but you believed it to be true, and with reason. Everyone believed it before you even interrogated him."

"He killed himself," Asrael growled. "And all the Council passed down as punishment was to assign me a temporary job, processing humans who'd crossed over. It was boring, but it was not a punishment."

Processing traumatized humans into Heaven was definitely a punishment. Torturously menial. But, personally, Gabriel hadn't thought Asrael deserved even that. Jaguriel might have been innocent in the murder of a fellow angel, but he'd been under investigation by the Internal Corruption Investigation unit for other sins.

Still, Asrael had felt the need for penance, and he'd sworn to do better at his regular job as an interrogator, leading to the idiotic decision to increase his empathic ability through a sketchy spell. Gabriel could have told him it would go wrong.

And it had. His ability had increased a thousandfold, making him so sensitive to the emotions of others that it pained him, often leaving him overloaded and incapacitated.

"So, you did something foolish and can't be around humans or angels anymore." Gabriel shrugged. "So what? Like I said, you could have isolated yourself in Heaven, too. You'd have been in luxury. So why"—he made a gesture that encompassed all of the barren nothingness—"here?"

"Because the human realm has something Heaven doesn't." The light in Asrael's eyes sparked again. "Demons. I get to kill them here."

That was exactly what Gabriel had hoped Asrael would say.

Gabriel watched a dull gray lizard skitter across a boulder. In Heaven, reptiles sparkled. The earthly realm was so boring and bland. "What if I told you I know a place where your empathic abilities won't work, you can have anything you want, and you can punish demons all day long?"

Asrael snorted. "And where is this magical place?"

"It hasn't been built yet, but it'll exist as its own realm in the space between the human and demon realms. We're going to call it Sheoul-gra."

"I see." Asrael paused, and Gabriel felt a tingle spread across his skin. Asrael was reaching out with his empathic gift, probably trying to probe for sincerity...or deception. "What is Sheoul-gra's intended purpose?"

"To contain demon souls." Tired of squinting in the sunlight, Gabriel poofed a cloud into existence overhead, blocking the direct light and saving himself from a headache later. "Right now, when a demon's physical body dies, his soul is left wandering. You've been in isolation, so you might not have noticed that a growing number of demonic souls are wreaking havoc in human settlements, haunting people. Possessing them. They're doing the same in Sheoul. We've come to an agreement with Satan that will ensure souls are gathered and stored in a secure location presided over by a fallen angel."

"Intriguing," Asrael said in a cool, composed voice as if he didn't want to give away just how interested he was in the concept. "So, why are you telling me this?"

"We want you to run it."

Asrael might be more enamored with the idea than he was letting on, but he wasn't a fool, and he eyed Gabriel with a healthy dose of skepticism. "How many have already turned you down?"

"None. You were our first choice."

Asrael's mouth quirked in amusement. "You mean no one applied for the task."

Gabriel shrugged. They'd put out a call for volunteers, but apparently, ruling one's own hell realm wasn't appealing to any angels. No sane or qualified angels, anyway.

"No one of your caliber," Gabriel said truthfully. "We need someone honorable. Someone we can trust. Your history with Satan makes you a valuable asset."

"My history," Asrael mused. "I despised the bastard even before I uncovered his crimes, and he hates me for it. So you assume that I would side with Heaven in any future dispute."

There was no point in denying that the animosity between Satan and Asrael had played a large role in whom the archangels had chosen to rule this new realm, so Gabriel just nodded.

"Is that assumption wrong?"

"Probably not." Asrael looked up at Gabriel's personal cloud, and it swelled, growing darker as it filled with rain. "What would the job entail?"

"Mainly the reaping of all demon souls, as well as the souls of evil humans. You'll be bound to the realm, but you'll create a race of beings who will carry out your grim task on Earth and in Sheoul."

Rain began to pelt the ground. "You said 'mainly.' What else?"

"You'll mete out punishment, authorize reincarnations, and you'll have the power to destroy souls. We can discuss the specifics later. And…" Gabriel trailed off, unsure of how to present the next duty.

"And?"

"The human population is growing," he said, opting to ease the other male into this one. "More and more humans—and even a few demons—are critical to the future of this very planet."

Asrael nodded. "Primori."

"Yes. We've decided they need specialized guardians. Guardians raised among humans to enhance their understanding of the primitive beings our Creator seems to favor." Gabriel stopped the rain. "We want you to father these guardians with angels we send to you."

For a moment, everything went quiet. The rain stopped, and not even the wind stirred. Asrael's expression stilled, and Gabriel instinctively reached for his power. He wasn't even sure why. He was far stronger than Asrael. And yet, he sensed something inside the other male, as if a massive untapped well of strength were about to be unleashed. For the first time, he wondered if choosing Asrael for this was a mistake.

"Let me get this straight," Asrael said quietly. "You want me to fuck an entire race of beings into existence, create another race to collect souls, and torture evil demons?"

Gabriel sighed. Asrael was as blunt and unapologetic as his father had been. "That's an accurate—if crude—summary."

Slowly, Asrael's face turned up to the sky, and his sleek, black wings shot upward. He was the very picture of an angel who felt the call to duty.

Even if it was a shit job. One of isolation and evil and corruption.

But only one person in the universe could do it, and Gabriel suddenly understood that Asrael was that person. He hadn't made a mistake in choosing him. Any mistakes made from here on out wouldn't be Gabriel's.

They'd be Asrael's.

But that wouldn't stop Gabriel from keeping an eye on things.

"I accept." Asrael gave Gabriel a meaningful look. "But I won't create a bunch of new angels, and I'm sure I'll want to make changes to the contract."

Gabriel paused. He'd been sent to get Asrael's acceptance, but Asrael had only agreed to half of what they needed.

He gave a mental shrug. Heaven would get him to accept the terms of the deal later. "Then it's done."

Asrael nodded. "So, what now?"

The cloud above turned black and roiled across the sky, swallowing the blue and the sun. Asrael wasn't doing it, and neither was Gabriel. The wind gathered, screaming across the dunes and spinning up clouds of sand.

"What's happening?"

"It's an omen," Gabriel shouted over the shrieking wind. It was a sign that, for good or for bad, this was supposed to happen.

Lightning streaked overhead as he willed a scythe into his hand, its rustic handle carved from the trunk of a carnivorous death knell oak by a demon woodworker, its blade crafted by Heaven's best weapons-master.

He held out the scythe. "With this, you'll have the power to destroy and create. And your name," Gabriel called out, "is an angelic word that hearkens back to the negotiations with Satan over the great harvest of souls in the prophesized End of Days."

In his other hand, he willed a blade used to sever Heaven's power link from an angel's wings without completely removing them.

"When we're done, you shall, forevermore, be known as Azagoth, Reaper of Souls."

Chapter 1

It was a room few knew about, and even fewer had seen. Not even his mate had known about it until a couple of days ago.

In his quest to ensure that his mate never left him again, Azagoth had come clean about a lot of shit since Lilliana had returned to him two weeks ago, tanned, pregnant, and bonded to a hellhound. But the confession about the existence of this chamber had been a two-parter.

He'd also had to tell her what he planned to do in here.

Inhaling stale air layered with the stench of fear, pain, and sulfur, he trailed his finger over shelves laden with dusty potion bottles and clay pots filled with ingredients any sorcerer would kill their offspring to have in their possession.

But they'd do far worse than that for just five minutes with the object that made this chamber so…special.

It wasn't the pulsing, transparent cage in the corner, constructed from the veins of a shadow wraith. It wasn't the brimstone altar in the center of the room. It wasn't the glowing Symbol of Azagoth forming a giant scythe above the door.

It was the engine that fueled his realm, the furnace of eternal hellfire that formed the entire east wall.

Power radiated from the violet flames, evil power that beckoned Azagoth closer. Already, he felt its malevolence penetrate him, filling a well that had nearly run dry.

Loving Lilliana had opened his heart and allowed the evil inside to leak out.

Now, he had to let it back in.

But only for a little while.

He'd promised.

But the flames called to him, whispering like a lover whose orgasm would burn every ounce of good inside him to ash.

And that was the thing about evil…it felt amazing. It was incredibly freeing when you didn't give a shit about anyone except yourself. And in a world designed for pain, the more you liked doling it out, the happier you were.

Azagoth had been very, very happy for a very, very long time.

And then Lilliana had come along, exposing his emotions and making his heart beat, and for the first time in eons, he'd been the one to feel pain. He hadn't liked it very much, and he'd turned into a "ginormous asshat," as she'd called him more than once.

It had taken her saying goodbye for him to realize that he needed to let her in *more*, not less.

So, he'd told her about the room he'd flagrantly named the Genesis Chamber and the power it gave him. And he'd promised he wouldn't touch the flames no matter how much they enticed him. The charge he'd get from being this close would be enough to fuel what he was about to do.

As if it heard Azagoth's thoughts, a *griminion,* a three-foot-tall male wrapped in a black cloak, spilled out of the spiral staircase behind him and skittered over to the altar in the center of the room. The place where he'd been born.

Grateful for the distraction from the lure of the eternal hellfire, Azagoth patted the altar top. "Hop up here, Asrael. I don't think this is going to hurt. At least, not as much as your creation did."

Asrael, given Azagoth's angelic name, had been the first *griminion* and the mold from which all others were cast. Whatever was done to him was done to all *griminions*.

Which was why Asrael never left the safety of Sheoul-gra.

Heavy footfalls echoed into the room from the staircase, and a moment later, Hades ducked through the doorway, his blue Mohawk brushing the top of the frame and bringing down a cloud of dust.

"Why the fuck did you summon me during my weekly prison inspection?" He frowned at Asrael as he brushed dust off his bare shoulders. The guy had never liked shirts, which his mate, Cataclysm, bemoaned because she couldn't buy him some sort of traditional human garment called an ugly Christmas sweater. At least Hades was cool with pants, even if they were form-fitting, nausea-inducing, color-shifting things. "And what are you doing to him?"

Azagoth drew a glass vial and a plastic container from the bag he'd brought. "I'm upgrading my *griminions*."

Hades' gaze drifted to the eternal hellfire, longing flickering in the ice-blue depths of his eyes. Unlike Azagoth, he'd never touched the flames, but he still felt the infusion of evil and power it delivered. Sweat beaded on his brow and chest as he fought the pull, and in a jerky, uncoordinated motion, he swung back around to Azagoth.

"Upgrading?" he asked, his voice gruff with the effort it took to resist the hellfire. "To do what? How much more efficient can they be at collecting evil souls? They sense death within seconds."

Griminions didn't collect only evil souls. Sometimes, they brought *iffy* human souls as well, and it was up to Azagoth to sort them out. Keep 'em or send them for Heavenly processing, most likely into what some called Limbo, and others Purgatory, where they'd linger until Judgment Day.

But Hades' question was valid. In thousands of years, Azagoth hadn't made any changes to the little demon helpers he'd created. He hadn't needed to. With the notable exception of Satan, no one had ever threatened him or his family.

Things had changed.

"Imagine how much more efficient they'd be at gathering souls if they didn't have to wait for death?" Azagoth measured one precious drop of the liquid from the vial into a bowl made from a human skull. "If they had the capability to kill."

"They already have that."

"Only if I gift it to them individually." Even then, the ability to cause a heart attack or an aneurysm was only temporary. "I'm going to gift *all* of them. Permanently."

"Interesting." Hades watched as Azagoth used a pole to push the bowl just to the edge of the eternal fire. "But won't Heaven flip the fuckity-fuck out?"

"Yes." What Azagoth was about to do wasn't just forbidden; it was *epically* forbidden as his son Journey would say. He'd been on an *epic* kick lately, edging out *mucho* as his favorite—and much overused—word. "Which is why I'm not telling them."

"So…why are you doing it?" Hades wiped his brow as sweat began to drip. "I mean, I've always thought *griminions* should have had the power to kill from the beginning. But why now?"

Normally, Azagoth would be annoyed at being questioned, but

Hades had been with Azagoth for thousands of years, and whatever plans fate had for him, Hades was tied to them, as well.

Flames licked at the bowl, and the liquid inside, venom from Satan's fangs, began to steam. Azagoth drew the bowl back and carefully placed it on the altar next to Asrael.

"You said it yourself yesterday. Shit's getting weird. Bael's death will have consequences, and I don't trust Heaven."

He'd stopped trusting angels long ago, and now that he was no longer responsible for making Memitim, his usefulness might be waning in their view. He needed to be proactive to protect himself, his realm, and his family.

"You didn't kill Bael," Hades pointed out. "Cipher did. Moloc will want revenge on him, not you."

And wasn't that a sore subject? Azagoth had wanted that kill. He'd wanted to claim the death—and the soul—of the fallen angel who had murdered several of Azagoth's sons and daughters. Instead, Cipher had killed him, and Bael's soul had merged with that of his twin brother, Moloc.

"Moloc doesn't want revenge," Azagoth said. "He wants me to release Satan from the prison Revenant and Reaver put him in." And Moloc would do anything to make it happen.

Hades laughed, his fangs glinting in the light from the flames. "Obviously, you're not going to do that. So, why am I here?"

"I need your DNA." Azagoth took a pinch of freshly ground Soulshredder claw powder from the container he'd brought and sprinkled it into the steaming bowl. It hissed and sparked, and a few seconds later, black, foul-smelling smoke rose in a thin tendril that snapped at Azagoth with sharp little teeth when he tried to wave it away.

"Mine? Why?"

The tendril grew longer, its blunt head slithering toward Asrael. "Because the spell calls for it."

"It calls for my DNA." Hades gave him a flat look dripping with skepticism. "Specifically."

"Yes."

Now Hades' skepticism was practically puddling on the floor. "Where did you get this spell?"

The tendril disappeared under Asrael's hood. "From an Orphmage I blackmailed."

"Viscerog?"

"Yup."

Cursing, Hades scrubbed his hand across the top of his Mohawk. "That bastard hates me."

Azagoth snorted. "Probably why he said I needed to cut off a piece of your wing with a dull knife." He glanced up at Hades as he moved the bowl closer to Asrael. "He was very specific about the fact that the blade had to be dull."

"He's full of shit, you know."

"Maybe." Azagoth didn't bother to hide the amusement in his voice. "Probably. But he warned me to follow the recipe exactly. Otherwise, he said my *griminions* would turn into rot-toads. I definitely don't want that."

Asrael's alarmed, high-pitched chatter made it pretty clear that he didn't want that, either.

Hades cursed again, but his wings erupted from his back, knocking jars off the shelves and scraping the ceiling. "Here, you fucker. Maim away."

Azagoth took his sample with a quick flick of the wrist.

Hades walked off the pain as he wandered around the chamber, picking up jars and checking out the items so powerful or secret that Azagoth stored them here instead of displaying them in the room where he kept most of his valuable artifacts.

"You sure you're not going to use your enhanced *griminions* to go after your enemies?" he asked, pausing in front of a tray covered with a velvet cloth.

Azagoth dropped the bit of wing into the bowl. "You think I'd use them as my own private army?"

"The thought occurred to me, yes."

Hades was right. It was definitely something he'd do. The authors of his Sheoul-gra contract had been wise to forbid it. But Azagoth no longer cared about an agreement he'd signed thousands of years ago. He had too much to protect, and arming the *griminions* was more about safeguarding what he had than anything else. They were going to be his firewall, not his attack dogs.

"They are a defensive weapon," he said. "Not an offensive one."

For now.

"I see." Hades lifted the velvet cloth and inhaled sharply at the sight of the two feathers lying beneath it, one white and gold, the other black and silver. "Damn," he whispered. "With these..."

"With those, I could bring down Sheoul-gra's very foundations."

Hades pivoted around, his eyes glowing with intensity. "Are we still talking defensive weapons here? Because from where I stand, it looks like you're prepping for war."

"We do have less than a thousand years before Satan is released from prison and the End of Days begins," Azagoth pointed out, but it was a dodge, and Hades knew it.

"I'm not buying your bullshit," he growled. "But at least tell me you aren't going after Moloc. And that you won't do something stupid, like destroy Sheoul-gra or try to assassinate Reaver."

"Sheoul-gra is safe," Azagoth assured him. "As is Moloc. For now. And Reaver's an asshole, but he's one of the most powerful assholes in all the realms."

Reaver was also the only high-ranking angel to command a measure of Azagoth's respect. The guy's path from angel to Unfallen, then back to angel, and finally to Radiant, had given him a unique insight into the way all the realms worked. He'd proven to be immune to corruption, uninterested in politics, and willing to break the rules when needed.

Hades studied Azagoth for a heartbeat, his expression uncharacteristically serious. "You have a mate and a good life now, Azagoth. I do, too." His words were measured, carefully spoken, and yet...there was a note of warning threaded through them. He was a male protecting what was his. But so was Azagoth. "I...hope it stays that way."

"So do I," Azagoth said gravely. "And that's why I'm doing this. What's that human bit of wisdom? Hope for the best but prepare for the worst? Well, I'm prepping."

Suddenly, the eternal hellfire blasted hot, and Asrael screamed a gut-wrenching, pained sound that, just a few minutes ago, would have made Azagoth feel bad.

But the eternal hellfire had already done its job, smiting his empathy and filling him with the kind of evil that got off on pain.

He hated that it felt good. That it made him want more. That it made him want to step into the flames to amplify the feeling a million times.

Lilliana. Think about Lilliana.

Yes.

That was easy. So easy. Because, ultimately, Lilliana's love felt even better than this.

Chapter 2

If a fellow angel had told Lilliana just ten years ago that she'd someday be living in an upscale subdivision of Hell and would be pregnant with the Grim Reaper's baby, she'd have told them where to shove their halo.

And yet, here she was. Two weeks from giving birth and peering into a fountain that had been flowing with blood when she'd arrived in Sheoul-gra as what amounted to a mail-order bride.

Or a virgin sacrifice.

When Lilliana had first come here, wide-eyed and terrified, the realm Azagoth created had been a barren, cold, dead place that mirrored his heart. Evil had corrupted the former angel, twisting him into a beast. He'd been a demon wearing the face and body of a god.

But with her help and love, Azagoth's heart had started beating again, and as a result, his realm had bloomed into a land of life, filled with animals, plants, and Unfallen angels seeking refuge from the horrors of Sheoul.

There were also Memitim here, scores of them, the offspring of Azagoth and countless angels.

Angels who weren't Lilliana.

She'd gotten over that fact a while ago, mostly because she understood that making all those Memitim—a special class of earthbound guardian angels who had to earn their wings—had been Azagoth's duty for thousands of years.

It also helped that he'd despised the females, and they generally felt the same about him.

Most of Azagoth's adult sons and daughters had already earned their way into Heaven, but those who lived in the human realm or here in Sheoul-gra were still actively serving mankind as protectors of those who were meant to play crucial roles in the future of the world. And, recently, he'd brought in all the younger children from the care of their adoptive—and completely clueless—human parents. The youngsters, ranging in age from eight to twenty, had infused the realm with even more energy.

Energy that would be good for Lilliana's son or daughter.

She sank awkwardly onto a bench along the winding path that led to the Memitim training grounds and sighed as her bodyguard rushed over to help her.

"I'm not an invalid, Jasmine."

Jasmine, a four-hundred-year-old Memitim with the most beautiful honey-colored skin and golden eyes Lilliana had ever seen, grinned. "I know. But you're just so…ungainly."

Like her father, Jasmine always said exactly what she was thinking. It was both charming and annoying. Lilliana liked her though, despite the fact that her mother was a twat-faced bitch. Lilli had actually been glad when Jasmine was assigned as today's guard.

She just wished she didn't need one at all.

But she understood Azagoth's concern. A powerful enemy was targeting those closest to him, getting so close, in fact, that they'd murdered one of his sons *inside* Sheoul-gra. Azagoth had purged his realm of everyone but his offspring and a handful of trusted fallen angels who served him, but he still wasn't willing to take chances. He was so desperate to keep her safe that he was even happy about her new pet hellhound.

She looked around for the beast, but Maleficent had gone hunting earlier in the day, and it could be hours before she returned.

Jasmine gracefully sat down next to her. "How did you even get pregnant? I heard it wasn't planned. But isn't Azagoth supposed to be able to turn his fertility on and off?"

Yup, she said exactly what she was thinking.

Too tired to scold Jasmine for being rude, she looked up at the waxy-leafed trees that lined the pathway and marveled at their ability to survive here without real sunlight.

"He can," she said as a dove landed on a nearby branch. "Many angels can. But it's a conscious thing, and sometimes, fate intervenes."

Jasmine gave a dismissive snort. "You're such an angel."

"I hate to tell you this," Lilliana said, "but you are, too."

"Not like you. You even still have your wings." Jasmine scooted over to make room for the bag over her shoulder. "I mean, you have this goody-goody, everything-happens-for-a-reason thing going on. All I'm saying is maybe the baby isn't a product of fate or design or whatever, but is just the result of you and Azagoth getting carried away. It's kinda romantic, you know?"

Azagoth had a surprising romantic streak, but this kid was definitely not the result of it. No, Lilliana remembered the events that'd led to conception, and it had been raunchy and hot and…damn, she was ready for another night like that.

"Sure," she said. "Romantic."

Jasmine let out a dreamy sigh. "I can't wait to have sex with someone besides myself. I mean, I know Hawkyn got the Memitim Council to loosen the stupid restrictions on fornication, but I've gone this long, you know? Might as well keep enjoying my collection of battery-operated toys until I find *the one*."

She placed Lilliana's tote full of snacks, an iPad, some books, and her phone down next to her.

Lilliana wasn't even allowed to carry a bag. Azagoth's orders, of course. And since most of the Memitim were more frightened of him than they were of her, she couldn't get them to disobey him. She'd tried.

"Thank you for the graphic image," Lilliana said. "Do you know if Cat included treats for Maleficent?"

Jasmine's lip curled in distaste, revealing delicate fangs. "I can't believe Father lets you keep that filthy mutt."

"Your father doesn't *let* me do anything." Lilliana peered into the bag for said treats. Looked like Mal would be disappointed. "And Maleficent is neither filthy nor a mutt."

"Well, she's an asshole," Jasmine muttered.

Laughing, Lilliana pulled a bottle of water from the bag. "She is that."

Hellhounds hated everyone, especially angels. They were ill-tempered, vicious, and they drooled a lot. But somehow, Maleficent had formed a friendship with Lilliana during the months she'd stayed with the Horseman of the Apocalypse known as War and his hellhound-whisperer mate, Cara.

Unfortunately, Maleficent's feelings toward Lilliana didn't extend to Azagoth. Just last night, she'd found them facing off in the courtyard, snarling at each other.

At Lilliana's snapped, "Knock it off, you two," Mal had phased out, and Azagoth had growled, "She bit me in the ass."

He'd probably deserved it.

And…speaking of the devilishly handsome demon, Azagoth appeared at the crest of the path. His brilliant emerald eyes locked on her like a predator homing in on prey. Majestic pillars and towering, intricate statues lined the walkway, but Azagoth made them all seem small and insignificant as he prowled toward her, his lean, powerful body moving with impossible grace.

She shivered as her body reacted with heat and a low, deep ache made itself known at the sight of her mate.

Then the baby kicked, reminding her that she was under doctor's orders to avoid strenuous activity…and sex with Azagoth was definitely on the active, strenuous side.

It. Was. Fabulous.

Azagoth stopped near the bench. "Thanks, Jasmine," he said, the rich baritone of his voice flowing through Lilliana like warm honey. "Take the rest of the day off. I've got it from here."

Jasmine acknowledged him with a nod, waved at Lilliana, and flounced toward the dorms, all skinny jeans, hot pink heels, and attitude.

"I thought you'd be busy judging souls all afternoon." Lilliana patted the bench. "Have a seat."

He sank down next to her, his aged-whiskey scent mingled with a little smoky brimstone today. "I finished early and met with Hades in the Genesis Chamber."

She tried not to show her concern. Her *grave* concern. "Did you do what you talked about?" At Azagoth's pause, a chill went up her spine. "You did, didn't you?"

"I upgraded the *griminions* and gave them the power to kill," he acknowledged.

A knot formed in her gut. Azagoth wouldn't violate the *griminion* clause of his contract on a whim, but she'd still hoped that he would change his mind.

"What if Heaven finds out?" she asked, her stomach letting out a loud rumble despite being unsettled by her mate's casual announcement.

"They won't," he assured her as he reached into the bag. "I only did it as a precaution. As long as I don't order the *griminions* to kill, there's nothing to worry about." He plucked a carrot cake cupcake from one of the containers. "You need to eat." He eyed the treat, its top smeared with cream cheese frosting. "And this looks healthy. Ish."

"We're immortal," she pointed out. "Healthy is irrelevant."

"That demon doctor says otherwise."

That demon doctor was Eidolon, head of Underworld General Hospital, and he had already promised to be there if Lilliana needed him for the birth. She'd been unsure at first, but he'd delivered Cara's baby, as well as the children of two other Horsemen, and Azagoth's daughter, Idess. Heck, he, his brothers, and their UG co-workers had treated and/or saved the lives of countless people in Azagoth and Lilliana's circle.

That they had a circle made her smile. Although the separation from Azagoth had been difficult for both of them, they'd gained a lot more than they'd lost. Including friends.

Unfortunately, as part of her agreement with Heaven, she couldn't leave Sheoul-gra to see them. Only Reaver's interference had allowed her to stay with Cara temporarily, and he'd been clear that after the baby was born, she couldn't leave again except for the daily allowances of an hour of time travel.

"Eidolon told me that some species of immortals have strict dietary requirements to keep them healthy," she said. "The rest of us could survive on nothing but lard if we wanted to."

"I'll remember that next time I order a tray of snacks delivered to you." He shoved the cupcake at her.

She took it with a sigh. "Darling, I've eaten so much lately, I'm about to pop. People keep bringing me fattening food. Except Juliana. She brought me fruit. Who gives a pregnant chick fruit? I ate an apple to be nice, but I really wanted more of the chocolate cake Suzanne made me. Or the petit fours Maddox brought. And Emerico brought me Belgian chocolates from the same shop in Bruges where Jasmine got the chocolates she gave me."

That had been a surprise. She hadn't always been on good terms with Emerico. She shared a tense relationship with several of Azagoth's adult children, in fact. They were all so complex. Children of both good and evil, the only angels who had to earn their wings—they had a lot of resentment. And none of them, save Suzanne, had grown up in stable, loving homes.

After being told the truth of their existence, they were whisked away to training centers, where they spent decades training to fight demons and learning how to watch over their Primori charges. They also learned to fear and despise their father, and for good reason.

He used to be a real bastard.

He'd come around, even if many of his children hadn't. Still, some of them, like Jasmine and Emerico, were making an effort.

"Oh," she added, "I'm hoping Jedda brings me more of those divine little jelly mushrooms she smuggled out of the elf realm."

Ugh, all her babbling had made her hungry.

"Didn't Limos bring you pastries yesterday, too? Is it ironic that the Horseman known as Famine brought you food?" Azagoth pawed through the tote, and it struck her that she loved moments like these with him. They were just two normal people at their happiest, simply…enjoying life. "And what is this? Caramel corn? Why is it people think all pregnant females want is food?"

Laughing, and despite her protests, Lilliana unwrapped the cupcake as if she hadn't eaten in days. "Because it's true."

"Didn't you just say you're going to pop?"

She nodded because it was all she could do with her mouth full.

Smiling, he wiped a bit of frosting off her lower lip. The mere brush of his finger made her long for more. More of his fingers…in more places.

He could get a scoopful of frosting and paint it along the V-neck of her top, using his touch to sweeten her skin for the stroke of his tongue…

After the baby is born.

"Dammit," she breathed.

"Dammit, what?"

"Nothing. I'm just so ready to have this baby."

"Me, too." Standing, he took her tote in one hand and held out the other to her. "I have a surprise for you."

"Where are we going?" She let him help her to her feet, which spared her the awkwardness of trying to get off the stupidly low bench. "Because I gotta be honest, the only place I want to go is into labor."

He laughed, and her knees went weak. He was so damned handsome, and his rare moments of genuine amusement only made him that much more scrumptious. Like a carrot cupcake with extra frosting.

Oh, how she'd missed that when she was away all those months.

"I told you," he said as he led her up the path toward the building that housed the Memitim community center. "It's a surprise."

As they drew closer, the sound of laughter and the drone of voices grew louder.

"What's going on?"

He cocked a dark eyebrow. "You're not grasping the concept of a surprise, are you?"

"Really?" She pinched his ass playfully, loving how Mr. Cool and Collected jumped. "See? I get it." A sudden wave of nausea came out of nowhere, and she wobbled. Azagoth's arm shot out to steady her. "It's okay," she assured him, swallowing sickly until the sensation passed. "I get woozy sometimes."

"I don't like it. Maybe we should call Eidolon."

She blew him off. He'd call Eidolon for a burp. "Just open the door."

He threw open the door, and a chorus of "Congratulations," poured through the entryway. Dozens of Memitim and fallen angels dressed in their party finest surrounded them, their hands full of food and drink. Pop music drummed from the speakers on either side of a table laden with cake, a chocolate fountain, and elegantly wrapped gifts. Sparkling gold, green, and silver balloons, and streamers in the traditional color scheme of Heavenly birth celebrations decorated every available space.

Overwhelmed by love and happiness, she wrapped her arm around Azagoth's waist and held tight. This was not what she'd expected out of life in the underworld.

This was so much better.

Chapter 3

Lilliana woke to someone tap dancing on her bladder.

Groaning, she rolled over and bumped into Azagoth. Pleasantly surprised that he was still in bed, she ignored her need to pee and curled up against him.

She'd missed this so much while she was gone.

"Good morning," he murmured, his husky voice even more gravelly than usual.

"Morning." She snuggled into his shoulder. "I'm surprised you're not working."

He yawned. "You wore me out last night."

Smiling against his skin, she trailed her fingers along the hard ridges and deep valleys of his abs.

"I wanted to show you how grateful I was that you threw me a baby shower." And she'd done it without getting *too* active. Eidolon couldn't begrudge her *one* orgasm, right?

"Mmm." He pressed a kiss into her hair. "You must have been *very* grateful."

She slid her hand under the sheet and meandered her way to the curve of his hip. She might be a million months into her pregnancy, but her sex drive didn't care in the least.

"I'm still grateful."

He hissed as her knuckles brushed his shaft. "Not complaining."

It truly had been sweet of him to gather together the denizens of Sheoul-gra for a big celebration of food, drink, and games in the traditions of people from the human, demon, and angelic cultures. She'd suffered two more bouts of intense nausea and some cramps, but they'd passed quickly. What hadn't passed was Azagoth's concern.

Which was probably why he was still in bed with her.

It was cute the way he hovered. Annoying at times, but cute.

"I just want you to know that you're my life," he said. "Without you, I'm a monster."

"And what are you *with* me?"

He gave her a rare, boyish grin, made even more playful by his mop of bedhead. "A *happy* monster."

"I'm very happy about the happy." She rubbed her eyes and yawned.

"Things are good, Lil," he said. "I never thought much about being a partner, let alone a parent, but I want to do these things with you." He settled his hand on her belly and smiled with wonder. "This will be my first child born without a predetermined future. He or she can be anything. Do anything."

"Incredible, isn't it?" She pushed up on one elbow and leaned in to kiss his chest. She'd kissed every inch of him last night. Maybe she'd lick every inch of him this morning. "And our baby will be born to parents who love each other."

Determined to show him how much she loved him, she kissed her way lower. Her lips whispered over his nipple, but before she could taste him, a cramp wrenched her insides. She sucked in a harsh breath, her hand going to her belly.

"What is it?" Azagoth jackknifed up, his expression dark with worry. "Is it the baby?"

Fierce heat swelled beneath the surface of her skin as her abdomen tightened. "I think it might be Braxton Hicks," she said between panting breaths.

"What?"

"Cara had them." Closing her eyes to stop the room from spinning, she eased back onto her pillow. "They're like practice contractions."

She didn't remember Cara complaining about being hot and sweating buckets, though. Another cramp streaked through her, and she moaned. Cara *had* said they were painful, as if someone were squeezing her intestines.

This was more like someone was driving a red-hot blade through them.

"You're white as a ghost, Lilli."

Something's wrong.

No, nothing was wrong. She was being paranoid.

Azagoth rested his palm on her forehead, testing her temperature. "Are these Hicks things supposed to be like this?"

She heard the panic in his voice but not the words. Her ears were buzzing. Her head was pounding. And, suddenly, a wave of agony wrapped around her and squeezed so hard she screamed. Vaguely, she heard Azagoth call out her name as a warm gush spread between her thighs.

"Lilliana? Lilliana!" His voice droned in and out as the room began to tilt. There was shouting. More pain. Her thoughts fragmented.

And then, finally…nothing.

"*Zhubaal!*"

Terror gripped Azagoth as he shouted for his lieutenant, one of the few fallen angels he trusted with his—and his mate's—life. Naked and not giving a single shit, he tore open the bedroom door and shouted again. There was so much blood…so much.

"Zhubaal! Call Idess. I need a doctor. Now!"

Z had been sprinting through the long, dark hallway toward the bedroom, but he skidded to a halt as he whipped his phone out of the pocket of his jeans.

"And get Cat," Azagoth added. Cat was Lilli's best friend in Sheoulgra. And just as important, she was female. Surely, a female would know what to do. They had instincts and stuff. Right?

Lilliana cried out, and he rushed back to her, his heart surging into his throat.

At least she's conscious.

He told himself that was a good sign.

But the reality, as blood pooled on the mattress beneath her, soaking her white maternity nightshirt, said something different.

"What's wrong with me?" she whispered, her amber gaze glassy, reflections of pain and fear shimmering on the surface.

He gathered her limp body in his arms and tucked her head against his chest, soothing her the only way he knew how.

"I'm sure it's nothing," he said with confidence he didn't feel. "But a doctor is on the way." Azagoth hoped Idess could get Eidolon, but at this point, he'd welcome almost any healer.

He took that back. Heaven had offered to send a team to assist with the birth, but he didn't trust any of them. Angels were a last resort.

Lilliana looked up at him, her pale expression brimming with trust, and his heart both swelled with love and broke with terror. Gently, he stroked her chestnut hair, alarmed by how brittle it felt. Something was very, very wrong.

"I feel lightheaded," she whispered. "Am I bleeding?"

"A little," he said, utterly comfortable with the lie even though he'd sworn to be honest with her. She didn't need the stress of knowing she'd lost enough blood to kill a human. "Can you feel the baby?"

She swallowed. "No."

Closing his eyes, he reached out with his mind. He'd connected with the baby when Lilliana first came back. Had heard…no, *felt*…the child call him "father." Every night since then, he'd awakened with a peaceful sense of awareness that the baby was touching him. Not physically, but mentally.

Now that Lilliana was home, for the first time in his life, he looked forward to sleeping.

Hey, Baby Grim. You there?

He didn't expect a response, but it was still disappointing that there was nothing.

The sound of pounding footsteps echoed from the hallway, and a moment later, Eidolon, Idess, and Cat burst inside all at once. Two of Azagoth's sons, Journey and Emerico, followed but remained inside the doorway as silent, concerned sentinels.

Eidolon strode over, his gold-plated stethoscope dangling over a black scrub top embroidered with Underworld General's specialized caduceus on the pocket. Azagoth had never met the infamous incubus in person, but he was about what Azagoth expected: tall, darkly handsome, and athletic. Tools of the trade for a sex demon.

"What's going on?" he asked, his voice oozing with confidence and professionalism as he dropped a medical duffel onto the end of the bed. Azagoth wasn't sure if he was relieved or pissed off that the guy was keeping his composure when Azagoth was on the verge of losing his.

"She passed out," Azagoth said as he gently moved Lilliana off his lap and onto the mattress and a pillow, careful to avoid the blood as much as possible. "She was fine, and then she…" He trailed off, unable to voice the obvious.

"Hurts," Lilliana moaned. "Hurts so bad."

Eidolon gloved up and gripped Lilliana's wrist. The sleeve of glyphs on his arm, what Seminus demons called a *dermoire*, lit up as he channeled energy into Lilli. Every protective instinct Azagoth had screamed for him to make Eidolon stop, but he told himself that this wasn't a random demon channeling evil shit into her. Seminus demons possessed the ability to heal the body and the mind.

Of course, the same gifts that could heal could also kill. It was what made Sems as lethal as they were horny.

"When did it start?" Eidolon asked.

She swallowed, her throat working for so long, Azagoth reached for the glass of water she kept next to the bed. Eidolon shook his head.

"I've been nauseous for a couple of days," she said between panting breaths. "I mean, I've had episodes for my entire pregnancy, but it got worse a couple of days ago."

Azagoth froze as he shrugged into his robe. "You lied to me?"

"I told you it was nothing, and I didn't think it was," she snapped with so much strength that it lifted Azagoth's spirits. "And *you* lied about me losing blood, so you can suck on your outrage."

He laughed despite the situation. Lilliana never put up with his shit, and he loved that about her.

Eidolon adjusted his grip on her wrist. "What about the pain?"

"It started just after I woke up this morning." She shuddered and cried out, and another gush of blood puddled on the sheets.

"Dammit, Doc," Azagoth barked. "Do something!"

Eidolon's *dermoire* glowed brighter, and his expression grew grimmer. "This shouldn't be happening. There's no reason for it."

"No reason for what?" Azagoth's hands fisted at his sides as he fought to control his panic. "Fucking talk to me."

If Azagoth's bluntness irritated the doctor, he didn't show it, and Azagoth's respect for him bumped up a notch. "She needs to go to the hospital."

"No damned way," Azagoth growled.

"Reaver assured us that if she ever needed to go, she could. It'll be okay."

Angels—except Memitim and Reaver—couldn't step foot in Underworld General, but Lilliana's move to Sheoul-gra had all but destroyed her angel status, dirtying her wings just enough that she could temporarily go places most angels couldn't.

But that wasn't Azagoth's concern.

"I said no. Whatever needs to happen, it can happen here. No one is taking her from me again."

Eidolon rose to his feet, his steady, dark gaze holding Azagoth's. "I'm going to be blunt because I don't think we have much time. Do you want to lose the baby?"

The doctor's words were a gut punch. Azagoth wanted to destroy the bastard for even asking the question. Wanted to scream in frustration that this was happening. Obviously, he didn't want to lose his baby, but he was terrified of allowing Lilliana to leave. To go to a place full of strangers and demons and who the hell knew what else.

He'd just gotten her back.

"Father." Idess laid her slender hand on his forearm in a gentle plea. "She'll have the best care in the world. I promise."

"I have enemies," he insisted. "She'll be exposed. In danger."

"My hospital is protected by an anti-violence spell," Eidolon said in a soothing voice that shouldn't have worked on Azagoth but did. "No one can flash in or out. I can assign guards, or you can send your own. She'll be safe within UG's walls. You have my word."

Journey stepped forward, his booted foot hitting the floor like a clap of thunder. "I'll accompany her as a bodyguard. I swear, no one will touch her."

"I'll go, too," Emerico offered.

"Please, darling," Lilliana croaked. "It'll be okay."

He wanted to believe that. Was desperate to believe that. But even as he nodded in assent, he felt a sinking in his gut.

None of this was okay.

But losing the baby wasn't an option.

"Do it," he said roughly, catching the doctor's gaze. "And if you return my mate and child to me, I'll owe you a debt I can never repay."

Eidolon gave him a shrewd look as he gathered his bag. "You can expect me to collect. My hospital doesn't run on goodwill alone."

Azagoth's pulse hammered as he watched Journey gently gather Lilliana into his arms. She smiled weakly and captured Azagoth's hand before they started out the door.

"I love you," she whispered.

Azagoth still wasn't comfortable with emotion, so his voice broke a bit as he whispered back, "I love you, too." Somehow, he summoned the strength to release her so they could go, but not before he seized Eidolon by the elbow. "Remember, Doctor, someday your soul will be mine."

Idess's hand came down lightly on Azagoth's shoulder. "Threats aren't necessary, Father."

"I'm used to it," Eidolon muttered. "He isn't the first psychotically overprotective mate I've dealt with." The doctor paused at the doorway and turned to Azagoth. "Lilliana will get the best care in all the realms. You made the right decision."

Azagoth wasn't sure of that, but he nodded anyway.

And then, the moment the door closed, he fell to his knees and screamed.

Chapter 4

Eidolon wasted no time in getting Lilliana to the hospital. He burst out of the Harrowgate, followed by Emerico, Idess, and Journey, Lilliana draped in the Memitim's arms.

"This way," he called out, leading them toward the closest vacant exam room. Hospital staff scrambled out of the way as they rushed in.

"Everything will be okay," Journey assured Lilliana as he carefully placed her on the exam table.

Eidolon hoped the Memitim was psychic. Eidolon had treated a lot of powerful, top-of-the-food-chain patients and their loved ones, but Azagoth was in a category of his own. The Grim Reaper's reach was extensive enough in the physical world, but the fact that it went beyond that, past the grave, meant there was no escaping his wrath. Even if it took thousands of years, he would, eventually, nail your ass to the wall.

Literally and for eternity.

Putting those unsettling thoughts aside, Eidolon told the Memitim boys to wait outside. As he grabbed an IV kit from a cabinet, he called over a physician assistant, a cocky, young vampire named Drake with spiky, purple-silver hair.

"I need Blaspheme on this."

As an angel who hadn't gotten her wings yet, she was able to run UG's London clinic. She'd be invaluable in this situation with Lilliana.

Drake's lips, coated in black lipstick, dipped into a frown. "Uh, Dr. Blaspheme didn't show up for work today."

"What do you mean she didn't show up?" Eidolon handed the supplies to Meesa, a new nurse at UG. She had quit her job at John Hopkins after twenty years, following an unfortunate incident where a co-worker had seen her shapeshift into a lion. "Did she take the day off?"

"No, sir. She hasn't shown up in two days, and no one can get ahold of her. It's the talk of the hospital."

"And I'm just hearing about this now...why?"

"The clinic tried calling you," Meesa said, "but you didn't answer."

Shit, yeah. He'd turned his phone off while he was in Sheoul-gra. "Okay, we'll deal with that later. Get Gem." He paused. "And call Shade if he isn't on an ambulance run. If we can't get him, we need to start a transfusion."

Eidolon's brother, Shade, was a paramedic and had the ability to manipulate bodily functions. A little juice from him could keep a heart beating, lungs breathing, and blood forming.

Lilliana moaned. "I think I'm going to throw up."

Meesa rushed an emesis basin over as Eidolon helped roll Lilliana onto her side.

"Drake, I need labs. Test for everything, and tell them this is their number one priority." Summoning his power, he channeled the energy through the glowing symbols of his *dermoire* and sent it into Lilliana's body.

All around him, the sounds of a hospital—the beeps of equipment, the moans of pain, the retching of a pregnant female—faded away as Eidolon began to *see* inside Lilliana.

And it was disturbing.

Touching angels had always given Eidolon a case of the willies, but as a resident of Sheoul-gra and Azagoth's mate, Lilliana didn't affect Eidolon's senses as intensely as she would have if her wings weren't *dirty*. But it wasn't her Heavenly status currently punching Eidolon with a cold fist of dread. It was the shifting, undulating shadow of darkness encasing her womb and the base of each wing.

"Doctor." The urgency in Drake's voice startled him, and he glanced over at the rush of blood flowing onto the table.

Shit. He dove back into Lilliana with his gift, but it wouldn't penetrate the layer of darkness.

"I can't get to her womb or the baby." He cursed. "This isn't natural. It's not a known disease, but it isn't acting like a toxin, either. More like an infection. Or a virus."

A virus.

He wheeled around and hit the call button. "Get Sin in here.

Hurry!"

Eidolon's sister, Sin, was the only female Seminus demon in existence and had once caused a plague that'd threatened to put werewolves on the Endangered Species List. She'd since dedicated a lot of her time to learning everything she could about how viruses worked so she could use her unique gift to create cures...or make really, really lethal viruses.

His sister was a walking superplague.

Shade sauntered into the room in his paramedic uniform, a steaming cup of coffee in his hand. "What's going on?"

"She needs blood," Eidolon said. "Fast."

Shade tossed his coffee into the trash and had hold of Lilliana's wrist before the cup hit the bottom of the bin.

"I'm Shade," he told her, speaking in the gentle, confident tone that helped make him a great medic. "What's your name?"

"Lilliana," she whispered.

"Lilliana is Azagoth's mate," Eidolon added, taking just a second to enjoy the way Shade's hand jerked a little.

"Seriously?" he mouthed, and Eidolon nodded. *"Hell's fucking bells."*

Eidolon couldn't agree more.

A commotion in the ER signaled Sin's arrival, and she burst into the room. "I hear you're treating the Grim Reaper's mate. And she's knocked up? Holy shit."

Sin was as tactful and delicate as ever. "Lilliana," Eidolon said then gestured to his sister. "This is Sin. I consult with her from time to time. Her mouth has no filter, but she's the best at what she does."

Lilliana nodded weakly and closed her eyes. Shade was likely reducing her nausea and relaxing her system. What Eidolon wouldn't give for a dozen more Shades in the hospital.

He turned to Sin. "There's something inside her I can't identify. Whatever it is, it's causing a dangerous situation for the baby."

"She's still losing a lot of blood," Shade said in a low voice. "Is she a candidate for a C-Section?"

Eidolon shook his head. "She's an angel, remember?"

He'd learned the hard way that it was dangerous for demons to attempt to cut into an angel, let alone one pregnant with another powerful being's baby.

"Oh, yeah," Shade murmured. "Weird that she doesn't feel like one."

"That's what the corruption of Sheoul-gra will do to you," Drake announced, giving a sheepish shrug when everyone looked over at him. "It's what I heard."

"Oh, damn." Sin's alarmed tone had everyone whiplashing from Drake to her. "What the fuck?" She frowned, and her *dermoire,* a faded version of Eidolon's and Shade's, glowed brighter. "It's a weird mass of shit, but inside it, I can see some individual elements. It's like someone mixed chemicals and bacteria together, and then threw in a virus for fun…" She trailed off, her expression hidden behind a curtain of black hair. "The weird thing—well, the weird*er* thing—is that the substance isn't spread through her body. It's concentrated in the tissues of her wings. Only a few stray bits are attacking her uterus inside the black blob."

Lightbulbs clicked on in every corner of Eidolon's brain. Quickly, he stuck his head outside the room and gestured to Idess, who was waiting nearby with Emerico and Journey.

"Idess, we need a tissue sample from Lilliana's wing anchors. I was hoping to talk you through the process. I know you're not technically an angel anymore, but you're Memitim, and you're Lilliana's stepdaughter, so it should be safe for you to do it. Or at least safer than it would be for any of us." He lowered his voice. "If you'd rather not—"

"Of course, I'll do it." She smiled sadly. "I'll do anything for Lilliana."

It only took a couple of minutes for Shade to put Lilliana out and for Idess to get the sample. Eidolon handed it to Drake. "Run. Tell them to test for angelicant."

Drake took off in a blur of vampiric speed.

"Angelicant?" Sin dabbed sweat from Lilliana's brow with a wet cloth, freeing up Meesa to attempt an ultrasound. "What's that?"

"It's an oil of demonic origin. It's supposed to help angels enter regions of Sheoul they otherwise couldn't go."

"Lilliana wouldn't take anything like that," Idess said fiercely. "Never. Not while she's pregnant."

Eidolon searched Lilliana's pale, ageless face, creased with worry even in unconsciousness.

"She wouldn't," he said. "She didn't, I'm certain. There are safer ways for angels to venture into Sheoul, and angelicant isn't safe for any pregnant being." He looped his stethoscope around his neck. "The most common use of angelicant, mostly among demons, is as an abortifacient."

"So, someone was trying to kill the baby." Shade whistled. "Someone tried to kill the fucking Grim Reaper's unborn child."

"Who would do that?" Sin asked. "And why?"

Eidolon had no idea, but he did know that whoever was responsible was going to be very, very sorry.

Chapter 5

Groggy, her head pounding, Lilliana sat up in the strange bed. It only took a second to figure out where she was, given the medical equipment and supplies.

Journey and Maddox sat at a small table next to the bed, playing what appeared to be Uno. Journey saw her first.

"Lilliana!" He grinned and, as always, she saw Azagoth in him. Journey was as free with his smiles as Azagoth was stingy with them, but their genuine grin was the same.

Her hand flew to her belly, and both boys were at her side before she could let out a relieved breath that she was still pregnant under the hospital gown and sheet. As if the baby heard her thoughts, it gave her a couple of sassy kicks, and her eyes watered with gratitude.

"Emerico can't sit still for more than five minutes, so I took over for him." Maddox reached over and pressed the call button. "And Eidolon said to let him know when you woke up."

"Am I okay?" She wiggled her toes and fingers as if doing so meant that everything was cool. "Is the baby okay?"

Journey nodded, the black plugs in his lobes bouncing with every motion. "We don't know specifics. They won't tell us anything. But the doctor assured us that you and my little brother or sister will be fine."

Oh, thank the Maker.

"What about Azagoth?"

"He's been told," Maddox said as he handed her his phone. "But I'm sure he's going to want to hear it from you." He pointed to a duffel near the bathroom. "Cat sent clothes and stuff, too."

"Thank you." She smiled, so grateful to have such wonderful

friends and family to support her. "Thank you both for everything." She also gave silent thanks to Cat for making sure she didn't have to wear a hospital gown home.

A tap at the door interrupted her as she started to dial Azagoth, and she looked up from the phone.

"It's Eidolon," the doctor called out. After she'd given permission, he entered, a warm smile curving his made-to-please-females lips. He strode toward her, his tan, muscular physique making the black scrubs he wore surprisingly sexy. A rare breed of incubus, he was literally designed to tempt and please, and she totally got why so many angels had lost their wings for a night with a sex demon.

"How are you feeling?"

"The boys tell me the baby and I are healthy, but until I hear it from you, I'm going to be a wreck."

"I get it." He grabbed the chart from the end of the bed and carried it over to her bedside. The black glyphs extending from his fingers to his neck danced as his right arm flexed. "They're right. Your vitals seem normal for an angel, and so are the baby's." He paused. "Do you know its gender?"

She had her suspicions, but she'd kept them to herself. "Not for sure."

"Do you want to know?"

She hesitated for a heartbeat, but the decision wasn't that difficult. "I don't think so. I want Azagoth and I to find out at the same time."

"You could FaceTime him," Journey suggested.

"It's okay. I think we can wait another week or two for the big reveal." She turned back to Eidolon. "That's right, isn't it? We're still on track for an October fifteenth delivery date, right?"

"We are," he said, a little too solemnly. "But this has stressed your system." He glanced over at Journey and Maddox. "Could I have a minute with Lilliana alone?"

"It's okay, Doctor." She smiled at the boys with genuine affection. It had taken some time and tears to build relationships with Azagoth's kids, but she was very glad that they were in her and Azagoth's lives. Her mate had been alone for far too long. "They're family."

"Of course," he said. "But I really think I should speak with you alone." At his tone, her hair stood on end.

She nodded at Mad and Journey, and although it was clear they were reluctant to leave, they did.

"Wraith said he was coming by the hospital to say hi," Eidolon called after them. "You might find him in the break room."

She knew the boys wouldn't venture more than ten feet from her room, but she hoped they got to see Eidolon's brother before they left with her. Apparently, the demon had helped them a few months back when their sister, Suzanne, got into a dangerous situation with her Primori—now her husband—Declan. They'd been friends ever since.

Lilliana could hardly wait until the door closed behind them before blurting, "What's going on?"

Eidolon propped himself against the counter and set aside her chart, his expression grim. "Is there any reason you would have taken something that would allow you to enter parts of Sheoul forbidden to angels?"

"No." She blinked in confusion. What a bizarre question. "Why?"

"Because you have something in your system that does exactly that, and if you didn't take it, then someone gave it to you."

Now she was even more confused. "Why would anyone do that?"

Eidolon gripped the counter with white-knuckled force as if to brace himself for what he was about to say. "Because it causes fetal death, leading to spontaneous abortion."

"What?" She felt the blood drain from her face. "You said my baby—"

"The baby is fine. You were lucky. I was able to repair the damage to your womb, but your body still needs to heal. We couldn't remove the toxin, but we cast a containment spell to keep it concentrated in your wings, where it can't affect the baby."

This new information, along with her brush with death, had sapped her strength. She hugged herself as she leaned back into the soothing softness of the pillow. "How long will the spell last?"

"It'll last the entirety of your pregnancy, so you don't need to worry."

You don't need to worry. She knew Eidolon had intended his words to be comforting, but right now, she was scared out of her mind.

"Someone tried to kill my child." She hugged herself harder. "I think worry is justified."

"I know," he said softly. "I'm sorry."

Feeling bad for being snippy, she closed her eyes and composed herself. "So am I. I'm just shaken. And I wish Azagoth could be here." She looked up at him. "Does he know?"

"Idess informed him that you and the baby were both out of danger and told him that I'd call with details later." He paused. "I wanted to wait until you were awake."

Maddox's phone felt cold and heavy in her hand. She and the baby were healthy, but things could have turned out much differently. Someone had tried to kill her unborn child. Someone Azagoth trusted. Most likely someone living in Sheoul-gra, right under their noses.

Fear for her child and anger at the betrayal shook her to her marrow. "How was whatever it is given to me?"

"Most likely in an oral form. It was probably concealed in something you ate or drank."

Although that narrowed the suspect list down a little, she'd eaten a lot of food given to her by almost everyone she knew. Although…there was a chance that the food brought in from the outside could have been tainted by anyone who knew that she was the intended recipient. So, there was hope that no one she and Azagoth trusted was involved.

Please let that be the case.

"Will you please tell the boys to come back inside?"

Eidolon called Journey and Maddox back and then hovered protectively close, his sharp, speculative gaze shifting between the two of them.

"What's going on?" Maddox stopped next to the bed rail and stared across the mattress at Eidolon, returning the suspicious stare.

There was no point in keeping the information from them, not when she would need their help. "Someone slipped me a toxin that was meant to kill the baby," she said bluntly, a little amazed that her voice hadn't wavered.

There were several heartbeats of stunned silence, and then a lot of cursing. Journey looked as if he wanted to hit the wall. Maddox took her hand and gave it a comforting squeeze. It struck her that he'd never touched her before. He was definitely his father's son, his grip firm, his skin icy, the way Azagoth's used to be when she first arrived in Sheoul-gra.

"I swear we'll find who did it, Lilliana." Journey wheeled away from the wall, anger scorching his cheeks. "Doctor, how soon can she go back to Sheoul-gra?"

"As soon as she's ready," Eidolon said before shooting her a meaningful look. "But there's no hurry. Stay as long as you want to."

She wanted to go home. She wanted to go so badly it hurt, and she rested a protective hand over her belly. "I…I'm afraid I can't."

"Can't what?" Journey asked. "Go home?"

"Someone is trying to harm my baby." Saying the words made it real, and made her decision easier. "Possibly someone inside Sheoul-gra. If they got to me once, they could do it again. I can't go back until I know it's safe."

Maddox cringed. "Father won't like that."

"He'll understand."

"He's going to freak out."

Yes, he would, but not because she refused to go back to Sheoul-gra. He'd agree with her reasoning as long as he believed that she was safe. But he was going to go next-level Reaper when he learned that what had happened to her had been intentional.

"Epic freak-out," Journey muttered, and then he looked over at her, his gaze as hard and cold as she'd ever seen it. "And I don't blame him. Someone we live with, someone we trust, murdered at least one of his children and tried to kill another. Death at our father's hands won't be enough of a punishment, no matter who it is."

She shivered, recognizing the danger in her stepson's tone. It belonged to Azagoth, and it was the first time she'd ever seen this side of Journey. Gone was the laid-back goof who liked to surf and play *Dungeons & Dragons* with Cipher. In his place was a warrior. He'd grown up a lot in the months she'd been gone.

"So, where are you going to stay?" Maddox asked. "Here? In a fucking *demon* hospital?"

"This fucking demon hospital is protected by an anti-violence ward," Eidolon said calmly. "And the fucking demons who work here are trained professionals who—"

"Sorry, Doctor." Journey jumped in and tagged Maddox hard on the shoulder. "Mad here is a dick of epic proportions, and he's sorry he insulted your hospital. We appreciate everything you've done. What he meant to say was 'Lilliana, where would you feel safe?'"

Journey's rare attempt at diplomacy made her smile. He was usually the type to crack a beer and settle in to watch a tense exchange like it was a sport. No wonder he'd been entrusted with more Primori to watch over recently, including Suzanne's husband.

"If Cara and Ares are okay with it, I'll stay with them again," she said. "I can't think of anywhere safer than a secret, highly defended island belonging to the Horseman of the Apocalypse known as War."

Clearly still stung by Journey's rebuke, Maddox rolled a shoulder in a sullen shrug. "I dunno. The secret castle in Greenland that belongs to the Horseman known as Death is a safe bet, too."

He had a point, but she didn't know Thanatos and his mate well. And besides, she'd take a warm, lush Greek isle over a frozen tundra any day.

"Father is not going to take this well," Journey repeated.

Maddox snorted. "Yeah, well, imagine how much worse he'd take it if she died inside Sheoul-gra."

A tense silence engulfed the room at the cold reality of the situation. She and the baby could die if she went home. And even if she went to stay with Cara and Ares, someone still wanted her and/or her baby dead. Making matters worse, Azagoth would be furious, and when the Grim Reaper got angry, no one was spared his wrath. Not even himself. He had a tendency toward self-destructive behavior that terrified her.

Cramps twisted her fingers, and she realized that she'd been holding Maddox's phone so hard, it threatened to crack. This call would not be fun.

Stomach churning, she took a deep breath and dialed.

Chapter 6

Fury flowed in Azagoth's veins like molten lava, bubbling just beneath the surface, held in check by a thin, fragile shell of ice. Somehow, he hadn't exploded. Somehow, his beast hadn't broken free.

Somehow, someone had poisoned his mate and tried to kill his child.

In his own home.

"Azagoth?" Lilliana spoke in soothing tones, no doubt attempting to ease his pain and keep his inner demon at bay. "I can't come home. You know that, right? I can go to Ares' island. Just until Sheoul-gra is safe."

"I can have it safe in five minutes," he swore. "I'll get rid of everyone, and I won't let anyone inside ever again."

"Oh, darling," she breathed softly. "That's not the answer. It can't be just the three of us trapped there forever."

Yes, it can. On some level, he knew that thought was irrational. On a much higher level, he understood that his tendency toward extreme action was why he trusted Lilliana to make this decision.

"A?" she prompted, using the nickname that usually made him smile. "Are you there?" At his grunt of assent, she continued. "I'll call you when I get settled, and we can talk about it."

Talk about it? He didn't want to *talk*. He wanted to kill. He wanted to own the soul of whoever had dared to betray him. He wanted to rip the bastard to shreds with his bare hands, wait for him or her to regenerate, and then repeat the process over and over. Like squeezing one of those little stress balls, except with more begging and screaming.

"I'll find whoever is responsible, Lilli," he swore. "I want our child to be born here, not on Ares' island."

"Me, too," she murmured. "Please hurry." She paused. "I love you."

"I love you, too." Azagoth set down the phone, his body numb, his brain buzzing with rage.

"Azagoth."

He shifted his gaze to the speaker. He'd forgotten that the angel, code-named Jim Bob, was still standing in the library, his hand wrapped around a highball glass of Azagoth's best rum.

Azagoth hadn't even poured his own glass before Lilliana called. He reached across his desk for the bottle. "What?"

"What happened?"

He didn't bother with a glass. He wasn't feeling that fucking civilized. "Someone," he growled, "attempted to kill my mate and child."

Jim Bob slowly lowered the glass from his mouth. "Where?"

"Right here." He took a long pull from the bottle, reveling in the burn of the alcohol pouring down his throat. When his insides were sufficiently on fire, he slammed the vessel down on the desk so hard the shelves rattled. "They're okay, but they can't come back."

"Someone got to her *inside* Sheoul-gra?" Jim Bob let out an oh-shit whistle. "Where is Lilliana now?"

Azagoth shot his spy a look. His circle of trust was small, and Jim Bob wasn't included, no matter how long he'd known him or how much information Jim Bob brought him.

"She's safe," Azagoth said, leaving it at that. Jim Bob was probably well-connected enough to find out if he really wanted to, but Azagoth wasn't going to make it easy for him. Instead, he changed the subject to the reason Jim Bob had come in the first place: the rise of the fallen angel Moloc, and the massive surge in his powers after his soul was fused with his dead twin's. "You said you're here about Moloc. Why? Is Heaven up in arms because I sent a few souls after Bael?"

"Obviously. What you did was in breach of your agreement with Heaven, and it resulted in an already powerful enemy becoming even more powerful." Jim Bob's voice rumbled with irritation. Clearly, he agreed with his Heavenly brethren. "It was the last straw for your detractors. They claim you're reckless, unpredictable, and your reach is too great. They want you either brought to heel or put down."

"Fools." Azagoth reached out and idly stroked the petals of the living crystal rose Lilliana had given him as a gift mere days ago. "All of them."

Jim Bob peered into his glass as he swirled the rum around. "Those who want to see you castrated—figuratively, although I wouldn't rule out a few who are thinking in more literal terms—is a small percentage, but the movement is growing."

"I don't fear them." When Jim Bob cut him a look of dismay, he snorted. "What? You think I should?"

"No." Jim Bob paused as if rethinking that. "But you might want to stop flexing your muscles. You aren't invincible, Reaper. Remember that."

Few things annoyed Azagoth more than being threatened, and he surged to his feet. "I'm not afraid of Heaven's wrath."

Jim Bob nodded, almost as if he approved. "You've never been afraid of anything, have you, Azagoth?"

"He who hasn't known fear hasn't faced his demons," he mused, quoting a line from *Grim Reapings: The Making of Sheoul-gra*, by Zachariel, First Angel of the Apocalypse. It had been a good read, maybe a little too accurate when accounting Azagoth's time as Asrael, but hey, it had entertained him for a couple of hours.

"And have you?" Jim Bob asked. "Faced your demons?"

Azagoth laughed. "I *am* a demon, and Heaven had better remember that."

"You're an angel tasked with storing evil souls until they can be reincarnated," Jim Bob said as if Azagoth were unaware of his own fucking job description. "You were chosen by Heaven for a reason, but if you start breaking the terms of the agreement in order to go after Moloc, they'll terminate it. And you."

Yeah, well, if Moloc was behind the attack on Lilliana, there was going to be a lot of terminating going on.

Heaven could suck it.

And why the hell hadn't Lilliana called from Ares' place yet? He glanced at his watch. Son of a bitch. It had only been ten minutes since he'd spoken with her. She probably wasn't even dressed yet.

"Azagoth? Did you hear me?"

He waved his hand in dismissal. "Yeah, yeah. I fuck up, Heaven loses its shit. I get it." He didn't give a hellrat's ass right now. He had to uncover who had poisoned Lilliana.

Moloc, probably. And even if he hadn't, it didn't matter. Bael's half-soul had merged with Moloc's half-soul, and Bael had been responsible for the deaths of several of Azagoth's children.

So, Moloc would pay. And so would whoever had actually delivered the poison to Lilliana.

But who was it?

One of the fallen angels who had served him for centuries? One of the Unfallen who lived here, trading their services for protection from True Fallen angels who would drag them to Hell to complete their fall from grace?

One of his children?

The idea that one of his progeny would betray him should have brought denial and pain, but it had happened before. More than once. And, why not? Most had never met him, and those who had barely knew him.

His children had all grown up in the human realm, believing they were as human as those who raised them. The truth about their origins and their real parents only came when they were whisked away as adults by an older Memitim sibling to begin a life of angelic duties. They trained for years, learning to use their powers and to fight. They were educated on the histories of humans, angels, and demons…and they were taught to despise him.

A few had come to him over the millennia, back when his realm was a charred, blackened ruin that reflected what Azagoth had become. But after Lilliana arrived, more of his children showed up, some of them several hundreds of years old. They'd started training with the Unfallen, and eventually, Sheoul-gra had become a thriving community. Azagoth had even brought in every remaining child from the human realm. Just two days ago, he'd ordered the construction of a pool with a waterfall, a slide, and two diving boards to help them adjust.

So as much as he loved having his children in Sheoul-gra, he also knew it was a risk. They'd all gone through hellish childhoods, abandoned by their mothers to be raised by the worst that humankind had to offer, all to give them *perspective*, or some crap.

What it did was teach them to despise the beings who'd fucked them into existence, only to abandon them in the shittiest conditions imaginable.

Yep, he understood why Memitim might betray him.

But what if someone close to him had? Someone like…Zhubaal. Or Razr.

He shook his head, not wanting to go down that road. Not yet. It was far more likely that the person was outside his inner circle. Close, but not wholly trusted.

Someone like…Jim Bob.

He eyed the angel speculatively. Jim Bob had never given Azagoth any reason not to trust him…but that would be the goal of anyone trying to play him. "Did you give Lilliana anything recently?"

One tawny eyebrow arched. "Yes. My condolences for being mated to you."

"Besides that. Anything edible? A gift?"

"I'm not that nice."

Azagoth believed him, but he wasn't willing to risk his mate's life on the male's word. Jim Bob would remain a suspect until Azagoth had the person who tried to kill his child at the eviscerating end of his scythe.

And then maybe, just maybe, life could finally get back to normal.

Chapter 7

Underworld General's emergency department was almost always in a state of chaos. Which Eidolon figured was to be expected when its patients and staff members consisted of hundreds of species of demons, were-creatures, vampires, shifters, and fallen angels.

And most of them didn't get along. A lot of them had long-standing feuds between their kinds. Some were justifiably hated because their entire species were a bunch of dicks. Others had a predator/prey dynamic going on. Just today, Eidolon had treated a *quillminder* while the Dire Mantis who'd tried to eat him was being patched up one room over.

If not for the anti-violence spell, the place would be bathed in a lot more blood than it already was. But just because people couldn't bite, stab, or gut each other, didn't mean they couldn't scream their bloody heads off. Right now, at least five patients, two nurses, and a physician were engaged in shouting matches.

As if that weren't enough to make Eidolon long for a vacation, the hospital's Harrowgate, part of the transportation system that allowed underworlders to travel instantly to millions of other Harrowgates around the human and demon realms, had stopped working. And so had the gate that connected the New York-based hospital with the London-based clinic from which Blaspheme was currently AWOL for the third day in a row now.

The only other entrance was via the parking lot's concealed doorway that opened into a Manhattan parking garage on a busy street. And that meant demons who couldn't pass as human couldn't come or go unless they could teleport or make themselves invisible.

Naturally, tempers were flaring.

The hospital was going to have to start using the cover of ambulances to ferry people out of here when the vehicles weren't being used for active calls.

Eidolon was about to hand down the order to do just that when one of the technicians working on the Harrowgate called to him. The tech, a werewolf who worked at a human software company, stepped out, the physics of the gate making it appear as if he'd walked out of thin air from between two pillars.

"I think we isolated the problem." He rubbed his head, making his already unkempt blond man bun flop over. "Looks like there's a bug in the coding for the European continent."

"Can you fix it?"

Man Bun tapped the tablet in his hand as he spoke. "We're working on it."

That wasn't the answer Eidolon wanted to hear, but it was probably the best answer he'd get right now.

"Yo, E!" Wraith, Eidolon's youngest brother, and the only blond in the family—if only thanks to bleach—sauntered through the sliding doors from the ambulance bay and parking lot, his ancient leather duster kicking up around a battle-worn pair of combat boots.

Those were his hunting clothes, the weapons evident on his harness nothing compared to those that weren't visible. As a vampire *and* a Seminus demon, he had an impressive set of fangs and crazy vampire speed.

He cut through the crowd of patients in a dance of nimble steps and spins as if he were having fun. He probably was. Wraith had always been most comfortable in the middle of chaos. Often, *he* was the chaos.

Man Bun stared in awe before disappearing into the translucent, shimmering doorway of the Harrowgate. Wraith had earned his reputation as a legend, and he couldn't go anywhere without someone wanting to either "kill me or fuck me," at least, according to Wraith. Though from what Eidolon had seen, it was largely true.

Unfortunately for the ones who wanted to kill him, Wraith was protected by an invincibility charm, and those who wanted to fuck him found that he was one hundred percent fiercely devoted to his vampire mate, Serena.

"Not now, Wraith." Eidolon sighed. "We've got problems."

"No shit?" Wraith jerked his thumb toward the sliding doors.

"That's what I'm trying to tell you. Three fucking fallen angels just popped into the parking lot."

Cursing, because…seriously, what else could go wrong today, Eidolon started toward the parking lot but pulled up short when he saw Lilliana and her two ever-present bodyguards heading toward the Harrowgate. Maddox and Journey, both dressed in jeans and dark tees, flanked Lilliana, Maddox with a duffel slung over his shoulder. Lilliana glowed in a turquoise and white dress and sandals, her long hair pulled back with jeweled gold combs. No one would have guessed that just hours ago, she'd been close to losing her child.

"This can't be a coincidence," he muttered. "The day we have a VIP getting ready to leave, the Harrowgate shuts down, and fallen angels pay a visit?"

He met Lilliana at the *OUT OF ORDER* sign in front of the gate. "As you can see, we have a bit of a—"

"Clusterfuck," Wraith offered as he greeted Journey and Maddox with high-fives.

"*Situation.*" Eidolon shot Wraith a glare. "Although my brother isn't wrong," he admitted.

Lilliana's ever-present smile faded. "What kind of situation?"

"Our exits are temporarily inaccessible."

"So we're stuck here?" A shadow of worry darkened her expression. "Does this kind of thing happen often?"

"Harrowgate malfunctions are rare," he said. "But you'd be surprised how often jackasses hijack the parking lot."

"Word." Wraith swung back around to Eidolon. "Speaking of jackasses, I saw Revenant."

Interesting. Revenant's status as the King of Hell left him with no spare time, and no one saw him much anymore.

"Is he here?"

"Nah. He came by the house last night." Wraith bared his fangs at a pink-skinned Oni demon that had dared to bump into him. "Brought a book I guess Serena wanted to borrow from Blaspheme."

"Did he tell you why Blaspheme hasn't shown up for work in three days?"

"Nope." Wraith frowned. "I didn't know she was missing. Come to think of it, he seemed more dickish than normal."

An uneasy feeling settled over Eidolon. While the Harrowgate, parking lot angels, Blaspheme, and Revenant could all be unrelated,

Eidolon had learned to trust his gut, and his intuition said that everything was tied together somehow.

Lilliana wobbled, and Eidolon grabbed her, keeping her steady as he eased her onto a seat.

"Sorry," she said. "I just got a touch woozy. Guess I'm still a little tired."

"That's to be expected," Eidolon assured her. "You've been through an ordeal, and there's a lot going on. We'll figure out a way to get you out of the hospital as soon as possible."

"I'll get a couple dozen Memitim over here," Journey said as he dialed his phone. "They can distract the fallen angels while we flash Lilliana out from the parking lot." He scowled down at his phone. "What the hell?"

"What is it?" Lilliana asked.

"My phone's not working. No service on either the human or demon networks."

"Ditto." Maddox shook his phone as if it would help.

All around, people were suddenly complaining that they couldn't send or receive calls or texts. Eidolon's sense of unease became flat-out alarm as if every heart monitor in the hospital suddenly flat-lined.

They were trapped, and if the hospital's landlines weren't working, they had no way to call for help. At the very moment the Grim Reaper's pregnant mate was supposed to be leaving.

"Gem!" he shouted at one of his best physicians—also his sister-in-law—as she jogged toward him. "I need you to check—"

"Cell and landline service is down," she called out. Well, that took care of that. "And there are asshole fallen angels in the parking lot. They won't let anyone leave."

"I don't like this." Journey shifted closer to Lilliana, hovering protectively. "We need to get her out of here."

Wraith jerked his chin at the sliding bay doors. "I'll handle the angels."

Lilliana put her hand out to grip Wraith's sleeve. "Please, don't. I don't want anyone risking their lives on my account."

"She's right." Maddox shifted the duffel. "I know you have superpowers or some shit, and I've seen you fight, but those are fallens out there. You think you can take on one, let alone three?"

Journey's dark brows pulled together in confusion. "Yeah. I thought your invincibility mojo didn't work on angels."

Wraith grinned, his vampire fangs glistening. "Reaver tweaked it so I can battle the fallen. Pretty cool, huh?"

Eidolon had been furious about that. Wraith didn't need more excuses to be reckless. Yeah, Wraith had settled down considerably, especially now that he had a mate and son to go home to, but a well-fed predator was still a predator.

"But *we* could still kick your ass, right?" Maddox asked.

Wraith snorted. "You could try."

"Males." Lilliana huffed, and Eidolon chuckled despite the dire situation.

He liked her, and she seemed to be exactly what a male like Azagoth needed in his life. A strong soul with a gentle spirit. Someone who could stand up to him but also make him laugh.

Eidolon needed to get her back to the Grim Reaper safely. "Why don't we take you to my office to wait?" he said to her. "And, Wraith, I want you to sit this one out—" He broke off as Wraith sauntered out the doors to the parking lot. "Dammit."

"Oh, no," Lilliana whispered as, through the glass, they all watched Wraith walk toward the leather-bound trio, one fallen swinging a thick chain in his fist.

The other two, one male and one female, held flaming axes, and all three popped their leathery black wings at Wraith's approach. The female smiled, a sinister, knowing grin that chilled Eidolon to the bone and dropped a load of ice into his gut.

His feet moved even before his brain kicked in. He sprinted to the door, and as they slid open, he yelled, "Wraith, get out of there!"

Wraith turned, and as he did, Chainfist struck out, his weapon cracking against Wraith's skull with a sickening, wet crunch. Wraith launched into the air and slammed into the rear doors of an ambulance fifty feet away before landing on the pavement, blood pouring from his head.

That didn't just happen.

It couldn't have. Nothing should be able to touch Wraith...not unless he'd turned off the charm that made him invincible. But why would he do something that stupid?

"Wraith!" Eidolon started toward him, but he slammed against an invisible forcefield and the other two angels reached Wraith first.

Wraith suddenly pivoted on the ground, swinging his legs around to catch one of the evil assholes in the legs.

Way to go, bro!

The female angel crumpled, but the remaining male brought his axe down hard, broadsiding it against Wraith's ribs. Wraith's scream and the sound of breaking bones echoed through the parking lot—and Eidolon's head.

He watched helplessly as the two axe-happy angels hoisted Wraith up, hanging him by the shoulders between their bodies.

Blood poured down Wraith's face and neck, matting his hair, streaking his skin. Eidolon wasn't even sure he was conscious anymore. His body was limp, his head hanging loosely on his neck.

Chainfist swung around to Eidolon. "Give us the female."

Eidolon swallowed his rage, knowing he needed to play their game if he wanted his brother back. "I don't know what you're talking about."

"Azagoth's whore!" the guy yelled. "Give her to me, or your brother dies."

Eidolon instinctively looked back into the emergency department. The once unruly crowd was quiet now, all eyes on him.

Including Lilliana's. Horrified, she stood near the front, sandwiched between Journey and Maddox, her face pale, her hand covering her mouth.

"Now, demon!"

Fuck that. Eidolon might have to play the game, but he'd do it on his time schedule and his terms. He'd dealt with a lot of powerful assholes in his life, and he'd faced worse odds. With casual deliberation, he turned back to the fallen angel.

"You know that's not going to happen," he said calmly. "Let's discuss this. Release my brother, and—"

Wraith screamed, his head thrown back in agony. For a second, Eidolon didn't know why. Then he watched in disbelief as a glowing sword pierced his chest, thrust slowly forward from behind.

Right through the heart.

"No," Eidolon croaked. "*No!*"

Chainfist flung Wraith's body past Eidolon and through the double doors. "Let this be your first lesson," he said. "Tell everyone you know. Hell is getting a regime change. Discussion time is over."

The angels dematerialized, taking the forcefield and leaving devastation, shock, and horror behind.

Tears blurred Eidolon's vision as he stumbled to Wraith and sank to his knees beside him. Gem was there, and so was Chu-hua and

Vladlena, and others…he couldn't keep track of everyone trying desperately to save Wraith. But it was too late.

That space inside where he could sense all his living siblings, had emptied of Wraith. The gaping hole swallowed Eidolon, taking his hearing, his thoughts, his ability to function.

A roar of agony echoed through the hospital. *Shade*, he thought dazedly. It was Shade.

Eidolon watched in an almost dreamlike trance as his brother ran into the emergency department, one hand clutching his chest. He skidded to a halt, meeting Eidolon's gaze with one full of agony.

"Oh, gods," he rasped. "*Oh, gods!*" He hit the floor next to Eidolon, his arm glowing as he punched his gift into their brother. "Help me, E! *Fucking help me!*"

Knowing it was useless but wanting to ease Shade's pain as much as he could, Eidolon channeled his own Seminus healing waves into Wraith.

But neither of them could repair a heart split in half by an enchanted blade.

"He's gone," Eidolon whispered after what seemed like hours. "Fuck me, our brother is gone."

Shade's sobs filled the stunned, silent room.

"Eidolon?" Lilliana's shaken voice pierced Eidolon's shroud of pain. "I-I don't mean to interfere, but something strange is going on." She glanced down at Wraith, her eyes filled with tears. "*Griminions* haven't reaped his soul."

Shade lifted his head in jerky, drunken motions. "What?"

"*Griminions* sense death the moment it happens," she said. "They show up almost immediately. They should have been here by now."

"Maybe they have been," Maddox offered, his voice low and respectful. "You probably can't see them. Few can, outside of Sheoul-gra."

"I can see them," she insisted. "I think the baby has given me the ability, and I'm telling you, they haven't come."

"Maybe he's not dead." Journey's voice was threaded with hope. False hope.

"I'm a doctor," Eidolon said, his own voice ragged with defeat. "I assure you, my brother is gone."

"Then his soul is trapped." Shade dashed away a tear. "He must be in so much pain."

A soft, gentle hand came down on Eidolon's shoulder. It was Lilliana.

"We can take him to Azagoth." She crouched, aided by Journey, and took Eidolon's and Shade's hands. "He can release Wraith's soul. After Maddox and Journey drop me off on Ares' island, they can take him straight to Azagoth."

Eidolon didn't want to make this decision. He didn't want this to be happening at all. So, he was grateful when Shade nodded.

"We need him back when it's done," he rasped.

"Of course." She gave them both a brief hug. "I'm so sorry."

With that, Journey helped her up, and she left Eidolon and Shade to say goodbye to Wraith, something Eidolon used to think he'd have to do every single day.

Now that day was here, and he wasn't ready.

"Uh...sir?" Eidolon focused on Man Bun, who stood nearby, wringing his trembling hands. "I'm sorry. He...was a great...inspiration," he choked out, and Eidolon nearly bit out a bitter laugh. Wraith would have eaten that shit up. "And, ah...the Harrowgate is working."

It was time for Lilliana to go. Which meant it was time for Wraith to go.

Eidolon looked down at his brother once more.

No, he wasn't ready at all.

Chapter 8

Lilliana's heart was heavy as she stood inside the Harrowgate and punched in the code to Ares' personal island gate. She hadn't known Eidolon's brother, had only met him in passing a couple of times when he'd come to the island during her stay, but Ares and Cara had spoken highly of him—between the jabs. Seeing the devastation in not only Eidolon and Shade but also in the expressions of every Underworld General staffer had been truly heart-rending.

Journey held Wraith as he would a brother, his head bowed from hunched shoulders as he cradled the demon's big body in his arms. Even Maddox looked as if he were trying to keep his emotions in check—his jaw tight, his gaze distant.

The gate opened and, zombielike, they all stepped out.

Hot, humid air engulfed Lilliana in a welcoming embrace. After the events of the last twelve hours, this was exactly what she needed. Well, she needed Azagoth, but if she couldn't be in Sheoul-gra, then this was where she wanted to be. She loved it here. The warmth, the rhythmic, lulling pattern of the waves, the earthy scent of the olive groves, and the fragrant citrus air from the lemon trees Cara had planted a couple of years ago.

Lilliana inhaled, frowning when she didn't smell the lemons or the olives. Weird. She glanced around for the familiar landscape and mansion, but all she saw was pristine white sand, some scrub brush, and a few swaying palms stretching along a craggy coastline.

The hair on the back of her neck stood on end. "Uh…guys? This isn't Ares' island."

The very air around them charged with deadly electricity as Maddox armed up, twin scythes appearing in his fists.

Journey went on instant alert and swung around. "Shit. The island is warded. We can't flash out." He shouldered her like a ram, shoving her backward. "Into the Harrowgate! Hur—"

He broke off with a grunt. Something warm splashed her face and arms.

Blood.

Journey's blood.

Wraith's body fell from his arms and landed with a thud in the sand. Blood poured from Journey's neck, flowing between his fingers as he clutched at it. Shock and terror shone in his eyes as his mouth worked soundlessly.

"Journey!" she screamed, instinctively moving toward him instead of the Harrowgate.

"Run," he rasped as he dropped to his knees. "*Run.*"

His brilliant eyes grew cloudy, and then he collapsed next to Wraith.

As if a veil had been lifted, the island came alive with demons. They were everywhere. Darquethoths, with their razor-sharp teeth and onyx skin slashed with fluorescent orange. Screechers, their eyeless, pale faces consisting mostly of six-inch fangs. Others, things she didn't recognize and were too horrific to look at, formed a wall around her, blocking her from the Harrowgate.

"Lilliana!" Maddox's urgent voice was drenched with pain. She caught flashes of him slashing at the demons, blood splattering the white sand.

Terror became the air she breathed as she drew on her rusty angelic gifts and lit up the sky with lightning. Demons screamed as bolts charred them to a crisp or exploded them into raw chunks of gore.

"Maddox!"

She sent a spear of ultra-hot angel glass through a half-dozen demons, knocking them back...and that was when she saw him, one scythe still slashing even as he fell under an onslaught of monsters.

A moment of sadness turned into a renewed desire to live as she swung around, taking down a giant Ramreel demon with a summoned sword.

She could make it to the Harrowgate. She could clear a path and then—

Pain exploded inside her skull, and that was the last thing she knew.

Chapter 9

Patience was not something Azagoth claimed to possess. At all. In any measure known to the human, angelic, or demon realms.

When he wanted something, he wanted it *now*. Instant gratification.

And right now, he wanted his mate to call.

Where the hell was she?

"It's only been half an hour since she texted that she was leaving her room and heading to the Harrowgate." Hawkyn, one of Azagoth's most trusted sons and the Memitim liaison to Heaven, looked out over the newly installed playground where two of the youngest children from the human realm played. This was where Azagoth's child with Lilliana would play. Dammit. *Where is she?* "She probably got hung up talking to someone."

"Or she's at Ares' place and got busy catching up with Cara and forgot to let you know," Cat said. She'd been strolling down the cobblestone path toward the pond where Lilliana liked to spend hours reading when she spotted Azagoth with Hawk and Suzanne.

"See?" Hawkyn said. "Simple explanations."

Nothing was ever that simple. "If either of those things is true, then why hasn't Maddox or Journey answered your texts?"

Hawk shrugged. "If they're still at Underworld General, they're busy. If they're in Greece, Ares is probably grilling the shit out of them before he lets them roam around his island."

Probably? Definitely. Ares was as cautious as Azagoth when it came to newcomers. Mad and Journey might be Azagoth's sons, but Ares had lived long enough to know not to trust anyone based solely on his or her relationship to another.

Suzanne, still holding the basket of treats she'd brought for Lilliana, gestured to Azagoth's phone. "Why don't you text her?"

"Because I don't want her to think I'm obsessing." Azagoth's cheeks heated at the admission. "She already says I'm being overprotective and that I worry too much."

"I don't think a text would hurt." Hawkyn looked up from his own phone. "Just tell her you were thinking about her. When she gets the text, she'll realize she forgot to let you know she was safely at Ares' place."

Maybe Hawk was right. Dammit, Azagoth wasn't used to doubting himself or second-guessing his actions. But Lilliana was so important to him that he didn't want to screw up in any way. He'd lost her once; he couldn't lose her again.

Ulrike, her long, platinum blond hair brushing the grass as she hung upside down from the monkey bars, smiled shyly and waved. He hadn't spent much time with his ten-year-old daughter or his eleven-year-old son, Obasi, since they'd arrived a couple of weeks ago, but they were starting to warm up to him. Obasi, small for his age and severely malnourished, had even taken Azagoth's hand for a moment. He hadn't spoken a single word yet, the trauma of being raised in a brutal Boko Haram camp still haunting him.

It was shit like that that had made Azagoth lose himself for a while. Lilliana had given him the ability to feel again, and he'd been unable to cope with the onslaught of pain, sorrow, and guilt for his role in the horrors his children experienced while growing up in the worst conditions the human realm had to offer.

It was why, despite objections from Heaven, he'd sent his adult offspring to find every last one of his children left in the care of humans, and instructed that they be brought back here to be raised by their real family.

This hell realm wasn't nearly as bad as the hell realm the human world had become.

Hawkyn's phone buzzed. A heartbeat later, Suzanne's did, as well. Hawkyn looked down, and his mouth fell open.

"Holy shit," he breathed, his face losing every drop of color.

"Oh, no." Suzanne slapped her hand over her mouth and let out a muffled sob. "Not Wraith."

Already jacked up with anxiety over Lilliana, Azagoth wheeled around with an impatient grunt. "What happened?"

Hawkyn looked up. "It's Eidolon's brother, Wraith. He's dead."

Wraith was *dead?* Unease centered in Azagoth's chest as the shock wore off. The demon had sent Azagoth a lot of powerful, evil souls over the years, and he'd made a lot of enemies. Hell, he'd pissed off half the demon population by helping prevent at least two apocalypses. This was going to send shockwaves through both Heaven and Sheoul, and there was no way his death wasn't connected to something bigger.

"Declan says…" Suzanne swallowed over and over again as if trying to hold back tears. "The family is devastated, and there's an issue with Wraith's…soul? I don't know what that means. Journey and Maddox are supposed to be bringing the body here."

"*Father!*" Jasmine topped the hill at a dead run, her jogging shoes tearing up the grass. She was freaked out and holding her wrist as though it hurt as she stopped in front of them. "Look."

She gestured to the angry red circular symbol pulsing on her forearm, a *heraldi* that linked her to the Primori she was assigned to protect. Yesterday, she'd had three *heraldis*.

Today, she had four.

"So…you don't want another Primori?" Hawkyn asked, as confused as Azagoth.

The more Primori a Memitim watched over, the closer they got to earning their wings and gaining admittance into Heaven. It was a good thing. The goal of every Memitim.

Well, *almost* every Memitim. Suzanne and Idess had both given up their chances to Ascend to Heaven in exchange for a life with their mates in the human realm.

"Of course, I want another Primori," Jasmine insisted.

"But?" Azagoth prompted.

Jasmine's eyes grew liquid, and a teardrop fell onto her arm as she looked down at the new *heraldi.* "It's Declan."

"Declan? That can't be," Suzanne said. "Journey is Declan's guardian."

Azagoth's heart seized in his chest. Declan had been reassigned. Which meant, Journey was dead.

One of his favorite sons was dead.

He stared at the *heraldi.* Maybe it was a mistake. Maybe Journey had earned his wings. There were any number of reasons the Memitim Council would reassign Declan to Jasmine.

Journey was with Lilliana.

The realization, piled on top of the pain of Journey's probable death, nearly brought Azagoth to his knees.

Still, he clung to hope, something he used to laugh at others for doing, as he fumbled around in his pocket for his phone.

It rang in his palm.

The caller was Ares.

Everyone went utterly still. Even the air became heavy and oppressive as if a storm were bearing down.

Heart pounding again, this time too fast, Azagoth answered, his voice clipped with barely controlled fear. "Ares. Tell me she's there. Tell me my sons are there." There was a pause. A long fucking pause. "Are they there?"

"That's what I was calling to ask *you*," Ares said, his voice tight as if he were trying to keep his emotions in check. "They haven't shown up. We thought maybe…maybe since they had Wraith with them, Lilliana changed her mind and went to Sheoul-gra. I assume you know about Wraith."

"Yeah." Azagoth scrubbed his hand over his face. His skin felt uncomfortable, itchy, stretched thin, and he wanted to break out of it. "Lilliana's not here." *Stay calm. Stay…calm.* "She must still be at the hospital."

"I called. They left fifteen minutes ago," Ares said gruffly, and fear made Azagoth's skin shrink. "There's more. Eidolon said Journey and Maddox couldn't flash Lilliana from the hospital parking lot because a bunch of fallen angels had taken up positions outside. They killed Wraith when he tried to get rid of them."

Fifteen minutes. Fifteen minutes was an eternity when something bad was happening. And fallen angels? What did they, or Wraith's death, have to do with any of this?

"How did they leave?"

"E said they used the Harrowgate."

If they used the Harrowgate, they could be anywhere in the human *or* demon realms. "I'm sending someone to the hospital," he said, hating the emotion in his voice. "Let me know if any of them show up."

"Cara will call you. I'm going to UG, too. We'll find your mate."

His mind barely functioning at this point, Azagoth mumbled some sort of thanks and disconnected.

"Hawkyn." He cleared his throat of the lump that had formed there. "Get to the hospital. Find Lilliana." His voice broke, the obstruction growing like cancer. "Please, son. Please find her."

Underworld General was a strange place, kind of human but mostly…not. Hawkyn didn't think he'd ever get used to seeing demons in scrubs.

It was never the happiest of places—hospitals generally weren't—but right now, a pall of sorrow hung over it like a shroud. Even the patients in the triage room, some of them sporting gruesome wounds or cradling broken limbs, were quiet as if they felt grateful to feel only physical pain.

"I can't wait to get out of here. This place feels like a crypt," Cipher said, which was accurate, if not especially sympathetic.

"You're all heart."

Cipher grunted. "I'm a fallen angel. Hearts are for you Heavenly types."

Hawkyn rolled his eyes. Yeah, Hawkyn had earned his wings, but as a Memitim liaison, he was still earthbound. And Cipher had recently—and forcibly—gone from being a neutral Unfallen with the potential to regain his wings to a True Fallen with no hope of redemption. And while evil would eventually work its way into his very DNA, he hadn't gone dark yet, so Hawkyn didn't accept his I'm-a-fallen-angel-with-no-heart bullshit.

"I know you're as worried about Lilliana and my brothers as I am," Hawkyn said. "So, drop the evil-tough-guy act." Hawkyn didn't wait for a response, grabbing the first demon in scrubs he saw—a gray-skinned Umber demon. "I'm here to see Eidolon. Know where I can find him?"

"He's…indisposed right now." The demon averted his gaze and looked down at his enormous boots, his massive shoulders slumping. "A death in the family."

"I know," he said, with as much sympathy as he could while still trying to impart a sense of urgency. "But this is important. I'm here on behalf of Azagoth."

The guy's gunmetal eyes flew wide. "The Grim Reaper? For real?" He shrugged. "Well, why the hell not?" He gestured at the hallway near the parking lot entrance. "He's over there with War." He lowered his voice to a conspiratorial whisper that still rumbled loudly enough for people in Guam to hear. "He's an actual Horseman of the Apocalypse."

"Is that so?" He clapped the guy on the back. "Thanks, man."

He and Cipher found the Seminus doctor standing near a drinking fountain with the big Horseman whose reddish-brown hair was grooved from the rake of his fingers. Hawkyn had met the guy a couple of times and had yet to see him without his leather armor, the breastplate embossed with the same horse symbol as the one on his skin. Except the warhorse on his forearm could come to life and crush your skull with a single blow from one of his dinner-plate-sized hooves.

Eidolon waved Hawk and Cipher over when he saw them. "I was just telling Ares what I know."

"I'm sorry about Wraith," Hawkyn said. "He was…unique. I wish I'd gotten a chance to know him better." He bowed his head in respect. "My father sends his condolences."

Eidolon offered a jerky nod of acknowledgment. His eyes were red-rimmed, and his face was ashen, but his voice was as steady and authoritative as ever.

"The Harrowgate malfunctioned this afternoon," he said. "And while it was being repaired, fallen angels showed up and blocked the parking lot exit. They wanted Lilliana. I…refused." The linked ring of glyphs around his throat that signified a mated Seminus male undulated as he cleared his throat of the rawness in his voice. "They killed Wraith in response."

Cipher swore softly, and Hawkyn echoed the sentiment. He'd be devastated if he were Eidolon. And once he got over his devastation, he'd hunt down those responsible and gut them with their own teeth. As a bonus, their souls would go straight to Azagoth, and he'd make them pay all over again. And again. And again.

For all eternity.

"My father said Lilliana used the Harrowgate," Hawkyn said after an appropriate pause. "But you said it was broken."

Eidolon nodded. "Technicians said it was a coding error or something, and they repaired the problem. Or so we thought. I was unaware that Lilliana didn't arrive in Greece until Ares showed up." He gestured to where the gate stood between two pillars, a shimmering curtain invisible to humans and inoperable in their presence. "As far as I know, she's the only person who's been reported missing after using it, but as a precaution, we're not letting anyone leave through it."

Ares gestured down the hall at the parking lot doors. "Are the angels gone?"

At Eidolon's clipped nod, Cipher turned to Hawkyn. "Sounds like we need to check out the gate."

Eidolon's phone rang, and he gave them the universal go-ahead-without-me gesture. As Hawkyn, Cipher, and Ares headed toward the Harrowgate, Hawk heard him answer the phone in an emotional rumble.

"Serena...I'm so sorry..."

Hawkyn tuned it out, too compromised by his own fears for his brothers and Lilliana to witness the fallout of someone else's private pain.

Once inside the Harrowgate, Ares punched in the sequence that would reveal the secret symbol and code box leading to his private island gate. It popped up, glowing a brilliant orange. As Ares reached for it, Cipher grabbed his arm.

"Wait. Don't touch it."

"What is it?"

Cipher studied the wall, his eyes bright with the challenge of a tech mystery. He'd always been happiest when he was messing around with codes and programs Hawkyn didn't understand, but now that Cipher had fallen angel powers, he was also able to *see* most magic in the form of code.

Unfortunately, because his wings weren't fully formed yet, his powers were limited.

"Someone overrode the coding," Cipher said. "I don't think it'll take us to Greece."

"Can you tell where it goes?" Hawkyn asked.

"Definitely the human realm..." He rubbed his chin as he studied the wall. "Somewhere in the Pacific." He shrugged. "It's gonna be a crapshoot."

Hawkyn rolled his shoulders, taking comfort in the weightless energy contained in his wing anchors. It wasn't time for the wings to come out, but he liked knowing they were there. He was still getting used to the things, and the power they brought with them.

"Maybe you should stay," he told Cipher. "This could be dangerous."

"Fuck that," Ciph growled. "My fallen angel powers might not be at full strength, but I can still fight." He gestured to Ares. "Plus, we have Mount Horseman with us."

Ares snorted and mashed his gauntleted thumb on the symbol. The gate opened, and blinding sunlight flooded the inside of the dark space.

They stepped out into a bloodbath.

Cipher inhaled sharply, baring his fangs at the sharp notes of blood in the salty air. "Where the fuck are we?"

Hawkyn studied the foot and hoof prints that churned up the sand and the slurry created by all the blood. Greasy, ashen stains darkened the beach, the remains of dead demons that had disintegrated the way they did in the human realm.

"I don't know, man. But, shit, this is—" Hawkyn broke off at the sight of a *dermoire*-covered arm poking out from beneath some bushes. His gut dropped to his feet. "Wraith. Fuck, that's Wraith."

They all stared for a moment, the sound of soothing waves seeming bizarre on an island so stained with blood. Finally, Ares stiffly walked over and solemnly, reverently, hauled the dead demon into his arms.

A cell phone fell from Wraith's hand and tumbled onto the sand.

Hawkyn reached for it.

"Don't!" Cipher kicked it, knocking the device into a clump of seagrass a few feet away. "There's a spell around it." Crouching on his heels, he poked it with a stick as if it were a viper. "Looks like it's a spell to make it invisible to everyone but someone with Azagoth's blood. Damn. That's some tricky shit."

"Then why can you see it?" Hawkyn asked.

Ares scowled. "See what?"

"It's a cell phone." Cipher poked it again. "I can't technically *see* it, but I can see the spell that surrounds it." He waved his hand over the phone, made a few gestures, and then picked it up. "Disabled it like a boss."

Hawk took the slender device from Cipher and turned it over in his palm. It was new. Cheap. Still had the plastic screen protector.

"Obviously, we were meant to find it," he said, staring at it like it was poisonous. Maybe he should borrow Cipher's viper-poking stick. "That can't be good." His queasy stomach agreed.

Ares barked out a curse. "You gonna turn it on? Or are you going to stare at it all damned day?"

"Yeah. Shit." He pushed a button on top, and almost instantly, a video started playing. The churning in his gut turned serious, and his hand began to shake. "No," he whispered. "Ah, no..." The phone fell from his hand as he heaved up everything he'd eaten for the last two days.

"Hawk?" Through his pain, he felt his friend's hand on his back. "What is it?"

"They're dead," he croaked. "Maddox and Journey." Tears burned in his eyes, blurring his vision.

"What about Lilliana?"

The image of her trying to fight her way out of a horde of demons before being struck down by an axe was like a bruise on the brain.

"She's gone," he whispered. "They took her. They fucking took her."

Chapter 10

Lilliana wasn't sure what woke her. The throbbing pain in her head, the nausea in her stomach, or the baby's urgent kicks in her womb.

Groaning, she shifted. Why was the bed so hard? And why did the bedroom smell like a sewer?

Fighting the urge to vomit, she sat up and peeled open her eyes.

Instant terror winged through her. She wasn't in Sheoul-gra. She wasn't in bed next to Azagoth.

She was on the filthy floor of a dais overlooking a dank, dark great hall strewn with straw and...body parts. Bile filled her mouth, and she lurched toward the edge of the platform. A sharp jerk around her ankle yanked her to a hard stop. Pain shot up her leg, but at least she didn't need to throw up anymore.

Laughter echoed throughout the chamber. Chills slithered up her spine as she risked another look around, taking in the throne of skulls that she was chained to.

This can't be happening. She closed her eyes. *This is a nightmare. It's just a nightmare. Wake up.*

The sound of footsteps rang in her ears.

Wake up!

"I'm glad you're awake, Lilliana." The slithery, smooth voice made every hair on her head stand up. "I feared my minions went too far and permanently ruined you."

A terrifyingly handsome, dark-haired male stepped out of the shadows, his boots and leather armor splattered with gore, his scaly black wings folded against his back. Someone else remained in the shadow of a statue of demonic torture, but she kept her eyes on the one moving toward her. He made a sweeping gesture that encompassed the mangled bodies lying about like broken dolls.

"I guess I tore them apart for nothing." A garnet glow lit the black of his eyes, and claws punched from his fingertips. She instinctively reached for her angelic powers, but to her horror, she couldn't so much as touch them. "The merge with Bael's half-soul makes me too impulsive."

The sudden realization of who he was stole her breath. But her shock veered quickly to hatred and fury. "Moloc," she snarled.

Moloc and his insane twin brother Bael, Satan's right and left hands, had shared a single soul until two weeks ago when Bael had died, and his soul had joined with Moloc's. The fallen angel brothers had been engaged in a cold war with Azagoth for centuries, but the battle turned hot when they started killing Azagoth's children.

Moloc's gaze sharpened and focused, pinning her in place with the force of his evil.

"Moloc is who I was before. Now that my and Bael's souls have joined, I am now called Moloch."

"That's…the exact same thing."

"I took a cue from *Paradise Lost* and added an *H*." He flicked a bit of gore off his breastplate. "So when our story is written in the great histories, the three of us are distinguishable."

That was the dumbest thing she'd ever heard, but Moloc or Moloch, it made no difference. The son of a bitch had abducted her and killed Maddox and Journey. "Azagoth is going to destroy you, no matter how you spell your name."

"He's going to do what I want if he wants you and your brat to survive," he snapped.

She wanted to stand, to face the bastard, but getting up would be awkward and sad, and it certainly wouldn't make for a show of strength. Instead, she casually leaned against the grotesque throne of skulls and looked up at Moloc with an *H*.

"You're demanding the one thing he can't do," she said. "He can't release Satan from his prison."

Moloch smiled. "We'll see."

He was a suicidal fool. "You don't know what he's capable of."

"What about what I'm capable of?" His words were clipped,

defensive. He didn't like being thought of as the weaker adversary. "Take a look at your shackles, bitch. Do you think just anyone could plan and successfully execute a plot to snatch the Grim Reaper's mate?"

He had a point. How *had* he done it? How had he known she'd be in the hospital? Unless...unless he was responsible for putting her there in the first place.

"You were the one who poisoned me!" she blurted. "You gave it to someone inside Sheoul-gra to give to me."

"I can see why Azagoth mated you," he said drolly. "So smart."

She ignored the barb as another thought came to her. "The fallen angels. The ones in the parking lot. They were yours, weren't they?"

He inclined his head in the shallowest of nods. "I had to force you to use the Harrowgate to Ares' place. My technicians rerouted the destination shortly before you were discharged."

Which must have been why the Harrowgate was out of order. Eidolon's techs had gotten it working again, but they hadn't fixed the bug in Ares' Harrowgate code. They probably hadn't even known about it.

The baby kicked, but she refused to acknowledge it, refused to draw attention to the fact that she was pregnant. Yes, it was blatantly obvious, but there was no sense in making an evil monster focus on it.

Keep him talking. That she could do. She wanted answers anyway. "But how did you know I'd be going to Ares' island?"

Bending over, he picked up what looked like a bloody claw. "You would have been stupid to go back to Sheoul-gra before the traitor was found, and no place would be safer than an island owned by War and defended by hellhounds." He dragged his tongue up the curved side of the claw, licking it clean of blood. "Besides, is Cara not your new bestie now? You two could bond over"—he gestured to her belly—"motherhood."

She hated that he knew all of that. The traitor inside Sheoul-gra had done his or her job well. "So, you had your traitor poison me in order to have me sent to the hospital. Well done. You almost killed the baby."

He snorted, and she swore smoke puffed out of his nose. "We gave you a calculated amount that the child could survive with Eidolon's help. But I really didn't care. The child isn't important. I needed you to be able to survive in Sheoul. The effects of the drug on the baby were inconsequential." He shrugged. "But since Azagoth's spawn did survive, I can use you both to get what I want."

A chill went up her spine at the raw hatred she saw in his black eyes. "I told you, he'll never cooperate."

"Oh, that's where you're wrong." He grinned and tightened his grip on the eight-inch claw in his hand as he moved toward her. "He absolutely will."

Chapter 11

Azagoth felt the moment Hawkyn and Cipher arrived back in Sheoul-gra.

Please let them have good news.

But no matter how much hope he held in his heart, he knew in his soul that nothing Hawkyn had to say would be good.

He'd spent the last fifteen minutes wearing a hole in the floor of his library, stewing in his own fear. He'd gotten a short break from the doom and gloom when he called Zhubaal in to bring him up to speed and ask him to investigate Lilliana's poisoning. The fallen angel was a total asshole, and very capable when it came to interrogations. Azagoth just hoped that he found the traitor quickly. His patience was running as thin as the barrier that separated Heaven from Hell.

There was a tap at the door, and a heartbeat later, Hawkyn entered, his steps heavy, ringing out like death knells.

The expression on his face said it all, and Azagoth felt his world crumble.

"Tell me," he said in a voice as broken as his heart.

"They never made it to Ares' island." Hawkyn stopped in the middle of the room, his arms hanging limply by his sides. "Someone rewired the hospital's Harrowgate. When they stepped out on some random Pacific island, a fallen angel and a horde of demons ambushed them." Raw emotion bled into his voice, and Azagoth braced himself. "Journey and Maddox are dead. Lilliana…"

No. Don't say it. Don't. Fucking. Say it.

"All we found was Wraith's body and…this." Hawkyn dug a phone out of his pocket and handed it to Azagoth.

Azagoth's hand shook as the screen activated. A video popped up, and he watched on unsteady legs as his sons were slaughtered, and Lilliana battled an overwhelming surge of demons. She'd put up one hell of a fight, and for a moment, he silently cheered her on, rooting for her, hoping against all logic that she escaped.

The video abruptly cut out, and a new frame filled the screen. He squinted at the dark picture. It was a live feed, but of what?

Lilliana. Oh, holy hell, no!

His blood froze at the sight of his mate huddled against a throne of skulls, her face buried against it, her arms wrapped protectively around her belly.

She was naked, her skin streaked with blood.

"Lilli," he croaked.

The feed cut out.

Despair crushed him, then a slow, torturous sensation of being pressed between two red-hot boulders took over. It stole his breath. His thoughts. His sanity.

"Someone hurt her...someone *dared* to hurt her!"

"Father..."

The room began to shift. The floor started to buckle.

"I have to find her." His voice was low, barely audible over the pounding of his pulse in his ears. "*I have to find her.*"

He had no plan, no way to locate her, but he knew he had to get out of here. Had to get out of Sheoul-gra. Fuck his contract with Heaven and Hell.

"Father, please, calm down—"

His roar shook the building. Fissures split the floor tiles. Cracks zigzagged across the walls. Bits of stone from the ceiling crashed down. Hawkyn covered his ears and shouted in pain.

Agony tore through Azagoth as his fury boiled the blood in his veins and scoured the skin from his body. Bones broke, and his jaw dislocated as his inner demon erupted, crashing through the ceiling and scoring the walls with his massive wings.

Azagoth's thoughts became muddled as pure instinct swallowed them. All he knew was the need to escape this hell of his own making.

Throwing his great beast head back, he screamed. Fire and light, tainted by black soot, streaked from his mouth, blasting a hole in the building. He shot upward, flying through smoke, dust, and rubble.

Escape. Escape. Escape.

Lilliana!

Azagoth shot skyward. The flap of his wings displaced the air with such force that branches broke from the trees below, and dust devils spun up along the carefully manicured trails that Lilliana loved to walk. The barrier between Sheoul-gra and the human realm lay ahead, invisible, its power of containment fueled by angelic grace, a blessed stone, and unicorn farts or some shit.

He spewed a massive stream of power. He'd blast a hole right through the bastard. Molten fire splashed into the barrier, spreading, splashing…but the forcefield held.

Enraged by his failure, he slammed into the barrier. There was a slight give.

Yes.

Circling back, he flew at it again. And again. And again. He hit it until he felt his bones snap. Until he was too exhausted to maintain flight. Until he wanted to die.

One last attempt…he needed one more.

He slammed into the barrier with everything he had left, shattering every remaining bone in his body.

He crashed to the ground like a meteor, sending a tremor through the earth, flipping benches and trees into the air as the ground formed waves from the epicenter of the crater.

Dazed, panting through the pain of regeneration, he clawed his way out of the smoking hole, coming up at the base of the altar both Heaven and Hell had insisted he install. Apparently, on the eve of Armageddon, he was supposed to choose a side and offer a sacrifice on its half-obsidian/half-pure-white marble surface to prove his allegiance.

Had he not sacrificed enough?

He blinked up at the monstrosity, at the blanket draped over what appeared to be a body lying on the altar's thick slab. Who was that?

Exhaustion and mild curiosity wore down his fury and, in response, his form began to morph. His claws receded into his fingers, and his scales melted into his skin. Oh, he was still on the fucking edge of insane anger, but this was the part where the fury chilled, growing icier and icier…and far more deadly.

He wasn't going to get out, not this way, but he *would* get his mate back. And he was going to make damn sure no one *ever* fucked with him again.

More level-headed now, he remembered Hawkyn saying something about bringing Wraith. Was that the Sem's body on the altar?

Azagoth climbed to his feet, his every move awkward thanks to bones still broken from the fall, and stumbled to the demon's side. Wraith was clearly dead, but beneath the cold flesh, just under the skin, his soul burned bright. Trapped. Furious.

This demon had spirit.

Wraith's fire drew him, sparked a need to draw from the unique bank of power only a soul—especially a strong one—possessed. He palmed the demon's forehead, frowning when he couldn't reach that fiery inner being.

What the hell?

"Father?" Hawkyn jogged over, dodging toppled statues and leaping jagged stones. "What is it?"

"Wraith's soul," he said, his voice rough, charred by the malevolent energy he'd used to blast the barrier. "I can't touch it."

"But you can release it, right?"

"No." And it pissed him off. He had the ultimate power over demon souls, especially inside his own realm.

Hawkyn brushed Wraith's hair out of his face. Azagoth had always admired his son's ability to feel empathy without being overwhelmed. It was something Azagoth hadn't been able to do...and something that had ultimately landed him here.

It was also what had chased Lilliana away for months.

"But you're the Grim Reaper," Hawkyn said. "Souls are your thing."

"Which means that someone more powerful than I am has claimed this one and tethered it to his physical body."

"More powerful than you?" Hawkyn solemnly considered that. "Reaver? He was friends with Wraith."

"Perhaps." And there could be any number of reasons why the most powerful angel in Heaven would tether a soul to a body. Azagoth didn't know what any of them could possibly be, though. Nor did he care. Not right now. "Take the body to Hades. He'll keep it safe until we can release Wraith's soul into the Inner Sanctum, or someone comes to claim it."

"Someone?" Hawkyn sounded aghast. "We can't let just *anyone* claim it."

"I have bigger concerns right now," Azagoth snapped. "My sons are dead, and my pregnant mate is being tortured. I have more important things to worry about than—"

A phone rang, and Hawkyn slid the ringing device out of his pocket. "You dropped this when you launched through the library ceiling."

It wasn't Azagoth's.

Sub-zero rage was the only thing keeping him calm as he took the phone he'd watched the video and live feed on and put it to his ear.

"Release Satan, and I'll release your mate." The words, spoken with an ancient Sheoulic dialect, came over the airwaves in a deep, sinister voice that Azagoth recognized. One he wasn't surprised to hear. Hatred curled in his belly.

"Moloc," he snarled. "You—"

"It's not Moloc anymore. It's Moloch. With an *H*."

"I don't give a fuck what you call yourself." Azagoth wasn't in the mood to play this nutbag's game of names. "Do you know what you've done?"

"No," Moloch said, sarcasm dripping across the airwaves. "I accidentally killed the Grim Reaper's brats, poisoned his mate, and kidnapped her."

"Return her now, and I won't torture you before I kill you." No, he'd have an eternity to inflict pain on the fucker while his soul resided on the worst level of the Inner Sanctum.

"I'm not afraid of you, Azagoth." In the background, Azagoth heard a whimper, and he prayed it hadn't come from Lilliana. "Release the Dark Lord. You have forty-eight human hours."

The line went dead.

Hawkyn went taut as Azagoth lowered the phone from his ear. "What did he say?"

"He said I have forty-eight hours to release Satan. He also said he's not afraid of me."

He felt icy hatred expand inside him, slowly at first, and then building to an avalanche of malevolence. He ran his tongue across one fang and savored the sharp sting, the metallic taste of blood he imagined to be Moloch's.

"But soon, he will be."

Chapter 12

When Idess arrived in Sheoul-gra, she was greeted by toppled statues and trees, buckled swaths of ground, and a half-dozen grim faces.

Not a good sign.

Jasmine, barefoot and dressed in multicolored harem pants and a midriff-baring black tank top, sashayed forward as Idess stepped off the portal's platform. "We're so glad you came."

Hawkyn nodded in agreement. "Thank you for coming."

Truthfully, Idess had been grateful when Hawkyn's text had given her a reason to escape the heartbreak in her extended Seminus family, if only for a little while. Her mate, Lore, had only known Wraith—and his other half-brothers, Shade and Eidolon—for a few years. But they, along with Lore's twin, Sin, had grown close. So close that when Idess and Lore wanted a child but couldn't conceive due to Lore's sterility, the brothers had volunteered to help.

Now, not only had their son lost his uncle, he'd also lost his birth father.

A crushing sadness wrapped around her at the memory of telling Mace about Wraith. Mace's brown eyes had filled with tears, and the first thing out of his mouth had been concern for his half-brother.

"Poor Stewie," he'd said. "He doesn't have another daddy like I do. I can share with him, Mama."

Losing Wraith had sent the entire family into a state of deep mourning, and as she looked around Sheoul-gra, it seemed that things weren't much better here.

Journey's and Maddox's deaths were an awful blow, but the fact that Lilliana was still alive left room for hope.

Which was why Idess suspected she was here.

"I'm not sure how you expect me to help with Father," she said. She couldn't even help her mate right now. Hugs and refills of the whiskey glass only went so far.

Jasmine gestured to the destroyed surroundings with a sweep of her arm, her dozens of bracelets tinkling delicately. "Take a look around. He did this. His mood isn't getting any better."

And why would it? A monster had his mate. "What's being done to locate Lilliana?"

"He's called in pretty much every favor owed to him," Hawkyn said. "The Horsemen are helping, and Cara has sent hellhounds on the hunt."

Her brother's tone was riddled with apprehension. "But?"

"But Moloch has raised an army of Satan's supporters with promises that he's going to free him. There are rumors that Revenant has been imprisoned— or destroyed, depending on who you talk to. Without Revenant around, no one fears his retaliation and they're flocking to Moloch's banner."

"Dammit," Idess breathed. "We've heard similar stirrings at the hospital. Eidolon asked all staff members to question patients about anything they've heard. He wants Wraith's killers, and he's convinced everything is connected."

"It has to be," Cipher chimed in, his eyes glued to his iPad. "The fallen angels were in the parking lot to force Lilliana to use the Harrowgate. We're not sure how Wraith's death and trapped soul play a part, but we'll figure it out."

She glanced up the ruined path to the fountain that had once run with blood, that had just yesterday run with crystal water. Now, it lay in ruins at the base of Azagoth's palace.

"Where is Father now?"

"He's in the Inner Sanctum." Jasmine's eyes flickered to Hawkyn, almost as if seeking permission to continue. And then she finished in a low, grave voice, "With a Charnel Apostle high priest."

Idess gasped. Charnel Apostles were evil even by Hell's standards. Demons who celebrated violence and pain with religious zealousness, their priests and high priests possessed powerful, murderous abilities. But that wasn't even the part that left her reeling. It was that no one was allowed in the Inner Sanctum except Azagoth, Hades, Cat, and the fallen angel wardens who ran the place. The millions—perhaps billions—of demons imprisoned there could take advantage of a visitor's physical form and the powers inherent to it. A single human fingernail could allow a soul to escape into the human world. A hair from an angel could be fashioned into a weapon capable of killing all the wardens.

"Why?" she asked, still stunned by the news.

"We don't know," Jasmine said, and everyone traded glances, their discomfort clear. "That's why you're here. He needs counsel, and he's not going to listen to any of us. He's suspicious of almost everyone, but he trusts you. And Hawkyn."

She cut a glance at Hawk. "Then why aren't you handling this?"

"Because I need backup, Idess." He looked exhausted. Everyone did. They had to know that the odds of getting Lilliana back weren't good. "I've already delivered bad news to him. As the offspring he's known longer than any of us, it's your turn."

It was such a sibling thing to say, and she actually smiled a little before crashing back into reality. And the reality was that she was going to be a sacrificial lamb. The daughter who got disinherited for trying to take her elderly daddy's keys away before he killed someone.

"Fine," she sighed as she shrugged out of her jacket and laid it across her arm. "You said in your text that you recovered Wraith's body. Has Father taken care of his soul? His brothers and sister would like him returned."

Hawkyn shook his head. "His soul is tethered to his physical form by someone more powerful than our father. Hades is watching over Wraith for now."

How bizarre. Poor Wraith. Who would have messed with his soul? And why?

A minor tremor shook the ground, and Hawkyn looked up sharply. "You should go to Father."

This was not going to be pleasant.

Hawkyn fell into step beside her on the walk to Azagoth's office. They had to take several detours around objects, clearly the wreckage of Azagoth's wrath. She didn't bother asking what it had been about. His mate and unborn child were in danger; she was surprised the damage wasn't worse.

Then she saw the courtyard.

Chunks of roof, soot, and a thick coat of dust covered everything in sight. The inside of the palace was even worse, with collapsed walls and several broken living statues. She'd never felt sorry for the evil beings

Azagoth had encased in stone and put on display in his Hall of Souls, but she couldn't help but wince when she had to step over some poor jackass's shattered torso. That had to hurt.

"You should see the library," Hawkyn said, kicking aside a stone head with two broken horns. "I have a feeling there's going to be a lot of collateral damage before all of this is over."

When powerful beings battled, there was *always* collateral damage. "Who do you think gave Lilliana the poison?"

Hawkyn's expression became even grimmer and more troubled than it already was. "I don't know. I still can't believe anyone here would do that."

"I'm surprised Zhubaal hasn't expelled all but essential personnel."

"Father told him not to let anyone but me and a couple others leave Sheoul-gra." Hawkyn stopped to let them into Azagoth's office. "Only Memitim whose *heraldis* have activated can go to protect their Primori. He doesn't want to give whoever poisoned her a chance to get away."

Made sense. And, man…she did not want to be around when he caught the bastard. Azagoth was going to make whoever it was wish they'd never been born. She shuddered as Hawkyn walked to the far wall and opened the portal to the Inner Sanctum.

"Have you ever been inside?" she asked.

"Just once, and only in the gateway area. I can't even tell you what it'll look like because it changes all the time. That's where Father should be. I can't imagine he'd take anyone, let alone a Charnel Apostle, to one of the rings."

No, she couldn't imagine that, either. Azagoth, out of necessity, had very strict rules regarding who could enter the Inner Sanctum, and no one was allowed unless accompanied by him or Hades.

"Maybe we should summon Hades," she suggested.

He shook his head. "Don't need to. The portal will alert him to activity. If Azagoth isn't right inside with the demon priest, Hades will be there shortly to kick you out."

"Then I should get going." She hesitated, a sudden, disturbing thought popping into her mind. "Hawk? What if our father has taken the demon to one of the rings?"

Shadows flickered in his bright green eyes, turning them into a forest at night. "Then things are even more serious than I thought."

"Got any tips?"

"Yeah. Don't get dead."

It was something Wraith would have said, and she smiled sadly as she stepped through the doorway and into one of the strangest areas she'd ever seen.

Endless, parched gray earth stretched as far as the eye could see, interrupted only by six stone buildings that resembled mausoleums, one newer than the rest. There was definitely no Azagoth or Charnel Apostle priest.

What she did notice was a crimson aura surrounding one of the buildings. Weird. Was that where Azagoth had gone?

A rumble rose, shaking the ground. Footsteps? She spun around to see Hades in the distance, coming at her quickly, even though he appeared to be walking. How was he doing that?

Get out.

His voice boomed inside her head.

Get out now!

Shit. Without thinking, she sprinted to the crimson-ringed mausoleum.

"Idess! No!" This time, his voice wasn't inside her head. It was practically in her ear.

She darted inside...and stepped out into a realm so horrifying, so grotesque, that she started to turn back.

Until she heard Azagoth's voice.

Swallowing bile, she eased her way between blobs of bloody, quivering flesh the size of dump trucks, and skeletons that writhed on the ground. Things skittered and slithered underfoot, and twisted, bloated beings with their organs on the outside moaned as they hung from thorny crucifixes.

She rounded a wall of snapping teeth, jumping backward when a fang caught her sleeve. Shit. She rubbed her arm as she peered beyond the wall and caught sight of her father on the edge of a cliff. The Charnel Apostle stood next to him attired in something straight out of *Mad Max*, including his helm, which appeared to be fashioned from the skull of some sort of humanoid creature.

Azagoth watched as the priest chanted in Sheoulic, his bone staff glowing as he held it aloft. What was he doing?

Suddenly, something grabbed her and covered her mouth. She couldn't scream, couldn't even see as she was spun and dragged into some sort of gooey cocoon. Panic frayed the edges of her control as visions of herself being slowly digested or chewed into burger meat filled her head. Then, Hades was there, his blade cutting through the rubbery arms that held her.

"Fool," he whispered harshly as he tugged her free. "This is no place for anyone who isn't evil, let alone an angel."

She was no longer an angel, but now wasn't the time to argue.

Hades bared his fangs at her, teeth much larger than the ones on the wall. "Let's go before Azagoth knows you're here."

"I already know." Azagoth's voice, little more than a serrated growl, came from every direction, blowing Idess's hair like a gust of wind. "Bring her to me."

Oh, no.

Cursing, Hades glared at her and brought her before Azagoth as he stood at the precipice overlooking a valley. A gorge filled with demons. Thousands of them. Tens of thousands.

The disappointment in his expression combined with the angry flames—literal flames—in his eyes, made her mouth go as dry as the desiccated husk of whatever creature currently lay at his feet.

"So, you're the chosen sacrifice."

She swallowed. "W-what?"

"Your brothers and sisters. They chose you to spy on me and then talk me down if you discovered I was doing something crazy."

Relieved that he wasn't being literal and needing a blood sacrifice for whatever he was doing here, she tried to muster a little dignity after being manhandled by first a carnivorous, stinky plant, and then by Hades.

"It's not like that," she said, even though it was. "Everyone wants to help. We want to get Lilliana back."

"That's what I'm trying to do."

She eyed the demon priest, his chalky skin made paler by his black lips and dead, black eyes. "By doing what, exactly?"

Azagoth gestured to the legions of demons below. "By enlisting their help."

She had a bad feeling about this. "Father, surely there are other ways." She turned to Hades for help. "Right?"

"Fuck that." Hades held up his hands and stepped back. "Don't put me in the middle of this shit. I just work here. For free, I might add."

The priest droned on, the crowd below chanting with him, and she caught a few stray words. But she couldn't have heard what she thought she did. She listened more carefully as the priest's chant grew louder and more frenzied. When it all finally clicked into place in her head, she gasped.

"He…he's giving them the power to kill."

Hades' head whipped around to Azagoth. "I thought it was just the *griminions*."

The *griminions*, too?

The air went bitterly cold as Azagoth took Hades by the throat. "And I thought you didn't want to be in the middle of this shit." He bared his fangs, discouraging any further comment before releasing Hades and turning his focus back on Idess. "Priest-boy here is giving a hundred thousand souls the power to make a single kill and possess the body of their victim after *griminions* collect the soul. Then they'll punch through Moloch's defenses and rescue Lilliana."

Holy shit. The plan was ballsy, brutal, and a huge middle finger directed at Heaven. She couldn't let him do this.

"But, Father, Moloch has millions of supporters now. Even if your freshly re-souled soldiers get through the lines, even if they rescue Lilliana, Heaven will—"

"What?" Azagoth snarled. "What can they do to me that they haven't already done? I'm finished playing by their rules."

She wrung her hands, unsettled by his recklessness. "They'll destroy you!"

"*They'll bow to me.*" His wings erupted, casting long shadows down into the valley of demons below. "Kill the first demon you see," he shouted. "Any demon. I don't care."

"Father." Idess snared his wrist, pleading with him. "No. Please. We have demon friends. My mate and son are demons."

Azagoth snarled and turned back to them. "Evil demons only. Go! Reap!"

The Charnel Apostle thrust his fist into the air, and a blurry portal appeared against the face of a craggy cliff. The demons charged toward the opening, their bloodlust so thick in the air she could taste it on her tongue.

She shouldn't say anything. She should keep her mouth shut. But that wasn't how she was made. Azagoth was making a mistake, and someone was going to pay the price.

"Heaven isn't going to let this stand," she said softly. "It's one thing to take out an enemy. It's another to release a hundred thousand souls and allow them to kill a hundred thousand people."

"Do you truly think I care?" He gazed out over the hell he'd created, his profile as harsh as his surroundings. "Without Lilliana, I am nothing. Nothing matters but getting her back." He waved his hand in dismissal. "Get her out of here, Hades."

She didn't protest. Simply let Hades guide her back to Azagoth's office, where Hawkyn was waiting. The moment Hades shut down the portal and disappeared, she filled her brother in on everything.

Hawkyn listened, his expression growing more concerned with every word. Finally, he closed his eyes and rubbed them with his palms.

"Fuck me, I know what I have to do," he murmured. "Fuck!"

"Hawkyn?"

He didn't appear to have heard her. "He's going to see it as a betrayal."

"See what as a betrayal?" She seized his biceps and forced him to look at her. "Hawk, what are you going to do?"

His gaze met hers, the gravity in his emerald eyes sending a chill of dread up her spine. "I'm going to rat him out to Reaver," he said. "I'm going to turn him in to Heaven."

Chapter 13

"Sup, Lil?"

Lilliana blinked at the sound of the feminine voice as light flooded the chamber she'd been shackled inside for...a century, maybe? It was probably no more than a couple of days, but it felt longer. A lot longer.

"I brought something for you to eat."

She groaned, expecting a bowl of curdled gore or a maggot-covered shank of mystery meat. But the fallen angel, a backstabbing female named Flail, put down a wooden trencher with a sad but not terribly disgusting-looking cheese sandwich and a bruised, shriveled apple.

Lilliana sat up, tugging at the scratchy, stained tunic she'd been given to wear. She tried to be nonchalant and dismissive of the food, but her stomach betrayed her with a growl that echoed inside the cramped chamber.

Still, she resisted the urge to fall on the food like a starving lion on a dead gazelle.

Flail closed the heavy chamber door and used her power to increase the glow of the single torch on the far wall. "I was actually kind of sad when I found out that Moloch had managed to abduct you," she said. "You were always decent to me in Sheoul-gra."

"That was back when I thought you were an ally." Lilliana used her foot to shoo away a shoe-sized hell roach as it skittered toward the sandwich. "Now that I know you were the enemy all along, I wish I'd spit in your traitorous face."

Flail smiled, a malevolent baring of fangs. "I'll bet you do." She stomped on the roach and nudged the plate of food closer. "I didn't have to bring you this. Moloch said to let you starve."

Lilliana gingerly propped herself against the spikes jutting out of the wall and said nothing. Flail was toying with her, waiting for her to ask the obvious question of *"then why did you bring it?"* Lilliana could toy right back.

When it became clear that Lilliana wasn't going to budge, Flail stepped on the sandwich, squashing it beneath her spiked-heel boot like she had the bug.

"You ungrateful bitch." She lifted her foot, the top slice of bread sticking to the sole of her boot. "I just thought you'd like to feed the baby."

"The baby and I are fine. But thank you for caring," she added, her voice dripping with sarcasm.

Flail kicked the flattened bread across the tiny cell. "Eat it or don't. I don't fucking care. Maybe you like the idea of growing weaker and weaker until you're a pathetic wisp that can't die. I've seen it happen, you know. Immortals who are too stubborn to do the things they need to do to function. It's sad. And stupid." She shook her head, making her long, dark hair swing loosely around her biceps. "Oh, so stupid! Why would anyone choose to endure such endless torment?"

"The kind of endless torment I'm enduring right now?"

"You laugh, but don't you think you should stay strong? For the kid?" Flail asked. This was ridiculous. Flail didn't give a shit about the baby. "I didn't poison the food. If I wanted you dead, I'd do it myself. Eat."

Lilliana eyed the offerings. She really was hungry, and Flail was right. She needed to stay strong until Azagoth could rescue her.

And he would. Of that, she had no doubt. She also had no doubt that Moloch would come to regret kidnapping her and murdering Azagoth's sons.

Casually, she reached for the apple. Studied it. Gave it a sniff. Flail watched, amused, as Lilliana finally took a tentative bite. It was mealy, dry, and sour, but it was the only thing she'd eaten since she'd gotten here, and the only thing she'd been offered that resembled food.

It was delicious. She had to force herself not to moan in ecstasy as she gobbled it down to the core.

"Now," Flail said with a slight smirk. "Let's talk business."

There it was, Flail's real reason for being here. Lilliana took a bite of the cheese-topped bread while the fallen angel pulled a phone out of her pocket.

Flail held out the cell. "I'll let you talk to your mate if you promise to tell him to release Satan from his prison."

She nearly choked on her sandwich at the continued absurdity of these people. "Releasing Satan will jump-start the Apocalypse. Azagoth will never do that."

"Listen to me, Lilliana." Flail's voice held a note of urgency, her gaze dropping to Lilliana's belly with such intensity that Lilliana wrapped her arms protectively around it. "If you can't convince Azagoth to do this, you and your baby are going to suffer horrors you can't even imagine." She shoved the phone closer. "You have to try."

Lilliana laughed, the acoustics in the room making her sound a little demented. "You *almost* sound like you care."

Angry red splotches bloomed in Flail's cheeks. "Let's get one thing straight, you fat whore. I don't give a shit about you or the little fuckstain in your belly. My only desire is to serve the Dark Lord and revel in the End of Days." She jammed the phone back into her pocket. "And it would be best for everyone if Azagoth did things the easy way." She spun gracefully toward the door, but before she stepped out, she looked back over her shoulder. "Think about it, but don't take too long. Moloch gave Azagoth forty-eight hours to act, and he's eager to take the next step. I promise you won't like it. Get some sleep. You're going to need it."

Chapter 14

Azagoth had spies everywhere. They had monitored demon, human, and angelic activity for eons. They'd kept him up to date on politics, natural disasters, and every war that had been fought since the day he'd cobbled Sheoul-gra together from the remnants of the universe's creation.

In less than twelve hours, they'd be reporting on the start of a battle he'd put into motion by releasing a hundred thousand souls to fight for him. Cara was sending five thousand hellhounds, and with Ares commanding the army, they would win.

He waved away the spy who had just informed him of something new—perhaps important, perhaps not. Moloch had a strange, frequent visitor, one who he said, "reeked of Satan's blood," which Azagoth assumed meant that the visitor was one of Satan's unholy spawn. Too bad his spy hadn't had a name to go with the description.

It was also too bad he couldn't have texted the info. Technology had been the greatest thing ever for his spy network, but some species, like the Malibites, couldn't use it, whether for religious reasons or because their physiology didn't allow it.

Malibites couldn't touch anything electronic or it would short out their memories. He wondered if that included battery-operated things like sex toys. Then he pondered if one of Lilliana's toys could short *him* out and get rid of all of these fucked-up days.

He should be with his mate, preparing for a baby. Instead, he was in his new war room, prepping for the fight of his life.

Preparing *and* pacing the fuck out of the floor. His boot strikes clapped like thunder, rolling in waves around the polished stone walls of his rarely used great hall, its arched ceiling, and six massive entrances barely letting the sound escape. The demonic gargoyles perched atop the four corner pillars kept watch, their crimson eyes glowing.

As far as he knew, they'd never moved from the obsidian pillars they'd been carved from, although Lilliana speculated that they came to life at night like the exhibits in that museum movie she'd made him watch.

Someday, though, they would fly, at least according to the angel who'd carved them with the tools of a dead demon sculptor. They'd serve as protectors when the walls of Sheoul-gra came tumbling down. "At the force of the Beast's will," the angel had said.

Yeah, well, there were still over nine centuries to go before Satan was free, so the gargoyles would just have to wait. Azagoth wasn't going to make it happen any sooner. Satan hated him, had tolerated him running Sheoul-gra, but Azagoth had no doubt that the bastard was just biding his time until he could someday strike at Azagoth in the most painful way possible.

"Please, Father." Suzanne stepped in front of him as he made his five-thousandth pass around the room. Over on the table that could seat a hundred, his phone, laptop, and Moloch's cell sat silent. "You need rest."

"I can't rest while my mate and child are suffering."

"They need you whole." She handed him a steaming cup from the tray next to his electronics. "Have some tea. I made it myself."

He didn't drink fucking tea. Who the hell did she think he was? The Queen of England?

"Come on," she said, completely oblivious to his glare. "Let me at least get you to your room for a shower and a change of clothes before the battle begins. Dress for success and all that."

Suzanne had always had the spunky, positive attitude of a Disney princess, but at least what she proposed was halfway reasonable. And maybe it would get her, Hawkyn, Cipher, and Jasmine off his ass about getting some rest. No, he didn't *need* it, not in the way mortals did, but quiet time and sleep helped speed up healing...both physical and mental.

The thing was, he didn't need to heal jack shit. What he needed was his mate.

"I have to talk to Zhubaal. He said he had an update about the investigation." Azagoth started to put the cup down, but Hawkyn blocked him. Where had he even come from?

"I just came from talking to him. He emailed you a list of

everything given to Lilliana since she got back, and who gave it to her. He's interrogating everyone."

Azagoth arched a brow. "Even you?"

Hawkyn growled. "I was the first." He gestured to the cup. "Now you don't have an excuse not to go with Suzanne."

Grimly amused, because Z was a hardass bastard when he was in mission-mode, Azagoth downed the tea, which could have used a shot of whiskey to make it palatable, and handed the cup back to Suzanne.

"I can find my way to the bedroom." He swiped both phones from the table. "If you hear anything about *anything*, let me know immediately. I'll be back in ten."

On the way to his room, he checked both phones for updates. There wasn't any low-level chatter about his forces building in Moloch's territories yet, but the underworld was definitely talking about the rash of demons falling dead and then rising again as completely different people.

Griminions were gathering the souls of those who had been forced out of their physical bodies by the souls he'd set free, and so far, they'd brought in almost seventy thousand. Which meant that thirty thousand of the bastards he'd released hadn't found a suitable demon to take over.

"Hurry up, you picky fuckers," he muttered as he entered the bedroom.

The door closed, and a huge, instant weight lifted from his shoulders. This room had never been his favorite place in Sheoul-gra, but since Lilliana's arrival, it had become his sanctuary. The place where he could relax. Where he could lose himself in his mate. Where he could forget what he was and be who he *wanted* to be.

Fighting a yawn, because why not—it seemed like he was fighting everything lately—he stripped off his clothes and hit the shower. His mind still spun with a thousand thoughts, but under the hot spray, his body turned to rubber. Damn, it felt good. He hadn't showered since Lilliana went missing. He was still covered in dust and his own blood. Hell, his horns were still accessorizing his head, as he discovered when he tried to shampoo his hair with Lilliana's coconut-scented frilly stuff…just because he wanted to smell her on himself.

Fuck, he was a disaster. No wonder everyone had been trying to get him to take a break.

Filth sluiced off his body, and by the time he felt clean, his eyelids were drooping. What the hell—?

"Suzanne," he growled. "Damn you."

She'd drugged him. Maybe not with an actual drug, but with her cooking mojo. His culinarily talented daughter could infuse food and drink with emotions or the ability to relax or be more creative, have more energy…she was expanding her powers constantly.

He didn't bother drying off. He was going to get dressed and ream Suzanne a new one.

Right after he parked his ass in Lilliana's favorite chair and composed himself.

Sinking down, he lay back and closed his eyes. He'd rest for a minute, just long enough to get his kids off his back.

Damn, he was tired. Physically, he could go without sleep for centuries. He'd go insane, sure, but he could do it. He knew because he'd done it once, a couple of thousand years ago.

Mentally, though, he needed a recharge, no matter what he'd thought about that earlier. Anger and hatred had sustained him for days, and it would continue to fuel every decision he made until Lilliana was back.

Background noises and thoughts faded as thoughts of Lilliana filled his mind. He drifted, his memories giving him his first moments of peace since this nightmare had begun.

"Azagoth?"

He leaped to his feet, startled by the sound of Lilliana's voice. "Lil?"

He spun around toward the doorway and froze at the sight of her standing inside it. She wore a shapeless, stained, gray tunic, but her hair was perfect, hanging in smooth ringlets, her skin rosy, her eyes bright.

She flew into his arms. Her scent, vanilla and jasmine, surrounded him. "I'm here. How am I here instead of inside Moloch's dungeon?"

This couldn't be real. But he couldn't let her go. "I don't care how," he murmured into her hair. It smelled like coconut.

"I think…" She pushed back slightly and looked up at him. "I think we're asleep." She dropped her hand to her flat belly. "But it's not a dream."

He frowned. "You think we're dream walking? Or astral projecting?"

"I think the baby is making it happen."

That was entirely possible. Females pregnant with a powerful child often temporarily inherited the baby's abilities. "If that's true, how will we know if this is real or not?"

She thought about that for a second. "I know." She gestured to her chest of drawers. "When you wake up, open my lingerie drawer. In the very back, there's a little red box. It's a gift I was going to give you when the baby was born. If you didn't know about it before just now, then that's proof that this isn't all a dream."

He supposed that was true, but he didn't like how she'd framed the argument, that she *was* going to give it to him.

"You'll be here when the baby's born, Lilliana." He kissed her, losing herself in the warmth of her sweet lips. "I'll find a way to bring you home."

"I know," she murmured against his mouth.

He lifted his head and took in the sight of her, memorizing every eyelash, the curve of her jaw, the graceful slope of her nose. He should have spent more time admiring her before. How wasteful he'd been these past years.

"How will *you* know this is real?"

"I don't need proof," she said. "I can feel it through the baby." Her eyes grew bright, the way they did when she was excited about an idea. "Azagoth, we can use this."

If this was real, and not some kind of trick, then yes, they could. "First, I need to know how you are. I saw video—"

"Shh." She put a finger to his lips. "The baby and I are strong. But please tell me you have a plan to get me out of here. Don't tell me what it is, though, just in case this *is* some sort of trick, or Moloch is somehow listening in."

Damn, he loved how in sync they were. "I'm working on it now. But can you tell me anything that might help? Did Moloch tell you who betrayed us?"

"I asked him, but all he said was that I'd find out eventually. He's so awful, Azagoth. Totally demented. He actually added an *H* to his name so history would differentiate between Moloc and Moloch, as if anyone gives a crap."

"I know," he ground out. "He sent out an official announcement over the demonweb. A fucking diatribe about how his good friend John Milton misspelled Moloc in *Paradise Lost*, but that it must have been fate that he'd added an *H*, because now the universe would witness the rise of Moloch. The guy is a narcissistic lunatic."

He was *far* more unstable than Azagoth had anticipated.

Lilliana nodded absently, and when she spoke, there was a hitch in her voice. "I'm sorry about Maddox and Journey." At his choked-up nod, she went on. "I don't know if this is helpful or not, but Moloch said he had everything planned out, from my admission to Underworld General to my plan to go to Ares' island afterward." Pulling away, she moved toward the glass doors leading to the balcony. "And Flail's here. With Moloch, I mean. Can you get some background on her? Anything from her past as an angel, maybe?"

Flail. That *bitch*. She'd betrayed them more than once, and he was certain she was behind the death of at least one of his children. "Has she hurt you?"

He was already planning to kill her, but if she'd harmed Lilliana in any way, he'd take a long time doing it.

"On the contrary, she's being nice." Lilliana pulled the curtain away from the balcony doors, letting in daylight. There was no sun here, but the endless sky above kept to the day and night schedule, the brightness during the day directly in tune with Azagoth's mood. Right now, it was as brilliant as the noon sun in any desert. "It's most likely a ploy to get me to cooperate, but she has the advantage of knowing more about me than I know about her."

"I'll get whatever you need." He came up behind her and wrapped his arms around her midsection, tugging her close.

"I need you." There were tears in her voice, and his heart broke open, spilling agony all through his chest cavity.

"Soon," he promised. "I will do anything to get you back."

"Is that why everything outside is destroyed?"

He gazed out at the field of debris and the scorched, scarred land. His realm really did reflect what was going on in his life, didn't it?

"I tried to get out."

"Oh, darling," she whispered, turning into him. She settled her head against his chest, and he felt wetness drip down his skin. She was crying, and he felt so damned helpless. All he could do was hold her.

And feel like an utter failure.

How he wished he could go back in time, to the very beginning, to the day Gabriel had come to him with the opportunity to do something for the sake of all the realms.

He'd still have done it, but he'd have made some substantial changes to the contract. Although, in truth, it wasn't the original contract that was the problem. The issue was that Heaven kept changing the rules. They'd left things hazy enough in the contract that they always found ways to change shit.

Initially, there had been an escape clause, a way for Azagoth to retire if he ever wanted to. And then he'd pissed off the wrong archangel dickhead, and the asshole had successfully petitioned to have the clause struck from the contract, and a containment stone installed to keep him from breaking out.

It had been a betrayal that'd put an end to Azagoth's cooperation with Heaven.

Fuckers.

Lilliana sniffed. "Oh, hey," she mumbled against his chest. "This is a dream. I don't need tissue!" She looked up at him, smiling, no watery eyes or red-splotched cheeks. "And, check it out. No shapeless tunic that I think might be made from stinging nettles and hornets."

She stepped back, and despite all the shit running through his head, he got an instant erection.

She was as naked as he was, an exquisite example of the female form. He'd been with a lot of females, from succubi to angels who sat on the high councils, but none of them could compare to Lilliana. He loved her curves, her full, heavy breasts with their dusky nipples that pebbled beautifully under his tongue. Her narrow waist that flared into softly rounded hips made for his hands to grip as he licked between her thighs and made her whimper for more.

Holy hell, he wanted to do so many things to her right now, things he hadn't been able to do since she'd gotten back. Pregnancy and all that.

But in dreams, they could do anything.

Anything.

Abruptly, there was terror etched on her face, and the nettle tunic was hanging limply from her shoulders.

"I…shit, I think I'm waking—"

"Lilliana?" He reached for her as if holding her would keep her with him. "*Lilliana!*"

His hands closed on empty air.

Wretched, miserable grief heaved out of his chest in a massive sob as he came awake, alone in his chair. The impact of her loss hit him harder than before, like a kick into a bruise, and he lurched to his feet.

It felt so real. Her presence. Her scent. His pain.

It *was* real.

He could prove it.

Desperate to confirm that he'd been with Lilliana, that she was just a dream away, he yanked open her lingerie drawer and pawed through the neatly folded layers of panties and camisoles. In the very back, beneath a pair of lacy purple underwear he'd bought her to replace the ones he'd torn with his fangs, was a little red velvet box.

Exactly as she'd said.

Holding his breath, he opened it.

Inside was a pendant shaped like a scythe. His hand shook as he took it out of the box. It was exquisite, a gold blade with an emerald staff. Very carefully, he turned it over, and his eyes stung at the inscription.

Father of Souls.
Father of Angels.
Father.

It was real. The dream had been real.

Closing his eyes, Azagoth clutched the pendant to his chest.

He knew for a fact that the universe used signs to warn and to guide. He'd created one himself. Every angel had to weave a sign of some sort into a human's life as part of their final non-Order-specific training. But universal signs were bigger than that, woven into the fabric of existence at the moment of creation, their patterns constantly being reworked with the fluidity of time and history-altering events.

Lilliana's visit had been a sign. His hope hadn't been for nothing.

He was going to get her back.

Chapter 15

"You look like you went a dozen rounds with a hellhound. And lost."

If that was the case, then Reaver felt like he looked, but he still gave Metatron a weary glare as he approached the highest-ranking angel in Heaven. "We've got trouble, Uncle."

Reaver had once thought the ebony-haired archangel was his father, but a memory restoration had changed that. It had changed a lot of things. Fortunately, most of those things had been for the better.

Dressed in jeans and a crisp white, untucked dress shirt, Metatron stood on his palace's spacious deck and looked out over the Sea of Tranquility, a Heavenly body of crystalline water where every sea animal to have ever existed in the human realm swam in peace and harmony with all others.

"I feel it," he said. "A disturbance."

Reaver couldn't resist saying something Wraith would say. Seemed appropriate right now. "In the Force?"

"No. What?" Metatron shook his head in that exasperated way he always did when Reaver baffled him with human pop culture references. Which was a lot, and something Reaver had only become aware of since he'd gotten his memory back. "In the underworld. I thought we were finally past this. I thought we had a thousand years of peace ahead of us."

That had been the general assumption when Reaver and Revenant had trapped Satan and ended a decade of near-apocalypses and instability in the realms.

Reaver should have known it was too good to be true.

"It's Azagoth. Moloch abducted Lilliana and killed two of

Azagoth's sons." Reaver moved to the very edge of the clear deck and looked down at the pink dolphins playing just beneath the surface of the water. As awful as the news was that his friend Lilliana had been kidnapped by a sadistic monster, it got worse, and he had to take a deep breath to say the rest. "And Wraith is dead."

Metatron swore, an indication of how stunned he was by the news. Met rarely cursed. "I'm sorry, my son. I know you cared for the demon. He was one of the few decent ones. A legend even among angels." A muscle in Metatron's strong jawline twitched as he clapped Reaver on the shoulder with a firm, reassuring grip. "Tell me everything."

It took a minute for Reaver to gain his composure, and a few more to fill Metatron in on all the upheaval. His uncle listened, his expression as neutral as a stone. After Reaver had finished, Metatron considered the news in silence for a little while.

"Do you believe Moloch will kill Lilliana if Azagoth doesn't release Satan?" Metatron finally asked. "Is he truly that stupid?"

"I wondered that, as well," Reaver said. "I asked Harvester. She knew Bael and Moloc better than anyone." As Satan's daughter and a former fallen angel, Reaver's mate was a gold mine of information and sure to be one of Heaven's greatest weapons against him in the Final Battle. "She said Bael was an unpredictable, reckless moron, but Moloc was smart and shrewd. Now that the two are merged as one, it's hard to say how stable Moloch is, but she thinks he won't hesitate to kill Lilliana. Azagoth will assume the same thing."

"Even so," Metatron said, "Azagoth swore he wouldn't release Satan."

"He did," Reaver acknowledged. "And Azagoth has always abided by the spirit of the agreement, if not the letter." Kind of like Reaver. No, not even close. Reaver didn't even abide by the spirit. "But this is his mate and child."

"It's *Satan*," Metatron snapped, wheeling around to Reaver. "I'd sacrifice anyone to stop his release from happening."

Reaver cocked an eyebrow. "Aunt Caila?"

"She'd understand," Metatron said bluntly, and yeah, any angel would. According to prophecy, Satan's release from prison would trigger a cascading series of events leading Reaver to break the seals of the Four Horsemen and usher in Armageddon. But no one knew why he'd do it, and it wasn't supposed to happen for almost a thousand years. "Have you talked to Azagoth?"

That was the first thing Reaver had tried after he got off the phone with Hawkyn. "He's not taking my calls, and he's sealed off Sheoul-gra."

Metatron swore again. "What's he up to?"

"Apparently, he's trying to break out."

Metatron paled. "We can't let that happen." A communication portal the size of a dinner plate opened out of thin air in front of him. "We need to assign a legion of battle angels to guard the containment stone."

Reaver waved the portal away. This needed to stay between him and Metatron. "I've already done that." Covertly. "Azagoth's not going to escape by breaking the spell that contains him. But he won't stop looking for a way out. And in the meantime, he has a lot of weapons at his disposal."

Hawkyn hadn't said what weapons, exactly, but he didn't have to. Azagoth could blackmail anyone he wanted, simply by threatening their eternal soul. If that didn't work, he had other kinds of blackmail material on an alarming number of powerful humans and almost every demon alive—provided by the souls he interrogated when they arrived in Sheoul-gra.

Metatron stared at Reaver. "Where's Revenant in all this? How could he let Moloch take over?"

"I don't know. He hasn't responded to my summons." Reaver jammed a frustrated hand through his shoulder-length, blond hair. "He's got his own shit to deal with. Everyone is plotting against him. Someone tried to abduct Blaspheme a few months ago, and just last month, some of Satan's whelps got together and tried to bring Revenant down. They got closer than he liked while doing it."

"What happened to those who attacked him?"

"Ah, yeah, fun story. After torturing and killing them, he preserved their bodies, sewed them together, and mounted them on the bridge to Satan's castle. He ordered them to remain for a thousand years so they'd be on display for Satan to see." Revenant had a vengeful streak. "The weird thing is, he didn't keep their souls."

"*That's* the weird part?" At Reaver's shrug, Metatron sighed. "Did he send the souls of Satan's bastards to Azagoth?"

"Yep."

"A message? A gift?"

"No idea." Reaver shook his head. "I'm worried, though. Blaspheme hasn't shown up to work in days, and Revenant is missing in action. At best, I don't think we can count on his help. At worst, he's involved somehow."

Metatron had been intermittently gazing out at the sea, but now his eyes cut sharply to Reaver. "Involved?"

"It can't be a coincidence that he's missing as this is happening," Reaver pointed out. "And not long ago, I altered Wraith's invincibility ward to include protection from fallen angels." The demon had proven to be a loyal friend and an invaluable asset for Team Good, and Reaver had wanted to keep him safe. "Wraith was killed by a fallen angel, but just before he died, he said he'd seen Revenant, who is one of the few people who could remove the protection I gave Wraith."

"Any principality or archangel could do it. Why would *he* do that?"

And that was the million-dollar question. Revenant had grown up in Sheoul, tortured and believing that he was something he wasn't. Some in Heaven didn't think he could possibly be anything but pure evil, but Reaver knew better. There had been a lot of hate between them for a long time, but that was over. Reaver trusted his brother.

"I'm sure he had a good reason."

Metatron leveled Reaver with a grave look. "We have to inform the Archangel Council. Maybe even the Angelic Council or the Council of Orders."

"No!" Reaver barked and then tempered his voice. He might, technically, be Metatron's equal in many ways, but Uncle Met commanded—and deserved—respect, not only because of his station as the Creator's mouthpiece and right-hand man but also because he was the most decent angel Reaver knew. "Not yet. We can fix this."

"Before Azagoth releases Satan?"

"He's not going to do that."

"Why?" Metatron's voice was edged with doubt. "Because he told you he wouldn't?"

"No. Because he hates Satan."

Metatron's gaze shifted to his palace and the balcony above, where Caila was entertaining a giggling group of friends. "More than he loves his mate?"

"I have no doubt Azagoth will stop at nothing to save Lilliana," Reaver admitted. "But he knows that if he releases Satan, Satan will kill Lilliana. He can't risk it."

"What do you suggest we do then?"

"I can talk to him," Reaver said. "Hawkyn requested information about a fallen angel named Flail. I'll use that as an excuse to get to Azagoth."

A flock of gulls squawked as the birds circled the palace, looking for handouts from Caila's guests, and Metatron had to raise his voice to be heard. "You said he sealed off Sheoul-gra."

"Hawkyn will open it to me if I can convince him that I'm not there to destroy his father."

It shouldn't be a problem; Hawkyn wouldn't have contacted Reaver at all if he weren't sure Reaver could handle the situation without killing anyone.

"And if Azagoth is out of control?" Metatron asked. "Will you destroy him?"

"Isn't it a little early to be discussing that?"

Metatron rolled his shoulders, probably not even aware he'd done it, but Reaver knew he was testing his wings and his powers, feeling them out at the thought that shit might get really fucking biblical real soon.

"He can't be allowed to release Satan," he said, fire in his tone. "And he can't be allowed to escape Sheoul-gra."

"Would escaping be such a bad thing?"

Reaver wasn't Azagoth's biggest fan, but the guy had been trapped for thousands of years. He'd proven that he was capable of wrangling souls and navigating the politics of both Sheoul and Heaven. He'd chilled out a lot since getting mated, too. Seemed like it wouldn't be a big deal if he lived where he wanted and commuted to work.

Metatron appeared troubled that Reaver would even ask such an apparently insane question. "Yes, it could be bad."

"Why?" Reaver asked. "I mean, I get that he's an asshole, but a lot *bigger* assholes are running around loose."

Like the fallen angels who had killed Wraith. He clenched his fists, wishing he was out hunting them right now.

"Azagoth signed contracts," Metatron said. "Contracts sealed with the powers of Heaven and Sheoul. We don't know what kind of damage we'd take if he made that big of a breach."

Sounded kind of minor to Reaver, but he knew well how seriously Heaven took broken rules and breaches of contract. They also weren't fond of Heaven being damaged, which was why Revenant, while technically welcome here, wasn't...*welcome*. His presence destroyed everything around him.

"Okay," Reaver said. "Let me grab the info on Flail and give Hawkyn a call. I'll let you know what happens. And, Uncle?"

Metatron inclined his head.

"I want this to stay between us for now."

Silence stretched. Not even the gulls called out, and Reaver started to sweat. Metatron had always been fair and by-the-book, which was probably part of why Reaver had been such a rule breaker as a youth. And beyond. Hell, he still was, he just wasn't as reckless about it now.

Responsibility was a bitch.

"For now," Metatron finally said. "But be ready to be called to testify before any number of high councils. This isn't going to stay quiet for long, and there are a lot of people who would love to see Azagoth gone."

That made no sense. "What did he do to make anyone want him gone so badly? As Asrael, he was a hero. If not for him, Satan and his acolytes could have destroyed everything."

"People have short memories," Metatron said, his mouth quirking in the first smile Reaver had seen from him all day. "Especially the mates of the females Azagoth bred Memitim with."

Reaver laughed. Yeah, he could see how jealous mates might not want reminders that their lovers had, before mating them, been bedded by the Grim Reaper.

Reaver sprang his wings, and gold glitter floated through the air. "Thank you, Uncle."

"Just..." Metatron gripped Reaver's shoulder and gave it an affectionate squeeze. "Be prepared."

"Prepared for what?"

"For the worst." Metatron's voice lowered into what some called his God Voice, a resonant tone that vibrated the air when he brought proclamations or messages from the Creator. "Satan cannot be freed. If that means Azagoth must die, so be it."

Yeah, Reaver got the message.

He'd have to be the one to do it.

Chapter 16

Hope isn't for fools.

Hope isn't for fools.

Azagoth told himself that over and over but, not unexpectedly, it didn't help him feel better any more than getting fucked in the ass by a quill troll would make him feel better.

An hour ago, he'd been confident of victory. Moloch had, according to Azagoth's sources, an army of millions, but his supporters were spread all throughout Sheoul-gra. Only a fraction was guarding his castle. Ares' battle plan had looked solid, if not foolproof.

Until they started getting credible reports that Moloch had taken Satan's palace from Revenant.

If that were true, Lilliana could be held in either stronghold, and the odds of victory had taken a dive. They'd been forced to pursue Plan B, splitting Azagoth's army in two, and giving Ares' brother Reseph command of one of them. They'd attack both fortresses simultaneously and hope like hell they had enough soldiers to do it.

Fuck. This was not how Azagoth wanted to do this. Both Horsemen were legendary warriors, their skill in battle unequaled in all of history. But looking at the campaign, all laid out on a giant map that covered every inch of the hundred-seat command center table, wasn't the most inspiring thing ever.

Moloch's armies spanned four regions, with pockets of troops in nearly all the rest. That the bastard had been able to so easily gather demons who should have been loyal to Revenant was disturbing…and also unfortunate.

Azagoth cursed and knocked over one of the thousands of D&D

figures Cipher had brought to represent the armies.

Moloch's forces of little green plastic orcs, goblins, and imps took up far too much real estate. Azagoth's hundred thousand demons were represented by far fewer silver plastic trolls, and the five thousand hellhounds Cara had sent were on the map as black dire wolf figures. The two remaining figurines were the ones he focused on, a hand-painted elf ranger, and a human fighter who looked remarkably like their doubles, Reseph and Ares.

The two Horsemen known as Pestilence and War would lead the charges, and once they got close enough, they would retrieve Lilliana—with the help of Azagoth's spies inside the fortresses. At least, that was the plan.

Ares said that things rarely went as planned.

Fucking Horseman and his frank, honest assessments. Azagoth flicked the fighter figurine onto the floor because that was what mature males with control of their emotions did.

If Lilliana were here, she'd give him a look full of, *did you really just do that?*

If she were here, he wouldn't have done it.

Getting his shit together, he picked Ares off the floor. In truth, the guy's frankness was what made him valuable as an advisor. There was nothing more useless than a sycophant who told him only what he wanted to hear. But just this once, it would have been great if Ares had sugarcoated the pill he'd given him before he and Reseph left to stage for the battle.

"We'll be severely outnumbered." Ares gestured to areas of the map near Moloch's castle. "Here, here, and here." He moved several feet down the table and waved his hand over Satan's territory, which Moloch apparently now held. "We're not outnumbered here, but I doubt Reseph can get past the natural geological barriers, and even if he does, there are a lot of things worse than a demon army protecting the palace." He gripped the sword at his hip and swung around to Azagoth in a smooth, crisp turn. "You're going to lose your entire army with no guarantee that I'll get in."

It was not what Azagoth wanted to hear. "It's the only chance I have, Ares," he snapped. *"What would you do?"*

Ares ran his thumb across the sword's pommel as if remembering the thousands of battles he'd fought, the millions he'd killed. "I'd do exactly what you're doing," he said. *"But I'd do it knowing that even with the hellhounds Cara's sending, the chance of success is maybe…fifty-fifty."*

"You're just a ray of fucking sunshine, aren't you?"

"Did you want me to blow smoke up your ass? Because that's not my kink, and I'd rather not pop my cherry with the Grim Reaper."

As irritated as Azagoth was, he had to admire the guy. He was a brilliant tactician, a warrior who commanded respect, and a fierce defender of those he cared about. There had been a time when Ares, along with his three Horseman siblings, believed that Azagoth was their sire. He wondered if they'd been relieved when they learned the truth, that Reaver was their father.

Father.

He reached up and fingered the scythe pendant Lilliana had given him, taking comfort in the connection they'd established and experienced. Could they do it again? If he laid down on the floor right now and closed his eyes, would she be there?

He'd never wanted to sleep more in his life.

A tap at one of the door columns brought him sharply back to the present.

"Enter," he called out as he glanced at his watch. The rescue attempt would begin in thirty-four minutes.

"Azagoth."

"Reaver." Summoning his power, Azagoth spun around to the south entrance with a hiss. "Why didn't I sense your arrival?"

Reaver strode toward him in jeans and a black tee, his blond hair shorter than the last time he'd seen him, his expression far less angry. "The last time I was here to spank your ass, I figured out how to conceal my signature."

The last time Reaver was here, he'd delivered a warning not to fuck with Moloch. Something told Azagoth that attacking Moloch might count as fucking with him.

"Who let you in?" As if he didn't know. Only Hawkyn and Z could open the portal, and Z would die before doing so without permission.

Reaver didn't answer. "I hear you want information about Flail."

"You could have sent a text."

"I could have. But I wanted to see if I could help."

Although Azagoth didn't doubt that Reaver would do what he could for Lilliana, he did doubt that helping was his sole reason for being here, and Azagoth called him on it.

"You wanted to make sure that what I'm doing to get Lilliana back isn't violating my contract." Azagoth gestured to the map, figuring…what the hell. If the angel could help, at this point, he'd take it. "I've got two Horsemen going against Moloch, leading hellhounds and legions of demons I command." It wasn't a lie. He did command his secret re-souled army, but he'd also gotten an influx of demons who'd joined his cause, some mercs for pay or those who owed him, and even a few who knew he had blackmail material on them.

Reaver narrowed his eyes at him. "How did you get my sons to risk themselves for you? If you threatened them—"

"I didn't, you winged jackass. They volunteered. Reseph likes a good fight, and Ares wants to help Lilliana. I'd have had all four Horsemen, but Limos and Thanatos are hunting the fallen angels who killed Wraith. Thanatos caught one, so he's...busy, and Limos said she'd drop in and help fight if she didn't bag a fallen angel of her own by the time the battle starts. So, yeah, you can help. How about you destroy Moloch and his armies and then grab Lilliana? That'd be great."

"You know I can't do that."

"I know you can go almost anywhere in Sheoul you want to go. Just as Revenant has access to Heaven."

Reaver studied the armies surrounding the fortresses. "I'm not merely forbidden to enter any region held by Satan, I'm *incapable* of it. And since Moloch holds the lands for Satan, I don't have access to his fortresses."

"You can wipe out his armies beyond the regions he holds."

"Not inside Sheoul. There are rules, Azagoth." Reaver's gaze held his, the Radiant's look edged with a warning. "You'd do well to remember that."

Azagoth laughed at Reaver's arrogance. "Rules? You, the greatest rule breaker in all of history, are lecturing *me* about adhering to protocol?"

Reaver shrugged. "You're catching on."

"Go fuck yourself," Azagoth growled. "I haven't broken any rules."

"No? Did you not give your *griminions* the power to kill?"

Azagoth's jaw damned near hit his boots. Somehow, he managed to keep his composure, even as his mind raced to figure out who had betrayed him.

"It was a long-overdo upgrade," he said. "Hardly anything to get worked up over. And I did have the demon lawyers at Dire and Dyre look over my contract. They think the section on *griminions* is vague enough to allow some play." Heaven had fucked him over with the vague thing, and Azagoth figured it was his turn to twist a clause in his favor. "You should know, I'll fight any attempts by Heaven to find me in violation of the contract."

"Don't bullshit me, Azagoth." Reaver crossed his arms over his chest. "What you did was illegal, and you know it."

Cipher had set up dozens of noncombatant figurines around the map, some chosen to represent specific people, some more generic, and Azagoth picked up one with wings as he paced slowly, opposite the table from Reaver.

"You said you were here about Flail."

The smug jackass pulled out his cell phone, tapped angrily, and then shoved it back into his pocket. "I emailed the file."

"Then you'll be leaving, I assume."

"Right after you assure me you aren't going to release Satan from the prison I put him in."

That Reaver was concerned was a no-brainer. He and his twin, Revenant, had pissed off the most powerful, infamous, grudge-holding fallen angel in existence. Of course, they wouldn't want him walking out on parole nine hundred and some odd years early. Azagoth got that. He wasn't Satan's Facebook friend, either.

"I won't release him from his prison," Azagoth promised.

"And how can I trust that, given that you've already broken a contract signed in your own blood?"

Azagoth squeezed the figurine so hard, its wings pierced the skin of his thumb. "I told you, *griminions* are a gray area."

"And what of Part III, Section II, Paragraph I, which specifically states that you cannot, using any means or method, release souls from Sheoul-gra unless they are to be reincarnated? Is that a gray area? I warned you, Azagoth. After you released souls to go after Bael, I warned you not to do it again. Specifically, not to go after his twin."

Yeah, Reaver had warned him, all right.

If you kill him, all that you know, all that you are...will be destroyed.

Which was why Azagoth had given strict orders to capture Moloch, not kill him.

"You don't need to worry about Moloch."

Reaver swiped a hand over the map and grabbed a handful of silver game pieces. Azagoth's army. "But I do need to worry about the hundred thousand souls you released."

Son of a bitch.

There was no point in denying it. There was no point in anything except getting Lilliana back. "It's not worth ruffling your feathers over.

Most of them will die in battle and return to Sheoul-gra."

"Don't bullshit me!" Reaver repeated, his white and gold wings flaring, and his body glowing with power. "You broke at least three rules, and you did it on a huge scale. You released souls, you gave them the power to evict the souls of living demons, which ultimately gave you a hundred thousand more souls, and then they took over the physical bodies. What you've done is *beyond* forbidden."

"And I'd do it again," Azagoth yelled back, charging up his own power. Reaver could kick his ass, but Azagoth would fuck him up hard before it happened. "It's my wife and child!"

"I can't keep protecting you." Reaver swept his arm across the map, wiping it clean. "Right now, this is contained. But it *will* come out, and I don't know what's going to happen."

"What is it you want me to do, Reaver?"

Reaver inhaled deeply, and his wings settled against his back. "I want you to win the battle, and I want you to get Lilliana back. She doesn't deserve this. None of you do."

Azagoth crushed a figurine from Moloch's army under his boot. "Then maybe you could find your brother. He could end all of this."

"Well, gee, I hadn't thought of that," Reaver said with a roll of his brilliant blue eyes. "I don't suppose you know where he could be?"

As if Azagoth hadn't given that very question a lot of thought. "Depends on if he gave up his reign willingly or not."

"He didn't. He's imprisoned somewhere. I know he is."

"Then that narrows down the places he could be." Azagoth flicked his finger, and all of the figurines on the floor jumped back onto the map. "In order to trap someone as powerful as Revenant, you'd need a container as strong as the one you created for Satan."

"There are few who can create one like that."

Azagoth nodded. "I'm aware of that." He willed the figurines to fight, playing out a battle on the table that he was guaranteed to win. "But one already exists. There's just one catch."

"What do you mean?"

The hellhound figures took down a skeleton army guarding Moloch's north wall. "A few thousand years ago, some fallen angels who were pissed off at Satan built a prison hidden inside a temple, but there were a few snags."

"Such as?"

"Well, Satan got wind of it, for one. But the real problem is that it's a voluntary trap." At Reaver's raised eyebrows, he continued. "Its power comes from the victim's desire to be inside it."

"Who would *want* to be inside it?"

Azagoth used to wonder the same thing. Now, he knew. "Anyone whose mate was being used as the bait."

"Do you know where it is?"

"Inside a temple in the Ca'askull region. Getting there is a journey many don't survive, and only a handful know it was built to house the trap. The snare itself is like the Abyss in Heaven." It had, in fact, been built using materials from Heaven, a dirty little secret Azagoth had learned when he questioned the original builders, one of whom still resided on the second ring of the Inner Sanctum. "You can only find it if the need is great enough."

"Revenant's need would be great if he believed his mate was inside," Reaver said grimly. "I've got to find that temple."

"You can't. The trap was built with the secret help of angels. I don't know who. It was designed so an angel could lure Satan inside and still get out after it'd closed. But when Satan got wind of the temple's purpose, he claimed it in his name."

"Which means, it's his property, and even I can't get to it," Reaver snarled. "Damn it." He cursed again. "I still have to try."

Azagoth wished him luck. He looked at his map and revised that thought. He wished them *all* luck.

They were going to need it.

Chapter 17

The Fourth Horseman of the Apocalypse, the legend known as Thanatos to friends, and Death to everyone else, wasn't notorious for his generous spirit or tendency to dole out mercy. Nope. Thanatos was proud to be renowned for the exact opposite.

The fallen angel hanging in his dungeon could testify to that. The fucker would definitely agree that killing Thanatos's best friend drew out the very worst in Death.

He wiped his hands on a bloodstained rag as he climbed the winding stone steps to the castle's main residence where he lived with his mate, Regan, their children Logan and Amber, and dozens of vampire servants. There was also a bison-sized hellhound running around somewhere, but Thanatos hadn't seen Cujo since this morning when Logan had been slipping the beast bites of sausage from his breakfast plate.

The heavy wooden door at the top of the stairs swung open as he reached for the handle.

"Hey, bro." Limos, the Horseman called Famine, stepped aside, her Hawaiian-print sundress swirling around her slender thighs. "Regan said you were downstairs. Thought I'd see if you needed help."

Help? As if. "My name is Death. I think I've got this."

Inhaling the mouthwatering aroma of baking bread coming from the kitchen, he closed the dungeon door and engaged the lock. Regan would be furious if one of the kids found their way down there. Something about scarring them for life and maybe being out of car seats before they were allowed to play with iron maidens and torture racks.

Kids these days were so sheltered.

"Well, what has he told you so far?" Limos followed him as he headed for the washroom, her steps so light, he didn't even hear them.

"I only started questioning him a few minutes ago, but he's given up the names of his accomplices and the fucker who hired them to make sure Lilliana left Underworld General via the Harrowgate instead of the parking lot." He washed and dried. "As suspected, it was Moloch."

"Fucking perv," Limos muttered, her violet eyes sparking with outrage. "He used to come and check my chastity belt, you know, for *fit,* back when I was living with Mommie Dearest." She wrapped a strand of long, black hair around her finger and tugged angrily. "He was so disgusting. I finally shoved a fork in his eye. Hoo boy, he was *not* happy."

That made Thanatos chuckle. While Reseph, Ares, and Thanatos had grown up in the human world, unaware that they were the product of a union between the angel Reaver and the succubus Lilith, Limos had been raised with their mother in Sheoul. Promised to Satan as his bride when she was just an infant, she'd been forced to wear a chastity belt from the moment she could walk.

Thanatos would have eye-forked any sick bastard who wanted to check it for *fit,* too. Good for her.

He patted his pocket. Dammit, he'd left his phone in the dungeon. He headed back, Limos still on his heels. "Any news from the battle? Last I heard, Ares had just led the initial charge."

"I have news," she said, "but you're not going to want to hear it."

Wasn't that par for the course? He unlocked the dungeon door. "Lay it on me. I've sensed large-scale death for hours."

Normally, he'd be drawn to the scene, but dealing with the fallen angel had been enough to satisfy his bloodlust for battle.

The sound of his boots and Limos's flip-flops echoed off the tight, narrow walls as they descended into the dank underbelly of his fortress.

"Ares led Azagoth's army against the forces surrounding Moloch's keep, and he was kicking ass." The icy temperature as they descended made Limos's breath visible as she spoke. "But then Moloch brought in a dozen fallen angels and a hundred thousand demon soldiers through a giant temporary Harrowgate."

That made Thanatos halt in his tracks so fast that Limos bumped into him. "How is that even possible?"

"No idea." She gave him a nudge to get him moving again. "And Reseph couldn't even get within a thousand miles of Revenant's fortress."

Ares must be furious. The only thing he hated more than losing a battle was losing a battle to a fallen angel.

"Reseph's assault was pretty much doomed from the beginning," Than said. "No one has ever taken Satan's castle by force. But the attack on Moloch should have gone better. I mean, Ares is *War*. If he were a *Dungeons and Dragons* character, he'd get plus-three modifiers to all his ability scores." He reconsidered that. "Except charisma. He'd take a big hit there. And he'd get a proficiency bonus on every roll just because of his name." Well, his name and several thousand years of killing people in battle.

"If you're trying to say that Ares has the tactical advantage against anyone, in any and all wartime situations, just say it." She huffed. "You don't have to get all weird and nerdy."

Thanatos smiled sadly. Wraith had been the one to get him into role-playing games, and before his death at the hands of the fucker in the dungeon, they'd been planning a game with Hawkyn, Journey, Maddox, Emerico, Cipher, and Declan.

Oh, yeah, the fucker in the dungeon was going to pay.

"What about the hellhounds?" he asked. "Ares should have been able to take Moloch's castle with a legion of those things."

"They refused to fight."

He halted at the base of the stairs and glanced back at his sister in disbelief. "Hellhounds. *Hellhounds* refused to fight."

"I know, right?" Limos gave an incredulous shrug. "Ares thinks it's because Moloch's army is basically Satan's army, and hellhounds won't fight Satan."

Well, fuck.

He ducked through the archway to the torture chamber, the stench of piss and fear drowning out the last lingering notes of baking bread. His phone was on the table next to all his fun medieval tools—he was something of a collector, really—and as he reached for it, he heard a wet thud followed by a grunt. He turned to see Limos, standing on a crate, nose-to-nose with Curson as he hung by his mangled wrists.

"Why did you kill Wraith?" Limos cut a punch to his gut. "Tell me, you piece of shit."

The angel flashed blood-streaked fangs. Well, *fang*. Thanatos had knocked out the other one hours ago.

"Because we could," Curson snarled. "The demon hunted us for long enough."

Thanatos drew in an uneasy breath. He'd warned Wraith that taking out fallen angels for sport would earn him some powerful enemies. Wraith hadn't listened. "*Hunters gotta hunt*," he'd said, completely oblivious to the risks and consequences he could face.

Arrogant fool! If Wraith were here now, Than would beat some sense into him. He'd make the idiot understand how his loss would affect his family, his friends. Thanatos.

Grief squeezed his heart, crippling him for a moment as Limos grilled Curson. He didn't care what she did to him. Limos had cared for Wraith, too.

"How did you kill him?" Punch. Grunt.

Grin. "A sword through the heart."

Enraged by the flippant answer and the sickening glee in Curson's smile, Thanatos shoved past Limos and slammed his fist into the bastard's sternum, delivering a solid, bone-cracking blow to his black heart.

"How?" he demanded. "Wraith was immune to damage from fallen angels."

It took Curson thirty seconds to stop wheezing. "Moloch assured us"—he gasped again—"that was no longer the case."

"And how did Moloch know that?" Limos asked, and Curson clammed up, clenching his jaw and staring in defiance. "How?"

She jammed one cheery yellow fingernail under his chin, and a couple of heartbeats later, his muscles started to dissolve beneath his skin as his body digested itself. Curson's deep, resonant scream came from his very soul.

"This is famine," she growled. "Soon, you'll be nothing but skin and bones and gnawing agony. Tell me how Moloch knew Wraith's charm had been disabled, and I'll stop."

"He arranged it," Curson blurted. "Stop! Please...stop."

Pleased with herself, Limos stepped back and brushed off her hands as Curson went limp with exhaustion, his ribs showing where they hadn't before.

"That's not something he could just...arrange," Thanatos said. "Not when a Radiant angel is the one who bestowed that immunity on him. So, who did Moloch get to remove the enchantment?"

Curson said nothing, trying to catch his breath, but when Limos took a step forward, he remarkably found his voice.

"One of the only people besides Reaver who could." The fallen angel lifted his wobbly head to give Thanatos a weary smile of contempt, and Thanatos's heart lurched. *Don't say it. Don't say it...* "His twin, your uncle. Revenant."

Chapter 18

The shackles around Lilliana's wrists chafed with every sharp tug made by the scrawny, twisted demon dragging her down the torch-lit hallway. Her bare feet kept tripping over the uneven flooring, and it was a miracle she hadn't taken a tumble yet.

"Where are we going?" She yanked on the chains, earning another violent tug that sent her careening into the wet, slimy wall.

She didn't know why she even tried. The twisty bastard hadn't said a single word since fetching her from her cell.

But he really didn't need to. She had a sick feeling that she was about to face the consequences of Azagoth's failure to release Satan by Moloch's deadline. Fear, so intense she could smell it coming out of her pores, made her even clumsier as Twisty hauled her into the great room she knew well by now.

When she wasn't in a filthy cell, she was chained to the skull throne, forced to watch the depraved activities of Moloch's guests and servants. That was when she was lucky. When she wasn't…

She shuddered. She could take any amount of torture she was subjected to…she'd suffered at the hands of a monster before. What she couldn't take was the thought of her baby suffering, and she wasn't sure how much longer it could remain in the safety of her womb.

Not that there was a choice, obviously. But that didn't mean she couldn't keep repeating, over and over, "Stay inside, little one. Stay inside where it's safe."

Twisty wrenched the chain and swung her into the middle of the room…and into a crowd of demons and fallen angels, all of them sporting heinous, fresh injuries. Some snarled at her as if it were her fault that they were missing limbs, while others leered or wagged their forked tongues at her in obscene gestures.

God, she wished she was asleep. In sleep, she was happy. Safe. And Azagoth might be there. Or Maleficent.

At first, Lilliana had been startled to see Mal flickering on the periphery of her dreams. Then she remembered Cara mentioning that bonded hellhounds could communicate through dreams, and while Mal had never given Lilliana a *hellhound's kiss* to create the bond, Lilliana still felt a connection with the beast.

Mystical bonds aside, Lilliana had tried to get close to Mal in her dreams, and Mal had clearly wanted to get to Lilliana, but it was as if there was a hundred-yard-thick force field between them. Maybe the lack of a true bond had kept them from being able to communicate in the dreams, or maybe Maleficent's abilities weren't powerful enough to reach Lilliana. It would make sense, given that her small size and lack of physical and supernatural strength had made her an outcast among her kind.

Cara had said that if not for her and the safety of Ares' island, hellhounds would have ripped Mal to pieces long ago.

Twisty clamped his three-clawed paw down on the back of Lilliana's neck and forced her to the ground, where he clipped her chain to a drain grate that was already gurgling with the blood of the injured demons.

Terror spiked as the crowd parted and scrambled backward, and she knew Moloch was coming.

"Your mate has been a bad boy." The grotesquely distorted architecture of the room, reminiscent of a charred skeleton that had been stretched and warped, amplified Moloch's voice into a terrifying entity of its own.

But that was nothing compared to the sight of the big male, his three-foot horns dripping gore onto his bald head. His armor, as grotesque and skeletal as the chamber's architecture, glistened with blood splatter, and the cracks in his gauntlets were caked with bits of flesh and hair.

Stark fear clawed at Lilliana on a level so primal, she forgot how to breathe. *Inhale. Inhale. Inhale, dammit!*

Somehow, she didn't pass out or piss herself. Somehow, she raised her head and met Moloch's black gaze with defiance. "Not naughty enough. You're still alive."

She paid for that with a backhand that knocked her back so hard that her shoulders nearly dislocated when the chain jerked her body. Welcoming the pain throbbing in her wrists, shoulders, and jaw because it chased away the terror, she braced herself for the next blow.

"I fucking told him not to try anything stupid. So, what does he do? He tries something stupid." Moloch bit out a handful of curses in Sheoulic. "He and his Horseman buddies slaughtered thousands of my men."

Lilliana had a hard time feeling bad about that. Still, she offered her most insincere condolences. "I'm so *very* sorry."

That earned her another backhand and a subsequent throbbing cheek to match the first one. "You *will* be sorry." The crazy in his eyes dimmed a little, a sign, she'd learned, that meant the Moloc half of the soul had more influence than the Bael half. Both were dangerous in different ways, but she preferred to deal with the slightly more stable personality of Moloc. "Azagoth will be even sorrier. Heaven isn't going to be happy about what he's done."

She snorted. "I don't think Heaven will care that he snuffed some evil scum."

Flail strutted up next to Moloch in thigh-high boots, her fine mesh catsuit revealing pretty much everything. "I think they'll care that he re-souled tens of thousands of demons to do it."

"He...re-souled them?" Lilliana couldn't hide her shock. Or her disbelief. Azagoth possessed the ultimate authority to send demon souls to be reincarnated, but he couldn't give souls corporeal form, nor could he gift souls with the ability to take over physical bodies that already housed a soul. "He couldn't. He doesn't have that power."

"Apparently, with the help of a Charnel Apostle, he does," Moloch said.

Lilliana wanted to deny that he'd use a Charnel Apostle for anything, let alone a forbidden ritual, but she also knew the lengths Azagoth would go to in order to get what he wanted. At this point, her only play was to get as much intel as possible in case she could connect with her mate again in dreams.

"How do you know this?" she demanded. "Your spy inside Sheoul-gra?"

Moloch suddenly and violently went down to his haunches and grabbed her by the throat, his metal-covered fingers digging painfully into her skin. "I captured some of them." He bared his teeth, strings of saliva stretching from his upper jaw to the lower, his fetid breath burning her eyes. "Your mate released thousands of souls from Sheoul-gra with orders to kill and possess bodies before breaching my fortress, capturing me, and rescuing you. I told him not to fuck with me. I *warned* him."

"I tried to tell you, Lilliana," Flail said, her voice strangely soft. "You should have called Azagoth."

Still in Moloch's grasp, Lilliana struggled for air. "It wouldn't have mattered," she gasped, wrapping her arms protectively around her belly. "He's not going to release Satan. He's not going to give you what you want."

"Oh, but he will," Moloch began, his voice as silky as warm blood. "Especially if I start sending you back." Releasing her, he drew a wicked, jagged blade from the sheath at his hip. The primal fear roared back.

"Piece by piece."

Chapter 19

Hawkyn didn't want to do this.

Of all the news he'd delivered in his life, this was the worst. His father had already been dealt a blow when they learned that his army of re-souled demons had failed to take either of Moloch's strongholds.

Azagoth also had to know that Hawkyn had not only ratted him out to Reaver, but that he'd also let Reaver inside Sheoul-gra. Strangely, his father hadn't even addressed it yet. One would think that was good news; Azagoth hadn't gone nuclear. Cool.

One would be wrong.

When Azagoth didn't freak out, it was scary as fuck.

Raised voices drifted down the hall from the war room as Hawkyn approached. What a shitty day. And it was about to get worse.

Two blows, back-to-back. And now for the knockout punch.

Taking a bracing breath, Hawkyn adjusted the duffel over his shoulder and walked into Azagoth's command center.

The place was a zoo, packed wall-to-wall with proven allies, spies, assassins, and a couple of Moloch's minions, who were oblivious to the fact that Azagoth knew they were enemies. They'd be provided information Azagoth and Ares wanted leaked.

At the center of the room, hovering over the map of Sheoul-gra, was Azagoth.

In a room full of giant people and legends, he stood out in a modified form of his beast, his horns curling behind his head, his eyes aflame with hellfire, his skin a deep blood-red.

Hawkyn felt the moment Azagoth's gaze lit on him, the scorching heat burning like lasers where it landed.

Hawk knew better than to look directly into his eyes.

"I need to speak to my father," Hawkyn barked. "Everyone out."

For a couple of heartbeats, no one moved. Several looked to Azagoth for guidance, but when all he did was stare at Hawkyn, they hastily scurried out through the multiple doorways.

The fire in Azagoth's eyes burned brighter now. Brighter *and* bigger, the flames all but licking his eyebrows. He'd turned the heat down at least, allowing Hawkyn to look at him.

Not that he wanted to.

"We're going to strike again," Azagoth said, his voice smoky and full of demonic resonance. "Reseph is going to unload a pestilence on Moloch's forces here"—he gestured to a grouping of plastic orcs—"and here." He wiped out the second group with his hand. "Dracxis will lead a team of assassins through the broken line here—"

"Father."

"What? Whatever it is, say it quickly. We have to attack again before Moloch regroups and hurts Lilliana. We lost the gamble, but we hurt him. Ares says he won't expect another attack so soon—"

"Father!" Hawkyn laid the giant duffel on the map, knocking over vast swaths of armies. "It's too late."

"What's too late?"

Hawkyn swallowed. "Moloch sent this."

Azagoth went utterly still. A chill spread through the room, growing so cold that streaks of frost formed on the floor. Then, in a blur of motion, Azagoth crossed to the duffel and unzipped it.

The floor tiles cracked under the polar temperatures that plunged the room into a deep freeze.

Azagoth's shock and pain turned the very air brittle as the color drained from his skin, and his horns and claws receded. His wings...they didn't retract. They shriveled.

"No," he whispered. "Ah...no."

Azagoth swayed, and if not for Hawkyn bracing him against his chest, his father would have sunk to the floor.

"That bastard." Azagoth peeled away from Hawkyn and stumbled to the bottle of whiskey at the end of the table. "That...*bastard!*"

"Father." Hawkyn cursed the tremor in his voice. "Moloch said...he said that if you attack again, it won't be a piece of Lilliana he sends in a bag. If you want to know what you'll get next time, he suggested you refer to *Paradise Lost.*"

In *Paradise Lost*, Moloch had a thing for child sacrifice.

With a bellow of fury, Azagoth wheeled around. "Ares!" he roared, and the Horseman, who must have been right outside the door, stepped inside. "Call off the attack. No one is to go near Moloch. No one."

Ares hesitated for a moment, but after a glance at the duffel and Hawkyn, he wisely nodded and slipped out of the room.

"Father? What can I do?"

Azagoth held up his hand in a leave-me-alone gesture as he walked toward the south exit, his gait unsteady. "Sleep," he rasped. "I need to sleep."

Sleep? They were in the middle of a crisis, and the Grim Reaper wanted to take a damned nap?

Hawkyn felt Jasmine's approach, appreciated her comforting presence next to him. "What's going on?"

"I don't know," he said. "But I think things just got a whole lot worse."

Chapter 20

Lilliana ran along the seashore in a hot pink bikini, her bare feet splashing in the waves as the water lapped at her toes. She inhaled, taking in the salty air and the fresh scent of the citrus groves that dotted Ares' Greek island.

She'd jogged daily when she lived here, until her eighth month of pregnancy when she'd had to walk instead. She came to a stop, kicking droplets of sand and water onto her calves. This was a dream, but it was real.

Her hand went to her belly. Flat.

Right. This was the baby-power again. The dreams always started like this, and she had to remember what was happening. Maybe Azagoth would be here this time.

Please, please let him show up.

She rolled her shoulders, thankful that the pain of having her wings sawed off was gone. At least here in the dream world. Back on the cold floor of her cell, the agony was unbearable.

And yet, some of the pain wasn't physical. A lot of it, actually.

She was going to die. She knew that, and she'd made peace with it. Well, maybe not *peace* exactly, but on some level, she'd accepted her fate.

What occupied her thoughts and terrified her beyond belief during every waking moment was concern for the baby. It couldn't be born in Sheoul. There were monsters and misery around every corner, and the biggest fiend of all was Moloch.

Imagining what he would do to the innocent child of his enemy— easy to do since Moloch had described it to her in graphic detail—had left her shaking and vomiting for hours afterward.

And if, somehow, she was able to get it out of her head, her thoughts turned to Azagoth, and what he would go through if he lost them both.

When she first met the Grim Reaper, he'd been cold, all but dead inside. Ironically, he'd been emotionally numb because he'd once felt *too* much. As an empath of extreme sensitivity, he'd been pummeled by the emotions of others, and losing the ability had given him peace and freedom.

At least it had until Lilliana had awakened his emotions again. It had taken time for him to get them under control, and it was still a daily struggle. What would happen if he lost himself to grief and anger?

She was afraid she knew the answer to that.

It would consume him. It would destroy everything he'd built, everything he loved.

"Lilliana?"

Grinning, almost giddy at the sound of Azagoth's voice, Lilliana spun around in the wet sand, only to be greeted by his expression of sheer devastation.

She launched herself across the distance and into his arms, desperate to comfort him, to keep him from falling into self-destruction. "It's okay, Azagoth. I'm okay."

"Your wings," he croaked. "I'm so sorry. I'm so…sorry."

"Shh." She framed his face with her hands, forcing him to look at her. "They'll grow back. It's okay," she said, even though it wasn't.

Her wings wouldn't grow back until she got out of Sheoul, and she wasn't one hundred percent sure they'd fare better in Sheoul-gra.

"I know how much it hurt—"

She hushed him with a kiss. "I didn't feel anything." Another lie. She wondered if he'd taste the deception on her lips. "Flail did something to dull my senses."

"Why?" His voice rang with justifiable skepticism. "Why would she do that?"

Lilliana thought back to Flail's visit the other day in the cell. The fallen angel had come back twice more with edible food to convince Lilliana to call Azagoth, and both times, she'd refused. Flail's pattern had been the same, first to plead, and then to get angry and throw around insults—and some of Lilliana's dinner.

But she hadn't once hurt Lilliana. During Moloch's sadistic taking of Lilliana's wings, as she was being held down by half a dozen handsy demons, Flail had even threatened them all with disembowelment if they hurt the baby.

"Because the baby can only be used against Azagoth if it's healthy, of course."

Those had been her words, but every once in a while, between screams, Lilliana had caught a glimpse of Flail, and she hadn't seemed to be enjoying herself like everyone else in the chamber.

No, it had been so exciting for some of the demons that her de-winging had turned into an orgy.

She hated Hell. A lot.

"I don't know why Flail would do anything to help me," she said, and that, at least, was the truth. "She's been oddly nice. I'm sure she wants something."

"Fuck." Azagoth wheeled away, his gaze cast down at the sand. "I've failed you in so many ways."

"Failed me?" She moved around to face him. "None of this is your fault, Azagoth."

"All of it is my fault." He looked up, but not at her. His gaze, burning with pain and a tiny, alarming crimson spark of hatred, took in the crystal-blue-green sea, going somewhere she couldn't follow. "The things I've done, the enemies I've made, all of it has led to this. I've endangered you and everyone I care about."

"You can't think that way." She gripped his arm, wanting his full focus, but he was still somewhere over the water. "You're the Grim Reaper. You had a job to do, and you've done it well and without any incidents for thousands of years. You've done things the way you had to. The battle between Heaven and Hell is what stirred things up. *They* are the ones changing the rules of the game."

"This *game*," he spat. In the distance, steam rose from the sea. "I'm so tired of it."

"You've been dealing with life and death for so long—"

"That's not the game I'm talking about." He broke away to pace the beach. "Death...that makes sense to me. Physical forms only last so long. At some point, they have to release the soul. It's so...basic." He jammed his hands through his hair and snarled. "But the rest of it, always having to watch your back, always being pressed between two powers and millions of factions. If I could run away with you, build a life somewhere together where no one could touch us unless we wanted that..." His gaze lit on the sea again. "Ares has it right."

He was dreaming of something they could never have, and it broke her heart. "His island is crawling with Ramreel demons and hellhounds," she pointed out in a sad attempt to make Ares' island sound less great than it was. "Not to mention all the friends and family that pop over at all times of the day and night."

She shut up, realizing that she was actually making the opposite argument. Fortunately, Azagoth didn't seem to notice. He'd stopped pacing and was back to making the water steam.

"Ares isn't responsible for millions of souls or keeping the balance between good and evil. The people who visit him do so because they want to, not because they *need* to. He doesn't have to spend eighteen hours a day with evil souls so contaminated with filth that it makes him feel dirty no matter how many showers he takes." The surface of the sea began to boil, and his voice lowered, scraping the bottom of the deep trenches below. "Sometimes, after I've wrung information from a really foul, fucked-up demon, I can't even touch you. I'm too…stained, and you're too pure."

He was going to a dark place, and if she didn't drag him toward the light, he'd get lost in it.

"Darling?" She moved to him, willing away her swimsuit as she walked. "I don't know how much time we have. Make love to me."

It wasn't an offer. It was a command, meant to snag his attention and trigger his natural impulse to meet a challenge.

He swung around, and she willed away his clothes, as well.

Holy damn, but he was remarkable. Supple, bronze skin stretched tight over lean muscles that rippled in all the right places and begged to be kissed, squeezed, scratched, and bitten. Powerful arms and shoulders that flexed as he squared his stance in the sand.

"What?"

"You heard me." She sauntered up to him, planted her hand on his breastbone, and rolled her hips, brushing them up against his. "Make love to me."

His eyes, once aflame with anger, now smoldered, and his arousal stirred against her belly. "I know what you're trying to do."

"And what is that?" She trailed her fingers downward, tracing his ribs and abs.

His chest expanded on a sound that was something between a purr and a growl. "You're distracting me."

The pad of her thumb brushed the tip of his erection, and he hissed. "Distracting you?" she asked, a mix of innocence and vixen.

He pushed his erection into her belly, but it felt almost mechanical, like his body was on board, but his mind was still mired in darkness. "From my anger."

Dammit, he wasn't giving her anything to work with here. "Your anger is what's going to save me," she said. "All I ask is that, no matter what happens, you don't become the monster you used to be."

"I won't." He took her hand and pressed a deep kiss to her palm. "I promise."

She believed him. At least, she believed he intended to keep his promise. For now, that would have to be good enough.

Slowly, deliberately, she licked her thumb, watching his expression grow hotter as she smoothed it over the head of his cock. And yet, there was still a distance in his gaze that she couldn't close.

She could fix that.

Taking him in her fist, she dropped to her knees. She held his gaze with hers, wanting him to see everything she was going to do to him. She'd give him a show that would fill his memories with more than regrets.

Her mouth watered as she pressed a lingering kiss to his shaft. The taste of him, smoky and hot, sent a shiver of lust straight to her core. She tongued him, little dabs up and down the length of his thick erection.

"Darling," he whispered, his voice fading to a moan when she took one plump testicle into her mouth and sucked gently, well short of the intensity he liked.

She was going to tease the hell out of him.

She licked and sucked her way to the other one as she slowly pumped her fist up and down his shaft, the sound of the rolling waves and his short, choppy breaths urging her on. He thrust his fingers into her hair, his touch tender as if he were afraid to hurt her.

Was that why he was being so distant? He was worried about her fragility?

That did not work for her.

She shot to her feet and flared her wings; which, thankfully, still existed in the dream world. Azagoth's expression turned thunderous, and she knew he was thinking about the fact that they'd been torn off. She didn't give him time to obsess. She launched upward and hooked her thighs around his neck, using her wings to hold her aloft.

Now he'd be too busy to worry about treating her like she was made of glass.

He looked up at her, his eyes creased with wickedness. "This is new," he murmured, his hot breath caressing her sensitive flesh. "Can it still be called sitting on my face?"

She didn't answer, was too busy gasping as his tongue pierced her center. Oh...yes! She nearly forgot to flap her wings, but he caught her by her waist and held her upright in his strong grip. It occurred to her that this was a dream, and she probably didn't even need to use her wings, but it was just so...damned...erotic.

He purred as he lapped at her, using the flat of his tongue to make slow, long passes from her core to her clit. Waves of pleasure washed over her, intense and hot.

"Azagoth," she breathed, crying out when he changed up his torture and concentrated on nibbling at her pulsing nub.

She was almost there...almost...

Suddenly, the island spun, and she was upside down in the air, Azagoth's mouth still working between her legs as they drifted above the water in a modified sixty-nine. Oh, that clever Reaper.

Gripping his thighs, she took his cock in her mouth and sucked hard. He bucked his hips with a muffled shout, but the sinful, deep probe of his tongue never altered its mind-blowing rhythm.

Pleasure spiked, her climax sending her hurtling right to the edge of sanity. A sting of pain as Azagoth bit into her inner thigh amplified her ecstasy and triggered another muscle-melting orgasm.

He came with her, his hot jets spilling into her mouth, his hips pumping frantically, spastically.

But they weren't done.

He was still coming when he pulled out of her mouth and spun her around so her legs locked around his waist. His come splashed on her belly as his mouth found hers in an urgent kiss that tasted like her blood and arousal. And then they were airborne, his great wings carrying them high into the sky.

Higher, above the clouds. Through the upper limits of the stratosphere into the eerie silence of space. With a roar, he drew back his hips and thrust inside her. She screamed at the incredible sensation of him filling her, and then she screamed again when he wrapped his wings around them and dove back toward Earth.

They shot downward like a missile, spinning in a cocoon of uncontrolled lust. He thrashed against her, his cock stroking tissue already primed for him with every rapid-fire thrust of his hips. The whine of the wind and the pressure from the fall overloaded all her senses, freeing her to do nothing but feel this incredible thing he was doing to her body.

"Lilli," he shouted, throwing back his head in a display of fierce, male ecstasy, his fangs bared, the tendons in his neck straining.

She came again just as they hit the low deck of clouds, and once more as Azagoth flared his wings and stopped them from crashing into the ocean. He made a slow, graceful roll and drifted on an air current as they caught their breath and savored the last, waning pulses of pleasure.

"I love you," he whispered.

"I love you, too," she said for perhaps the millionth time, but for some reason, this time felt like it was the most important.

Because it might be the last.

Chapter 21

Azagoth held Lilliana as they floated back down to the beach. He wanted to lay in the surf and make love to her again, this time with the waves lapping at their bodies, and the hot wind caressing their skin. What they'd just done had been intense and wild, satisfying a need to release some aggression and passion.

Now, he wanted slow and seductive, just to show Lilliana how much she meant to him. He'd worship every inch of her body so she'd understand that she was his world. Sheoul-gra, a realm he'd built from the ground up, meant nothing compared to her.

"That was amazing," she murmured as they stretched out on the sand. "I want to just lay here and be with you, but we need to talk before something wakes us up."

She was right, but damn if that didn't fuck the mood. He flopped back with his arm behind his head to stare at the sky.

"I told Hawkyn that if anyone wakes me up, they'll be welcoming visitors on the landing pad for a month."

She pushed up on one elbow to look down at him. "That doesn't sound too bad."

"They'll be doing it as statues," he clarified.

"Ah. So, everyone in Sheoul-gra is being very quiet right now."

"Exactly."

She laughed but sobered quickly. He wondered if she was thinking about being awakened. The terror she must experience every time she opened her eyes. Anger at the horror she was experiencing rose up, but he tamped it down, not wanting to upset her.

"I need to know about Flail," she said. "Do you have any information that will help me dig into that psyche of hers?"

"Maybe." He reached over and played with a lock of her silky hair. "Did I ever tell you that Maddox was her nephew? It's one of the reasons I allowed her into Sheoul-gra." He'd always been careful about who was granted entrance to his realm, and he'd been *extremely* particular about those he employed. Flail had done odd jobs, mostly acting as a procurer of things promised, which pretty much meant that she was a glorified collections agent.

She'd been one of the best.

But she'd also been a spy for Moloch, and she'd been responsible for dragging Cipher into Sheoul and imprisoning him for Moloc and Bael. So, she had to die.

"Wait." Lilliana sat up all the way, her full breasts flushed and bouncing just enough to be a distraction. "You knew she was Maddox's aunt, and you never told me?"

"Why would I?"

She gave him an incredulous look, the one females always gave when they thought you were an idiot. "You slept with her sister."

"And that's relevant…why?"

Her mouth opened. Closed. Then she gave a dismissive sniff. "It just is."

Interesting. "Does my past still bother you?"

"Your past? That's a curious way of saying you fathered thousands of children with hundreds of females." She was suddenly wearing her fluffy navy robe, and he wondered if she'd done that consciously or not. "And, no, I'm not bothered by your past. I'd just like to know when people are related to you. Or related to the angels you had in your bed."

Yeah, it *totally* sounded like she was cool with it.

"So, what else do you have on Flail?" she asked, blatantly changing the subject.

He just wished talking about Flail wasn't it, no matter how important it was.

"She was close to her sister Ellandra," he said. "But after Maddox's birth, Ellandra apparently became withdrawn. Her family couldn't help her, and one day, she walked into the Abyss."

Lilliana shuddered. "The Abyss," she whispered. "Oh, my."

Yeah, that had been crazy news, courtesy of Reaver. The Abyss was an almost mythical place on the Other Side. It was said that only those who had truly lost the will to live could find it. Anyone who entered was never seen again. Angelically speaking, it was considered suicide, although some insisted that the Abyss wasn't instant death, but the entrance to another dimension. Basically, it was a way to get a new start.

"Was Flail an angel at the time?"

He shook his head. "She was fallen, but she and Ellandra kept in contact. Seems Ellandra wasn't ready to give up on Flail. In fact, it was Ellandra's support of her sister that got Ellandra sent to me."

Ellandra had confessed that little tidbit to him as she stood, trembling in his bedroom, waiting for him to rape her or something. At that point, he'd told her to go. He wanted his bedmates willing, and if they were sent to him as punishment, there was no consent. He might be evil, but he had standards.

To his surprise, she'd come back, and when she did, she'd begged for his participation. She'd believed that bringing a Memitim into the world would be her redemption.

Turned out, it was her ruin.

A warm breeze stirred Lilliana's hair as she turned her face to the sun. She deserved to have this kind of life. She deserved to be in the sunshine whenever she wanted to be. Instead, she was stuck inside Sheoul-gra.

No, she's trapped in a dungeon in Hell, and it's your fault.

He growled, and Lilliana's hand came down on his. "Hey." She tapped him gently. "Tell me why Flail was expelled from Heaven."

Grateful for the lifeline, he took her hand in his. "She lost her wings because she was part of a mini-rebellion of young angels who despise humans. She took it upon herself to kill a few she felt deserved to die."

She nodded. "I remember that. Well, I don't remember her, specifically, but I know there's been a movement brewing for a while. There have been a number of small rebellions over the last couple of centuries. The last decade has been especially active." She cocked her head and studied him for a moment, the sunlight glinting in her amber eyes. "Did the humans she killed really deserve it?"

"They were murderers and rapists. So, yeah." Flail had provided a lot of evil human souls for Hades to play with in the Inner Sanctum.

Azagoth filled Lilliana in on a few more details he wasn't sure would help, but he didn't want to leave anything out, just in case. When he exhausted his Encyclopedia of Flail, Lilli leaned over and kissed him.

"Now, tell me how *you're* doing. How is everyone handling things? I know the loss of Journey and Maddox must be so hard." She squeezed his hand. "I can't stop thinking about them. And Wraith. They all died trying to help me."

He couldn't imagine what she'd gone through, having to watch them die, and he cursed. "I hate this. Everyone does. They're all looking for ways to get at Moloch. Thanatos and Limos are hunting the angels who killed Wraith, while Ares and Reseph are scouting for ways to get into Moloch's stronghold without a military assault." He eyed her. "You *are* at Moloch's, right? He hasn't taken you to Satan's castle, has he?"

Lilliana's silky hair swung around her shoulders as she shook her head. "I heard him say something about a new occupant."

A new occupant? "Is Revenant back?"

"Someone else." She idly dug holes in the sand with her finger. "Moloch doesn't seem happy about it. I kind of got the impression that Moloch thought the guy was working for him, but now he's the one taking orders."

There was a new player in Sheoul? Interesting. "Do you have a name?"

"I heard Moloch call him Drakiin, but it almost seemed like an insult."

Azagoth snorted. "Because it was. It means *larvae* in Sheoulic." That didn't, however, mean that it couldn't be his name. Demons were fucking bizarre and disgusting. "Have you seen this male?"

"I've never seen his face." She shuddered. "He's evil, though. And cold. It seems to come in…waves."

"Waves?" His gaze automatically shifted to the ocean, which was completely oblivious to their plight. "What do you mean?"

"It's weird. One minute he's just lurking in the background, barely noticeable, and then it's like he becomes radioactive. The evil that radiates from him affects everyone around him. I've never felt anything like it before."

He inclined his head in a slow nod. "That tracks with some of the reports I've gotten."

"Any luck finding out who poisoned me?"

Wishing he had more to offer, he gave what he had. "Zhubaal is questioning everyone who brought you anything to eat or drink. So far, nothing is tripping any alarm bells, and he's not happy." No one was, but Z took his job seriously, and when it wasn't going well, he was *intense.* "I just wish he'd have saved Hawkyn for last when he's really pissed off and worked up."

Her brow arched in surprise. "Why? What did Hawkyn do?"

Azagoth reined in what would have been an epic—fuck, he missed Journey—and vulgar tirade. "Nothing much. He just told Heaven about my *griminion* upgrade, my escape attempt, and the fact that I released a hundred thousand demons to fight Moloch."

Lilliana's eyes went full saucer. "What? You're kidding. No. He wouldn't do that."

"Yeah, he fucking did. Reaver showed up and gave me a load of Heavenly shit." Needing a release for his fury, he dug his fingers into the sand and sent a blast of energy through the shore, turning the surface around them to glass.

Lilliana didn't bat an eye or miss a beat. Man, he loved this female. "What did Reaver say?"

"He said he's trying to keep Heaven from striking at me." He ground his molars, annoyed that Heaven thought he needed to be policed.

She let out a sigh of relief. "So, he's on our side."

"No one in Heaven is on our side."

"Darling, don't you see? That's why Hawkyn went to Reaver. He knew you needed help."

"If he had concerns, he should have come to me first," Azagoth bit out. "If he wasn't the Memitim liaison with Heaven, I'd banish him."

He didn't like the smile she concealed behind her hand.

"What?" he demanded.

"It's just…" She reached out and cupped his cheek. "You could still banish him, and you know it. But you won't because you love him and need him, and you know he was doing what he thought was best, even if it was wrongheaded."

"He betrayed me." It was that simple.

"I know loyalty is important to you, but please, don't be hasty in your decision about what to do with him. Hawkyn is as loyal as they come. He might have made a mistake, but his heart was in the right place, and with things being the way they are…you can't afford to alienate him. We need to be strong and united for what's coming. But we'll win. *You'll* win, Azagoth, and then no one will be stupid enough to screw with you ever again. We'll be free."

He loved her strength, her conviction. But he would never be free.

He would always be confined inside Sheoul-gra, the hell he'd built for himself, to atone for all his sins. What was worse, even after Lilliana got out of Moloch's dungeon, she'd still be imprisoned. The cage would just be more pleasant, and her jailor would be Azagoth.

But she'd at least be alive.

"I'll do whatever I have to do to get you out of there, Lilliana. I promise."

"Except release Satan, right?" She pegged him with a don't-go-there look. "That's the one thing you can't do."

"I'm aware."

"Are you?" She puffed up, and he braced himself for a Heavenly lecture. "Azagoth, the human experience is on a timetable. They've got another thousand years to achieve their goals. You can't mess with that. If Satan gets out of his prison early—"

"Yeah, yeah." He rolled his eyes and recited the standard line every angel learned in the cradle. "Humans have until the End of Days to perfect their souls and gain an immortal life on the Other Side. Those who don't experience all there is to experience over the course of several human lifetimes, whether because they procrastinated or because the Apocalypse comes early, will end up on Earth for Satan to play with for all eternity. I get it. I just don't care. I'm evil, remember?"

She huffed. "This is serious, Azagoth. How many billions of souls will suffer on Earth because they didn't get the entire thousand years to live more lives before the Apocalypse?"

Angels annoyed the shit out of him, but it was cute when Lilliana let her angelic indignation out to play every now and then.

"I know," he said, trying to smooth her ruffled feathers. When she snorted and shook her head, he figured that was a sign that he'd failed. "What?"

"It's just that sometimes you act on instinct and don't think about the consequences of your actions." She smiled, but that didn't take all the sting out of her words. "I love your instincts, and I love how you're willing to do anything for me, but I don't want you, or anyone we love, to pay a high price for getting me out of here. We've already lost too much."

A strong wind kicked, blowing sand and putting white caps on the waves. Overhead, a dark storm cloud rolled in, blotting out the sun.

"Lilliana? Why are you doing this?"

"I'm not," she said, looking up. "I thought it was you—oh, no!"

She started to fade. Lightning lit up the sky as she flickered in and out of existence.

"No! Lilliana!" He reached for her, knowing it was useless. And just like the last time, his hands closed on empty air.

Just like before, she was gone.

Chapter 22

Azagoth's body felt heavy, his mind sluggish, as he lay in bed, unable to find the strength to climb off the mattress. His throat was sore as if he'd been screaming in real life the way he had after Lilliana disappeared. He'd searched the island in a futile attempt to find her, hoping she would get the chance to fall back asleep, that she was awakened by a distant sound and not some demon assaulting her.

She didn't come back, and he'd shouted for her until he woke up, sweating and shaking, not knowing how he could possibly face another day without Lilliana. Worse, he didn't know how to change that reality. His attempt to rescue her had failed, and while he and Ares had put together several plans, executable at a moment's notice and in quick succession, he couldn't implement any of them without guaranteeing his child's death.

But if he didn't come up with another solution—*any* solution that didn't involve releasing Satan—his child and mate would die.

And if they died in Moloch's territory, their souls would be trapped for eternity in a hellish existence, tortured by demons, forced into slavery or, worst of all, imprisoned inside statues.

Entombing souls inside objects, or their own bodies, wasn't widely considered to be the worst way to spend eternity, but Azagoth knew otherwise. Being trapped in the darkness, helpless, unable to communicate, with only one's mind as company…no one came out of that sane.

According to the Charnel Apostle who'd helped him release his army, it took as little as a decade for insanity to set in, depending on the species. And in thousands of years of experimentation by Apostles, not one individual made it out whole after five decades. Azagoth thought about the hundreds of demons imprisoned inside statues or their own bodies in his Hall of Souls and figured they'd be extremely insane by now. Some were thousands of years old.

The newest would be Moloch.

But only after a couple of decades of torture.

The thought of stringing Moloch up by his balls was the push Azagoth needed to climb out of bed when all he wanted to do was sleep—just in case Lilliana was sleeping, too.

Soon. He'd take a nap as soon as he could.

Moving woodenly, he showered and dressed, choosing a pair of jeans and a black T-shirt, casual clothes he usually only wore when he and Lilliana went on their mini-vacations with the *chronoglass*.

Those precious moments were the only reason he had any sense of freedom at all, and they couldn't happen without her.

Before she'd agreed to stay inside Sheoul-gra and be his mate, she'd been an angel with one of the rarest gifts of all: time travel. Using the *chronoglass* as a tool to focus her power, she could open a portal to the human realm's past that lasted exactly one hour. There were rules, of course, but even if they did nothing but sit in the middle of a cornfield, Azagoth was happy.

He was fucking happy to sit in a cornfield in 1948, Nebraska.

If Lilliana didn't come back to him, he'd never sit in a cornfield with her again. They'd never again stand atop Mount Everest and shout into the wind. They'd never have another chance to ice skate together in Sweden.

There would be so many nevers.

Pain sliced at him with acid-tipped claws. He pulled himself together and tore open his bedroom door. The hall was empty of even the dust and debris from his escape attempt. There was no one there to look at him with pity. No one to avert their gaze. No one to walk on eggshells as they scrambled to get out of his way.

He wasn't sure if he was relieved or disappointed.

He went straight to his office, but when he opened the door, he drew to a halt so fast that his heart slammed into his ribcage.

Someone had set up an altar of marble, on top of which sat a red satin cloth where Lilliana's wings lay. The tasteful display, so carefully done, took his breath.

He wasn't sure how long he stood there when he heard footsteps approach.

"I hope that was okay," Hawkyn murmured from behind him. "Cat and I wanted to honor her."

Unable to speak, Azagoth nodded and moved over to the altar. He hadn't seen her wings since last night, which he could barely remember. He'd been so wrecked, so utterly devastated, that his mind had shut down.

It still wanted to. He brushed his fingers over the silky feathers, remembering how easily he could seduce her with a single stroke along the arch.

"Father, it wasn't my intention to bother you, but Maleficent is outside. She's been there for a full day now. It's freaking everyone out."

"What's she doing? Terrorizing people?"

"She's just...lying there." Hawkyn remained in the doorway, giving Azagoth space. Maybe out of respect, perhaps because he'd fucking betrayed his father and didn't want to get too close. Either way, wise choice. "By the pond where Lilliana goes to read. She doesn't move. Not even her eyes."

Azagoth had heard that sometimes hellhounds could communicate through dreams, and he wondered if Lilliana and Mal had been in contact. But if so, wouldn't Lilli have said something about it? He'd also heard that hellhounds could shut down, their broken hearts leaving them in a comatose-like state.

Just when he'd thought he couldn't relate to the mangy mutt.

Shit. Now, he had to help it.

Very gently, he gathered up Lilliana's wings and brushed past Hawkyn.

"He might have made a mistake, but his heart was in the right place."

The memory of Lilliana's words stopped Azagoth in his tracks.

"Hawkyn is as loyal as they come."

Yes, he was. Most of Azagoth's children were terrified to stand up to him, but a few, the ones closest to him and the most trusted, had gotten to that point *because* they stood up to him. Their honesty, while brutal at times, was the reason he respected them and kept them close.

Hawkyn was one of them.

Azagoth did a half-turn back to his son.

"Hawkyn."

Hawk pivoted around, his shoulders squared as if he were prepared to take a blow. "Yes, Father?"

Unexpected warmth trickled into Azagoth's heart at being called *Father*. Not many of his children called him that, and it startled him every time.

"You betrayed my trust." To Hawkyn's credit, he merely inclined his head in acknowledgment. Azagoth continued. "I believe you did what you thought was right. What you thought you had to do."

"Yes, sir."

"You. Were. Wrong," Azagoth growled. "Fortunately for you, you fucked me over *because* you're decent, which is the only reason you're still here. That, and because you're one of the few people I mostly trust, and I can't afford to alienate you."

"I'm not sure what to say." Hawkyn eyed him with suspicion, probably expecting to feel the slide of a blade between his ribs. Azagoth wasn't exactly known for his ability to forgive or forget. "Are we good? You're not going to roast me slowly on a giant spit or trap me inside a statue?"

"You violated my trust by confiding in an ally. You didn't betray me to Moloch." Whoever had would suffer the horrors Hawkyn had described. "We're...good. But don't do it again."

Azagoth headed outside, still gently cradling Lilliana's wings. The Memitim had cleaned up a lot of the structural damage he'd caused, but he still had to negotiate a few downed trees as he walked up the path toward Lilliana's pond.

He could have flown, or even flashed himself there, but he needed the walk. Needed to see his realm, even if it was slowly decaying, the plants wilting, the grass dying, just like his heart.

He approached Mal the way he always did: with caution. But Hawkyn was right. She just lay there, staring off into space. He wasn't even sure she was breathing.

"Hey, girl." He stopped at her side and crouched next to her. She didn't move, but a distressed whimper, barely audible, issued from her throat. "I know how it feels."

Slowly, because no one in their right mind wanted to startle a hellhound, he placed Lilliana's wings in front of her. For a moment, nothing happened. Then the beast's nostrils flared. Her eyes, once unfocused and empty, sparked to life, and she blinked as she lifted her massive, black head.

When she saw the wings, she stretched toward them, sniffing and whining, and then she looked at him and growled. He wasn't sure how he knew the growl wasn't directed at him, but he did, and in that moment, he had an ally.

"You smell Moloch on those wings, don't you?" Tentatively, he reached out and stroked her shoulder. She went so taut at his touch that he froze, but a few heartbeats later, she relaxed, and he gave her another long, gentle stroke. "I don't suppose you can break her out of his prison."

Even if she understood him, he doubted she could get inside Moloch's keep. Everyone in Sheoul warded their homes to prevent against unwanted visits from hungry hellhounds. Even if Maleficent could get into the dungeon, she was genetically incapable of harming an authorized agent of Satan except in self-defense, and it seemed that with Revenant missing, Moloch was now Sheoul's caretaker in Satan's name.

Still, resolve burned in her eyes, and he realized that, yes, she did know Moloch's scent. Which meant that she knew who had hurt Lilliana…and, quite possibly, she understood where to find her.

Mal pushed to her massive paws.

"I know I should try to stop you," he said softly. "Lilliana would be angry if I didn't try to keep you from danger. But I want—I need—her back, and if you can help…" He let out a shuddering breath. "Please, Maleficent."

A look of understanding passed between them, and as she dematerialized, he wondered if he'd ever see her again.

Then he wondered if he'd ever see Lilliana again, and he broke down. There, on the edge of Lilliana's pond, he lost it, knowing that nothing would ever be the same.

Chapter 23

They came from out of nowhere, ambushing Reaver as he materialized near the entrance to Ares' mansion.

Harvester had come with him today because, as she'd argued, "I'm the Horsemen's Heavenly Watcher *and* their stepmother, so they have to put up with me. Plus, I want to see Aleka. I haven't seen Cara and Ares' daughter in days."

There was no dissuading Harvester when she wanted something, and besides, she knew more about the inner workings of Sheoul than anyone, and her insight could be valuable.

If she could keep from antagonizing everyone.

Ares, Reseph, and Thanatos surrounded them before they'd even taken ten steps.

"Any news about Lilliana?" Ares asked. He was dressed in khakis and a gauzy, beachy, Greek-style shirt, but even without armor, he looked every inch the warrior he was. And he was as tall as Reaver, so there were a lot of inches.

"You probably know more than I do," Reaver said. "The last time I saw Azagoth, the battle hadn't even started yet."

There was nothing beachy about Harvester's form-fitting black dress, but that didn't stop her from kicking off her heels and planting her feet in the sand. "I heard from my sources that your army was defeated, and your hellhounds cowered and refused to fight."

Shit. Reaver didn't know anyone with less tact than Harvester. Not even Wraith could compete.

The sound of the waves caressing the shore grew uncomfortably loud as Ares stood there, a muscle in his jaw twitching, storm clouds brewing in his eyes. Just as Reaver was about to smooth things out, Ares shook his head as if an altercation with Harvester wasn't worth it.

"You're right about the battle," he said. "But the hounds did *not* cower. They wanted to fight. They wanted to so badly, but they couldn't. They're still pissed off and looking to tear shit up, so if you feel like you need a fight, have at it. I know I'd bring popcorn."

Thanatos, in black jeans and a henley that covered the 3D tattoos on his arms, thrust his fingers through his shaggy blond hair. "That's not the worst of it."

"Not even close," Reseph added. "We were with Azagoth, a bunch of us, planning another sneak attack while Moloch's forces were still reeling."

Ares nodded. "We wanted to hit hard when he wasn't expecting it, and before he hurt Lilliana."

"We were too late," Reseph spat. "The fucker cut off her wings and sent them to Azagoth. Moloch said that if we attacked again, the baby would pay."

"If I were still a fallen angel," Harvester growled, "I would go to Moloch now and rend him limb from limb while I drank his blood and promised him eternal pain."

"I love how descriptive that was," Limos chirped as she walked up to them from inside the house. She looked ready to hit the surf in board shorts and a swimsuit, her long, black hair up in a messy bun, the few stray wisps held back by the sunglasses pushed up on top of her head.

"Do you really think it was descriptive?" Harvester asked. "I was trying to tone it down. Reaver says I sometimes need to read the room better before I speak." She frowned. "I am truly sad about Lilliana. Losing her wings inside Sheoul will weaken her immensely. She must be in excruciating pain."

A raw ache erupted in Reaver's shoulders as if his body remembered the time Harvester had held him captive in her fallen angel lair inside Sheoul and sawed off his wings.

He shot her a glare. "You think?"

A breeze blew her midnight hair around her face as she turned to him. "I am genuinely sorry. No matter how big of an asshat you were, you didn't deserve that."

"Ah, thank you? I think." He gave her a sideways glance. "You also smashed me under a mountain."

She barked out a laugh. "Yes."

Ares rolled his eyes and waved for them to follow him toward the house. "Stay for dinner. We're having a seafood boil. We can talk while we eat. Jillian, Regan, Arik, and all the kids will be here soon." He glanced over at Reaver. "Have you seen Serena yet?"

Reaver shook his head. "I was supposed to go by the house, but I had to cancel."

"What's more important than visiting Wraith's widow?" Thanatos's voice pitched low with disapproval, and Reaver had a feeling he wasn't dealing well with losing his friend. The Horseman might be known as Death, but he hadn't had to deal with it personally much at all.

Harvester popped her sunglasses up to give Than a level stare. "Don't talk to your father that way."

Thanatos's lips peeled back, revealing fangs he usually kept hidden. "You're not my mother."

"And too bad for you," she snapped. "Because I wouldn't have abandoned any of you." She paused, thinking. "Except maybe Reseph." She jabbed her finger at Thanatos. "And I can still take you by your ear and shake some sense into you." She demonstrated that by using her power to lift Thanatos by the ear to his toes before dropping him again, the twin braids at his temples slapping against his cheeks as his boots hit the pavers.

"Okay, you two, knock it off." Reaver took Harvester's hand and turned to Thanatos. "I had to cancel my visit with Serena because the Angelic Council summoned me."

"Oh, shit." Limos spoke around a lollipop she'd just shoved into her mouth. "About Azagoth?"

He nodded. "Word is starting to filter up about the trouble."

"How much do they know?" Ares asked.

They knew way more than Reaver had expected. "They're aware that Moloch has Lilliana, and that Revenant is missing. They're guessing that Moloch is using Lilliana to secure Satan's release, but they don't know for sure." Neither Reaver nor Metatron had confirmed the theory. Doing so would almost certainly guarantee a swift decision to have Azagoth destroyed in order to prevent Armageddon. "The good news is that they don't know what Azagoth has done to retaliate, so they don't know he's in violation of his contract."

"What happens if they find out?" Reseph asked.

Nothing good. "The Council of Orders will get involved."

The CoO, the highest authority in Heaven save the Big Guy, would act on a breach of contract, and they had never been known for mercy or generosity. If something was so monumental that it landed on *their* desks, they figured it needed to be dealt with swiftly and decisively. There was no such thing as *going light.*

It was they who had made the decision to erase and rebuild human memories—more than once. It was they who wiped out the advanced civilization of Atlantis after they decided it was a bad idea to use angel DNA in order to evolve humans more quickly.

It was they who would give the order to destroy Azagoth if the time ever came.

"So the Council of Orders is bad." That from Limos.

Harvester nodded. "Very bad."

"Speaking of bad." Limos bounced on her toes as they started up the mansion steps. "Did you know we caught one of the fallen angels who killed Wraith?"

Reaver stopped dead in his tracks. "Who?"

Thanatos shoved his sleeves up as if preparing to punch someone, and the stallion glyph on his forearm stomped its hoof. "A cocksucker named Curson."

"Curson," Reaver repeated. "I never met him."

Harvester snorted. "He is such an arrogant, craven piece of shit." She paused, looked at Than. "Is? Or *was?*"

Limos answered with a grin. "Was."

"Cool." Harvester high-fived Limos. "As I was saying, he was a shitbag. He used his status as one of my father's original followers to get whatever he wanted in Sheoul. Even though they had a falling out a few hundred years ago. Such a prick. What did he say?"

"That he and the other two fucks in the parking lot work for Moloch," Thanatos said. "They knew Wraith had lost his immunity charm because Moloch arranged it."

Reaver had suspected as much. "Did he say how?" The shifting, fleeting glances the Horsemen gave each other made Reaver nervous. "Tell me."

"It was Revenant."

Dammit! Although Reaver had considered that possibility for a split-second, he hadn't truly believed his brother could have had anything to do with Wraith's death. It was still possible that Curson was lying or that he'd been intentionally fed the wrong information, but Reaver had to admit that it made sense. No one else could have gotten close enough to Wraith to remove the charm without him knowing about it.

"He wouldn't have done it without a good reason," Reaver said, hating that he sounded defensive and petty.

"Like what?" Ares stopped at the front door and turned to Reaver.

"I don't know. But something's going on with him and Blaspheme. She hasn't shown up for work at the hospital, and no one can get ahold of either of them. No one has seen Revenant since—" He broke off as something Eidolon said came back to him. "Shit."

Harvester had been playing with her diamond Tiffany key necklace, but now she stilled. "What is it?"

"Before Wraith went out into the parking lot, he said he'd just seen Revenant." The doctor had been choked up, his voice destroyed by grief, and Reaver had barely understood him. "Eidolon said Revenant stopped by the house to give Serena a book. He thought it was strange because Blaspheme had been missing, and Rev didn't bring it up at all."

Limos popped the lolli out of her mouth. "Can't you sense him or something?"

"Only if he's in Heaven or if he summons me from the human realm. I've tried summoning him, reaching out with my mind, everything I can think of. Nothing."

"Moloch abducted Lilliana and is using her as a bargaining chip," Harvester reminded him. "It's not a stretch to think that he did the same to Blaspheme to get what he wants out of Revenant."

Reseph backhanded a mosquito. Apparently, even Horsemen got bitten. "Why would Moloch want Revenant to destroy Wraith's invincibility?"

"Moloch didn't give a shit about Wraith," Thanatos said. "He wanted the fallen angels to help him, and that was their price."

"Maybe," Reaver said. "But there's more to it than that, or Revenant wouldn't be missing. Moloch needs Revenant out of the way so he can take control of Sheoul until Satan is freed from his prison."

"You think he's trapped Revenant somehow? But he's so powerful."

"Revenant and I trapped Satan," Reaver pointed out. "Nothing is impossible."

But, man, the idea that Rev was imprisoned was sobering. If Revenant could be taken down, Reaver could, as well.

"So, what are we going to do?" Limos asked.

"I'm still hunting the fuckers who killed Wraith," Thanatos said. "One down, two to go. As soon as dinner is over."

Reaver was so on board with that. "We also need to find Revenant. He can kick Moloch's ass, get Lilliana back, and keep Azagoth from doing something that will get him put down by the Council of Orders."

Harvester chewed her bottom lip for a second. "What book?"

"What?"

"What book did Revenant take to Serena?"

Reaver frowned. "Eidolon didn't say. But maybe we should find out." He looked at the Horsemen and squeezed Harvester's hand. "We'll be back."

He didn't give anyone a chance to argue or ask questions. He flashed off the island with Harvester and materialized on Wraith and Serena's porch. He'd been here just last month, pounding beers with Wraith and Shade as they watched the kids play in the yard.

Sadness swamped him. Maybe he hadn't needed to be at the Angelic Council meeting as early as he had. Perhaps he had, selfishly, been glad for an excuse to not pay Serena a visit yet. Because, no, he did not want to be here.

"I can see it," Harvester said quietly. "Their grief. It's like a gray aura surrounding the house."

He didn't see it, but he sure as hell felt it.

Eidolon's mate, Tayla, opened the door before he could knock. She looked less composed than usual, her burgundy hair covered by a baseball cap, but her smile, while not as bright as usual, welcomed them both.

"It's good to see you." She gave each of them a brief hug. "Come in. Runa's here, too. We don't want Serena to be alone right now."

"How's she doing?" Harvester asked, her voice thick with rare compassion. She'd liked Wraith and his impulsive, non-repentant nature.

"Not good." Tayla's green eyes, red-rimmed from crying, began to water. "She's holding it together for Stewie, but barely." She gestured to the bathroom. "Excuse me. I need a moment."

There had been a time when Tayla and Wraith had hated each other, but they'd eventually learned to tolerate one another. More recently, they'd become close, and this was clearly taking a toll on her.

They found Serena in the kitchen, sitting at the table with Runa, and after a round of hugs and some sobbing, Reaver finally found words of condolence.

"I'm so sorry, Serena. If there's anything I can do—"

"Can you bring him back?" Her question was genuine, expected, and it nearly shattered his composure.

"I wish I could," he said roughly. "If it was a matter of rules, I'd break them. But I simply don't have the ability."

She dabbed her eyes with a tissue, the lack of Wraith's mate mark, a replica of his *dermoire* on her left arm and hand, a stark reminder of what she'd lost. What they'd all lost.

"Do you know why his soul is trapped? Is he suffering?"

Reaver didn't know the answer to either question, and he didn't want to hurt Serena more than she already was, so he sat next to her and took her hand.

"Hades is making sure he's as safe and comfortable as possible."

"But I don't know Hades," she sobbed. "He doesn't know Wraith, and—"

"Actually, he does know Wraith." Reaver caught her gaze, wanting her to fully understand what he was about to say. "They met after a battle once. Wraith mouthed off, and they were like best friends. Trust me, Hades is a..." He tried to come up with a word that worked for the guy. Good? Nah. Decent? Nope.

"Dutiful male," Harvester finished, saving Reaver several awkward seconds.

Reaver nodded. "He takes his duties seriously, and he will treat Wraith with the utmost respect."

"Okay." Serena blew her nose, and Reaver waited until she was done to bring up the reason they were there.

"Serena...Wraith said Revenant brought you a book. What book?"

She pointed to a tome on the counter. "It's weird. I didn't ask for it, so I don't know why he brought it."

Harvester picked it up and frowned down at it. "*Into the Abyss.* Hmm. I've read this before."

Abyss. Why did that word keep coming up? "What's it about?"

Harvester turned it over in her hands. "It's about an angel whose mate went missing and the lengths he went to in order to find her. He goes total John Wick. Loses his wings and everything." She flipped it open, and a piece of paper fell out, but she caught it with her power and floated it up to her hand. "It's from Revenant."

Reaver surged to his feet, his heart pounding. "What's it say?"

"It says he's sorry, and to give this note to Reaver." She shrugged and handed it to him.

The instant he touched the sheet, an electric buzz shot up his arm, and more hastily scrawled words formed on the paper. His gut sank as he read.

I fucked up, bro. I gave Moloc and Bael too much freedom, and by the time I realized my mistake, it was too late. Moloch has Blaspheme, Reav. I did what I had to do to keep her alive. I want to fix it, but I have to find my mate. Forgive me.

Rev

"Well?" Harvester came up behind him. "What's it say?"

Feeling the weight of everyone's stares, Reaver looked up. "It says he's in trouble. And if he's in trouble, we're *all* in trouble."

Chapter 24

Revenant trudged through the knee-deep boiling river, an endless fucking body of water whose banks of hardened lava were even hotter than the water itself. Steam rose all around him, burning his skin, his nostrils, his eyes. Like the flesh on his submerged legs, the steam injuries healed almost instantly, which allowed him to get burned again. The endless cycle of pain was brutal, but he kept moving. Kept working his way toward his mate.

"Go to the source of the River Scaldera and climb the steps of the Temple of Tremors. If you love your female enough, you'll find her."

Moloch didn't even have the balls to tell Revenant to his face where he could find Blaspheme. He'd sent a lackey, who was now minus *his* balls.

It was a preview of what would happen when Revenant got ahold of Moloch.

That son of a bitch!

Revenant should have destroyed him long before this. He should have taken out any demon or fallen angel who might even *think* of posing a threat to him. Now, the bastard had amassed an army of demons, the size of which hadn't been seen before. And if Azagoth caved, Satan might be freed to take command.

It was a disaster of near-biblical proportions, way ahead of schedule.

Water rushed around his legs, but the river had narrowed and grown more shallow. Even the banks, blackened with ash, no longer glowed beneath the thick layer of cooled rock. Ahead, through the thinning steam, he saw a massive temple, carved from an entire mountain.

Despite the circumstances and the excruciating pain, he stared in awe. It must have taken tens of thousands of demons thousands of years to build. He'd heard stories, of course, but as one of the many places in Sheoul that were inaccessible via conventional means, like flashing, he'd never come. Not even the thriving tourism industry run by Skimmer devils who operated boats that could navigate the scalding waters could have gotten him here. Not that that option had even been available to him. Moloch's forces had slaughtered all the boat operators and destroyed the vessels. Apparently, Moloch had wanted Revenant to slog through the river for days before reaching the temple.

Fucking dick. Revenant was going to boil Moloch's balls in a pot over a bonfire. Right in front of him.

Then there'd be a weenie roast.

Revenant glanced back at the endless ribbon of steamy river as it cut through the mountains and valleys, and he wondered how many times his legs had been boiled to the bone during the journey.

At first, he'd flown. At least, he'd tried. A powerful, constant downdraft had kept him from sailing above the vapor, and it hadn't been long before the heat singed his wings, and the steam saturated his feathers. Shriveled and waterlogged, they could no longer support him, and he'd plunged into the roiling waters after only a few miles of flight.

I'm coming, Blaspheme.

Step after agonizing step, he got closer to the great staircase. The river narrowed, winding toward the steps where it disappeared beneath them, presumably continuing to its source somewhere under the temple.

Steam swirled around Revenant as he finally stepped out of the water and onto a stone step. His legs wobbled, and he went down to his knees, his body trembling, his lungs taking in great breaths as his body demanded a moment to heal.

There was no time for that. Not when Blaspheme could be suffering untold horrors. He tried to stand, and when his legs failed him, he crawled.

Gradually, as he heaved himself upward, sensation returned to his extremities. Normal feeling. He came to his feet, his legs shaking, but yeah, buddy, he was on his way to not feeling like a poached salmon.

He looked up. Down. Let out a thousand different curses.

He'd been crawling up the steps for hours, and he'd barely made a dent in the distance. The staircase stretched endlessly, disappearing into noxious clouds from the volcanoes.

"Fuck. Me," he breathed.

Rolling his shoulders, he felt a tingle of health deep inside his wings. He popped them and let out a whoop of sheer joy. The feathers were still a little curled, and he might fly as if he'd had a few too many shots of tequila, but his wings would get him to the temple entrance halfway up the mountain.

He launched, the powerful flaps of his wings carrying him drunkenly upward. He hit a formidable downdraft, probably designed to prevent exactly what he was doing, but he punched through it and burst through the entrance. A sudden loss of lift made him drop like a bomb, and he hit the floor of the temple in a tumble of limbs and feathers.

As he shoved to his feet, shadowy, wispy creatures squeezed from out of the mouths of the stone effigies. He didn't know the species, but the evil literally oozed from them in strings of black goo. It was some seriously fucked-up shit.

"You're here for the female?" the entities whispered in a single voice that made him think of a knife slicing through meat.

He summoned an elemental sword. Its blade burst into flame as it took on the character of the surroundings. "Where is she?" he growled.

"If you want her, you'll find her."

The things chattered, an eerie, ear-shattering sound that ended abruptly when they wisped themselves back into the statues.

"No! You bastards! Come back!" He wheeled around the room, looking for them, searching for anyone or anything. There was nothing here but tiled walls, mosaics of pain and suffering.

Releasing the sword, he raced along the walls, feeling for openings. He searched the floor for trap doors. He launched upward, high into the rafters made of some sort of smooth stone, but there was no way out from there, either.

Okay, he'd blast his way out.

Bringing the entire force of his power to bear, he hurled a personal creation, a boulder of what he affectionately called *gutenbad*, at the ceiling. A ball of pulsing, blackened evil surrounding a core of Heavenly goodness hit the structure with an ear-shattering boom. The mountain shook, and boulders—real ones weighing tons—came crashing down.

Shit! Flapping his wings as hard as he could, he slammed a force field overhead, and the stones were deflected and sent down the side of the mountain. When the rumbling finally stopped, he blasted away all the debris.

But nothing had changed. He could get out, but to go where? He was already at the entrance to the temple.

If you love your female enough, you'll find her.

Okay, well…he loved her. He loved her so much that if he didn't find her, he'd die trying. And if he found her dead, he'd die at her side.

If you want her, you'll find her.

"Of course, I want her!" he shouted to whoever was listening. "Blaspheme! Blaspheme, baby, where are you?"

He brought himself to a clumsy landing and ran around the room again. He must have missed something.

"Blaspheme!"

He had to have missed something!

"*Blaspheme!*"

He threw himself against the tiles, dug at them with his fingers until the walls were streaked with his blood. Finally, he wasn't sure how much later, he fell to his knees with a scream. He pitched forward, cracking his forehead against the floor.

"Please, Blaspheme," he croaked. "Please help me find you." Rage, terror, and despair all collided, and he threw back his head and screamed. "Anyone…*please!*"

Darkness overwhelmed him, and he collapsed.

When the lights came back on in his head, he blinked, disoriented. The room…still the same. But…no.

He scrambled to his knees. Over there…a doorway. He gave one flap of his wings, bringing him to his feet. The doorway, pulsing like bloody flesh, beckoned him with the sound of a beating heart.

Blaspheme's heart.

He didn't know how he knew that. He just did.

He paused at the doorway and reached out with his mind, hoping to connect with her, desperate to get to her. When he was met with nothing but the cold emptiness of his own mind, he went solid *fuck it* and stepped through the gaping maw.

Inside…inside was a fucking nightmare. What the everliving…*what* was going on? The cavernous area, awash in white and ivory, stretched endlessly, its high ceilings braced by glittering columns of crystal. The spongy ground could have been made of marshmallow, and as Revenant walked, he half-expected unicorns to greet him.

Seriously. What. The. Fuck?

"Revenant?"

He spun around at the sound of Blaspheme's voice, and when he saw her standing near an obelisk that appeared to have been carved from quartz, he nearly collapsed with relief. She was still wearing the pink scrubs she'd been abducted in, her blond hair falling in tangled ropes over her face.

He launched at her, had her in his arms in half a heartbeat.

"I'm so happy to see you," he breathed as he peppered her with kisses. Her cheeks, her forehead, her jaw. "Are you okay?" Her mouth. He kissed her over and over. "Did he hurt you?"

She gave him a reassuring smile that did little to actually assuage him. "Moloch didn't do anything I couldn't handle."

He growled. "What does that mean?"

"It means his goons threw me around a little," she said. "But no one really wanted to mess with the King of Hell's mate, you know? Not even Moloch."

They were still going to die horribly. Everyone who had dared to touch her. Revenant held her close as he looked around at the bizarre Cinderella Stay Puft mashup happening here.

"What *is* this place? And how are you here if it can't be found without great need?"

"Skimmer devils brought me upriver on a boat and then hauled me up the stairs. Took forever." She paused. "Is that how you got here?"

"Moloch destroyed them and their boats. So, no."

She looked genuinely troubled by that. "The Skimmers were actually kind of nice. They put padding under my shackles to keep me from bleeding." She shook her head in disgust. "Anyway, they left me inside the temple. I needed a way out, and at some point, a weird, fleshy door opened. And...here I am."

She pulled away from him and placed her hand on the crystal obelisk. Under her palm, golden light bloomed, spreading upward in tendrils that snaked their way to the top.

"Moloch said it was designed a long time ago as a secret prison for Satan."

Revenant ogled the weirdness. "This? Whoever built it really believed that a room built from what, a child's imagination, could hold Satan?"

"It was built using materials mined from the purest parts of Heaven." She removed her hand and replaced it with his. Instead of golden light, dark, inky clouds formed under his palm, but even as they tried to spread, they were swallowed by the crystal. "My mom used to tell me stories about a mysterious prison that used Heavenly energy to render evil inert. I guess this is it." She shrugged. "My mom's a conspiracy theorist, but she got this one right."

Blaspheme's fallen angel mother, Deva, was a whack job. But, obviously, whack jobs got lucky with their conspiracies now and then. He'd have to ask his mother-in-law what she thought about Bigfoot and the Loch Ness Monster.

"According to both Moloch and my mother, Satan got wind of it, and no one ever tricked him into coming here. Thanks to prophecies, he knew that he'd be imprisoned someday, and he thought this was the one that would spell his doom." She looked up at the crystal ceiling, the graceful arches twisted in places as if the builders hadn't been able to tame the materials. "He even tried to have the entire temple destroyed, but it was built inside a morabuble."

Morabubles, spaces where the barrier between realms weakened and allowed one realm to push slightly inside the other like a hernia, caused bizarre anomalies where normal rules and natural laws didn't apply. If this one shared a border with Heaven, the materials could have been passed through the barricade, and the barrier could, theoretically, prevent evil, even some as powerful as Satan's, from destroying it.

Instantly, Revenant checked his power. Reached deep. Not a spark. It was like reaching around in empty pockets for a dime.

So, it was a prison, all right. Just not Satan's.

It was Revenant's.

Chapter 25

Lilliana wanted to sleep.

It was all she wanted to do. She wanted to escape this literal hell for just a little while, and she wanted to see Azagoth again. But every time she curled up on the cold floor and started to drift off, a squeezing sensation wrapped around her abdomen, and the baby started kicking up a storm.

Stay in there a little longer, kiddo.

She talked to the baby as she lay there, rubbing her belly, trying to keep him or her inside for as long as she could.

She couldn't give birth here. She couldn't.

Your daddy will get us out of here soon. Just…hold on.

But what if Azagoth couldn't rescue them in time? What if she gave birth early?

Oh, God.

She blinked back tears. She had a plan, but it was a long shot.

The door to her cell opened, and before she could even sit up, a hulking demon that smelled like raw sewage grabbed her chain and hauled her to the courtyard outside the castle. In the human world, there would be grass inside the stone walls.

Here in Moloch's territory, there was mud and ash.

Sewer Demon chained her on a gallows platform so she could watch the horrifying things the demons did, and where they could do horrifying things to her.

Usually, they just threw things, thanks to Moloch's orders to not completely destroy her. Had to leave her alive, or Azagoth wasn't going to cooperate, of course.

She spotted Flail standing near a firepit where Moloch's goons were roasting something humanoid over the flames. Azagoth had said that she was Maddox's aunt. So far, Lilliana hadn't found Flail's weakness, but if she had one, it might be her nephew.

Her family, who had died at Moloch's command.

Lilliana's belly tightened again, and she sucked in a harsh breath.

"What's the matter?"

She jumped at the sound of Flail's voice right next to her ear.

"You shouldn't scare pregnant females like that," Lilliana muttered.

"I brought you this." She held out a burned hunk of meat on a charred bone.

"Ah..." Lilliana glanced over at the roasting dude. "No thanks..."

Flail lowered her voice. "This is labrynix. It's kind of a demon goat." She pointed to another pit fire on the other side of the courtyard. "Take it, or you'll end up with a bowl of leftovers, and I can't guarantee they won't belong to that human."

Lilliana's gut lurched, but she took the hunk of meat from Flail. The fallen angel hadn't brought her anything that had made her sick, and what she delivered was far better than the unidentifiable grotesqueness that her guards always offered.

"Thank you." Damn, she hated feeling grateful to Flail. Though maybe that's what the fallen's game was about: Stockholm Syndrome.

Lilliana wasn't going to fall for it. She would never feel compassion for her captors. Not Flail, not any of these scum.

Flail gestured to Lilliana's swollen belly with the mug of ale in her hand. "It won't be long now."

She looked down at the outline of the little foot pushing up at her through her hornet-weave stinging nettle frock. "What makes you say that?" she asked, encouraging a conversation instead of what she really wanted to say, which was closer to, "*No shit, you evil skank.*"

"I was with my sister before she gave birth."

"Your sister...Maddox's mother?"

Flail's lashes fluttered with mild surprise. "You know about that?"

Now it was Lilliana's turn to be surprised. "Do you really think Azagoth doesn't do background checks on everyone that visits Sheoul-gra?"

Flail took a gulp of ale and wiped her mouth with the back of her hand. "So, my sister fucked your husband, yet you allowed me there?"

I didn't know. Lilliana played it off as though she had. "I never liked you, Flail, but my allowing you there had nothing to do with your sister. I got over my insecurities about all the females Azagoth took to his bed a long time ago. The past is the past."

Although, really, she might have said no to Flail had she known the truth. From now on, *she* would be the final say in who got to spend time in Sheoul-gra. Azagoth would just have to deal.

Assuming she got out of here alive, of course. A shiver of terror spread over her skin in the form of goosebumps, but then Flail started talking again, and annoyance replaced her fear.

"Huh. I don't think I'd be as gracious." Flail sniffed. "Or stupid."

"See, *that's* why I don't like you," Lilliana muttered.

Flail laughed. "What's Azagoth like? As a lover, I mean."

Lilliana nearly choked on her spit. "What the hell kind of question is that? Do you honestly expect me to answer?"

"My sister was terrified of him." She held out the mug of ale to Lilliana, who waved it away. "So terrified that she ran away the first time she went to Sheoul-gra."

Well, that was interesting. "The first time?"

"She went back," Flail said with a shrug. "It's considered both a sacrifice and a divine duty if you're chosen to bed the Grim Reaper and make Memitim. Well, it used to be until you came along."

Now, Lilliana was genuinely curious about Flail's sister. "How many times did she go back?"

A shadow passed across Flail's expression, and for a moment, Lilliana feared she'd lost control of the conversation. But after another gulp of ale, Flail spoke.

"Just the once. She was only pregnant one time." She inhaled a ragged breath, clearly still troubled by wherever this story led. "And she loved the baby. Loved it so much that she refused to give it up to vile humans." Angry crimson blotches bloomed on Flail's cheeks. "The Memitim Council forcibly took him away. She never recovered."

"I wouldn't either." Lilliana couldn't keep her voice from trembling. Moloch would take her child when it was born. Maybe she could exploit Flail's pain a little, prep her for what Lilliana was about to propose. "To know you couldn't protect your baby, to know it would likely suffer..." She shuddered, and it was absolutely genuine. "Is that why your sister walked into the Abyss?"

Flail hissed, baring wicked, sharp fangs. "How the hell do you know about that?"

"Azagoth knows more than you might think."

Her abdomen squeezed hard, and she dropped her meat-club to the ground without having taken a bite. Spiny hellrats snatched it up before it even had a chance to roll to a stop.

"Shit," she breathed. This baby wanted out, and it wouldn't be long. She had to put her plan into motion.

She looked up at Flail in desperation. "Flail...I think this baby can help get Moloch what he wants."

Flail cocked a dark eyebrow. "How?"

Here we go. "When this baby is born, send her or him to Azagoth as an offering of good faith."

"Good faith? Good faith for what?" Snorting into her mug, Flail took a chug of ale. "No, I'm sure Moloch has plans for the brat. Imagine what Azagoth will do to ensure the safety of his precious mate and child. Seeing you in pain is one thing. Seeing an innocent infant—"

"No!" Lilliana grabbed Flail's arm in a frantic attempt to convince her. "Listen to me. That will guarantee Azagoth won't help Moloch. I can't even begin to tell you how nuclear Azagoth will go if you hurt his newborn child. But if Moloch makes a two-part deal with Azagoth, giving him the baby as a down payment, and me as the full payment, Azagoth will do it. He's a dealmaker, and he's a stickler for the terms of an agreement. It's Moloch's only chance."

Flail looked at her with pity. "Do you really think Azagoth believes Moloch will release you?"

"I don't know."

Now, Flail was looking at her with pity *and* skepticism. "Really?"

The baby kicked, and nausea bubbled up in Lilliana's throat at her inability to protect it. "No."

"You know you're not getting out of here alive, right?" Flail ran a slender finger around the rim of her mug, toying with it. Toying with Lilliana. "If Azagoth doesn't release the Dark Lord, Moloch will kill you. If Azagoth does release Satan, Moloch will offer you to him as a plaything. You're dead either way."

Lilliana looked at her. "But my baby can live." She swallowed dryly, then went for a shameless manipulation. "Wouldn't you have wanted someone to help your sister?"

"Nice," Flail said, raising her mug in salute. "That was so subtle."

"I can't afford to be subtle," Lilliana snapped. "This baby is going to be here any minute, and I don't want him or her to suffer for

Moloch's twisted pleasure. I mean, the bastard killed your nephew. Your sister's beloved son. Aren't you angry? Don't you want revenge?"

With a roar, Flail backhanded Lilliana so hard she fell backward, hitting her head on a stool meant for the unlucky hanging victims to stand on before having it kicked out from beneath their feet. All around, demons broke out in laughter.

"You don't get to question my anger," Flail yelled. Then, just as quickly as she went ballistic, she calmed down, squatting next to Lilliana and lowering her voice. "I'll see what I can do. But don't get your hopes up. Ever since Moloc's and Bael's souls merged, Moloch's had a real hard-on for torture." She patted Lilliana on the head as if she were a pet. "Try to get some rest. You're going to need to be strong for whatever comes next."

Lilliana had told Azagoth the same thing. Now it seemed like such a stupid thing to say.

Flail was seriously ready for the End of Days. She was sick of the fucking humans, and she was ready to be done with angels, as well. It was time for the Dark Lord to lead the charge and take the earthly realm from the Creator's dumbest experiments.

Humans were so damned stupid.

Not as stupid as you are.

Her random thought, as annoying as it was, might be accurate. She was actually considering asking Moloch for something she shouldn't care about at all. No, that wasn't entirely true. She did care, not for the child, but for the cause. If she asked him to deliver Lilliana's child to Azagoth, it would be because she truly believed her proposal would be the best way to get him to comply with Moloch's wishes.

Yes, that sounded good.

But she doubted she'd bring it up. She really didn't give a flying shit about Lilliana or the brat.

She found Moloch in the Garden of Night, a spookily spectacular garden full of flesh-eating plants, poisonous vines, and wicked black flowers. He was pouring blood into a container of irises as he spoke in low, hushed tones with a shadowy figure nearby. Moloch had loved gardening before Bael's soul joined the party, but now he spent more time torturing people. So even though she wasn't a fan of horticulture—or horrorticulture, as Moloch accurately called it—she figured that finding him here was a sign that he wasn't letting Bael's insane side take over completely.

"What is it?" Moloch asked, not looking up.

The shadowy person melted away before she could see his face, or even what he was wearing. The last two times she'd seen him, he'd been in black leather pants and a hoodie with the hood up. This time, she'd gotten a glimpse of hair, although she couldn't tell the color. On the light side, she thought.

And he was cold. So cold.

Flail stared at the sudden empty air. "Who *is* that guy? He's been lurking around for days."

Moloch moved the watering can to the next plant. "You don't recognize him?"

"I've never seen his face." She watched Moloch lick a drop of blood from the watering can's spout.

"He doesn't have one. Not yet." He straightened and turned to her, and she fought the urge to shrink back. The black pools of hate that were his eyes scorched her skin where they landed, and she wished she'd worn something a lot less skimpy. "He's of the Dark Lord's blood. He wants to know how Lilliana is doing."

So, one of Satan's bastard sons was part of this. She wondered how big a part. Who was pulling the strings in the race to Armageddon? Moloch? The bastard? Another player she hadn't met?

"Is that a question?" she asked. "Because you see her as much as I do."

He cocked his head and smiled. Again, she fought the desire to back up. Back up and run. "That's not true, is it? I think you feel bad for her."

A chill sank deep into her muscles. There was nothing deemed more worthy of punishment in Moloch's world than compassion. She was definitely not asking to send Lilliana's infant away. Hell, no. Moloch could eat it in a stew for all she cared.

"She amuses me, is all," she said hastily. "And I might be able to get her to talk. She knows more than anyone about Azagoth's secrets."

Moloch's expression revealed nothing that clued her in to whether or not he believed her.

"I have something to show you." He gestured for her to follow him along a winding path. "My new scarecrow."

He stopped in front of the pole where he was always putting up a newly impaled thing. She looked up.

Oh, Dark Lord…

Flail swallowed bile over and over. *Don't vomit. Don't vomit. Don't fucking vomit.*

"That's not his entire body," Moloch said in a pleasant, la-dee-da voice that filled her with terror. "Just his skin, stuffed with straw. It's beautiful, isn't it? That'll keep those pesky crows away."

Maddox. Oh, Maddox.

"There are no crows here." It was her voice, her words, but she didn't know why she spoke them. There were so many other things she could have said. Like, "*You fucking piece of shit, I'm going to slaughter you.*" Or, "*You told me he survived the ambush.*" Or, "*You promised you wouldn't kill him.*"

"No," Moloch said, studying her as she fought for the right balance of expectedly outraged yet not homicidal. "There are no crows here. There have been reports of a hellhound lurking around, though. Nasty things."

Bending over, he started watering a blackberry bush whose thorns dripped poison that burned like a mother.

You fucker, I hope you get pricked.

He was going to pay for this. Not right here, not this minute. But it would happen.

And, screw it, she was going to get Lilliana's kid out of here so it wasn't next week's garden ornament.

"How dare you?" she ground out. "We had a deal. I work for you, and in return, you don't do…*that*"—she gestured to the Maddox scarecrow—"to my nephew. We're on the same team, Moloch. I want Satan released as badly as you do. That's why I'm spending my time listening to Azagoth's whiny little bitch of a mate. I'm hoping she can tell us something useful. I have one idea that might work. But who knows?"

Moloc would never have taken the bait she'd just set out, but Bael would have. Would Moloch?

Intrigued, Moloch looked over his shoulder at her. "Tell me."

She steeled herself. Bael's influence had turned Moloch unpredictable, and he was just as likely to listen to her as he was to disembowel her for fun.

"Right now, Azagoth has no reason to believe you'll release Lilliana after he frees the Dark Lord. All you've done is torture her and piss him off. I spent enough time with him in Sheoul-gra to know that for a fact. I suggest that you send him a good-faith gesture."

Moloch straightened, the watering can at his side. "Such as?"

"When Lilliana gives birth, send him the infant."

The look he gave her was pure, *are you crazy.* "And give up two hostages?"

"You said yourself that you didn't care if the angelicant Lilliana took killed the child," she pointed out. "The goal was always to get *her* into our hands. We've got her, and so far, nothing you've done has convinced Azagoth to comply. And why is that? It's because he can't be dealt with by force. Ask Heaven. They'll tell you." Moloch was listening, no longer focused on his dumb plants. Encouraged, she kept pitching. "He's a businessman. He negotiates, Moloch. He makes deals, and he's not known for breaking them."

Unlike Moloch.

"Offer him the baby as a down payment on Satan's release," she continued, "with the full payment of Lilliana after it's done. What will it hurt to try a new tack?"

He actually appeared to consider it, and then he snorted. "You've been spending too much time with Azagoth's whore. I think you need to remember what you are."

"I despise the weak little bitch," she snapped, although, in truth, she had to hand it to Lilliana for one thing. There was no way Flail would survive being trapped in a tiny realm populated with her mate's offspring...and still be sane.

But while the stories of Azagoth's cruelty went far beyond the borders of Sheoul-gra, Flail also knew some lesser-known tales. Like how, when her sister had gone back to him after running away the first time, he'd refused to touch her until she was ready. And while Flail doubted that he'd done it out of nobility or decency, she'd seen enough during her time in Sheoul-gra to believe he took his duties seriously, and the only thing he'd ever expected of others was that they do the same.

Ellandra had actually come away from Azagoth's bed in good spirits. In fact, for the first few months afterward, as she grew Maddox in her womb, she was the happiest Flail had ever seen her. But as reality began to settle in, and Ellandra realized she would have to give up the baby and place her child in the hands of the worst humanity had to offer, depression and despair had set in.

Flail was only glad that her sister wasn't around to see what Moloch had done to her son.

"And what if I ask you to kill her when the time comes?" Moloch asked.

"It would be my greatest honor," she assured him. "But, my lord, this isn't about Lilliana. It's about starting the Great Cleansing, the End of Days, and to do that, we need Satan to be free. The child is disposable to you. Why not use it to bring Azagoth to our side?"

"You've convinced me," he said, and she exhaled in relief, unaware that she'd been holding her breath. "You've convinced me you need to remember that you are a fallen angel who once nailed a human's heart to a wall while he was still alive." Moloch's slow, malevolent smile froze her in place as her relief turned to terror. "Take off your clothes. I haven't heard a female scream in hours."

Chapter 26

Lilliana had her first contraction only moments after Moloch's games began. He called them games, but really, they were just trials of people Moloch considered traitors that ended with the guilty parties being executed in creative and gory ways.

She'd been forced to watch for hours at Moloch's side, made to endure his constant threats to put her on trial next. Every time someone died, he'd asked if she'd like to join them. When she said no, he laughed. When she said yes, he said no. And when she ignored him, he raked his claws across her face or punched her in the head.

He was a real fucking gentleman.

At least her misery and the spectacle had allowed her to disguise her labor discomfort as disgust or the pain of being struck.

But nothing could mask the sheer terror of knowing that her baby was almost here, and she would have no way to protect it.

Finally, as she moaned quietly through an intense contraction, he signaled to a guard to have her taken away.

"Your weak constitution annoys me," he said. "But it'll make Flail's job easier."

Flail's job? She didn't ask, didn't want to delay being taken away from this awful place. Granted, she was going to another terrible place, her cell, but even that cold, smelly box was better than this, where the stench of fear, burning flesh, and entrails left her swallowing bile.

Pain wrenched her belly as she shuffled toward the cell, a burly demon on each side, their armor scraping the stone walls as they walked. As they rounded the corner to her cell, a gush of liquid spilled from between her thighs and ran down her leg. One of the demons laughed.

"Look, Oog, she pissed herself. Angels are cowards."

If she weren't about to drop a baby on the floor right now, she'd punch the brute in the face. As it was, she breathed through a contraction and told herself to let it go. It was a good thing if the demons thought she was a coward. They'd let down their guard if they didn't see her as a threat.

Oog snorted like a boar rooting for truffles and shoved her inside the cell so hard, she stumbled and hit the floor, twisting so her shoulder and hip took the brunt of the impact instead of her belly.

"Assholes!" she yelled as the door slammed closed. "You dick—"

She broke off as pain wrenched her insides. Everything from her pelvis to her shoulder blades screamed in agony as if she were being stretched on one of Moloch's racks.

"No, please no," she moaned as she sat up and rubbed her belly. "Stay in there. Please—" This time, the scream was audible, breaking from her throat.

Water. She needed water. Panting, she looked around, but even the bucket filled with gelatinous brown muck was gone. Sweat and tears mingled and dripped down her face as the contractions ripped her in half, one coming right on top of the other now.

She pushed to her hands and knees and concentrated on breathing. In. Out. In. Out. For hours. Or maybe ten minutes. She couldn't tell.

The door creaked, and she was too scared to look. So terrified and in so much pain, that she couldn't contain a wail of despair.

"Oh, fuck."

Lilliana wasn't sure if she was relieved that the newcomer's voice belonged to Flail or not. Lilliana hadn't seen her since she'd talked to her about getting the baby out of here, and some small part of her didn't even want to know Flail's decision.

A yes meant she might never see her baby again.

A no meant she might have to watch her baby die.

She needed a yes, or she'd go mad.

She opened her eyes. The fallen angel was standing in the doorway, a phone in one hand, and a pair of garden shears in the other.

"Flail," Lilliana moaned as another contraction tore through her. "It's the baby."

"Son of a bitch." Flail wheeled around and fled, the sound of the door clanging shut echoing through the room.

Lilliana hated that skank, but right now, she hated being alone more. She was supposed to have her baby at home, surrounded by people she loved. Azagoth was supposed to be here to offer encouragement and welcome his son or daughter with his strong arms. She was supposed to bring this child into the world in a place of safety.

None of that was going to happen.

The door banged open again, and Flail rushed in with an armload of towels and a stool.

"Here." She placed a folded towel on the floor next to the stool. "Kneel on this and use the stool to brace yourself. My sister said this was the easiest way to do this. It'll just slide right out."

Somehow, Lilliana didn't think it would be that simple, but even if it were, it would only bring the child into this horrible world sooner.

Lilliana panted through a contraction. "I...don't want...what's easiest."

"Are you a fucking idiot?"

Lilliana's arms and legs shook with the effort to keep from pushing. "Tell me Moloch agreed to send the baby to Azagoth." She cried out as the instinct to bear down overwhelmed her.

No, no, no!

"Not...exactly."

Lilliana broke down into sobs, her limbs collapsing beneath her. That had been the one hope keeping her going. Keeping her from going completely insane. If something happened to her baby, she'd die. She had no doubt that she'd lose her sanity and her will to live. Right now, for the first time, she understood Azagoth's self-destructive streak.

"Lilliana? Shit, it's going to be okay." Flail rolled her onto her back and shoved a towel beneath her head, and even through Lilliana's physical and mental agony, it struck her as an oddly compassionate thing to do. "Just push, okay, you dumb bitch?" She thrust Lilliana's thighs apart. "Push!"

"No one is ever going to ask you to be their labor coach," Lilliana screamed as she bore down, her body overriding her will.

"It's coming, Lilliana," Flail said. "I see the head. Push."

Lilliana roared as she pushed, the tearing, searing pain spurring her on. Tears of sorrow streamed down her face.

The tears should be ones of joy, making this all so much worse.

"Another push. Now, Lilliana."

Lilliana shook with the effort, her lungs expelling a shout as her body expelled the little life she'd kept safe for all these months.

"Got it," Flail breathed. "It's a girl. You have a daughter."

A cry rose up, the most beautiful sound Lilliana had ever heard as Flail wrapped the baby in a towel. "Ooh, glad I have the garden shears," she said. "I came here to torture you a little, to try one more time to get you to call Azagoth, but you had to go and drop a kid."

Someone pounded on the door. "Flail?" A deep, booming voice vibrated the air. "Is the morsel born? I will tell Moloch, no?"

Sheer, stark terror screamed through Lilliana. *Morsel?*

Flail hesitated, and Lilliana reached for her, gripping her hand as the fallen angel tucked the baby against her.

"Please," Lilliana mouthed. *"Please help her."*

Flail glanced at her and then turned to the door. "Yes," she called out. "Report to Moloch."

Lilliana screamed and grabbed the shears. It didn't matter that she stood no chance of getting out of Moloch's castle, let alone out of the cell. She couldn't let her baby be taken away yet. She'd fight until the end. Until she was dead.

The shears ripped from her hands and clattered against the spiked wall. "Listen to me, you stupid twat!" Flail glanced nervously between Lilliana and the door. "I'm going to get her to Azagoth, okay? But I have to go *now* before that guard tells Moloch the baby is here."

Flail held up the bundle so Lilliana could see her daughter—her beautiful little face with Azagoth's nose and her eyes.

"Let me hold her," Lilliana pleaded. "Just for a minute."

"There's no time." Flail opened the door, but before she left, she looked back at Lilliana, sadness swirling in the dark depths of her eyes. "And, trust me, holding her will only make it harder." She cursed. "I'm a fucking idiot."

And then she was gone, and Lilliana sank to the floor, slick with birth blood, a profound sense of loss sapping what was left of her strength. Numb, unable to function, she wrapped her arms around her knees and rocked.

Without the baby, she wouldn't be able to communicate with Azagoth. In a matter of seconds, she'd lost both her lifelines.

And her hope.

Chapter 27

Eidolon had always been one to work through his grief. The more he mourned, the harder he worked.

He hadn't left the hospital in days. Not since it'd happened.

Tayla and their son had gone to stay with Serena and Stewie for a while, and he had no desire to go back to an empty home where all he'd do was think.

Shade hadn't come *back* to work since it happened. Funny how all Eidolon's siblings handled grief differently.

Lore's pain was silent, but he was always there. Sin was vocal, but distant. Wraith had killed. Eidolon healed.

Shade dwelled, openly parsing through his agony and anger. Right now, he was spending a lot of his time with Gem's mate, Kynan, and the Demonic Activity Response Team, as they spent the majority of their resources on the hunt for the last remaining fallen angel responsible for Wraith's death. Apparently, Limos and Reseph had bagged the second male this morning.

Eidolon hoped the Horsemen were making the bastard regret ever hearing Wraith's name. Much like Eidolon regretted how he'd handled the situation that had gotten Wraith killed.

When he wasn't busy, he ran Wraith's death over and over in his head, as though the what-if scenarios could play out in the past and bring his brother back from the dead. What if he'd physically restrained Wraith? What if he'd gone out to handle the fallen angels himself?

What if they'd just freaking waited ten minutes for the Harrowgate to be fixed?

Except the gate hadn't been fixed. Lilliana would still have been abducted, and that only made the whole thing worse.

His cell dinged as he negotiated the dim hospital hallways on his way to x-ray, where he'd sent a *blanchier* demon with a broken leg. It was a text from Gem.

There's a fallen angel with a baby here to see you. You should hurry.

A fallen angel. He was getting really fucking sick of fallen angels.

He reversed course and jogged toward the emergency department. As he rounded the last corner, he nearly slammed into Gem and Thanatos. The Horseman had been here a lot lately, keeping everyone up to date on his quest to make everyone responsible for Wraith's death pay in blood and pain. Eidolon was grateful for the guy's dedication and devotion to Wraith. It had been a mystifying friendship, but one that had rounded out Wraith's life.

The ache of losing Wraith would never go away, but Eidolon could take comfort in the knowledge that, for a while, Wraith's past had lost its grip on him. He'd made a good life with his mate and son, and he'd fleshed it out with a job he loved, and friends who made his exploits seem tame.

Fucking fallen angels.

Gem gestured through the ambulance bay doors at a female in black battle armor standing in the parking lot. Her dark, leathery wings were tucked behind her back, the crests rising high above her head. In her arms was a squirming bundle he assumed was the baby Gem had mentioned.

"She said she'll only talk to you."

Thanatos quirked an eyebrow at Eidolon. "Something you want to tell us?"

"I can only impregnate my mate." Which wouldn't happen for a while. Tayla was content with one child, and his Seminus instinct to reproduce was suppressed. Right now, even his sex drive, the thing that made him an incubus, was curbed, thank the gods. Sex could only distract from grief for so long, and then it opened a floodgate of raw emotion.

"Ignore E," Gem told Thanatos. "He doesn't get humor or teasing."

"I get it," he said. "I just don't acknowledge it. There's a difference."

Gem gestured to Eidolon. "See?"

Thanatos nodded. "Wraith always said he was 'starched.'"

A big hole in Eidolon's heart threatened to swallow him, but he shook it off, concentrating on the situation at hand. "Who is this fallen angel who will only talk to me?"

Shadows flickered in Gem's eyes as her demon half stirred. "She said her name is Flail, and she's covered in scars."

Gem's inner demon, a Soulshredder, could see scars—physical and emotional—that were invisible to everyone else. As a half-breed, she wasn't bound by her instinct to use her knowledge of the scars' existence to torment and traumatize people. She didn't need to feed off their fear and misery to survive. But she still possessed the raw desire to rip deep into those scars and bring the bearers screaming to their knees. Both she and Tayla had inked restraining tattoos on their throats to help them control the demon within.

Some days went better than others, and today, the gleam of desire was bright in Gem's eyes.

"Tell her to come inside."

"I already have," Gem said. "She refused."

"Don't go, E," Thanatos warned. "It's probably a trap. I'll do it. I'm equipped to fight a fallen angel. You're equipped to..." He looked Eidolon up and down. "Fuck her."

"What did I tell you about Eidolon's sense of humor?" Gem gestured to the female outside, oblivious to the fact that Thanatos hadn't been trying to be funny. "She also said if you don't come out alone, you and *only* you, she'll hurt the baby."

The female stared. Glared. Tapped her foot. Produced a dagger and held it menacingly close to the infant.

"I guess that's my cue," he said. "Stay here." He started toward the door, pausing as it opened. "Unless she tries to kill me. Then kick her ass."

Thanatos touched his finger to a mark on his throat, and his armor, some sort of pale bone plate, folded into place, instantly covering his leather pants and Deadpool T-shirt.

"For Wraith." He cast Eidolon a considering glance and then shrugged. "And you."

"Watch it, Horseman," he said. "I delivered both your children out of the goodness of my heart and the threat of an excruciating death. The next one will cost you a new hospital wing."

Thanatos's deep laughter rang out as Eidolon walked through the sliding glass doors and met the female near the two parked ambulances.

"I'm Eidolon."

"I know." The female held out the baby, wrapped in a bloody towel. "Deliver this to its father."

He gathered the mewling infant in his arms. It was a newborn, probably only minutes old, still wet with its mother's birth blood.

"Who is the father?" The child blinked up at him with the clearest amber eyes he'd ever seen. "Who is its mother? You?"

She scowled. "Do I look like I just gave birth, you idiot demon? How can you be a renowned physician?" She gave a sound of disgust and then gestured to the baby. "The brat's father is Azagoth. I assume you know of him."

Eidolon sucked in a shocked breath and then looked back down at the child. "Yes." Holy shit.

"Tell him this is a good-faith gesture. As soon as he does Moloch's bidding, Lilliana will be returned to him." She paused. "Tell him to hurry. She's not doing well."

Eidolon looked up sharply from the baby. "Where is she? Let me see her."

Both Flail and the air went deadly still. "You don't get to demand shit, demon."

He cradled the infant close, tucking it protectively against his chest. "Dammit, if she's suffering from complications of childbirth, she needs a doctor."

As an angel, Lilliana should heal from most illnesses and injuries on her own, but angels didn't regenerate as quickly—or at all—inside Sheoul. She might not die, but she could be enduring unspeakable suffering.

Flail gave a bitter laugh. "Do you honestly think Moloch cares about her health?"

No, but he probably should. Azagoth wasn't someone to be trifled with. "Just tell me how she is."

"She gave up her child before she even held it," she snapped. "How do you think she is?" With that, the fallen angel dematerialized.

Fuck.

Ignoring stares from bystanders, Eidolon hurried inside and hit the nearest exam room, Gem and Thanatos on his heels.

"Close the door," he told them.

"What's going on?" Thanatos peered over Eidolon's shoulder as he placed the baby on the exam table. "Whose kid is that?"

"It's Azagoth and Lilliana's." Eidolon peeled open the towel and smiled. "It's a girl."

"Aw, a little Reapette." Gem fetched a warm, wet cloth and began to bathe her as Eidolon checked her vitals and channeled a thread of power into her little body to make sure everything was somewhere on the scale of normal for her species.

Which was difficult, considering he wasn't even sure what her species was. Her mother was an angel, but no longer considered *Heavenly*, and her father was neither an angel nor a fallen angel, but something in between.

"Did the fallen say how Lilliana was doing? Or where she is?"

"She wasn't exactly forthcoming." Eidolon reached for a thermometer. "But it doesn't sound like Lilliana is doing well."

"Damn," Thanatos breathed. "I should have gone out there with you. I should have grabbed that bitch and made her talk."

Gem looked up from the sponge bath. "So, what now?"

Eidolon thought about it for a moment. "Call Idess. She's going to want to meet her new sister."

And then she'd have the bittersweet task of delivering the baby to its father.

Eidolon didn't envy her at all.

Eidolon was exhausted.

But resting meant thinking, and thinking meant reliving Wraith's death.

He threw out a few choice curse words as he shoved open his office door, and when he saw who was waiting inside, he threw out a few more.

"It's gonna get crowded and awkward on that couch when I lay across your lap," he said.

Shade snorted as he sprawled out across the cushions in his black leather pants and jacket, one booted foot on the floor, the other dangling.

He looked like hammered shit, as if he'd been on a week-long bender of booze and brawls. It was how Wraith used to look on a daily basis before he mated Serena.

"If you're tired, you can go home, you know."

Eidolon eyed the desk chair, but if he sat down, he might not get back up. "Tayla and Sabre are with Serena. The apartment is too empty." Tay had even taken the dog and ferret. There was absolutely nothing at home to keep his mind occupied.

"Then come to my place. Sin and Con are there. Lore, too." Shade sat up, his movements jerky as if he had to force his body to cooperate. "He said you called Idess to the hospital."

A whisper of warning tickled the back of Eidolon's neck at the hint of disapproval in Shade's tone. His brother wasn't here for no reason.

"What's this about, Shade?"

"I'm just wondering what was so damned important that you had to call Idess away from a family gathering. Not everyone's a workaholic like you."

"Well," Eidolon said flatly, too emotionally depleted to put up with his brother's attitude. Wraith's death had hit Shade harder than anyone, but they were all suffering, and Eidolon wasn't going to let Shade take his grief out on him. "A fallen angel dropped off a baby like some kind of evil stork. Turns out, it's Azagoth's daughter. I thought Idess would like to meet her little sister and take her to their father." He threw in a bit of snark just because. "Was that against the Seminus code of family gatherings?"

"Shit." Shade jammed his hand through his black hair and fell back against the couch. "Where's Lilliana?"

"According to the fallen angel, she's still imprisoned." Man, he felt for Azagoth, and that was a sentiment Eidolon never thought would enter his head.

"This is so fucked-up." Shade rubbed his eyes with his palms and let them fall into his lap. "Has Azagoth freed Wraith's soul?"

"I don't know, but it isn't as if he doesn't have his own problems." Eidolon didn't want to talk about this. He wasn't ready, and he didn't know if he ever would be. He glanced at his watch and swung toward the door. "I have to get back to work."

"The fuck, E?" Shade shot upright again, this time with no trace of the earlier awkwardness. "Are you serious?"

"I'm not a well-known prankster, Shade." Eidolon reached for the doorknob. "You're the one who always agrees when Wraith says I'm starched."

"He's dead," Shade rasped. "He's not still here to say that shit."

"I'm aware of that."

"Are you?" Shade's voice was quiet. Low. Begging for a

confrontation, and Eidolon happened to be in the right mood to give it to him.

"Spit it out, brother." Eidolon rounded on Shade. "What's up your ass?"

Shade shoved out of his seat. "What's up my ass? Wraith's dead, and all you can think about is work."

"It's what I do, Shade."

"Yeah, it is," he growled, getting right up in his face. "It's what you always do. When people need you, you're always there for them, aren't you? All these patients, they can count on you. But when can your family count on you, E?"

Eidolon stared, unable to believe what his brother had just said. "Excuse me?"

"You should be with us," Shade said, giving his chest a knuckle tap. "Instead, you're hiding behind your work."

"I'm not hiding." Even as the sentence came out of his mouth, he knew it was a lie. Well, he wouldn't use the word *hiding*, but he was definitely avoiding.

Avoiding having to deal with Wraith's death.

And Shade had called him on it. "Bullshit. You feel guilty because you got him killed, so you're burying yourself in your job like you always do."

"*I* got him killed?" Eidolon asked, incredulous. "Are you fucking kidding? Wraith's cockiness got him killed, and you know it. How many times have we had to haul him out of a fire of his own making?" He let out a bitter curse. "Hell, I didn't expect him to live this long."

Stepping closer, his boots hitting the floor like gavels, Shade bared his teeth. "You didn't have to let him challenge the angels."

The fact that Shade spoke the truth hit Eidolon in his already bruised heart. Though instead of getting pissed off and defensive, he closed his eyes and confronted the dark place inside him that he'd been avoiding.

Wraith's arrogance had been overshadowed only by Eidolon's.

Eidolon had grown up with the Judicia, a race of highly educated demons dedicated to logic and justice. Wraith had accused him of having a superiority complex because of it, which Eidolon had denied. But what if Wraith hadn't been wrong? What if Eidolon's ego and certainty about his intelligence had put Wraith at risk?

"You're right." Eidolon lifted his lids and looked his brother in the eye. "I thought I could talk down the fallen angels. My arrogance…" He swallowed a sudden lump of grief in his throat. "My arrogance got him killed."

"Ah, hell." Shade's arms came around him. "It wasn't your fault." His big body shuddered. "Fuck, man, of all the brothers we've lost…" He trailed off, his shoulders heaving on a ragged breath. "I don't know if I can recover from this one."

"You will," Eidolon said, forcing an even tone when he really wanted to break down. "We all will."

"How?" The desperation in Shade's voice galvanized Eidolon, bringing out his instinct to heal.

"Our families. Our mates, our kids." Eidolon pulled back from his brother. "Come on. Let's go to your place and be with them."

Physician, heal thyself.

He just hoped it was possible.

Chapter 28

Azagoth stood in the Inner Sanctum's dark underbelly, a cave-like structure where nightmares came to life. All around him, cracks invisible to everyone but Azagoth and Hades had formed in the walls that separated the space from Sheoul.

Hades was concerned that evil souls might try to escape.

Azagoth didn't give a shit. He no longer gave a shit about anything that wasn't directly related to getting his mate back.

Fortunately, he had the best minds working on that, including all the Horsemen and Reaver's mate, Harvester, who, as a former fallen angel and a daughter of Satan, knew intimate details about her father's kingdom and his loyalists. She'd requested entrance to Sheoul-gra this morning and had given him a lot of useful information about Moloch. Including the fact that he had one weakness: a female he'd kept as an object of his obsession for centuries.

She'd killed herself a hundred years ago, and if Azagoth could locate her soul in the Inner Sanctum, he might be able to use her against Moloch.

Hades and his crew were searching the rings at this very moment.

And Cipher had made progress in his attempts to hack Moloch's spell-based security system surrounding his territory. Unfortunately, Moloch had learned from Bael's mistakes that had allowed Cipher to escape his clutches, and every time Cipher found a back door, Moloch's techs closed it.

Still, Cipher had managed to access one of Moloch's cameras, and for a single, precious minute, Azagoth had seen Lilliana at some sort of public spectacle. She'd looked miserable, but despite the grainy video quality, the spark of defiance in her eyes had been obvious, and his heart had swelled with pride.

His mate was a badass. But that knowledge was nothing new.

"Hey, boss."

Hades' rumbling voice coming from behind Azagoth made him groan. "Why do I get the feeling you're checking to make sure I'm not doing something crazy?"

"I dunno. Maybe because you keep coming down here to do crazy shit, like free a hundred thousand of the evilest souls in Sheoul-gra?"

Ah, right. That.

"You can chill. I'm not breaking rules today." No, he was just *planning* to break them.

No, *planning* wasn't the right word. He was really setting up a contingency plan. A hail Mary. A nuclear option.

"I'm just here to deliver a message," Hades said. "I was topside, talking to Z. Idess is here to see you."

"Tell her I'm busy."

Hades leveled him with a look laden with meaning. "You really want to see her."

Azagoth's heart leaped into his throat at Hades' tone. He flashed to the Inner Sanctum's exit and practically dove through the portal into his office.

It was empty. Shit.

He tore open the door and found Zhubaal standing in the hallway, a silent sentinel. "She's waiting for you at Lilliana's reading spot."

Azagoth flashed there.

Idess was sitting on the bench at the edge of the pond, its waters murkier than they had been yesterday. The grass was faring no better under the influence of his moods, turning brown and crunchy like the leaves of the surrounding trees.

His daughter's back was to him as he approached, but when she heard him, she stood and turned around. She was holding something squirmy wrapped in a zombie-print blanket.

"This had better not be an attempt to make me feel better with a kitten or a puppy."

Idess's smile was tinged with sadness. "She was brought to Underworld General this morning." She pushed aside the blanket to reveal a tiny little face. "Flail brought her. Eidolon ran a genetic test to be sure." Idess stroked a wispy black curl of hair. "Lilliana gave birth.

This is your daughter."

The ground beneath Azagoth tilted violently. He stumbled back a step, catching himself on a cherry sapling.

"Oh, Lilliana," he whispered. All he could do was stare at the little miracle.

"She's perfectly healthy." Idess took a step closer to him. "She just had a bottle."

She moved even closer, and Azagoth took an involuntary step back, his palms sweating, his pulse pounding.

How could this be happening? Lilliana was supposed to give birth here in Sheoul-gra, surrounded by friends and family, with Azagoth at her side. Instead, she'd been forced to deliver their daughter in Hell, most likely in a dungeon under brutal circumstances.

And that was the best of the realistic scenarios. The others were too gruesome to think about. And yet, they kept running through his mind.

"What...what about Lilliana?" he croaked, his gaze glued to the infant. She had her mother's pure amber eyes. Azagoth's black hair.

"Flail indicated that she's alive. Moloch sent you the baby as some sort of goodwill gesture. A down payment of sorts. Do what he wants, and you'll get Lilliana back next." She held out the bundle. "Do you want to hold her?"

He wanted to hold her tight and never let her go. His hands trembled as he took her, but the moment she was secure in his arms, his body relaxed, and his mind calmed. His entire life, his entire being had been for this moment. This child.

He had feelings for all of his children, some negative, some positive, some neutral. He'd never even met most of them. He'd formed bonds with several, and he loved them deeply. Idess. Suzanne. Hawkyn. Maddox. Journey. There were more, some of them, like Emerico and Jasmine, standing nearby even now, trying to pretend they weren't curious about what was going on.

But this child was the first to be born out of love, not duty. And as tiny and innocent as she was, she was surrounded by a strong aura of power so pure that it was clear, visible only because of the slight flicker.

"This is the first time I've seen a neutral aura," he said, his voice choked. "I know they're common to children born of one fallen angel and one Heavenly angel, but by the time I see them, their auras are dark with evil."

"Since I lost my Memitim status, I rarely see auras at all." Idess ran her finger over a curly lock of hair with a wistful smile. "Heaven is sending milk for her."

His head snapped up. "What?"

"Only until Lilliana comes back." Idess gestured to a diaper bag on the bench. "There's formula in there until the milk arrives."

"No," he growled. "I don't want anything from Heaven."

"Father, it's vital that she ingest angel milk right away, especially if she's here in Sheoul-gra. She needs the protection from evil."

"I said no!" The baby stirred, and he lowered his voice. "I don't trust them."

Those bastards wouldn't send anything to Azagoth unless there was a price attached or it served their agenda. And they *always* had an agenda. He wouldn't put it past them to poison the milk or infuse it with some sort of spell.

"You'd rather see her aura go dark by the time she's two weeks old?" Idess had raised her voice, but as more people gathered, she lowered it and pivoted closer. "Father, I get it. I do. Angels have screwed with a lot of lives. But so has the evil that comes out of Sheoul. Look what it did to you, and you were hundreds of years old, battle-hardened, and with a mission when you came down here. What kind of chance does a complete innocent who hasn't been inoculated against the ravages of malevolence stand?"

Azagoth looked down at the fragile life in his arms, and he pretty much just tumbled into the pools of purity that were her eyes. His heart swelled as she blinked up at him, so trusting, so unaware of the turmoil going on all around them.

Dipping his head, he pressed his cheek to hers. His world narrowed and focused, becoming entirely about her. Her tiny fingers brushed against his lips and chin before wrapping around his thumb. She clung to him, and he to her.

He needed her so badly, but she needed him more.

For months, Lilliana had protected this little miracle, and now it was his turn. And for the first time, he realized that protecting her meant more than keeping her out of physical danger.

It meant keeping her out of spiritual danger, as well.

Idess was right. He hated it, but what she said made sense. As the product of a union between good and evil, it wouldn't take much to tilt the baby's alignment one way or the other. Given her proximity to evil so early in her development, and without the divine influence of her mother or the natural protection offered by an angel's milk, his infant daughter didn't stand a chance.

"Fine," he said. "But I want Cipher to inspect everything Heaven sends." Actually, he would have Cipher check out everything and everyone from now on.

Nothing was going to get close to his family ever again.

Chapter 29

Reaver hated meetings. Any kind of meeting. Especially those in Heaven.

Fortunately, he didn't get invited to many, thanks to the fact that pretty much everyone resented that he'd once been disgraced. An Unfallen angel screwup. And now, he was the most powerful Heavenly angel in existence, save Metatron, although much of Uncle Met's power and authority came from his status as The Mouth of God.

But this meeting was different, and for once, he was glad that he hadn't been left out. The higher level the meeting was, the higher the stakes and the more Reaver wanted to be in the know.

There was no higher level than the Council of Orders. Consisting of three representatives from each of the twelve Orders, the Council began the new session with Metatron at one end of the table, attending not as part of the archangel delegation, but as God's witness.

As the lone Radiant in an angelic Order of his own, Reaver sat at the opposite end of the table.

This was a room slathered in opulence and full of the most powerful beings in the universe. It was a showcase of wings, in which everyone coveted everyone else's because they were bigger or shinier or prettier. And it was a display of the who's who in the world of angels.

If ever Reaver or Revenant needed to be destroyed, the Council of Orders, with their combined powers, could do it.

The CoO meetings made Reaver nervous.

He glanced around the table, trying to get a read on everyone as they sat there in their formal, white robes, the colors of the trim signifying their Orders. Red for the cherubim, blue for the hosts, yellow for the aeons. Metatron's robe was striped with all the colors of all the Orders, including Reaver's gold.

Stern faces looked back at him, and he wondered who would speak first.

Finally, Jophiel, a senior throne and Metatron's best friend spoke, his sterling eyes grave. "As many of you might have heard in your Order meetings or in the urgent Angelic Council gathering, it seems that the Grim Reaper has been engaged in forbidden activities."

Damn. Reaver had hoped the news hadn't gotten out yet. The less Heaven knew about the situation in Sheoul-gra, the better.

Muriel, Second of the Order of Dominions, tapped her jeweled nails on the table. "One of our reliable sources claims his mate, Lilliana, was abducted and is being held for ransom."

A murmur rose up, quieting when Camael, First of the Order of Powers, spoke. "Our sources say the same thing."

A virtue Reaver didn't know well, Barbiel, closed the book he'd been pawing through. "Who would be so stupid?"

"The fallen angel, Moloch," Muriel said as she reached for one of the fruit bowls and pierced an apple with her fingernail.

"He's taking revenge for Bael's death?" Barbiel asked, which told Reaver that the idiot knew nothing about Bael and Moloc's shared soul. Or the fact that it was Cipher who'd killed Bael, not Azagoth.

Although it wasn't for lack of trying on Azagoth's part.

"No." Camael shifted uncomfortably in his seat, his glossy cream wings ruffling against his orange-trimmed robe. "Moloch is threatening to kill Lilliana and her unborn child if Azagoth doesn't release Satan."

The room fell silent. Camael averted his gaze, the eternal shame of his Order weighing heavily on not only his shoulders but also on that of his companions seated to either side of him.

Satan had belonged to the Order of Powers, and nearly half of the angels who defected with him had also belonged to the Order.

Abruptly, the room exploded with curses and questions until people were on their feet, yelling at each other. Reaver was pretty sure the seraphim and principalities were about to start a brawl.

"Quiet!" Jophiel slammed his fist down on the table. Fruit bounced out of the bowls and rolled down the table in a display of brilliant colors visible only in Heaven. "We're here to decide on a course of action, not to tear each other apart."

Reaver shot Jo a grateful look. Like Metatron, Jophiel had a good head on his shoulders, and a rare ability to put aside personal bias when looking at an issue.

Unlike pretty much everyone else in the room. Including Reaver.

Jophiel cleared his throat in the thick silence. "What we know so far is that Lilliana is in Moloch's custody, and Azagoth has violated his contract by releasing demon souls directly from the Inner Sanctum. And this wasn't the first time."

Now, all the shocked eyes turned to him. Camael looked relieved to have the pressure off his back.

"When was the first?" Phaleg, a super-douche from the Order of Angels, gripped the table so hard, his knuckles turned white. "I demand to know!"

Jophiel smiled at Reaver and made a dramatic ask-him gesture.

"Thanks, Jo," Reaver muttered before addressing the accusatory faces staring at him. All but Metatron, who already knew the whole story. "It was a few weeks ago. He did it because Bael murdered several of Azagoth's children."

"How many souls did Azagoth release?" Phaleg demanded.

Reaver gave a casual shrug in an attempt to minimize the impact. "A handful."

"A handful on *that* occasion," Jophiel flared his cinnamon wings in irritation. "But this most recent transgression went beyond what could be considered a reasonable, if still illegal, response." He caught an azure maidenfruit before it rolled off the table and tossed it back into the bowl. "He released a hundred thousand souls this time, and he gave them the power to kill or possess bodies and eject the host soul."

There were a few gasps. Phaleg shoved to his feet and leaned across the table at Reaver. "And you. You obviously knew about the first instance long ago. What did you do to punish him?"

Reaver gave him a level look, daring him to lean in closer. "I handled it."

"Handled? How?"

"It doesn't matter." Gabriel, the archangel who had made Azagoth and Sheoul-gra his personal project from the beginning, stood. "Our concern now is how to fix this."

"This isn't recoverable," Muriel said. "Azagoth must be destroyed. Now that he's not breeding Memitim, we don't need him. Hades can take over Sheoul-gra."

"Disagree." Metatron shoved to his feet in a rare display of temper.

"There has to be another way."

Camael arched an eyebrow at Metatron. "Do you have any ideas? Or any divine guidance?"

"Of course, I don't."

"Then I say we put him down like a diseased troll." Camael turned back to the table. "And take out any Memitim who side with Azagoth. We don't need anyone getting any ideas about revenge."

"What about Lilliana?" Gabriel asked, his resonant voice stilling conversation. "Do we kill her, too? The baby?" His multicolored locks of hair brushed his shoulders as he shook his head. "And you forget that he's put safeguards in place to prevent us from killing him. If we do that, all souls in Sheoul-gra will automatically be released."

That seemed to give everyone pause. Finally, Michael, seated next to Gabriel, spoke up.

"Only if he's executed *inside* the realm." Michael braced his forearms on the table and focused his gaze on the digital map of Sheoul-gra that suddenly appeared in the air. "All we have to do is get him out. And if Lilliana and the child are still alive, we'll bring them here. With her knowledge, Lilliana is invaluable to us. The child may be, as well."

"The child is a product of Sheoul-gra," Phaleg said. "Evil. We can't allow it in Heaven. If it's still alive, we must kill it."

"It's still alive." Royelle, a cherubim who was a mother to at least four Memitim, poured a glass of silver glacier wine from the crystal pitcher in front of her. "The newborn girl is, in fact, in Sheoul-gra with Azagoth," she said, and Reaver struggled to hide his shock. "Idess put in a formal request for mother's milk for the child not two hours ago." She smirked. "She went through the Memitim Council, hoping to keep the news contained. Idess has always been naive."

The baby had been born? How had it gotten to Azagoth? And where was Lilliana?

"We can't do this," Reaver growled, drawing on his power, ready to take on all these assholes at once if he had to.

"And we can't let Azagoth use demon souls for his own purposes," Phaleg snapped back. "His powers are meant to be limited to his realm. He signed a contract. Whatever happens to his kid is a direct result of *his* choices. He's forcing our hand."

At the murmured agreement rising up around the table from several councilmembers, Reaver surged to his feet, his wings flaring. "I won't *let* you do this!"

"Just because you're the Radiant, it doesn't mean you're in charge." Muriel studied her half-eaten apple, still impaled on her nail. "There are rules, and there is a hierarchy, just as there has always been, *Yenrieth*."

Uriel, the newest member of the Archangel Council, shot Reaver a glare. "He ignored all of that as Yenrieth. Do you think Reaver suddenly cares about rules now that he's the Radiant?"

"I care." Reaver waved the map out of existence. "But Azagoth's contract is due for an update. He's handled his duties admirably for thousands of years. Don't forget that he volunteered for that shitty job. These are unusual circumstances, and he can't be expected to—"

"To what?" Phaleg interrupted. "Honor the contract he signed?" He wheeled around and pointed at Gabriel. "You know him, you know the terms of his contract. What is the punishment for releasing a hundred thousand souls?"

Gabriel folded his hands over his robe's purple sash, all casual as if the topic bored him. But the shards of ice in his pale blue eyes said the exact opposite.

"The punishment is to be decided by the Council of Orders," he said. "But there's no requirement that he die for it."

"It doesn't matter," Camael said. "We can't take the risk that he'll release Satan."

"He won't," Reaver insisted.

Jo cast his solemn gaze at Reaver. "Can you guarantee that? Can you ensure that he's not taking the key down there right now, and that Armageddon isn't going to start tonight?"

No, he couldn't guarantee anything. He didn't believe Azagoth would do that, but Reaver also knew what insane lengths he'd go to to save Harvester. Hell, he *had* gone to crazy lengths to save her. He'd broken about a million rules and risked his wings and his life.

But he hadn't come close to starting the Apocalypse.

Azagoth could do that.

"Even if everyone here agreed that Azagoth has to go, you can't get to him." Reaver assessed each member of the Council in turn, trying to gauge who might be convinced that this was a terrible idea, and who was already getting their pen ready to sign Azagoth's death warrant. "He's locked down Sheoul-gra. By the time you got inside, he could have barricaded himself inside the Inner Sanctum where angels can't go."

Uriel gestured to Barbiel. "Barb has a team of blights ready to go."

Reaver shuddered. Blights. The angelic equivalent of police K-

9s…if police dogs were hellhound-shark hybrids with the power of an angel. The creatures could link to any angel—the more powerful the angel, the more powerful the blight. A pack could bring down Azagoth and tear his soul to pieces.

The risk to the host angels was high, however. They felt every injury, and if their blight died, the shock could render the angel unconscious for months.

Gabriel shook his head. "We're not doing this. Let me talk to him."

Camael didn't back down. "You have no say. You're here because Azagoth and Sheoul-gra were your projects, so your advice and expertise are valuable. But you need to recuse yourself from the vote."

"My ass," Gabriel snapped. "I will not agree to this."

"As Camael just noted," Phaleg said coldly, "you don't have to."

Metatron stood, unfurling to his full height…and maybe a couple of extra inches. "What you are proposing, destroying Azagoth, his family, and everything he has worked for for thousands of years, is not something that should be decided rashly. What Azagoth has done has worked to keep the human realm safe, and Satan's influence to a minimum. What happens when he's gone?"

"Things might be chaotic for a while," Uriel acknowledged. "But Hades is…competent. He'll grow into the role. It is, after all, who should have been given the job in the first place." He said that with a meaningful look at Gabriel.

Gabriel threw up his arms in exasperation. "Hades wasn't even born yet. But, hey, don't let facts get in the way of your narrative."

Uriel tugged angrily on his robe, the breast embroidered with his moon and stars crest in purple thread. The narcissist had all of his clothes marked with his insignia. "Raphael told you to suspend your Sheoul-gra project. He saw that it wasn't time."

"Raphael is a traitor," Jo said, clearly taken aback by the invocation of the archangel's name. "And you'd best remember that if Azagoth frees Satan, Raphael will be freed, as well. And he's probably both insane and evil by now."

"He wasn't a traitor back then," Uriel pointed out, a little petulantly. He'd been friends with Raphael, and of all the archangels, he'd taken the news of Raphael's betrayal the hardest.

Camael banged his fist on the table, putting a crack in the thick wood and making the spilled fruit bounce. "What's done is done. The past matters not. We're dealing with a crisis *now*. Stop being fools. It's clear that what we're proposing is extreme, but so is the threat to all the realms if Azagoth frees Satan in order to save his mate. This is one risk we cannot take."

Another murmur of assent rose up, and Reaver felt sick. "And what, exactly, are you proposing? How will you destroy Azagoth? He's not opening the gates of Sheoul-gra for just anyone. And what about the child? Are you truly going to kill her?"

Jo spoke up. "I don't think it's necessary to destroy the child," he said. Look at that. Someone wasn't drooling over the prospect of killing a baby. "But Azagoth needs to go."

"The child cannot be allowed into Heaven." Phaleg raised his voice, dead set on this course of action. "And if we don't put it down, it could grow up to seek revenge."

"Do you not think any of Azagoth's children, the thousands of them, won't do the same?" Metatron asked. "We can't kill them all. They're angels."

"Memitim will understand," Uriel said. "Most hate him. We calculate that no more than a hundred will protest, and of those, most are earthbound Memitim who haven't yet earned their wings. We can easily put down a small rebellion from them."

Gabriel's head swiveled around to his fellow archangel. "Who is we? And why would they feel the need to calculate a potential rebellion? How long have you been planning to destroy Azagoth?"

Uriel snorted. "Some of us have wanted him gone since he first started refusing to father more Memitim. When he took Lilliana as a mate, it was the last straw."

Unbelievable. Reaver cursed. "This is why I hang out with demons. They're more honorable than any of you."

Phaleg hissed at him. "Once again, you show why you don't deserve the gift of being the Radiant." He addressed the room, rising into the air to tower over the audience. "I propose that we use the opportunity to deliver milk to get inside Sheoul-gra to destroy Azagoth. And for those too squeamish to put down the child, you can place it with a family who will never know its parentage. Any objections? From anyone other than Reaver, Metatron, and Gabriel?"

Not a single person objected.

"This is a mistake," Reaver growled. "I'm not Azagoth's biggest fan. The bastard threw me into the belly of a demon and left me there to be slowly digested. Plus, he's a giant tool. But what you're talking about should be a last resort. We didn't even discuss other options."

"There are no other options."

"Then there's no reason for me to be here." He stormed to the door, but as he threw it open, Camael cleared his throat.

"Don't do anything stupid, Reaver. Stay out of the way."

Reaver almost laughed. Staying out of the way wasn't his specialty. And doing stupid shit was totally in his wheelhouse.

It was as if these idiots didn't know him at all.

"Do it," someone whispered.

A warning tingle made the base of his skull itch. What the—?

Clamps powered by the collective energy of the Orders wrapped around the base of his wings, and just like that, his powers went neutral, and he crashed to his knees.

"Stop!" Metatron shouted. "This isn't necessary."

"Don't worry," Uriel said. "It's only temporary. Just until we take care of Azagoth." He tweaked Reaver's nose on the way out the door. "We can't have you warning your buddies now, can we?"

Well, apparently, he'd been wrong. It seemed these idiots knew him *very* well.

Chapter 30

Lilliana didn't know how long it had been since she'd given birth. Time had become irrelevant, measured only by the meals her guards brought, which she left uneaten in the corner. She had no idea if Flail had successfully gotten out with the baby, and if she had, where her little girl was now.

Curled up in a little ball, Lilliana cried for the millionth time, praying she didn't die before she found out what had happened to her daughter.

She and Azagoth hadn't even settled on a name.

A fat tear plopped to the floor just as the door creaked open. Blinking, Lilliana wiped her eyes with the back of her hand and sat up.

Clad in head-to-toe black leather and cloaked in shadow, Flail stood in the doorway and scowled down at Lilliana.

"Pathetic," she said.

"My baby," Lilliana croaked, her throat parched. "Where is she?"

"I assume she's with Azagoth by now." Flail's voice sounded raw, as if she'd been screaming as much as Lilliana had. "I left the squalling little toad at Underworld General."

Days' worth of anxiety escaped Lilliana like air from a popped tire.

"Thank you," she whispered. "Thank you so much."

"I didn't do it for you. I did it for my sister." Flail paused. "I think you actually would have liked her. If she hadn't fucked your mate, anyway. But didn't you say none of that bothers you?"

Lilliana licked her dry lips, but her tongue scraped like sandpaper.

"That's what I said."

"You're not a very good liar." She turned to leave, and Lilliana gaped.

Half of Flail's face was missing, leaving muscle and bone exposed to the air.

"Flail," she gasped. "Your face…"

"My punishment for taking the baby to Azagoth." She shrugged. "Moloch's done worse."

"I'm sorry—"

"Save your pity for yourself," Flail snapped. "You're going to need it."

She slammed the door closed, leaving Lilliana blessedly alone and smiling. Her baby was safe. Eidolon would have seen to it that she was delivered to her father. Azagoth was probably, at this moment, holding her in his arms. It would be the first time he'd ever seen one of his children as an infant.

Joy at the thought mixed with sorrow that she couldn't be there. That she would probably never hold her child.

It must have been hell for all the females who gave up their children to be raised as Memitim. It had even driven Flail's sister to seek out the Abyss.

All this time, Lilliana had assumed that the females sent to Azagoth were cold as ice, calculating, duty-bound broodmares. Of course, it didn't help that one of her first—and worst—experiences with Azagoth's past had come early in their relationship, just months after their mating ceremony.

She'd been excited about the birth of the realm's first litter of rabbits, and she'd rushed to tell Azagoth.

Lilliana smiled and opened the door to Azagoth's office.

"Oops, I'm sorry—"

She stopped mid-stride at the sight of Azagoth, hip propped casually against his desk, arms folded over his chest, across from a seated female. A stunning, dark-skinned beauty in a white dress far more suited to a cocktail party at the Playboy Mansion than a meeting with the Grim Reaper.

"It's okay." Azagoth waved her in. "This is probably something you should hear anyway."

"What is it?" As she walked over, the female gave her a bored smile as if Lilliana weren't worth more energy than that.

"Lucielle was just saying that if more Memitim are needed, she'll volunteer her services."

Surely, Lilliana hadn't heard that right. "I'm sorry...what?"

Lucielle stood, her gold heels adding an extra three inches to her already model-tall height. She could look Azagoth in the eye. And now Lilliana was imagining their eye-level sex.

"I meant no offense," she said, all stately and queen-like as if Lilliana weren't the damned queen in this room. "It's just that Azagoth and I have a history of producing some of the most beautiful and extraordinary Memitim. You've met Jasmine, I'm sure."

Jasmine...Jasmine... Right, Azagoth's newly arrived, drop-dead gorgeous daughter, who seemed to hate Lilliana.

Lilliana stood there like a goosed cow, her thoughts so fractured she couldn't get them to make sense. "Y-yes. Yes, of course."

What was even happening here? It was like a bizarre dream. Did this chick not know that she and Azagoth were mated?

"I was about to give her my answer when you walked in," Azagoth said. "Perhaps you'd like to do the honors?"

Why, yes. Yes, she would. But all she could focus on was the fact that they had children together. This female and Azagoth had slept together. More than once.

So, instead of hauling the skank out by her thick, shiny braids, she asked, "How many?"

"How many what, dear?" Lucielle asked sweetly. "Children? Two hundred and twelve." She looked back at Azagoth and smiled, all lipstick and blowjobs. "The Grim Reaper and I go way back. Thousands of years before you were born." She raked Lilliana with her gaze and gave a meh *shrug. "You could join us. I'm very open to new things."*

Okay, that was enough. Lilliana was done.

DONE.

"Get out," she snarled, pointing at the door. "Get out now. And tell all your broodmare friends that Azagoth is no longer available for stud."

Azagoth laughed. He thought this was funny? He should be tossing Lucielle on her ass. He should be telling her that he was mated now and that he loved Lilliana and only wanted her. And that her offer was an insult to their vows.

"Broodmare?" Lucielle went erect with indignation, her chin coming up so she could look down her narrow, perfect nose at Lilliana. "Being chosen to create, within our bodies, a unique class of angels from the seed of—"

"Out!" With a thought and a fling of the arm, Lucielle was yanked off her feet and tossed into the hall. A slam of the door kept Lilliana from having to look at her

stupid, dumbfounded face. Then, because doing that had done nothing to ease the hurt Azagoth had caused by not being outraged, she palmed one of the jade figurines on his desk and hurled it to the floor, where it shattered into a dozen pieces.

"Was that really necessary?"

She wheeled back around to Azagoth, who was still sitting there like a statue, one dark eyebrow cocked.

"Was it—what? Are you kidding me right now?" she demanded. "You should have kicked her out. That...that skank*...propositioned you right in front of me. That female you fucked in our bedroom over two hundred times!" At least Lilliana had gotten rid of the bed.*

"Calm down," he said. "We didn't use the bedroom much."

Her mouth fell open. Closed.

She left it that way, because if her mouth opened again, well...he'd regret it more than she would.

Spinning on her heel, she marched out.

But not before giving him the universally understood glare for, "You're sleeping on the couch tonight."

She'd been so angry. Neither she nor Azagoth had apologized, and they'd eventually gotten past it.

But had they really?

She'd sworn she could deal with all the females he'd bedded, and she had. After all, she rarely saw any of them. Azagoth had put out a notice that they weren't welcome in Sheoul-gra, except for under extreme circumstances, and they'd listened.

So, it wasn't that she was dealing with the issue; it was that the issue hadn't been an issue at all.

Not...really. But even that wasn't true, was it? She was constantly surrounded by the evidence of Azagoth's sexcapades. Memitim were everywhere—walking, talking mementos.

She thought about living with them, how difficult it was sometimes. They could be jerks, some more so than others. She'd always written it off as it being their resentment of their parents or their circumstances, but what if...what if she were to blame for a lot of it?

What if she'd been giving standoffish vibes from the beginning?

It was possible that she hadn't been the most welcoming at times, and she'd probably been less patient than she could have been. Hell, there was no sense sugarcoating it. She'd been downright chilly and abrupt with many of them.

Oh, God. If she ever got out of here, she had some apologizing to do.

If she ever got out of here.

Azagoth sat in the rocking chair in the bedroom, his sweet little angel in his arms. A sweet little angel with a cry that could wake the souls in the Inner Sanctum. Razr's mate, Jedda, had taken to calling her Raika, a word in Jedda's native elven language that meant *hellmouth*.

As unflattering as that was, it was accurate, and the name had stuck. For now.

"I wish your mom were here," he murmured to his daughter.

She cooed around the nipple of the bottle he was using to feed her. No angels had shown up with milk yet, but hopefully, he'd hear something soon. Hawkyn had gone to the Memitim Council to check on the status of the request.

He looked down at his little girl and couldn't believe that he was actually holding one of his own infant children. Had he known how in love one could fall with a baby, he'd have fought from the beginning to have his children raised in Heaven instead of with the worst people humanity had to offer.

There were a lot of things he'd do differently if given a chance.

There was a tap at the door. "Father?" Jasmine's voice drifted through the thick iron and wood. "Jim Bob is requesting entrance, and Hawkyn said the milk should be here within the hour. He's bringing it himself."

Good. The bastards had insisted on bringing it themselves, but that had been a firm no-deal for Azagoth.

"Tell Jim Bob no, and that he can text if it's important," he called out.

"I'll tell him, but he's pretty insistent. Also, Suzanne will be here momentarily. She wants to cook supper. I'll give her a hand if she needs help."

Jasmine didn't like to cook, but she'd stepped up since Lilliana had been gone. She'd even offered to babysit, but he'd had no need. His child wouldn't leave his sight until Lilliana was home. Still, he appreciated Jasmine's offer. Sometimes, it was hard to believe that she'd come from Lucielle.

Lucielle had been one of the handful of angels who hadn't hated every minute of being in his bed. Not that they'd used his bed much. She preferred porn-worthy locations and creativity, using him as an outlet for pleasures she couldn't get from stodgy, uptight angel types.

She was one of the few who acknowledged that she enjoyed fucking him, and he was pretty sure that fact, more than any *honor* bullshit, was the reason she had kept coming back.

It was definitely the reason she'd come back and wrecked his relationship with Lilliana for a few days.

Azagoth sat on the edge of his desk, annoyed that Lucielle had been here for five minutes already, and she still hadn't told him why. He didn't think she had, anyway. He'd tuned her out for a couple of minutes while he fantasized about his new mate.

Last night had been hot.

Damn, Lilliana was eager. She'd grown bolder with her sexual demands, and last night, she'd wanted it rough and dirty.

He'd been okay with that.

"...so, as I was saying," Lucielle droned on, "a few of us would like to continue our relationship with you...as mothers of Memitim, of course."

Huh. She'd really gone there.

"So, even though I'm mated, you want to keep fucking me," he said flatly. "To get pregnant, of course."

She uncrossed and re-crossed her legs, flashing a lot of toned, flawless thigh and a glimpse of the shadowy place in between. Did she really think he was so easily seduced? He took that back. If Lilliana ever did that, he'd have his face between her thighs before she could cross her legs again.

"The creation of divine beings destined to protect the future of mankind is both a calling and a mandate that reaches beyond all other convention and law. Many of us are true believers in the mission of the Memitim, and if you recall, many of us are mated to mates who also believe in the cause."

So, basically, they had open marriages and were using extreme interpretations of angelic guidelines to justify them.

Also, Lilliana would be moaning his name by now.

"What's the saying, Lucielle? Be honest in your sin, else you add three more sins when you lie to yourself, to others, and to the Almighty? You and your mate want to screw other people? Nothing wrong with that. Just admit it instead of using some sacred duty as an excuse."

"If I admit it, is that a yes?"

It was a hard no. In fact—

The door whipped open, and Lilliana started inside, looking incredibly sexy in worn, frayed jeans, a plain white tee, and white flip-flops. Lucielle's polished, sterile perfection had nothing on the natural, classic beauty Lilliana achieved without even trying.

"Oops, I'm sorry—" She stopped mid-stride in the doorway, her gaze flitting between him and Lucielle.

"It's okay." Azagoth waved her in. He probably should send Lucielle on her way, but he was curious, morbidly so perhaps, to see what Lilliana would do. She claimed to be at peace with his past, but his past had an ill-timed tendency to become the present with alarming frequency. And always when his children were around. "This is probably something you should hear anyway."

"What is it?" Lilliana came over, looking a little hesitant. She'd been here for months, but so much of his world was new to her. She didn't know the players, she didn't know the politics, and she didn't know jack shit about the mothers of his children.

"Lucielle was just saying that if more Memitim are needed, she'll volunteer her services."

Lilliana blinked in confusion. "I'm sorry...what?"

Lucielle came gracefully to her feet, her tight dress hiked high on her thighs. Lilliana would look so much better in it. The way she looked better out of it.

"I meant no offense," she said in the unruffled, breathy drawl she used when she proposed some new way to screw.

Which was what she was doing with Lilliana. Screwing with her. He couldn't wait for Lilli to unleash on her. He'd been on the wrong side of Lilliana's wrath a couple of times, and it was not pleasant.

Lucielle continued, all satin and knives. "It's just that Azagoth and I have a history of producing some of the most beautiful and extraordinary Memitim. You've met Jasmine, I'm sure."

"Y-yes. Yes, of course."

Shit. Lilliana needed a lifeline.

"I was about to give her my answer when you walked in," Azagoth said to her. "Perhaps you'd like to do the honors?"

She ignored him, keeping her gaze glued to Lucielle. "How many?"

"How many what, dear?" Lucielle's voice dripped with saccharine. "Children? Two hundred and twelve." She shot him a smile that was the oral equivalent of uncrossing her legs. He knew what that mouth could do. And it wasn't anything Lilliana couldn't do better. "The Grim Reaper and I go way back. Thousands of years before you were even born." She gave Lilliana a cool once-over. "I suppose you could join us. I'm very open to new things."

"Get out," Lilliana snarled, pointing at the door. "Get out now. And tell all your broodmare friends that Azagoth is no longer available for stud."

Azagoth laughed.

"Broodmare?" Lucielle bristled. "Being chosen to create within our bodies a unique class of angels from the seed of—"

"Out!" Lilliana flung out her arm, and Lucielle catapulted through the air, right through the doorway.

The door slammed shut with a resounding bang that rattled the artwork on his walls. Then Lilli picked up one of his jade horse figurines and shattered it on the floor.

"Was that really necessary?" he asked. Throwing an annoying angel out on her ass was one thing; destroying a four-thousand-year-old demon carving was another.

Lilliana rounded on him, her eyes spitting fire.

"Was it—what? Are you kidding me right now? You should have kicked her out. That…that skank…propositioned you right in front of me. That female you fucked in our bedroom over two hundred times!"

Whoa. He'd only meant the figurine, but clearly, it didn't matter. She was pissed, and not just at Lucielle. He'd gotten rid of most of the evidence of his past, the sex furniture, the toys…and she'd burned the mattress. But he supposed the bedroom was still…the bedroom.

"Calm down," he said gently. "We didn't use the bedroom much."

And boy, was that ever the wrong thing to say. Over the course of the next couple of days, he'd learned that his library couch wasn't comfortable and that it wasn't wise to tell an angry female to calm down.

He still thought the entire episode was amusing, but as he thought back on it, he realized that he should have tried to see it through Lilliana's eyes. From her perspective, she'd been ambushed by a female who wanted to have sex with her mate, and a male who thought the whole thing was funny and flattering. And she wasn't wrong. He'd been so used to females wanting him only for what he could give them— power, notoriety, favors, babies—that it was refreshing to be wanted for *him*. Okay, they didn't want *all* of him. Just his dick. But, still.

Instead of laughing, he should have reassured her. He should have made it painfully clear to both Lilliana and Lucielle that the only angel who would be bearing his children, the only one he would ever sleep with again, was Lilliana.

Abruptly, his senses screamed an alert, drop-kicking him out of his reminiscing. Someone powerful had just entered Sheoul-gra.

While it was on lockdown.

Again.

He was going to kill Hawkyn.

And, maybe, whoever had come through the portal.

Chapter 31

Azagoth launched into the air from his balcony, Raika still in his arms. She looked up at him, utter innocence and trust in her big eyes.

"Don't worry," he murmured. "Daddy's going to keep you safe."

He soared over his grounds, flying toward the portal. He saw Suzanne below and dropped down, landing softly behind her.

She whirled around with a startled yelp, but when she saw Raika, her shock turned to a broad smile. "Hey—"

"Here." He handed Raika to her. "I need to handle something."

She looked past him and nodded. "Hi, Jim Bob."

Jim Bob? "What the fuck?" Azagoth turned so fast, he nearly whacked the angel in the face with a wing. "Who let you in? Hawkyn?"

Jim Bob shook his head. "It doesn't matter. What are you doing to save your mate?"

"What?"

"What. Are. You. Doing?" he demanded. "Moloch is going to kill her if you don't release Satan. So, what is your plan?"

The immediate plan was shaping up to include kicking Jim Bob's ass.

"Watch your tone, halo. You don't get to demand anything of me."

"Dammit, Azagoth!" Jim Bob moved forward with the sudden speed of a striking snake. "I need to know what you're going to do!"

With a thought, Azagoth lobbed a barrage of summoned blades at the angel. They struck with barely a whisper, a hundred daggers that would slice downward with agonizing slowness, shredding their victim like a cheese grater.

The force of the blades' impact knocked Jim Bob into the last standing remains of the gazebo Azagoth had destroyed during his bid to escape.

"Get Raika inside!" he barked to Suzanne.

But as he turned back to Jim Bob, something yanked him off the ground before slamming him back down so hard, his body left a crater. Suzanne got blasted several feet away, was sprawled on the ground, but Raika was still cradled safely in her arms, and she gave him a we're-okay wave.

Fury lit him like a torch. No one but Azagoth and Lilliana could wield power in his realm. No one but Reaver and Revenant, anyway, and certainly not to that extent.

"How?" he roared as he burst upward, firing a summoned spear of hell-forged blood iron.

Somehow, Jim Bob had rid himself of the blades, but he couldn't avoid the dead-center blow from the spear. He screamed and dropped to his knees. Steam rose up from around the spear where it was buried in his chest, and blood poured down the shaft as he fell forward, impaled off the ground. His head dropped, his face hidden under the hood of his charcoal robe.

"How did you get in here?" Azagoth stormed toward him. "And how the fuck are you using power in my realm?"

Jim Bob coughed, spraying blood on the ground. "I helped you build Sheoul-gra, you ass," he rasped in a voice that was no longer his. A voice Azagoth hadn't heard in thousands of years. "Did you really think I wouldn't make sure there was always a way in for me?"

Utterly speechless, Azagoth willed the spear away. Jim Bob dropped face-first to the ground. Groaning, he rolled onto his back. The hood fell away, revealing a new face and a luxurious head of hair in all the shades of mankind.

"Gabriel?"

Azagoth nudged him with his boot, and the archangel sat up, clutching his still-burning chest. "That weapon was unnecessarily harsh."

Yeah, it was harsh. It was an anti-angel weapon explicitly designed to cause devastating wounds or finish off an already severely wounded angel. But Azagoth was done fucking around.

"I disagree," Azagoth snapped. "And I don't need to ask why you kept your identity a secret. But why have you been sharing information with me in the first place?"

"Why?" he asked, incredulous. "I'm a bit invested in your success, asshole. Plus, you're my source for a lot of shit that goes on in both realms."

"Why now?" Azagoth asked, still reeling at the revelation of Jim

Bob's true identity. "Where were you for thousands of years?"

"I was behaving." Gabriel coughed and spat blood. "Being a good little archangel. Then, a few hundred years ago, I started seeing dark portents. I figured it might be a good time to get acquainted again."

"Archangel?" Suzanne, who was supposed to be safely inside with Raika, drifted closer. "You're the *archangel* Gabriel? *You* gave Declan his tattoo?"

Azagoth nearly gave himself whiplash looking between the two of them. "Tattoo?"

Crimson splotches bloomed in her cheeks, and Azagoth suspected that she'd just revealed something she wasn't supposed to. Gabriel gave her a pained go-ahead nod.

"Declan and I needed information about the set of wings tattooed on his back," she explained, still shooting Gabriel sheepish glances. "We found the artist in a shop in San Francisco. The guy who did it was Jim Bob. Er…Gabriel."

Azagoth narrowed his eyes at the angel. "Let me fucking guess. The tat is enchanted somehow, and it's probably an angelic tracking device. Is Heaven so boring now that you have to spend your days tattooing humans?"

"Have you been listening?" Gabriel said in an angry rush, although the coughing fit afterward took some of the bite out of his tone. "A shitstorm is coming, Azagoth. Some of us are preparing. We're tracking down those who have angelic DNA. We're getting humans ready for the truth of our existence. We're doing everything we can to get our players ready for the End of Days. And that means keeping Satan in his cage until the very last minute."

"So that's why you're here? To stop me from releasing Satan?"

"I'm hoping I don't have to." He wheezed, and blood bubbled between his fingers as they covered the chest wound. "I came to warn you."

Gabriel leaned back against the rubble. The injury hadn't closed at all. Even in the human realm, it wouldn't have closed yet, but there would be signs of healing. If Gabriel didn't return to Heaven soon, his powers would drain, and he'd be trapped here.

Which was going to happen, anyway. Azagoth couldn't think of a better hostage than an archangel. Which was probably, in part, why Gabriel had come as Jim Bob. That, and he couldn't let anyone in Heaven know he was in contact with Azagoth. Heaven had strict rules about who was allowed to contact him, and even stricter rules about who could step inside Sheoul-gra.

"Warn me about what?"

"The Council of Orders. They've sanctioned your destruction."

Azagoth went cold inside. Fucking Deep. Freeze. "Did they?"

"Azagoth, listen to me—"

"My lord!" Razr ran toward them from the direction of the portal. "There are two angels requesting entry. They say Hawkyn was called to business, so they're bringing the milk for Raika."

"It's a trick," Gabriel warned. "I guarantee they've done something with Hawkyn. If you don't respond, or if you refuse, they'll try breaking through your portal security."

Snarling, Azagoth wheeled around to Razr. "Don't respond. It'll buy more time than refusing. Get Cipher. Tell him to monitor the portal enchantment." Razr took off, and Azagoth spun back to Gabriel. "What else are they going to do?"

"I don't know. They kicked me out of the meeting after they disabled Reaver."

"What did they do to Reaver?"

"They used their collective power to restrain him. They were afraid he'd warn you."

"They weren't worried about you?"

"They don't know I've been in contact with you." He closed his eyes and took a couple of deep breaths before continuing. "But they were worried enough to assure me that if I tipped you off, I'd answer for a high crime."

Stunned by the news, Azagoth took a step back. A high crime was punishable by anything from imprisonment in torturous isolation to execution, but the most common punishment was expulsion from Heaven.

Gabriel had risked everything to warn Azagoth that, once again, Heaven was going to fuck him over.

His phone rang, and he snatched it out of his pocket. He didn't recognize the number, but the moment he answered, he knew the voice on the other end of the line.

"You know what I want, Azagoth," Moloch said. "Release Satan now, or Lilliana will be in my bed tonight and dead by morning."

"You bastard," he breathed. "If you touch her—"

"Oh, *I'm* not going to touch her. That's what the hot pokers and maces are for."

"You're going to die screaming," he swore. "You will beg me for mercy, and I will *laugh*."

There was a long, tense silence, and then Moloch said quietly, "You should know that your angel buddies sent an assassin to kill Lilliana. Just FYI. Oh, and Azagoth? I just changed my mind. You have until the Hour of the Crone to release the Dark Lord."

He looked at his watch. The Hour of the Crone, the three A.M. strike of the clock at Mount Megiddo in Israel, when the barrier between all the realms was the weakest, and supernatural powers were at their greatest. It was less than two hours away.

"If you don't, Lilliana will die within minutes. I'll save my hot pokers for when I get your daughter back."

The line went dead.

Hot, rabid anger built like a summer storm in his chest. His inner beast vibrated with the need for release as he rounded on Gabriel.

"Moloch said you sent an assassin to kill Lilliana," he snarled. "Is it true?"

"Possibly." Gabriel swallowed. "Camael said they had a spy inside Moloch's organization. Low-level, a pissant fallen angel guard or something. He said he couldn't get Lilliana out, but he could kill her."

Of course. If Lilliana were dead, Moloch would have nothing to hold over Azagoth, and Heaven wouldn't have to worry about him releasing Satan."

Those bastards. Those cheating, lying, holier-than-thou *fucks*. Fury seared his thoughts to ash.

"You helped me," he said in the deep, smoky voice of his beast, "and now I'll help you. Get out. Get out before I change my mind."

A massive quake shook the place. The angels were trying to force their way in.

He was done. He was fucking done with this. Sandwiched between two massive armies, he saw one way out.

The world was going to burn, and he was holding the match.

Chapter 32

Feral rage rolled through Azagoth's body in great tremors as he stood at the precipice of an endless void, his gaze locked on the spinning crystal cube suspended over the empty space. No sounds came from inside the cube, but then, he figured that any screaming, moaning, and crying had taken place in the first months of imprisonment.

He flexed his clawed fingers at his sides as he stared at the prison meant to hold Satan, King of Demons, his son Lucifer, and one traitorous archangel, for another nine centuries and change.

The evil soul of the fallen angel who'd birthed Lucifer was in there, too, her decaying physical remains keeping the other three company.

Right now, Azagoth could free them all.

And kick off the prophesized End of Days *way* early.

But he'd have Lilliana back.

Unless Moloch killed her anyway, or worse, saved her for Satan.

A dark surge of energy swallowed him, billowing up from the void.

Release me, and I will return Lilliana to you.

Satan's voice was an echo wrapped in pain inside Azagoth's head. Glorious pain, like an orgasm that went on for too long. And beyond that, there was recognition, an awareness of Satan's unique energy…and his mind.

As dark as the demon's energy had been in Heaven, it was a drop of piss compared to the ocean of malevolence it was now.

"How do you know about Lilliana? Who have you been in contact with?"

And how the fuck could he be in contact with anyone?

I knew I was going to be trapped someday. Do you not think I had multiple contingency plans for the event? Azagoth. Asrael. Listen to me, my old friend. Together, we can break your contract. You give me my freedom…and I'll give you yours.

Azagoth panted through the exquisite agony of Satan's voice…and his words. Freedom. It was something he'd had only once in his life, when he'd isolated himself in the human realm. He'd been lonely, far too empathic to interact with anyone, but he'd been free of everything, including obligations.

We'll remake Sheoul-gra in the shadow of the shattered human realm, and it will be a paradise for souls. It will no longer be a place of punishment, but a new Eden, where my demons will feed on the souls of the humans forsaken by angels. You will operate it with no oversight from Heaven, and you will be free to come and go.

Azagoth moaned. Yes.

Release me! I'll give you the freedom to live anywhere.

Yes! Wait, no. He shook his head, trying to get the voice out of his mind, droplets of blood flinging from his nose to splatter on the cliff.

Lilliana suffers while you hesitate.

"Damn you!" he screamed, hating himself for what he was about to release on the world. "Promise you won't harm her. Promise no one will harm her, or any of my children, *ever*, or I walk."

I swear it, Asrael.

"Convince me, Prince of Lies." Somewhere deep inside, beneath the demon scales covering his beast body, he didn't want to be convinced. Being convinced that Lilliana would be safe from Satan meant releasing him and bringing about destruction on a truly biblical scale.

I can practically feel your tender-skinned mate's pain as you dither.

"Convince me, damn you!"

Azagoth could feel Satan's agitation. Now, they were getting somewhere. This…this was where he was truly a master. An extraordinary empath, he'd been the one to discover Satan's deception and the plot to overthrow Heaven's leadership. He knew how the male thought. How he felt.

Azagoth knew his buttons.

"Convince me why I should believe you'll spare my family when you vowed to bring me to my knees. When you threatened to start killing Memitim if I didn't stop creating them. You despise me. So, tell me why I should think, for one fucking second, that you will keep your word."

Despise? You fool, I don't hate you. I owe you my eternal gratitude. I lost Heaven, but look at what I built! A kingdom of my own, power beyond imagination. Religions both exalt and fear me. I have more power over humans than God does. Don't you see, Azagoth? You were my savior. Be my savior once again.

"That's pretty convincing," he said gruffly, because it was, and it was tilting him back into dangerous territory.

I'll need your cooperation in our new world, so why would I betray my word?

That was probably true, but still...fuck, he just needed one reason to not do this. Only one. He had to keep the Prince of Lies talking, even though every second could mean more suffering for Lilliana.

I'm so sorry, baby. "If I do this, I want Moloch delivered to my door. Alive."

Done. And then I will slaughter that faithless pig, War, and I'll grant you his island. Lilliana and your daughter would love that, wouldn't they?

They would. Lilliana would bloom like a rose on an island of her own, in the sun and away from the malevolence of Sheoul-gra. But not...not Ares' island.

Not because he was dead.

Azagoth didn't want that. Releasing Satan would get Heaven off his back, seeing as how they'd be busy fighting a war. And it might save Lilliana. He'd be killing two birds with one stone.

But he'd also be killing a lot more than birds.

What kind of world would his daughter grow up in? What kind of hell would all of his sons and daughters live in?

A remote calm settled over him at the clarity of his thoughts. Sometimes when he became overwhelmed by the emotions of others, it left him empty. Clear. Too often, it was the opposite. But this was what Satan's emotions had always done to him, even when his evil was just a drop in the sea that swallowed it.

He couldn't release Satan. Only a fool would trust him, especially one who had been lied to.

Satan *was* communicating with someone. Somehow, he was getting information from outside.

"Tell me, Satan, who are you talking to?"

I told you! No one.

"Then how do you know about my daughter?"

There was silence, and then an enraged shout. *Asrael. Asrael! Release me!*

No. This wasn't the answer. This would make him the biggest

villain in history, the one to destroy prophecy and the world.

He had one other option.

He'd still be a villain, and he'd probably lose everything he had, everyone he loved, and most likely his own life.

But those he loved would be safe. The human realm would be safe.

"Yeah, you know what? Fuck off."

Fuck off?

"Want me to say it again?"

Lightning filled the dark space all around, tearing the darkness to shreds. Azagoth looked around, stunned. This shouldn't be happening. Satan shouldn't have this kind of power. Not the kind that could command electricity, not the power to communicate with someone outside.

There had to be a crack in the cage.

A bolt of lightning stabbed Azagoth with a zillion degrees of agony, burning his flesh, searing his mind. He heard screams, his own, he thought, as his blood vaporized inside his veins. The bolt snapped back upward, leaving Azagoth on his hands and knees, smoke curling into the air from his charred body.

A shriek of fury blasted through Azagoth's eardrums. *Release me, you cocksucker! Do it, or so help me, when the Lamb finally sets me free, you will be the first person I come after. And when I'm done slaughtering your sons and raping your daughters in front of you, I will fuck your mate until she's dead! And then I'll—*

Roaring in rage, Azagoth summoned everything he had, every ounce of power available to him, and sent the cube tumbling into the void, the blackness swallowing it in a disturbing, slow ooze.

"Thanks for the heads-up, fucker."

As Azagoth unfurled, ash falling to the ground and revealing healed, strong flesh, Lilliana's voice echoed in his head.

All I ask is that, no matter what happens, you don't become the monster you used to be.

He wouldn't. Oh, fuck no.

He was going to become a brand-new monster.

Chapter 33

1:02:46

Azagoth had one hour, two minutes, and forty-six seconds left to release Satan.

Which meant he had just over an hour to get his affairs in order because setting the evil fuck loose wasn't an option.

He held his daughter against his chest, feeling her heart tap against his and committing it to memory. His inner demon had been in command when he'd returned from Satan's prison, but the moment he saw Raika asleep in her cradle, Cat watching over her, he'd calmed. Holding her had brought him completely down.

Well, not completely. Inside he was raging, ready to do what needed to be done.

Soon. Just a few more minutes...

Raika wrinkled her nose and yawned, her little fists waving in the air. He pushed aside her blanket and ran his fingertip over the downy material of the demon duckie pajamas Eidolon had sent.

The demon was mourning his beloved brother, and he'd still taken the time to send a gift. On a shortlist of demons Azagoth respected, Eidolon was at the very top. Azagoth couldn't return Wraith's body to the doctor, but he *would* bring an end to Wraith's suffering, one way or another.

Raika reached for him, and he dipped his head, letting her touch his face as he inhaled her fresh, clean scent that went beyond the baby soap Cat had used to wash her. She smelled pristine, deep down in her soul, and somehow, he knew she hadn't lived before.

New souls were beyond rare, a once-per-century kind of thing, and he wondered what was in store for his daughter. She had so much potential.

Her gaze met his, and he couldn't deny the intensity of the love that surged through him. She deserved better than being born in Hell. He'd failed her, and he'd failed her mother.

He was done failing. And he was willing to pay the ultimate price to keep it from happening again.

There was a knock at his office door, and Azagoth didn't have to wait for Ares to call out to know that he and Cara were in the hall. He'd felt Ares enter Sheoul-gra, and he'd taken those last precious moments of time alone with his daughter to memorize every detail about her.

Another knock. A death knell, Azagoth supposed.

"Enter."

Ares and Cara came inside, and while Cara closed the door, Ares, his leather armor creaking, strode across the room.

"Fucking angels," he growled.

"Obviously, your hellhounds took care of them."

Calling Cara for a hellhound assist had been a stroke of genius. Hellhounds despised angels, and the hounds' king, Cerberus, had a particular affinity for Hades and the Inner Sanctum. Chasing angels from Sheoul-gra's entrance had probably been great sport for them.

Ares snorted. "A thousand hellhounds against a hundred angels? It's a great distraction, but Heaven's going to send backup. We don't have much time."

"Azagoth." Cara smiled politely, but she was wringing her hands like she had a dripping towel between them. "It's great to finally meet you in person." It was a lie, but it was nice that she tried. "I'm just sorry it's under these circumstances. Tears filled her eyes as her gaze dropped to the bundle in Azagoth's arms. "Can I do anything to help? Anything at all?"

"It's why I asked you here." Somehow, he said that without his voice cracking.

Raika cooed, and pain took his breath. Her mother should be here. This shouldn't be happening.

"Her name is Raika," he said, and this time, he couldn't stop the emotional warble in his voice. "I don't know if Lilliana will like that."

"It's beautiful," she assured him.

"It means *hellmouth*."

Cara contemplated that for a heartbeat. "Well, I heard her crying in the background while you were talking to Ares on the phone. Seems appropriate." She smiled. "Can I hold her?"

He swallowed. Panicked. He didn't want to let her go.

"You don't have to," she said quickly. "It's okay."

Buck up, asshole. Lilliana's waiting, and Moloch isn't going to bite his own head off.

"No, please." Very carefully, he placed Raika in Cara's arms, and the sense of loss nearly drove him to his knees. He backed away before he snatched Raika back. "I asked you here because what I'm going to ask affects you both." He gestured to the series of paintings depicting Sheoul-gra's history. "For thousands of years, my realm sat empty. Then I filled it with fallen angels to help me, and Unfallen who sought safety, and finally, Memitim. But I've come to realize that Sheoul-gra should always have remained empty."

He looked at the space on the wall meant for art reflecting Sheoul-gra as it had been just days ago. Green, undamaged, full of life.

"Things have to change. My realm is no longer safe, especially from me."

"What is it you want from us?" Ares asked, getting straight to the point, as usual.

Azagoth finally turned away from the wall. "I want you to take in the refugees from Sheoul-gra. Your island is safe, secret, and secure. They can build apartments and a training facility on the opposite end of your island. You'll never know they're there."

Cara looked up from the baby as Ares stared, processing for a moment.

"Damn, Reaper," he said under his breath. "When you want something, you want something big."

"I know it's a lot to ask," Azagoth said. "But I want my family to be safe."

"What happens if we say no?" Cara asked.

Please, don't say no. "The Unfallen will be at risk of being dragged into Sheoul. The Memitim will go back to living the way they did before they came here, hiding among humans or staying in smaller training camps. The youngest will be safest in those."

He glanced over at his wet bar and decided that now would be a good time to open the thousand-year-old rum given to him by craftsmen from the Grimmon region of Sheoul.

"I'm sure you need to discuss it." He gestured to the door as he crossed to the bar. "Feel free, but don't take too long. I have a hard deadline."

Ares nodded and moved for the door, and Cara started to hand over Raika.

Azagoth backed up. "No, please keep her." He hoped they didn't notice the way his hand shook as he reached for the bottle. "She's probably sick of me."

"Are you sure?"

He didn't look at them. "Positive."

They stepped outside, and he slumped against the bar as he unsealed the bottle. He couldn't put it to his lips fast enough.

He embraced the burn, welcomed the smoky bite of the brimstone beds the liquor had washed over on its way to the bottle. It scoured away what nothing else could: the last, clinging remnants of his emotions.

Only one thing could bring them back, and he was going to get her or die trying.

Ares had lived a long time. He'd done everything, seen everything. Nothing surprised him anymore.

The Grim Reaper had just shocked the shit out of him. Cara as well, if her wide-eyed worry was any indication.

"What was that?" she asked in a hushed voice. "What's going on with him?"

"His mate is being held by a sadistic demon," he said, his voice bordering on a snarl. "He's prepared to die for her."

Ares could feel Azagoth's pain to his bones. Reseph, when he'd become the evil version of himself known as Pestilence, had taken Cara once. The sick things he'd planned to do to her before he killed her, the way he'd hurt her in front of Ares…it had turned Ares into a male bent on one thing: getting her back. He would have sacrificed anything, including himself, to save her.

Cara's lips pursed as she shifted her gaze from the baby to him. "Do you think she's okay?"

"I don't think Moloch is stupid enough to kill her before the deadline. But he *will* do it." He shook his head in a futile attempt to rid his mind of the memory of Cara, bruised and bleeding, at Pestilence's feet.

"We have to help him," she said as she rocked Raika. This was the first time they'd been away from their own month-old daughter, and Cara was clearly missing her. "The island can support what he's asking."

It could, and Azagoth was right; they'd rarely even see the Memitim and Unfallen. But, shit, the analytical part of his brain that couldn't stop running disastrous scenarios through his head was in rapid-fire mode. Someone inside Sheoul-gra had killed one of Azagoth's children, almost killed another, and helped arrange for Lilliana's abduction. Until the person was identified, the idea of letting so many unvetted people near his family made Ares jumpy.

"If you think it's a security risk," she continued, being psychic or something, "I don't think there's anything to worry about. Nothing is getting through your Ramreels and my hellhounds."

Nothing was getting through *Ares*.

"And," she added because she was evidently on board with this, "if our island ever comes under attack from outside forces, imagine how much help a hundred Memitim will be."

Ares cursed to himself, knowing he'd lost the battle but acknowledging that he hadn't fought too hard. He and his siblings owed Azagoth, each in their own way, and his island was large enough to accommodate five times that many Memitim and Unfallen.

"You know exactly what kind of arguments will sway me."

Cara blinked up at him, all mock innocence. "Me? Manipulate you? I would never."

This time, he cursed out loud. "Come on. The Grim Reaper is waiting."

He held the door open for Cara, and the moment they entered, he sensed a change in the air. Azagoth was standing in front of the tunnel in the wall that allowed him to view the passage of souls his *griminions* brought, holding a half-empty bottle of liquor loosely at his side. He was ushering them through too quickly to actually assess any of them, but Ares wasn't about to call him on it.

Not with the way his horns were out, and the fire in the hearth had gone so cold that Ares could see his breath.

He swung around, his eyes nothing but midnight marbles filled with flame.

"Your answer?" His voice boomed, rolling upward from the pits of Hell itself.

"We will welcome your people," Ares said. "When do you want this done?"

"Now. I need you to take them with you when you go." He turned back to the souls. "Zhubaal will serve you well if you let him. He's loyal and not yet completely infected by evil. Although, now that I think about it, he might do better with Thanatos. He prefers the dark and northern climates."

"Now?" Ares blurted. "With no time to prepare—"

"Now."

"I don't understand this, Reaper," Ares growled. "What's going to happen when we're all gone?"

Azagoth wheeled around, the flames in his eyes putting out enough heat to take the chill out of the air, and Ares stepped up, instinctively putting himself between Cara and the male. Azagoth wasn't as calm as he appeared to be. Everything they saw was an outer shell. A zombie. The real Grim Reaper was raging inside.

It was time to go.

"What about Raika?" Cara asked. "Who's going to take care of her?"

Clenching his fists even as claws erupted, Azagoth closed his eyes. When he opened them again, the flames had died down, suppressed by pain. "I was hoping you would."

"Of course," she said. "We can care for her for as long as you need."

Blood dripped to the floor from his punctured palms, but he didn't seem to notice. "What I need is for you to raise her as your own if Lilliana doesn't come back."

Cara gasped. Ares cursed. "Azagoth, listen to me. Whatever you're planning—"

"I'm planning to do what must be done. I don't know if Lilliana is even alive, and if she is, she might not be for long. Raika needs a mother, and she needs a father who can protect her. She needs sunlight. All my children do." The flames had reduced to hot coals, but the effort of keeping his inner demon in check was playing out in the tense set of his jaw, the strained cords in his neck. "Please, will you do this for us?"

Ares exchanged glances with Cara, and he knew they didn't need to discuss this.

"Yes," Cara whispered.

"Thank you." Once more, he turned away, but not before Ares saw a single tear roll down his cheek.

"Do you want to say goodbye?"

Azagoth shook his head. "I already did. And I'm afraid...I'm afraid if I hold her again, I'll never let her go." He inhaled a ragged breath. "Take her. Get her settled. Come back in five minutes. I need you to clear out my artifact room, too. Take everything. There will be items that will help in the Final Battle. Go. Go now. There isn't much time."

"Azagoth."

Azagoth turned, his wings erupting and scraping the ceiling like fingernails on a chalkboard.

Ares wasn't sure what he had been about to say, but now he realized there was nothing *to* say. He'd spent most of his existence fighting. He'd won countless battles over those thousands of years. Lost a few, too. And while he'd learned a lot from the losses, it was the wins that taught him the harshest lessons.

He'd stood with thousands of warriors of all species, from human to demons to angels, on the eve of war, knowing he wouldn't see many of them alive again. Death was always palpable before a battle, and sometimes, it wasn't even about the lives.

War had a way of ending more than lives. It ended dreams. It annihilated entire civilizations. It forced good men to commit atrocities, and it destroyed morality.

Even when you won.

Sometimes, *especially* when you won.

This was the eve of Azagoth's battle, and Ares knew that even if the Grim Reaper triumphed, nothing would ever be the same. What did one say to that?

Not a goddamned thing.

Instead, Ares put his fist to his chest and bent in a deep bow of respect.

As they used to say in my day, "may the gods grant you victory, and if not victory, then peace in death." Good luck, brother.

Chapter 34

Watching Ares and Cara leave with his daughter was the hardest thing Azagoth had ever done. He wanted to scream, cry, go on a destructive rampage that would never end. But Ares would be back in minutes to take everyone to his island.

Azagoth didn't have time for a breakdown.

The end is nigh.

Inhaling deeply, he released his wings and shot upward from his bedroom balcony.

Hear me!

He hadn't spoken, but he knew everyone in Sheoul-gra, save those in the Inner Sanctum, heard him. Dozens spilled out of buildings and the training arena. They looked up at him expectantly as he hovered several feet off the ground. From here, he could see much of his realm, from the hills and streams of the far-reaches to the new playground on his right, and his grand palace on his left.

Thousands of Unfallen and Memitim had lived here over the millennia. Inside this realm, angels and demons alike had kneeled before him. This had been his home, and these people had been his family.

One of the youngest, Obasi, climbed atop a broken pillar, toppled when Azagoth had tried to break his way out of Sheoul-gra. The fountain was still broken, its basin dry. And Lilliana's favorite statue, an early work of Michelangelo's that Azagoth had commissioned, lay shattered in a pile of rubble.

Everyone had been working hard to fix the destruction he'd caused, but it was too late. Some damage couldn't be repaired.

Some didn't need to be.

"Sheoul-gra is no longer safe. Ares is clearing a portion of his Greek island to create a new community where you can live and train in safety. Collect your things. Ares will be here in minutes."

In the stunned silence, he searched his brain for more words. He wished he had a meaningful speech to comfort them, but ultimately, he wasn't all that eloquent, and these were warriors. They were strong, and they'd thrive.

"Father!" Emerico stepped forward, pushing his way toward the front of the crowd. "You're truly kicking us out?" His brown eyes glowed with anger as he gestured to the buildings. "Was all of this a joke to you? Did you bring us here to assuage your guilt about the way you brought us into this world, abandoning us before our mothers even gave birth? And now...what? You lose your mate and no longer want to deal with us?"

"I'll bet you're keeping Raika here with you!"

That came from someone in the back, and following on the statement's heels was a chorus of agreement.

Unexpectedly stung, Azagoth lowered his voice. "I've failed you in a lot of ways," he said. "Kicking you out of here isn't one of them." A rabbit darted out from a bush, and he swept it up in a surge of power and dropped it into Cipher's arms. "And take the animals. They were gifts from Reaver."

Shouts rose up, questions that weren't going to be answered.

Azagoth flapped his wings and banked hard toward the portal, where Zhubaal and Razr were watching, their expressions as shocked as everyone else's. And yet, as Azagoth landed in front of them, Zhubaal came forward, all business.

"How can I assist with the move?"

Man, he'd hit the lottery when he brought Z on board. The fallen angel would be an incredible asset to whomever he chose to work with in the future.

"You're going with them." Azagoth ignored Z's subtle, disapproving growl. "You, Razr, your mates...everyone in Sheoul-gra."

"For how long?"

"Forever." The finality of it caught in Azagoth's throat. "Zhubaal, no one is ever coming back." He looked around at the realm he'd built. "Not to this."

Zhubaal stepped back in shock. "My Lord, have you discussed this with Hawkyn? I'm sure he—"

"My decision is made. I release you both from my service. You're free to do anything you want. You don't have to live on Ares' island with the Memitim. But Thanatos and Ares would both welcome you if you are willing to work with them. The End of Days is coming, and they could use all the help they can get as they prepare."

"Is there anything I can do to convince you not to do this?"

Azagoth shook his head. "Go. If you aren't out of Sheoul-gra by the bottom of the hour, you might not ever get out." He clapped each male on the shoulder, his claws digging in despite his effort to be careful. "Take care, my friends."

With that, he flashed himself away from there, because…fuck that. Fuck the pain.

It was time to cause it.

Chapter 35

Azagoth hadn't felt the weight of a sword at his hip in thousands of years. Not since he was an angel. Felt good. Felt right. Especially since the sword resting against his leg was the very blade he'd carried as an angel. It might be darkened with the malevolence of Sheoul-gra, but it could still behead someone from twenty yards away.

His scythe, however, had tasted blood much more recently. His gloved fingers curled in anticipation around the smooth wooden handle.

Not long now.

He gripped the bag in his other hand tighter as he waited for Hades in the Inner Sanctum's antechamber, his mind strangely calm. Ares had told him that on the eve of battle, his mind raced, his adrenaline pumped, and his blood ran hot. But that, in the minutes before the fight began, he found a quiet place. The cool distance needed to survey the game board and make sure all the pieces were in their positions.

This must be what Ares was talking about.

Oh, there was a deep, smoldering rage in Azagoth's heart just dying to break out, but it seemed to be okay with taking a moment to gather fuel before exploding.

Maybe his rage knew that the fuel would be worth the wait.

The air shimmered as Hades and Cat materialized. Several yards away, a thousand armed fallen angels formed a semicircle behind him. Malonius, a beefy warden at the Rot, Hades' torture prison, stood separate, Wraith's body in his arms.

Hades gestured for Cat to remain, and he strode forward, clothed, for the first time that Azagoth could remember, in actual garments. Black leather pants that were similar to Azagoth's, minus the buckles. A matching jacket over the top of a tee with the words, *WHAT DOESN'T KILL YOU DISAPPOINTS ME*. Holsters and harnesses crisscrossed his body, holding swords, daggers, throwing stars, and an axe.

Azagoth nodded approvingly. "Clothes are an interesting choice."

"Right?" Hades shot an annoyed glance at Cat, who grinned sheepishly in her own similar battle gear. "She thinks I should wear stuff when I go outside of Sheoul-gra." He lowered his voice to a conspiratorial whisper and tugged at one of the harnesses. "Plus, these things chafe bare skin. I would have worn a shirt anyway. Just not the unicorn and rainbow one she got me."

"I heard that," she called out. "And it's a unicorn *skeleton*."

Despite the dire circumstances, Azagoth snorted with amusement. Lilliana had gotten him the T-shirt he was currently wearing too, as a joke. And it was hilarious because he *had* enjoyed coffee from a cup made of the skull of an enemy. Not that he'd told her that. She probably wouldn't find it as funny as he did.

"Is everyone here?" Azagoth asked as Hades came to a rigid halt in front of him. "Every last one of your men?"

"Yeah. They're excited to fuck up a bunch of angels. You did mean what you said, though, right? After the battle, they get twelve hours of freedom."

They were going to get a lot more than that. He nodded. "You leashed them to you?"

It was Hades' turn to nod. "They have to respond to my summons within an hour, or unimaginable agony will drive them to me." He paused. "I know this is a last resort to keep Heaven from breaking in, but leaving the Inner Sanctum unattended..." He shook his head. "It's dangerous, man. And it's another violation of the contract—"

"It's handled," Azagoth broke in. There wasn't time to make up a bunch of lies or try to explain what he was doing. "Just go. Get out of Sheoul-gra. Leave Wraith with me."

He signaled to the *griminions* hovering on the periphery, and within seconds, they'd gathered Wraith's body from Malonius and carried him away.

Hades' eyes narrowed on him. "Why does it sound like you're telling us to evacuate, not sending us to fight angels?"

"Oh, there will probably be angels to fight." Cara's hellhounds were only going to hold off Heaven for so long. He handed Hades the bag and waited while the male opened it and removed a fist-sized crystal, its core glowing a brilliant violet. "This is eternal hellfire from Sheoul-gra's core, contained inside a stone mined from the Mountains of Galilee in Heaven. Take it with you. It's what will allow you to rebuild."

"Rebuild what?" Hades' eyes peeled wide. "Sheoul-gra?"

The smoldering rage inside Azagoth took flame as anticipation built. "Remember how you used to joke that humans got it wrong when they named you the ruler of the underworld in their various belief systems?" Azagoth laughed bitterly. "Joke's on us. Turns out, it was prophecy."

"Azagoth…" Hades growled. "What are you doing? What are you going to do down here?"

"That…I can't tell you."

A tense silence stretched as Hades seemed to grapple with his divided loyalties and the potential consequences of the choices he'd have to make within seconds.

"Please, Azagoth," Hades finally said. "We've never been the best of friends, and I've been a vocal critic when you're being a dumbass. But I've served you and the realm well. You owe it to me to tell me what you're planning."

Hades was rarely so laid bare, and if Azagoth weren't drowning in rage, he'd probably feel worse about this.

"I can't."

Disappointment in Hades' expression veered quickly to resolve. "Then I can't let you do it."

Azagoth glanced at his watch. Dammit. He didn't need this. "Don't try me, Hades," he warned. "Do *not*."

Hades inhaled deeply and let it out on a curse. "When you brought me in, you gave me dominion over the Inner Sanctum, told me to run it the way I wanted to." Hades' black, leathery wings burst from his shoulders, and behind him, Cat and the fallen angels tensed. "You made me swear an oath to protect Sheoul-gra. Even from you."

"I did do that, didn't I? Very short-sighted on my part." He sighed as the last vestiges of his civility began to turn to ash. "Ah, Hades, I didn't want it to go down this way—"

Hades didn't wait for Azagoth to finish his sentence before he struck out with a hammer Thor would envy. It sizzled with crimson lightning as it arced through the air, searing Azagoth's skin. He blocked the summoned weapon with his scythe, clenching his teeth as he held off the powerful blow.

"Don't fight me," he snarled. "Don't make me hurt you in front of your mate."

"This is my duty. I will not back down." Hades flashed behind him, and this time, his swing nailed Azagoth in the lower back. He felt his spine break, felt his ribs pierce his organs.

Felt his inner demon come fully online.

As he hit the ground, his beast erupted, horns and claws slicing through his skin. Hades had transformed, as well, his gray skin marbled with black veins, his eyes inky, his teeth gone piranha.

A need to draw blood and strip flesh from bone swallowed Azagoth in a wave of evil. This was who he'd been for most of his tenure here, and he embraced its return like a starving vampire welcomed a drunk who'd turned down the wrong alley.

He struck Hades with a barrage of summoned ghastbats that tore into his body, ripping away chunks of skin and muscle. Hades shouted in agony, and Cat screamed.

Shit. Azagoth whirled around as she charged him. As enraged as he was, he wouldn't hurt her. Not if he didn't have to.

Throwing out his arm, he put up a shield, blocking her and the fallen angels who had moved closer. It was unlikely the fallen would be a threat, but he wasn't going to take the chance.

Something struck him in the head, and he pivoted back around in time to take a second strike from a basketball-sized rock that Hades was using to show off his telekinesis skills.

It hurt, but it wasn't enough. Nothing Hades could do would be enough.

Blood dripping down his face, Azagoth flicked his wrist, and the ghastbats flew off. Hades stood there, mangled and bleeding, his head bowed, but anger burning in his eyes.

"I can't...let...you...do this," he said between panting breaths.

"I know." Azagoth's voice was little more than a smoky rumble. "That's why you will replace me. You've always been a male of honor."

With a thought, Azagoth dropped a blow to Hades' head that made the male crumple to the ground. Cat's scream of anger and agony wrenched his insides, but only for a second. He couldn't be sentimental. Emotions were more than useless right now. They were a hindrance.

He released the barrier and signaled for the fallen angels to pick up Hades.

"You asshole!" Cat yelled. "How could you?"

"Take him," he said, the iciness in his voice making her shrink back. "Sheoul-gra belongs to Hades now. Tell him to fix the crack in Satan's cage. And I apologize in advance for the mess I'm about to leave."

He launched into the air and gestured toward the exit portal. "You have six minutes to get out of Sheoul-gra. Go."

To get them moving, he blasted the area with a stream of fire and then chased them all with fireballs until everyone was gone.

And then he hit the portal with another fireball wrapped in a spell Cipher had given him. It splashed against the portal and spread, melting it like a marshmallow.

The Inner Sanctum was now sealed.

Chapter 36

The denizens of Sheoul had never been especially attentive to the politics of their realm. Or any realm, for that matter.

Which was why, as Flail stood atop the battlements of Moloch's stronghold, inhaling the musky scent of bloodlust and excitement, she was baffled by the army of millions gathering in the realm. Why were they so willing to fight for someone they'd never met or even heard of before now? What had Moloch promised them?

Movement along the wall below caught her eye, but when she looked, there was nothing there. Odd. She could have sworn she'd seen something big and black. Maybe the hellhound Moloch had claimed was lurking around. The things were attracted to violence and death, and while they couldn't fight against Satan's armies, they could defend themselves and their packmates, and they could eat anyone or anything that was already dead or dying.

Moloch would be wise to put out traps.

As if merely thinking his name had conjured him, Moloch materialized next to her. As subtly as she could, she put a couple of additional inches between them.

He looked out over the hundreds of thousands of bonfires that stretched over the Plains of Destruction and into the foothills of the Massacre Mountains. "Glorious, isn't it?"

"It is." She'd never seen such an army, and it gave her tingles to know she was witnessing history. She'd see to it that she played a starring role in the chronicles. And she could if he'd assign her to something besides babysitting Lilliana and overseeing the seizure of Satan's castle from Revenant. "But why?"

"Apparently," Moloch growled, "Azagoth isn't going to release Satan."

Interesting. She wasn't overly surprised at Azagoth's decision—after all, releasing Satan to save Lilliana's life would have been a total crapshoot. But so was defying Moloch. Her only partially healed face and the right side of her body could attest to that.

She turned to look at him in profile and, as always, was struck by how handsome he was. Even as he'd been burning the flesh off her cheek, she'd marveled that, if anything, he'd been even *more* attractive to her. The sadistic light in his eyes, the strength of his jaw as he clenched it, the erection she knew he'd use on her when he was done making her scream.

And how fucked-up was it that when he did bury his cock in her, she screamed again, but in ecstasy?

Hey, she was fucking evil. She was allowed to get off on pain. Even if it was her own.

She still hated Moloch for what he'd done to Maddox, though.

"If Azagoth isn't releasing the Dark Lord, what is this army about?"

"Azagoth isn't going to just sit back and let his mate's death go unpunished." He grinned. "But what he doesn't know is that I've put up wards to keep souls and *griminions* from entering my region. And if he somehow manages to take down my defenses the way he did Bael's, my army is equipped with weapons that fragment souls and force them to retreat while they regenerate."

She barely heard anything after the first sentence. "You've killed Lilliana already?"

"Do you care?"

"Of course, not." She sniffed, looking out over the army of millions. "I just wanted to watch. I hope she suffered."

Actually, the idea that Lilliana had suffered left Flail a little...well, she wasn't sure. She was fucking evil, and she liked it that way. But, sometimes, a clean kill was the better way to do things.

"She's not dead yet." Moloch reached into his waistband and withdrew a twisted dagger, its wicked edge glinting in the orange light from the torches on the battlements. It was an *aural*, one of the few weapons guaranteed to kill an angel or a fallen angel. "I'm assigning the task to you."

"Me?" she asked, startled. "I'd think you'd want the honor."

"I have preparations to make. And besides...I think you need to rid yourself of the lingering sentimentality you have for her."

"I don't—"

He backhanded her so hard, she fell back into the battlements and nearly tripped over them.

"Lying bitch!" he hissed. "Kill her. And when you're done, bring me her head. I want it displayed at the top of my flagpole for Azagoth's army to see."

"Yes, my lord," she gritted out as she took the *aural*. "As you wish."

"You still seem hesitant. Perhaps you need incentive."

Fear spiked, and the healing parts of her body screamed. "I don't."

"I think you do." His eyes shifted to the campfires and then back to her. "I don't trust you not to spare her out of pity, so I'll tell you what. Bring me her head, and I'll take you to see Maddox."

She'd been avoiding his garden for a reason. If anything, he'd just given her incentive to *not* kill the stupid angel. "I don't need to see your scarecrow again."

"That's just his skin," Moloch said slowly, relishing and savoring her horror. "He's still alive."

Her mouth fell open, and she had to force herself to snap it shut. "You...*skinned* him?"

He'd been alive and suffering all this time? She gripped the *aural* tighter as she battled the urge to bury it in Moloch's chest.

"It was necessary to expose his blood to Sheoul air."

Air? Blood? What had Moloch done to her sister's child?

"I don't understand," she ground out. "Why did you tell me he was dead?"

"Because he was." He shrugged. "Sort of."

His gaze turned toward Fearr, the fallen angel in command of a legion of Soulshredders, as she jogged along the battlements toward them. She'd woven poisonous barbs through her ebony braid, turning it into a creative weapon Flail wished she'd thought of. The barbs clanked against her armor as she approached, the axe in her hand dripping with blood.

The battle hadn't even started.

"My lord," she said, looking up at the man-sized raptor horrors that patrolled the skies. "I received a message from the Horsemen."

"What was it?"

"Curson's head. They said they have Falnor, as well, and they're coming for me next. Who would have thought killing a stupid Seminus demon would trigger the Four Horsemen like that?" She flipped her braid over her shoulder. "I don't know how old the message was, though. Falnor could be dead by now."

"Unfortunate," Moloch said, and Flail had to disagree. The fallen angel had been as stupid as Fearr was cunning. "Falnor was in charge of executing deserters."

Fearr grinned and lifted her axe. "I've assumed his duties."

"Well done." Moloch gave a dismissive wave. "Return to your post and watch your back. If Azagoth is stupid enough to engage me, Thanatos and Ares will be drawn to the battle."

Flail could only hope. Fearr was a brilliant warrior and evil's greatest ally. But, frankly, she was a cunt. Plus, she would be competition for the Dark Lord's affections someday. Flail wouldn't be sad to see her impaled on Thanatos's sword.

Just as Fearr gave a bow and dematerialized, one of Moloch's buddies, an ancient fallen angel who controlled the River Styx passages, landed lightly next to him, his ragged leather wings blasting her with a gust of foul-smelling wind. Expecting her own immediate dismissal, Flail turned to go but paused when Assailant spoke, his voice as serrated as his horns.

"I've received reports that Heaven has laid siege to Sheoul-gra."

Moloch threw his head back and laughed, his delight echoing off the distant mountains. "Good news, Flail. Azagoth is going to be busy for a while. You can take your time killing Lilliana. Spend at least an hour." A low, erotic groan billowed from deep in his chest, and she caught the acrid scent of his lust. "And get it on film. Azagoth should have a keepsake. And I'm running low on material for my porn collection."

Chapter 37

When Azagoth first designed the Inner Sanctum, he'd built five levels, sometimes called rings, or circles, in homage to Dante, who hadn't actually gotten much right about anything. None of the levels were based on sins, but rather on scales of evil as laid out by the Ufelskala.

He'd recently added a sixth level, one for the few demons who weren't evil at all. Just as some humans were truly, wholly evil, there were demons who were utterly and completely decent. The one constant the Creator insisted upon was balance, and everything Azagoth was tasked to do served the purpose of maintaining homeostasis in the human and demon realms.

The new level was pleasant in comparison to all the others, even though the hellish landscape was still reminiscent of Sheoul. Hades had tried to replicate the human realm atmosphere of Sheoul-gra, but the Inner Sanctum was too close to Hell-proper, the membrane between the realms too thin. Everything Earth-like, from plants to animals, to bodies of water, rotted and corrupted.

Azagoth's feet pounded the ground on the first level as he approached the center platform, the pulsing heart of each ring. The platforms were all connected, functioning as both the spine and the circulatory system of the entire Inner Sanctum. What was done to one level from the platform, was done to all.

He walked up the steps to the circular, fleshy pad that was large enough to support a crowd of hundreds as its heartbeat thumped under their feet.

But today, there would be only two.

Azagoth and Wraith.

The *griminions* had laid the demon's body atop the twisting main artery that fed blood through the pad before they, too, evacuated. The original *griminion*, Asrael, would join the Memitim on Ares' island, and the rest would find Hades. He was their master now.

Azagoth stepped onto the two-foot-diameter ruby eye in the very center of the pad. Almost instantly, energy infused him as he, along with Wraith, dropped through each level, traveling like a blood cell through an artery. He was connected here, his body becoming part of the Inner Sanctum's life support system, his mind aware of every individual soul.

He could mindfuck them all right now. He could put nightmares into all their heads. He could make every one of them cut off their own feet with dull knives. But today wasn't about fun.

On the last level where the worst of the worst were housed, he slammed onto the pad, sending a shockwave through the land like a nuclear blast. Waves of malevolent energy rode the blast, calling demon souls toward him like moths to a flame. They wouldn't resist. They couldn't.

Inside the leather pouch on his sword belt, the feathers he'd tucked away there began to burn.

Very carefully, he removed them.

He'd lifted the white one, shot through with thick streaks of golden glitter, off Reaver. The black one, its silver veins forming a delicate, lace-like pattern, had belonged to Revenant. In the human or demon realms, they'd be considered objects of unimaginable power.

Here in the Inner Sanctum, they were the *ultimate* power.

Let's fuck some shit up.

He released the feathers, letting them float as they wished. They hovered in front of him, spinning lazily, expectantly.

"*Infileus ehni slurnjia,*" he barked in Sheoulic. "Seek your power."

Abruptly, they began to glow, one surrounded by white light, the other crimson as they drew energy directly from their owners.

Yes.

The light surrounding each expanded, growing bigger and bigger until their energies mixed and engulfed him. Fire sizzled on his skin as he was lifted off his feet, his body arching so violently, his spine cracked.

"*Giarneri insa oriendi vestilo, iom ango du ensiliu tob unt tobu, holi unt unholi. Jal gia giarneri plaxionus!*" he shouted, aware that this could go horribly wrong. "I am a vessel of the universe, fill me with the balance of good and evil, of holy and unholy. Give me what I deserve!"

The feathers began to spin, faster and faster, shooting out bolts of lightning that struck far into the distance, shearing off tops of volcanoes and turning stagnant lakes into boiling pits of steam.

Suddenly, the feathers poofed away, and a burning, searing pain settled between Azagoth's shoulder blades. His world exploded in fire, pain, and ecstasy until he couldn't stand it anymore, and he shouted at the sensory overload.

And then it was over, and he was kneeling on the ground, naked, smoke drifting from his nostrils. Ash floated in the air that was now thick with the stench of charred flesh. He looked around, but there were no demons nearby, none except Wraith, and his body still lay there, all kinds of dead.

It was me. I burned.

The ash floating in the air was his skin, his organs, his bones.

He staggered to his feet and looked down at himself. He looked the same...but different. Years ago, when he'd been unable to feel anything, he'd taken tattoos from Thanatos, tats that were laden with emotion he wanted to experience. He'd burned several out, and many had faded or disappeared. But now, they were completely gone.

So was his sword. But his scythe was at his feet, and when he picked it up, a whoosh of eternal hellfire consumed the blade.

That was fucking awesome.

Power assailed him, shooting along every nerve ending. It was as if his entire body were a conduit to both Sheoul and Heaven. Their energies were mixing inside him, creating a well of fuel that was ready to detonate.

Demons began to drift toward him, drawn to his power. The massive crowd parted as Sarnat, the brother of the Charnel Apostle who had helped him release his soul army, strode toward him. He was big for an Apostle, and unlike most of his species of sorcerers, he'd been a warrior in his physical form. Here in Sheoul-gra, he chose, like most demons, to take the form and identity of his last life, and he even dressed the same. Armor, weapons, boots with blades in the soles, and a leather duster with a hood that concealed the wearer's face so nothing was visible but an inky black hole.

Sarnat pushed the hood back, revealing a long, gaunt face and pallid lips peeled back from tiny, sharp teeth. "Your back, my lord. It's smoking."

Azagoth willed a mirror into the air behind him, and when he looked over his shoulder, his breath caught. Wisps of smoke curled upward from an intricate glyph that had been burned into the skin of his upper back and shoulders.

A sword—*his* sword, he realized—swept down his spine, its pointed end reaching to the small of his back. Between his shoulders, two wings formed graceful arches on either side of the hilt. Each feather on each wing featured exquisite detail, but two feathers stood out in spectacular brilliance. On the right wing, a primary feather of glittering gold. On the left wing, a primary feather of sparkling silver.

Reaver's and Revenant's feathers.

It'd worked. It had fucking worked! No one had ever done what he'd just attempted—and accomplished. There'd been no blueprint, no testing. Just a lot of research into similar spells. He could have killed himself with what he'd done, or he could have burned out all of his powers.

He'd demanded to be given what he deserved. He could have just as easily been drawn and quartered.

Now, to put the results to the test.

Clothes. Clothes would be good.

And there they were. The clothes he'd put on to come down here. Except they looked as if he'd worn them to an apocalypse. His leather pants were faded and streaked with bloodstains that had to belong to him. His shirt was torn, his sword belt frayed, his gloves as stained as his pants.

He willed them clean and new.

Nothing happened. He tried again. Tried putting on different clothes. Nothing. He couldn't get jeans and a T-shirt, a suit, or a damned hockey jersey. All he could get was naked. Seemed his new powers had come with some weird restrictions.

Apocalypse chic, it was.

Now, he had to see what else he could do.

He turned to Sarnat. "Time to deliver on my end of the bargain that I struck with your brother."

"You're going to release me, yes?"

"That was what I agreed to when he helped me release the others." He summoned a trickle of what seemed like an endless vat of the silkiest, purest, darkest power. It flowed through his body like a drug, and he understood instinctively how to use it.

He just had to think it and then channel power into the thought. It was how he'd summoned the mirror. His clothes seemed to be on a separate circuit that he'd play with later. Right now, he wanted to make Sarnat a corporeal being in the demon realm, but without using reincarnation or by making him possess a physical body. Basically, he wanted to *poof* Sarnat—

The Charnel Apostle poofed. Gone. Only his armor, weapons, and clothing remained.

Shit. He'd have to work on that. It had never been *that* easy to destroy a soul.

Not that he gave a hellrat's ass. The guy had been so evil that he'd practically run the fifth ring. He'd have made a valuable ally but a relentless enemy.

He had excellent taste in coats, though, and Azagoth scooped up the duster from the ground, its buckles clinking. The hood might come in handy.

Demons had pressed in closer, and he was done wasting time. He needed to get this shit figured out.

He locked on to the closest demon, a Soulshredder whose snout was stuck in a perpetual sneer.

Take form.

The demon grunted and staggered backward. For a moment, it looked as if he might puke, and then his form flickered like a dying bulb. He held up his clawed hands and stared as his body went completely transparent.

Fuck, yeah.

Azagoth couldn't stop a fist pump of success that Journey would have been proud of. The Soulshredder might now be a ghostlike figure here in the Inner Sanctum, but in the demon and human realms, he'd be corporeal.

Azagoth did a repeat, this time with a group of ten demons. Then a hundred. A thousand. After a hundred thousand, he figured he was good to go.

Hear me.

His voice sifted through all the levels, to every corner and inside every cave in the Inner Sanctum. He felt the awareness of billions of souls, all tuned in to what he was going to say.

The walls between worlds are about to fall.

Storm clouds roiled overhead, and lightning sizzled between them.

I'm giving you form so you can once again live life in Sheoul. Take revenge on the ones who put you here. Find mates you left behind. Kill. Eat. Fuck. Do whatever makes your depraved selves happy.

All around, volcanoes erupted, the lava spewing into the clouds and lighting them on fire.

But first, you're going to destroy Moloch's armies.

Spreading his wings, he punched power into every cell of his body and plugged into the barrier between the realms. He held his scythe over his head, drawing on the eternal hellfire that fueled Sheoul-gra, the heat of it igniting the blood in his veins like gasoline.

The realm trembled. Massive claps rent the steaming air as cracks in the realm's structure expanded, fissures that had formed recently. Ruptures Azagoth had told Hades not to repair.

Even before Moloch abducted Lilliana, Azagoth had known something big was coming. Something he needed to prepare for. He assumed he'd been prepping for an apocalypse. Not *the* Apocalypse since he hadn't released Satan. But your standard, everyday kind of apocalypse that seemed to happen a lot.

Break apart!

A tremor shook the ground as more hairline fractures, visible only to him, began to form in the shimmering barriers. Explosions blew through the realm, drowning out the terrified screams of the demons.

Take form! he commanded as the barrier began to shatter. *Take form and take out Moloch!*

The barrier blew apart like a pane of mirrored glass, revealing a new realm of craggy, blackened mountains and expansive valleys framed by a dark sky and a roiling, twisting, crimson glow on the horizon.

Azagoth found himself standing on the drawbridge of a castle flying Moloch's flag, exactly where he wanted to be. Demons were swarming, setting up defenses, preparing for battle.

They didn't know the battle was already here.

He shot skyward, flying high to look out over the land. For as far as the eye could see, no matter how high he went, billions of demons were engaged in a bloody, violent battle. His army was pressing inward in a wave that would be here within minutes.

The gargoyles who had lived as statues for eons in his war room shot high into the sky before plummeting down to skim the top of a distant perimeter wall. Moloch's archers couldn't avoid being rammed right off the walls by the dozens.

Azagoth was free, and both Heaven and Hell were going to learn what that meant.

Chapter 38

Something was happening.

Lilliana wasn't sure what, exactly, but there was an electric buzz in the air, so strong that she could taste it as a metallic tang on her tongue.

She watched from her spot chained to the skull throne as demons charged through Moloch's main chamber, their armor clanking, and their weapons glinting in the flickering light from the massive hearth. A gray-skinned *rhino-fiend* nearly clocked her with a mace as he lumbered by, and she wished he could feel her glare on the back of his head.

She also wished her stare was a laser beam that could explode his skull.

She'd blast them all for what they'd done to her. To Journey and Maddox. To Wraith. To her daughter, who shouldn't be without her mother.

She'd never fully appreciated the bond between a mother and her child, but she got it now. The pain of being separated like this was more intense than anything she'd ever experienced. It went well beyond the physical ache of full breasts or the strangeness of an empty womb.

She didn't even know if her baby was okay. Flail could have been lying.

Someone shouted, and she forced herself to set aside her grief for now. There would be time for despair soon enough.

The demons bottlenecked near the doors, but a group of them parted and made way for Flail's entrance at the rear of the great hall. She looked ready for battle, her raven hair pulled back, her body protected by some sort of supple black leather armor that, no doubt, was a lot tougher than it looked. Fallen angels had a habit of fabricating their armor from demon hides, giving them various special protections depending on the species of demon that had been unfortunate enough to lose its skin.

"What's going on?" Lilliana asked as the fallen angel mounted the platform, her boots clomping on the steps.

"Moloch says Azagoth's attack is imminent," Flail said, and Lilliana couldn't help but shout a silent, *Yes!* "He's preparing for a couple million souls to swarm the land."

She cleared the top step, and the hair on the back of Lilliana's neck stood on end. She wasn't sure why. It might have been the way Flail was walking. Or how she looked at Lilliana. Or it could be the dagger-shaped bulge under her long, black cloak.

"It seems," Flail continued, "that Azagoth has made the foolish choice to not release Satan."

Lilliana wanted to sob with both relief and terror. It was good news. Amazing news that would preserve all the realms for almost a thousand years.

But it also meant that she was, most likely, going to die now.

And Azagoth…how would he handle her death? Would he revert back to what he'd been before she came along? Could having their daughter in his arms be enough to ward off the malevolence that had marked his thousands of years of existence?

Again, assuming that Flail hadn't lied.

Flail moved closer, and Lilliana instinctively reached for her power. Of course, it wasn't accessible, and the only thing the attempt accomplished was making her wing anchors throb. Her pulse picked up with every step Flail took. Casually, she gathered her legs beneath her and stood, trying to appear as if she was curious about the activity surrounding them when, in reality, she was madly plotting a way to fight back.

She could use her restraints as weapons. The chain would wrap around Flail's slender neck nicely. But Flail also had fallen angel powers at her disposal, while Lilliana was as helpless as a human. She'd have to act fast to grab what she was pretty confident was an *aural* beneath Flail's cloak.

"Flail?"

Flail looked around, her expression contemplative. "Hmm?"

"Moloch's going to kill me, isn't he?"

"No," she said, but Lilliana's relief only lasted a heartbeat. "I am."

Flail didn't look at her as she unhooked the chain that connected Lilliana to the throne and gave it a hard yank. "Come on."

Lilliana didn't budge, which made no sense. Flail could just as easily kill her here as someplace else. Maybe it was an instinct to not follow blindly to one's death. Perhaps the known danger was better than the unknown. Whatever it was, Flail didn't have the patience for it, and she yanked harder, dragging Lilliana off the platform.

"I have to film it, you stupid cow," Flail snapped. "I thought maybe you'd like a little privacy, but if you would rather these lowlifes watch and participate, I can just as easily do it here."

Oh, well, gee, wasn't that thoughtful?

But privacy meant that Lilliana would have a better shot at talking Flail out of this. It wasn't like Flail was reasonable or anything, but if she'd told the truth about the baby, maybe she had enough empathy to be swayed.

It was probably a foolish thing to think, but at this point, Lilliana was desperate.

"When you put it that way, I believe privacy would be lovely," she said, grimly amused by Flail's bewildered glance back. What? Lilliana wasn't allowed to be sarcastic *and* polite in her final moments?

She allowed Flail to walk her like a dog on a leash until they reached some sort of garden. It was beautiful, in an eerie, creepy way. All the plants were either black or dangerous, from the night-blooming roses with their deep green stems and silky, midnight flowers to the brilliant blue irises that turned black when they were hungry for blood.

"Am I to be plant food?" Lilliana asked, completely serious. There were big pod-things here that could digest her whole.

Flail shrugged one slender shoulder. "Nah. I was just thinking, creatively, that if I have to take a video of me killing you, I might as well have a dramatic setting. The tragic splendor of slaughter in a beautiful garden and all that. A bunch of demons jacking off to your pain is kinda tacky, you know?"

"Sure, sure," Lilliana said, her mind too busy working on a plot to truly listen. But she got the gist. Demons were disgusting, and Flail was a budding filmmaker. Neither of those things would get Lilliana out of her execution.

A shadow skirted one of the walls, moving so fast, Lilliana thought she might have imagined it. She mapped out the paths and doorways as they walked, and she noted the number of guards on the tops of the walls. There was a lot, but from the looks of things, she didn't need to worry. Their attention was entirely focused on something outside the walls, and the gargoyles battling raptor horrors overhead.

She stopped, jerking Flail to a halt.

"What the f—?"

"Shh." Lilliana smiled at the sound of the distant battle. "Do you hear that? Is that Azagoth?"

Flail dropped the chain. "Stay here." She flashed herself to the top of the wall and shoved a guard aside.

Because Lilliana wasn't an idiot, she tried to run. Unfortunately, Flail had tethered the chain to the ground, and she nearly dislocated her shoulders.

The shadow moved closer, fading out of view as Flail materialized and grabbed the chain, looking as rattled as the chain sounded.

"I don't know if that army belongs to Azagoth or not, but it's big. *Really* big. And corporeal." She cursed, seemingly talking more to herself than to Lilliana. "Moloch wasn't ready for this. He thought Azagoth would send souls. But there are millions of demons out there. Hundreds of millions."

A deafening boom lit the sky a brilliant red and shook the ground so hard, Lilliana stumbled. Stones crashed down from the walls around them, crushing plants and smashing branches off of trees.

He's here. Azagoth's forces are here!

"This is bad," Flail murmured as she looked up at the sky, which was sizzling with a webbing of lightning.

Another massive explosion sent a seismic jolt across the land, tossing Lilliana forward as Flail stepped backward. Without thinking, she shoved her hand beneath Flail's cloak and seized the weapon concealed at the small of the female's back.

Flail jammed her elbow back, catching Lilliana in the chin with a tooth-jarring blow. Lilliana wheeled backward into a potted spider plant, and she watched in horrified fascination as the pot crashed to the ground and hundreds of hand-sized spiders scurried toward her and Flail.

Flail hissed, kicking one and smashing another under her boot. And just as Lilliana scrambled away from one, its fangs dripping with flesh-dissolving poison, the entire bunch of them went up in smoke.

Flail lunged at Lilliana. "Give me the *aural*."

Lilliana put a row of growling pod plants between them. "How stupid do you think I am?"

Flail raised her voice over the brutal noise of battle as it came closer. "I can kill you without it, you know." To emphasize her point, she smiled, and Lilliana yelped in pain as her skin split in a dozen places, six-inch gashes opening as if she'd been struck with a lash. "It'll just take longer."

"Flail, please," Lilliana said, giving reason one last, desperate shot. "Let me go. Moloch doesn't have to know."

"He'll know because he ordered me to bring him your head."

Lilliana shook her head, hopefully not for the last time. "It won't matter. Moloch will be dead soon."

"How do you figure?"

A dark sense of both satisfaction and vengefulness came over Lilliana, and she smiled over the top of one of the weird black pods.

"Because Azagoth won't rest until he's dead. I promise you that. Moloch is a dead man. He just doesn't know it yet."

Suddenly, Flail spun in a circle, her gaze narrowed and searching. "Something is in here with us."

Okay, if Flail was worried, Lilliana should be, too. But for some reason, it really didn't matter.

Probably because she was going to die, and it didn't make a difference if it was by Flail's hand or in the jaws of some evil monster.

A black blur streaked through the garden and slammed into Flail, spinning her into a barrel. She caught herself before she went down and sent a volley of lightning bombs after the streak, but it phased out, avoiding every missile. Then it was back, hitting Flail from behind. Blood splattered, and for a moment, Lilliana wasn't sure where the blood had come from.

But as Flail rolled on the ground, her arm flopping at an unnatural angle, Lilliana realized that her hand was missing.

Red, glowing eyes watched from deep inside some sort of tentacled plant, and Lilliana couldn't contain a gasp.

Hellhound.

She couldn't tell if it was Maleficent or not, but it seemed to be on her side, and she took advantage. While Flail struggled to stand, Lilliana pounced.

Flail struck out with her stump, catching Lilliana in the face. The strike shattered the bones in her cheek, and she nearly passed out from the pain. Somehow, she managed to not drop to the ground like a sack of potatoes, and she returned the hit, swinging the chain in an arc that slammed the fallen angel bitch to the ground.

If Flail got back up, Lilliana knew she was dead. With no powers, she was basically a bug, and Flail was a bug zapper.

She dove on top of the other female, taking a hard jolt to her shoulder when she hit the ground, but she managed to wrap the chain around Flail's neck and pull it tight.

Flail snarled, and then Lilliana felt the fallen angel's power as her blood lit on fire. Everything inside her burned, and she screamed as smoke poured out of her mouth and nose.

Blindly, she reached for the *aural*, which had clattered to the path. She found it at the same time Flail did, and they struggled, Lilliana feeling the blade bite deep into her palm. Mercifully, the fire inside her had died out, but she was tiring, in pain, and her vision had gone double. Maybe triple.

"Bitch!" she cried as she put all her strength and desperation into wrenching the weapon away from Flail.

Got it!

She didn't hesitate. With a shout of determination, she plunged the *aural* into Flail's throat and thrust upward with all her strength. Flail's eyes shot wide in surprise, and she gasped, blood flecking her lips.

The merest hint of a smile curved her mouth. "Well done," she said in a pained whisper.

"For what it's worth," Lilliana said, "I don't enjoy this."

"It's okay…to…like it a little." Flail's breaths came in spurts as her body began to turn a sickly gray. "I did…fuck over…Cipher."

True. "Okay, I'm enjoying it a little."

Flail coughed sickly, the light in her eyes fading and, finally, extinguishing. If Lilliana were still pregnant, she'd have been able to see Flail's soul drift out of her body, and a *griminion* arrive to take it to Azagoth. She almost felt sorry for Flail then because Azagoth wasn't going to show mercy.

She slid the bloody *aural* free of Flail's body and fell back in exhaustion.

Suddenly, there was a tongue slathering her face, and foul-smelling hellhound breath searing her nostrils.

"Mal," she gasped as she dug her fingers into the beast's thick ruff. "I'm so happy to see you."

Mal had never been overly affectionate, and even now, she backed up and stood a few feet away, her tail wagging gently.

Bruised, bloody, and in excruciating pain, Lilliana considered her next move. First, she had to get rid of the nettle tunic that marked her as a prisoner. Flail's armor would do nicely as a replacement, and with the hooded cloak, Lilliana might even be able to get out of the castle.

And probably die in the battle.

But, first things first.

As quickly as her injuries allowed, she stripped Flail and donned her leggings and sports bra, both of which were a little tight, but that turned out to be a good thing, putting pressure on her wounds. The armor fit perfectly. Even the boots were a good fit.

"Okay," she said to Mal as she tucked the *aural* into the holster at the small of her back, "let's get out of here. I have no idea where we're going, but we're going to get there or die trying."

Chapter 39

Azagoth had never witnessed the devastation of an EF5 tornado in person. But he'd now seen what he could do with a cyclone that was definitely on the EF—Everyone's Fucked—scale. The Revenant feather on his back tingled as if to say, "*You're welcome.*"

He stood on the roof of the tallest of Moloch's towers, his wings spread, his beast body dripping with gore, and looked down on the destruction he'd wrought. The five-mile-wide monster tornado he'd spun himself into had cut a path through Moloch's forces, sucking up bodies and chopping them up like a giant blender.

So fucking cool. Epically cool, as Journey would say. Journey, who would never say anything again, thanks to Moloch.

"Moloch!" He shouted with his power, his voice booming through the valley, even over the sounds of battle. "Meet me, you coward."

A sinister blast of heat singed Azagoth's wings, and he wheeled around, sending a laser stream of compressed ice at the newcomer. The Reaver feather tingled, providing the juice and access to an angelic weapon that was devastating to evil beings, as Moloch's scream of agony proved.

That, too, was epically cool. So was the way the laser had taken Moloch's leg off at the knee.

"Who are you?" Moloch screamed as he flapped his wings in an effort to remain upright.

In his new, bigger, and improved beast form, Azagoth could swallow Moloch in two bites. Maybe one, if he made the other leg match the first.

Patience. Find Lilliana.

With a thought, he put away his inner demon. A heartbeat later, he stood before Moloch, clad in his charred leathers and cloak, his scythe burning in his hand.

"Who am I?" he asked, his voice dragging the very pits of Hell. "I'm death, and I've come for you, asshole."

Moloch gasped and lost every drop of color in his face. "Azagoth. How—? How did you—? How are you—?"

Azagoth roared in fury and flashed to him, taking the bastard by the throat. "Where is Lilliana?" he snarled.

Terror made Moloch's eyes bulge, but as he struggled in Azagoth's grip, the terror receded, and a demented smile turned up his cruel mouth.

"She's dead, you fuck," he bit out. "Really, really dead." He grinned, going completely still. "If you get off on snuff films, I'll share the video with you."

No!

He was too late. He was too late, and Lilliana had paid the price. Agony tore through him, mixing with rage and hatred and the need to destroy.

Azagoth lost his shit.

His heart screaming, and his blood boiling, he hurled Moloch off the tower and chased after him through the air, hacking at the fallen angel with his scythe as he tried desperately to escape. Azagoth listed the names of everyone Moloch had killed as he took small chunks out of him, tiny pieces from his legs, his back, his wings, until the guy looked like a blood-soaked, moth-eaten rag doll.

Moloch's pained screams fed all the darkness in Azagoth's soul, and when the fallen angel's ruined wings would no longer support him, Azagoth laughed as he tumbled out of the air and crashed to the ground.

He landed in a foot-deep slurry of tornado grindings, and when Azagoth landed next to him, his face was etched with fear. But as Azagoth raised his scythe to make the final blow, Moloch got that shit-eating grin again, and a surge of power lifted him off his feet and healed him in an instant.

Son of a bitch. Azagoth sought the source of the power, but it cost him. Moloch hit him with a pain weapon, a massive wave of agony that made Azagoth vibrate to his marrow. How had he done all that?

Then he saw the figure on the hill, soot-black armor and hood concealing all but the shape of a male. A big one. And he seemed to be sending power to aid Moloch.

It wasn't enough.

It was, however, enough to piss Azagoth off.

With a final, heaving roar, he pivoted around and punched two summoned daggers through Moloch's eyes.

"Now," he said, as the fallen angel cried out and stumbled back in a desperate scramble to get away, "your soul is mine."

Azagoth swung his scythe and took Moloch's head clean off his shoulders. The thing plunked into the demon McSlurry, and the bastard's soul screeched as it turned to smoke and faded away into nothing.

Well, fuck.

Azagoth stared at his burning scythe and made a note to never behead anyone with it if he didn't want to obliterate their soul. He'd really wanted to do horrible things to Moloch for a few centuries. He'd wanted to spend days at a time making him pay for destroying everything in Azagoth's life.

He'd lost his realm, his mate, his children. And, once Heaven got ahold of him, he'd most likely lose his life.

Not that it mattered. But until then, he was going to rampage. He was going to take out every demon who had fought for Moloch, and he didn't care if doing so would release millions of demon souls into Sheoul. With no Sheoul-gra and its Inner Sanctum, the souls would roam loose, wreaking havoc on every corner of Hell.

And Azagoth no longer gave a shit. Balance? Fuck it. Fuck everyone. His mate was dead, and he was a monster.

A sudden change of atmospheric pressure alerted him to a new presence, and he put Moloch's demise out of his mind. The bastard no longer deserved a single thought.

The figure he'd seen on the hilltop had moved closer, to within fifty yards. It flickered, and then was forty yards away. Thirty. Twenty. Ten.

Five.

Azagoth waited, his scythe's blade burning angrily, wanting to rend another soul into an inky wisp.

"'Sup, Azagoth." The male reached up and pushed back his hood, revealing a face Azagoth knew, even though it was missing a lot of skin. "Or should I say, Father."

Azagoth's legs wobbled, but somehow, he kept his cool. Somehow, he shoved his shock right back down into his gut as he stared at one of his favorite sons.

"Ah, Maddox," he growled, his disappointment veering quickly to soul-searing anger. "Come to Papa, boy. You're in for one hell of a spanking."

Chapter 40

Revenant stopped pounding his fist against the wall, a barrier he'd already gone over a thousand times in an attempt to find a weakness, as a strange tickling sensation curled in his spine.

"Holy shit," he breathed. "I think someone is drawing energy from me."

Blaspheme looked over at him, startled. She'd been on her hands and knees, going over the marshmallow floor again. "What are you talking about?"

He rolled his shoulders as if that would help. For the record, it didn't. "It's like a tiny trickle of power is leaking out of me."

"Where's it going?" She came to her feet a lot less awkwardly than he did whenever he tried. This place was weird. Just give him good old-fashioned filthy hellholes and shackles. "Why do you think it's being channeled to someone?"

"I don't know. I just do. It shouldn't be possible, but it's happening." An electric sizzle suddenly charged the air, and he looked around as if it were visible. "Do you feel that?"

She frowned. "It's like the power is fluctuating." She sucked in a sharp breath. "Rev?"

"Blaspheme!" He ran toward her, bouncing like a ball on a trampoline as she went to her knees. "Baby, what's wrong?"

"I—" She started panting, moaning, and holy shit, he was going to die if something happened to her. She was his life. His reason for not being an incurable, unrepentant asshole. "Oh...my..."

He fell to his knees beside her, sickened by her misery, terrified and...he froze. She didn't smell like fear or pain. She smelled...aroused.

Instant erection. Dicks had no sense of what was appropriate or inappropriate.

"Revenant," she whispered. Then she was on top of him, shoving him onto his back, her mouth on his, frantic.

"Hey," he said as she tore at his pants. "This might not be the place or time for—"

"Got something better to do?"

Well, no. She took him in her hand, and his answer shifted to "*definitely not.*" But still, what the fuck was happening?

"Blas? Sweetheart?"

"Shh." She straddled his thighs, and then her clothes were gone, and she was lowering herself onto his hard cock. He groaned, gripping her hips as her wet core swallowed him. "I don't know what's happening, but it's good. So good."

She rocked on him, and yeah, he'd agree with the *good* assessment. Hell, he'd agree with anything she wanted at this point.

He was seriously easy.

Adrenaline surged as she rode him, her head thrown back in an erotic display of female ecstasy. He loved the way her full breasts played peek-a-boo through her long, blond hair as they bounced with every pump of her powerful thighs.

The sight jacked him so tight, his balls damn near cramped. And when she reached back and stroked them while she squeezed her inner muscles, he came with a roar that made the marshmallow floor jiggle.

Which only intensified the orgasm with gentle vibrations that teased him from his ass to the tip of his cock.

She shouted as her orgasm tore through her, and he joined her with another, his hips coming off the ground so violently that she had to dig her nails into his chest to keep from being thrown off.

"Damn," he breathed, closing his eyes and letting the squishy floor support him like a giant pillow. Okay, maybe he'd been wrong about preferring a standard-issue prison cell. At least if sex was involved.

As he came down, he heard the soft snick of wings. Bizarre…he hadn't felt his emerge. No, they *hadn't* emerged.

He opened his eyes, and a set of violet-tipped white wings filled his vision.

Blaspheme was staring at them in shock. "My wings. They're filled with power. How can that be?"

Blaspheme was an angel, but she'd been born under unique

circumstances, and she'd never had full use of her angelic powers. In order for her angelic DNA to fully activate, she was required to take a trip to Heaven, something she'd never done, and hadn't planned to do in the foreseeable future. Full activation meant limitations on the places she could go...including Underworld General, where she was a respected physician.

"You said this place was built with materials from Heaven. Maybe after being here so long, your angel DNA woke up and gave you full angel status." Clearly, it had made her horny.

Her expression filled with horror and disappointment. "But I didn't want it. Revenant, this ruins everything. I won't be able to work at the hospital anymore."

"Maybe Eidolon can figure out a way for you to bypass the security system," Revenant offered. "He's pretty innovative."

Sighing, she climbed off him, and with a wave of her hand, she was dressed in jeans and a purple tank top, and he was cleaned and zipped up.

Wait. He frowned. "Blaspheme...you're using your powers."

"Of course, I am—" She sucked in a startled breath. "I *can* use them! Maybe it's all this Heaven surrounding us. It's filling me with all its grace."

He opened himself up to his power, and to his surprise, he could actually channel a trickle as the angel in him accessed the Heavenly fuel that had somehow become available. Still, with his usual Sheoulic fuel cut off, he didn't have enough power to do anything except maybe change his hair color.

"Do you think you can use your new powers to get us out of here?" He made an encompassing gesture that took in the entire room. "You said these materials negate evil energy. What about the Heavenly stuff?"

She looked up. "Can't hurt to try."

Closing her eyes, she stood quietly for a moment. Then, suddenly, the entire room began to glow. The crystal columns lit up with blinding gold and silver light, and the marshmallow floor solidified.

Blaspheme reached out and took his hand just as a massive crack snaked across the ceiling. The room shook, lightly at first, and then it became a rolling, bucking ride that had them scrambling to avoid toppling columns.

"Fly!" she yelled. "I think we can punch through the roof."

Sounded like a good plan to him. He popped his wings, squeezed her hand, and they launched. Instinctively, he tugged her close, prepared to shield her with his body, but his incredible mate did something just before they hit the ceiling that blasted a hole right through it.

They shot upward, clearing the building and hitting a hot layer of volcanic gas that choked them both. They coughed as they ascended, but as the gas thinned, a new sensation hit him hard.

So much was happening. Battle and death. Pain, suffering. And somehow, he sensed hundreds of millions of new souls. No, more than that. What the fuck?

"I feel so much…evil and chaos," she breathed.

"I know, baby." He powered through it, climbing higher. As soon as he could flash, he was going to Sheoul-gra. Azagoth was the only one who could possibly generate that many souls. Had he sent them after Moloch?

They hit a draft that pushed at them, forcing them down, but once more, he punched through it, and suddenly, he felt his ability to dematerialize infuse his soul. With Sheoul-gra in his thoughts, he engaged the flash.

Abruptly, the world fell away. He and Blas spun out of control in a strange vortex that stretched and swirled. A mist surrounded them, and beyond it, he could make out images of broken buildings. Was that…Azagoth's palace?

Shit. They had to get out of here before they got sucked into some unknown realm with no way out.

A quick thought later, he flashed them out of there to Ares' island. Which was utter chaos, as well, with more people running around than he'd ever seen before. Hellhounds, Ramreels, and *Memitim*?

What the everliving fuck?

Blaspheme wobbled as her feet hit the sand. "Oh, my God, Rev," she breathed. "What was that place?"

"I'm pretty sure it's what's left of Sheoul-gra." He spotted Limos, ready for battle in her Samurai armor, and he waved her over.

"Where have you been?" Limos stalked right up to him, a bundle of black-haired rage. He didn't even have a chance to defend himself before she hauled off and slugged him. Hit him hard enough to smash him into a tree. "And that's for Wraith."

Blaspheme didn't miss a beat, never mind that the love of her life had just been clocked into next week. "What happened to Wraith?"

Limos jammed her fists on her hips and glared at him. "You want to tell her, asshole?"

"We don't have time for this." He popped himself back onto his feet. "Sheoul-gra is gone."

"We—what?" The angry light in Limos's violet eyes snuffed out. "Did you say *gone*?"

When she said it, it sounded even worse. It truly was a disaster of biblical proportions. "It's destroyed. The souls, hundreds of millions...*billions* of them, are loose and swarming Sheoul."

"No way." Limos's gaze grew distant as she grappled with the enormity of the situation. "Oh, wow, that's why he evacuated everyone here," she breathed. "Even the animals. Holy shit."

"We felt a battle. Like, massive on the evil scale," Blaspheme said. "That has to be what broke the containment spell on our trap. Moloch must be dead."

"I don't know about that," Limos said. "But Ares and Thanatos were here until a couple of hours ago, and then they got called away."

Ares, as War, was drawn to battles, where he was compelled to fight. Didn't matter which side, as long as he got to kill. Thanatos, as Death, would have been drawn by the large-scale death toll. He could fight if he wanted to, but he was mainly there to lurk and be a nightmare.

And oh, shit, speaking of nightmares... "Tell me Satan isn't free."

Rev breathed a sigh of relief when Limos shook her head. "Azagoth refused to release him. The battle has to be his. Satan isn't free. Azagoth is."

"I'm assuming he went after Moloch."

"Moloch took Lilliana," Limos said. "So...yeah."

The fucker took Lilliana, one of the few angels Revenant actually liked? Well, good for Azagoth for going ghastbatshit crazy and going after Moloch. Too bad everyone in the demon and human realms would pay for it.

"How did he do it? How the hell did he destroy Sheoul-gra and get out with billions of demons?"

Limos shrugged. "I didn't even know he was out until you told me." She folded her arms over her chest and scorched him with a hateful glare. "Now, you gonna tell your mate what you did to Wraith?"

Blaspheme looked at him expectantly. Like she expected that she was going to be really pissed.

He braced himself for a verbal flaying and a few nights on the couch. "Moloch said he'd kill you if I didn't remove Wraith's invincibility charm," he said to her. "It was the only way he'd tell me where you were." He glanced at Limos. "How bad's Wraith hurt?"

"Lethally."

Blaspheme slapped her hand over her mouth. "Oh, no."

"It's okay," Revenant reassured them. "I tethered his soul to his body so I could bring him back." At least, he hoped he could. He'd never really tried.

"His body was in Sheoul-gra," Limos said. "Everyone thought maybe Azagoth was powerful enough to release his soul. Turns out, he wasn't."

Then why had Azagoth been powerful enough to break out of Sheoul-gra? How had he gotten the kind of power he needed to—?

Suddenly, Revenant's power drain made sense. Had his twin experienced the same thing?

"Where's Reaver?"

Limos was looking at the horse glyph on her arm, and he wondered if her hell stallion wanted out. "We haven't seen him for a couple of days," she said. "I don't think he even knows about the baby."

"What baby?"

"Lilliana's. Some fallen angel smuggled her out of Sheoul. Ares and Cara swore to raise her as their own if anything happened to Lilliana." She glanced toward the palace. "I don't think Azagoth plans to come back."

Son of a bitch. This was worse than he'd thought.

Blaspheme looked up the path, following Limos's gaze. "I'm going to go check on Cara and the babies." She looked back at Revenant. "You go do what you need to do. Sounds like there's a lot of shit to clean up."

That was an understatement. Millennia-long agreements were up in smoke, an entire realm had been destroyed, and Sheoul was about to become even more hellish than it already was.

He needed to see Metatron. Which meant he had to do something he'd sworn not to do again.

He had to go to Heaven.

Chapter 41

Reaver was really damned sick of being on his knees. At least Hawkyn had been allowed to walk around in the chamber they'd been locked inside, but then, the Memitim didn't have the power to break out.

The door opened, and Reaver nearly fell over when Revenant and Metatron walked inside. Every step Revenant took, left blackened scorch marks on the floor, and when he stopped, black veins spread from where he stood. It would take a lot of work to repair the damage he did to the realm with his mere presence, so the fact that he was here meant that circumstances were dire.

He cocked his head and looked down at Reaver. "Dude. Sucks to be you."

"Why are you here? What's going on?"

"And where have you been?" Hawkyn demanded as he crossed the room.

Metatron unsnapped Reaver's restraints, and he surged to his feet, extending his wings to work out the kinks. "We're taking a trip to Hell," he said. "Not you, Hawkyn. You need to join the other Memitim on Ares' island."

"Other Memitim?" Reaver froze. "Ares' island? What are you talking about?"

There was a long, grim silence as if neither of them wanted to be the one to share whatever they'd come to tell him. Finally, Metatron spoke up.

"Sheoul-gra has been destroyed," he said, his voice as grave as Reaver had ever heard it. He listened in stunned silence as the male continued. "All the Memitim and Unfallen evacuated to Ares' island.

Hades and the fallen angels who guarded Sheoul-gra are loose, and the billions of souls that were once stored in the Inner Sanctum are fully-fleshed demons, some of which have found their way to the human realm."

"In other words," Revenant said, "all hell has broken loose."

Reaver stared wordlessly, his mind racing with the significance of what he'd just learned.

"There's more," Metatron said. Because, of course, there was. "The collapse of Sheoul-gra blasted a hole through the barriers between all the realms. They're all leaking together and forming…we don't know what, but the blast destroyed the Valley of Eve here in Heaven. Thousands of lives were lost. The human realm fared better, but only because the tear in the barrier occurred in Australia. The entire continent is on fire, but the loss of both human and animal life is minimal."

Well, that was relatively good news. Several years ago, during the near apocalypse caused by the breaking of one of the Horsemen's Seals, Australia had been claimed as a demonic territory of Sheoul. After the demons had been banished, Australia reverted back to a human domain, but it hadn't been repopulated yet.

"What about my father?" Hawkyn rasped. "Where is he?"

"We think he's with his army in Moloch's region," Metatron replied before turning back to Reaver. "Every available angel is addressing the demons in the human realm. The rest of us are meeting at Megiddo to deal with Azagoth."

Hawkyn stepped closer. "Then I'm going with you."

"No." Metatron took a moment to grimace at the black veins crawling up the cloudy crystal walls as Revenant's evil spread. "We don't know what we might have to do."

"Which is why you need me there," Hawkyn said. "Is Lilliana safe?"

"We don't know."

"Then you *definitely* need me there. My father doesn't trust any of you, and for good reason. But he trusts me."

"Does he?" Reaver asked, and Hawkyn shot him an irritated glance. Reaver hadn't meant it as an insult. Hawk had done the right thing by coming to him, but he doubted Azagoth saw it that way.

"He thinks I betrayed him," Hawkyn admitted. "And I did. But he knows I would never allow him to come to harm." He leveled his emerald gaze at Metatron, his steady, sharp focus so like his father's that Reaver nearly smiled. "You want me there."

"I agree," Reaver said to Metatron. "If Azagoth has gone off the deep end, we need every advantage we can get." He paused. "Do you know how he managed to destroy an entire realm?"

Revenant flexed his wings. "I think I might. Have you felt something weird? Like a drain on your powers?"

"A drain? No, I—" Reaver broke off, rolling his shoulders. The kink in his wings…it wasn't a kink, was it? It was as if just the tiniest twinge of electricity were passing through his wing anchors. "Shit. That bastard got ahold of our feathers, didn't he?"

"That would be my guess."

Metatron scowled at the evil that was infecting the room. "We need to go before we have to tear down this entire building. Hurry."

He led them out of the building, following a trail of blackened footsteps. Already, angels were working to mitigate the damage Revenant had caused, and they glared at Rev as he passed.

"Don't do it, brother," Reaver warned him as they walked, but the sinister glint in Revenant's eyes said he wasn't listening.

Rev had been making an attempt to retrace his steps to minimize the destruction, but now, he grinned, shot the angels the bird, and made a few extra footprints on the once-pristine white floor.

It was something Reaver would have done too, despite the warning. They were definitely brothers.

Once outside, Metatron flashed them all to Mount Megiddo, a place of angelic significance and the site of thousands of meetings and battles between good and evil. The hilltop was packed with angels from all the Orders, with an extra-large helping of archangels, who always liked to think they were in charge, even though thrones held the Heavenly reins right now.

"Metatron," Uriel barked as he strode toward them, red-faced with fury. "You had no right to release them." He shot Revenant a scornful glare. "And you? You finally decide to show your face and—"

Revenant blasted him with a bolt of lightning so black it sucked in the light surrounding it. Uriel melted into a puddle at their feet.

"Don't get your halos in a twist," Revenant called out to the shocked crowd. "He's just…resting. He'll be running in full douche-mode again in a couple of minutes." He clapped his hands and rubbed them together in dramatic enthusiasm. "Now, what were y'all talking about?"

"I swear," Phaleg growled as he peered down at the Uriel puddle, "the Council of Orders is going to vote to exterminate you someday, and I'm going to lead the charge."

Revenant's malevolent smile accompanied a flare of his massive wings. "I think Uriel might be a little lonely. What say you, Phaleg? Wanna mingle your juices?"

"Enough!" Metatron barked. "The longer we stand around doing nothing, the more damage Azagoth is causing. Revenant can get us to him. We just need to figure out what to *do* with him."

"Isn't it obvious?" Michael said. "He must be destroyed."

"Fuck you," Hawkyn growled, and Michael had the good grace to look uncomfortable. "Maybe you unfeeling assholes would be cool with your mate's wings being delivered to you, but Azagoth was not. He wasn't okay with his kids being murdered, either. Crazy, I know."

The entire group erupted in curses and arguments, some advocating for a less permanent approach to Azagoth, while others were firmly in the kill-first-ask-questions-never camp. The most vehement of the latter group stepped forward as Uriel's puddle began to ooze into the shape of the angel.

Reaver was morbidly fascinated by that. Revenant had some interesting and creative abilities.

"Azagoth should have been destroyed long before this," Camael said. "He's been unstable for eons."

Gabriel came forward in golden armor that had been the envy of every angel since the first time he'd worn it in battle, and the light reflecting off it had turned demons to ash in a ten-foot radius. He'd never told anyone where he'd gotten it, but Reaver suspected it had been made by elves, which most angels didn't even know existed.

"Camael, the only reason you want Azagoth dead is because your mate fucked him, and your sad little ego can't handle it." While Camael sputtered in outrage, Gabriel addressed the entire group, his wings lifting him off the ground so he could see everyone. "Yeah, I see the truth. How many of you can't deal with the fact that your mates or your daughters made Memitim with Azagoth? Sorel? Jeriah? Metatron?"

Reaver's head cranked around so hard he saw double. "Uncle?" He stared in disbelief. "Aunt Caila?"

Metatron closed his eyes and let out a long breath. When he opened them again, his gaze was steady and unapologetic. "Caila gave birth to a Memitim before we were mated. Neither of us has regrets." He turned to Gabriel. "I do not vote to destroy Azagoth."

"Look," Revenant said, stepping forward. "I'm going to make this easy for all of you. I'll deliver you to Sheoul-gra, and we can take him down. But I won't let you kill him."

"But—"

"No."

"You can't—"

"I said, no. And the next asshole who argues gets the puddle treatment."

Phaleg stormed toward them. "How dare you threaten us? How dare—?"

Phaleg's puddle was a little smaller than Uriel's, but it was no less disturbing. Uriel shuddered and kept his mouth shut.

"You people are so damned stupid," Revenant said. "That's why angels always take it up the ass against fallen angels. Ever watch *Spaceballs*? Explains it perfectly. Evil will always triumph because Good is dumb." Revenant grinned and waggled his brow. "Fortunately for you, I'm evil. Let's go."

Chapter 42

There were few things Azagoth hated more than being betrayed. That he hadn't seen through Maddox's deception would haunt him for the rest of his life. It would sit there on the shelf next to Lilliana's memory and his grief. It would eat away at him.

And it would eventually burn everything that was left of his decency to cinders.

Eventually was for suckers.

He was going to burn it all down now.

He stepped closer to Maddox, amused when Mad stepped back and slipped on a skull. All around them, the battle still raged, but Azagoth muted the sound. All those screams of pain were annoying. He only wanted to hear those kinds of screams from one person.

"Lilliana is dead because of you," he growled, his voice dripping with barely contained rage. "Your own brothers and sisters are dead because of you. My entire realm is destroyed because of you. And once you're dead, that'll be because of you, too."

"C'mon, Pops." Maddox's hood fell back, revealing a face in the final stages of healing, although there was still exposed muscle around his temples and jaw. "Don't you even want to know why? Or how?"

"Don't care." He exploded a couple of dozen demons that had been creeping up on them. "Bend over, kid. It's time for the belt."

Releasing a shout of pure hatred, he blasted Maddox with the angelic equivalent of hollow-point bullets. Maddox screamed, his body jerking wildly, blood splashing to the already blood-soaked ground with every invisible hit.

Azagoth hit faster. Harder. Bigger. The bullets were fifty-cals now, and Maddox was blowing apart.

Die, fucker.

He swung his scythe, but instead of knocking Maddox's head from his shoulders, the blade caught empty air.

Azagoth growled and spun around.

"Where are you?" he called out. "Don't make me send you to bed without supper."

"Oh, now you play the dad card?" Maddox's ragged voice, steeped in pain, came from everywhere and nowhere. "Fucking deadbeat." There was a slight pause and a low chuckle. "But, hey, thanks for whacking Moloch. That fucker skinned me alive. Said it was necessary. Probably was, but he enjoyed it way too much."

How was Maddox doing the invisible thing? How was he doing anything down here? As a Memitim who hadn't ascended to earn his wings yet, he shouldn't have this much power. Despite what he'd told Maddox about not caring about the answers to his questions, he really was curious.

"Show yourself, Maddox."

A low, blood-soaked chuckle echoed through the air. "It's Drakiin now."

"Dumbass." Azagoth snorted. "Do you know what it means?"

"Do you know what it means?" Drakiin mimicked. "Fucking duh. It describes who I was before I learned the truth."

"And what is that truth, *larvae*?" Azagoth exploded a couple of demons who were coming too close for comfort.

There was a long, drawn-out, dramatic pause. "That you're not actually my father."

Well, that would explain a lot. "Yeah? Great. Makes it easier to absolve myself of any blame for what a piece of shit you turned out to be."

Azagoth stood still and let his gaze go unfocused. Sometimes invisible objects became visible when you weren't looking specifically for them.

"You're still my—you're my *father*," Drakiin blurted, his voice shrill. "But you're not my blood."

Azagoth nearly laughed as he turned slowly, his gaze still unfocused. Drakiin had sounded so disappointed in Azagoth's reaction.

"When I was a baby, the Dark Lord had my blood swapped out for his. He planned for the day he would need to be freed from prison, and he knew you'd be the person to do it. Moloc and Bael were in on it since the beginning." Drakiin's laughter surrounded Azagoth, and he clenched his teeth in irritation. "It was fun watching you freak out about them, when all the while, I was the one pulling the strings."

Azagoth blinked, ruining his focus. "You?" He'd assumed Maddox had been a lackey, not a boss.

"Not at first. I didn't even know I was a sleeper agent until Aunt Flail showed up to recruit me for Bael and Moloc's cause. She woke up my royal blood and didn't even know it." He laughed again, sounding stronger. Recovered from the barrage of angelic rounds. "Bael and Moloc, the idiots, thought they were in charge. Moloch thought he was going to rule Sheoul until Satan was released. He had no idea *I* was giving him his power. That I was getting orders directly from the Dark Lord, which included slaughtering my brothers and sisters just to piss you off."

Well, fuck. Satan *had* been in contact with someone. Maddox. And it had been possible thanks to Maddox's proximity to Satan's prison, as well as the crack that had allowed some of his power to leak out.

"But you know what was the most fun? Watching Lilliana eat the treats I poisoned. I'm just sorry the whelp didn't die."

Concentrating on keeping his temper under control, Azagoth went unfocused again, so ready to end this.

"What's the plan now?" Azagoth asked, figuring if he kept Drakiin talking, he wouldn't be attacking. Maddox had never been good at multitasking.

"Do you think the Dark Lord doesn't have countless contingency plans in place?" Drakiin asked, and there…Azagoth spotted a blur in the air. "I'm going to make a few of them go active. After I kill you."

Azagoth blasted the blur with a gazillion volts of everything he had. Drakiin shrieked, becoming visible, his body sparking and sizzling. This was it. This would end the bastard—

Suddenly, the ground beneath them erupted, and Azagoth was thrown into the air, pelted with boulders and corpses. He spread his wings and stabilized, but something struck one, and he spun wildly out of control, crash-landing against the side of a mountain.

He lurched to his feet and shook it off as his body healed. Where was Drakiin?

The ground below still shook, and he watched as a massive, scaly paw reached out of the crater left by the eruption. Then another paw, tipped with massive claws like the first. The extremities were followed by a snout the size of a school bus.

The skeletal thing climbed out of the pit, a pitch-black dragon-like beast with giant wings of leathery membrane and sharp bone. Its eyes burned as orange as the deepest firepits as it dipped its head and allowed Drakiin to climb onto its back.

Son of a bitch. He was *not* getting away.

Azagoth sent a hellspawned vortex at them, a whirlwind of fire and summoned demons that clawed and bit at Drakiin and the beast. The creature screeched and set its sights on Azagoth. It came at him in a streak of smoke, its gaping maw spewing lava.

Azagoth dove off a rock ledge, barely avoiding a splash of molten pain. Spiraling around behind the creature, he hit it from the front with another pass of the hellspawned vortex. The beast reared up, knocking its rider from its back.

Drakiin tumbled, and Azagoth took a steep dive, but just as he was about to snatch Drakiin out of the air, the beast caught him with his claws and whipped him right out of Azagoth's hands.

No. This ended now. It *all* ended now.

Azagoth had lost most of what mattered to him, and what remained, his children, were safe with Ares.

He had nothing left to lose, and if he destroyed himself in the quest to end Drakiin and the remnants of Moloch's army, so be it.

Rage mounted as he chased the bone dragon across hundreds of miles of lava beds and over mountain ranges as expansive as the Rockies. They weaved through valleys and canyons, and when the dragon skimmed a lake of offal, it threw up a wave that nearly knocked Azagoth out of the air.

All the while, Azagoth sent volleys of attacks, constantly knocking the beast off course, and nearly unseating Drakiin a dozen times. One particularly well-placed strike took off part of the dragon's back foot. The thing let out a bellow and banked hard to the left—directly into the path of a plume of volcanic ash.

This was Azagoth's chance. He pressed the creature forward, the onslaught of his powers driving the thing toward the mouth of the volcano. Drakiin fired off a dozen different weapons that shocked Azagoth with the strength of their potency, but no matter how many times they struck him, no matter how much he bled or was burned, he kept going.

His rage and need for revenge was everything to him.

Everything.

The dragon shrieked as the acid steam surrounded it, the ash clogging its throat and dissolving its eyes. It was headed for the crater, and Drakiin tried to steer it away, his desperation intensifying with every flap of the beast's wings.

And that, apparently, was Drakiin's weakness.

No wings.

Smiling darkly, Azagoth rammed a spear of lightning right up the dragon's ass. The thing screamed. Drakiin screamed. The beast's wings locked and, suddenly, it was rolling in a death spin. Drakiin held on, but Azagoth nailed him with another spear, and then Drakiin was tumbling, along with the dragon, into the mouth of the volcano as it spewed lava into the sky.

Azagoth sailed across the crater, dodging plumes of steam and bullets of magma, searching for signs of the dragon or Drakiin. The heat scorched him, and the gasses burned his eyes, but still, he looked. Finally, he accepted that proof of death wasn't likely. They'd probably burned instantly in the magma chamber.

They were gone, but Azagoth wasn't done. He wouldn't be finished until there was nothing left of the enemy army.

Nothing left of *him*.

Crimson rage took over. He blasted everything in sight.

He was destruction personified as he strafed the armies—Moloch's, his, it didn't matter. Everything needed to die.

"*AZAGOTH!*"

Dozens of voices rang out as one.

As Azagoth banked around, an invisible force pressed down on him like the sole of a boot on an insect. He was thrust, fighting the entire way, to the ground, landing on a hill just south of Moloch's castle. As his boots hit the dirt, he found himself surrounded by angels. Dozens of them. Hundreds.

Oh, and Hawkyn. Perfect.

Fucking angels. How were they here? How *could* they be here?

Revenant.

That guy continuously lived up to his name. And he was the only being besides Satan who could open a forbidden-to-angels region in Sheoul.

How desperate Heaven must be to trust that Revenant wouldn't suddenly change his mind and trap them all.

The current King of Hell strode toward him, cloaked in darkness.

"Chill out, soul boy," Revenant rumbled.

"Where the fuck have you been?"

"Long story, tell you later." Revenant halted a few feet away, and Reaver flashed in next to him. "Stand down.

"You're going to have to destroy me," he said, and naturally, a bunch of haloed assholes agreed. A couple even cheered. He flipped them off, a real shocker to some of the sheltered holies who'd probably never had anything but a cushy desk job.

"We're not destroying you, jackass," Revenant said. "But we are taking you into custody." He gestured to Reaver. "Well, he is. And the bunch of dicks we brought with us. But you get the gist."

Yeah, he got the gist. And they were about to get the same treatment he'd given Drakiin and his bad luck dragon.

"Father!" Hawkyn yelled. "Don't do it!"

Too late. Azagoth was going out in a hail of hellfire and blood. Before the delegation of angels could so much as blink, he knocked Hawkyn out of the way and brought down a storm of condensed evil on the rest of them. Acid, fire, electricity, and a fuckton of summoned demons crashed into the group, sending them scattering like bowling pins.

And then he saw the most beautiful sight.

Hades and his thousand fallen angels. Fuck, yeah.

The angels, still recovering from Azagoth's attack, didn't see the fallen angels coming. The two groups came together like a thunderclap, and the earth rumbled all the way to the distant mountains.

Something hit Azagoth, something that knocked him to his knees and made him scream as his skin burned, and his bones were ground into powder. He heard Revenant's low growl next to his ear, even though the guy was thirty yards away.

"My brother warned you. Now, we do this the hard way. Which is my favorite, if you really want to know."

Azagoth froze, surrounded by golden light produced by a million strands of Heavenly twine, the stuff of legend. Stuff that required the abilities of hundreds of angels and that hadn't been used on anyone since Satan.

Stuff that hurt so bad that all Azagoth could do was moan...and eventually, pass out. His very last thought was that he hoped he wouldn't wake up.

There was nothing to wake up to.

Chapter 43

Lilliana had no problem getting out of the castle. In Flail's armor and with her face hidden by the cloak's hood, she'd been able to jog through the place with a purpose that kept anyone from stopping her. Not that they'd even given her a second glance, not with the apocalyptic battle taking place outside.

The sounds of war had penetrated the thick castle walls that crumbled with every explosion, every earthquake. Screams, booming vibrations that made Mal whimper, and the clank of metal on metal had come from all directions. Once, Lilliana had even stopped to listen to a voice she could have sworn was Azagoth's.

How she'd wished.

Maleficent had phased during the journey, leaving her visible only as a flicker of shadow. They'd managed to clear both the stronghold and the moat before the battle forced her into a narrow space between two crumbling outbuildings. Lilliana had lifted a sword from the barrel chest of an ogre, and she'd been forced to use it several times. As injured as she was, as powerless as she was without her angel abilities, Flail's superstrong armor had kept her from taking more damage, and she'd managed to take down three demons.

She'd lost count of the demons Mal had killed, which meant that they were no longer considered a part of Satan's army.

Revenant was back.

She'd wanted to do a freaking dance when she realized that. And then it had occurred to her that demons were still demons, no matter who they fought for, and the danger hadn't gone anywhere.

"Okay, Mal, we need to get to a Harrowgate. Can you sense one?"

Preferably one that was really close.

Mal cocked her head, and Lilliana repeated her question, but she had no idea if the hound understood. Maleficent let out a little whine and slunk out from between the buildings. Lilliana followed, dodging demons and axes meant for her head.

They threaded through the battle for what seemed like hours, climbing over bodies and slogging through the carnage that was sometimes a foot deep. The worst of it was a field of minced gore that extended as far as she could see. She didn't even want to know what had caused that.

The fighting got thicker ahead, and...shit, she hoped that Mal was taking her to a Harrowgate. For all she knew, Maleficent was leading her to the local pub.

"Mal!" she said in a harsh whisper. "I think—"

She broke off as a tingle of awareness spread over her skin. She turned, gasping at the sight of an armored rider on a massive warhorse. The rider cleaved heads from necks as the stallion bowled demons over with his powerful chest and thick legs.

And it was coming directly at her.

Thanatos.

She called out, but he kept coming, his sword poised to strike.

Something hit her like a train, yanking her arm as it jolted her out of the way. She felt the stallion's breath on her face a split-second before she saw fur, teeth, and blackness, and then blinding light as her feet hit sand.

Mal released her, but damn, her grip was going to leave tooth dents in the armor. Worth it for a save, though.

She took heaving gulps of fresh air that smelled like ocean and citrus, but she figured it would be weeks before she got the stench of Sheoul out of her nostrils.

Covering her eyes with her arm as she rubbed her wrenched shoulder, she tried to figure out where Mal had brought her.

It took about two seconds.

Ares' island. *Yes!* With a sob of relief, she threw her arms around Mal. "Why didn't you flash me from the garden hours ago, you strange animal?"

Mal didn't reply, and Lilliana realized she hadn't asked Mal to bring her here. It hadn't even occurred to her. She hadn't thought hellhounds could flash people, but she supposed it made sense since they were able to transport their live prey between the realms.

The hound put up with her hug for a couple of heartbeats, and then she backed out of the embrace and slunk off into the bushes. It broke Lilliana's heart the way it had when she'd lived here and had to watch the beast be harassed and bullied by the others. She was small for a hellhound, about half the size she should be, and hellhounds weren't known for their accepting natures.

After making sure that Mal was okay, she charged up the path and the stairs to the palace. One of the Ramreel guards blocked her as she reached the landing, but when he recognized her, he smiled. It was the first time she'd ever seen one smile, and it was a bit unsettling. Goat-headed things should not bare their teeth like that.

"Lilliana," he said gruffly. "We thought you were dead."

She'd thought the same thing a couple of times. "Surprise."

"Wait here." He jogged away, his hooves clacking on the stone pavers.

She waited, her face to the sky, taking in the sun she had truly believed she'd never see again. And, actually, this could be the last time. Once she was back in Sheoul-gra with Azagoth, she'd be back to abiding by the terms of her agreement with Heaven, and she wouldn't be allowed to leave. Especially if Azagoth were punished for releasing souls.

"Lilliana!" Cara shrieked in delight and ran toward her. "You're alive. I can't believe it!"

They embraced, laughed, cried, and when they finally pulled apart, Cara looked Lilliana up and down. "I love the new look. Badass." Her brilliant smile faded a little. "Oh, honey. Are you okay? How did you get away from Moloch? Where's Azagoth?" Before Lilliana could decide which question to answer first, Cara gave Lilliana's arm a little squeeze and guided her toward the front door. "I'm sorry I'm bombarding you with questions. Let's go inside."

A Ramreel met them with a tray of cold drinks, and Lilliana practically pounced on the guy. She drank a glass of lemonade and a rosewater iced tea before Cara even took her first sip. All she could think was that the servant had better not bring snacks, or she was likely to eat the tray, too.

Cara ordered sandwiches and gestured to the seating area off the kitchen, but Lilliana waved her off.

"I can't," she said, reaching for her third drink. "I'm too anxious. I need to get to Sheoul-gra. For some reason, Mal brought me here instead."

"Yeah, about that…" Cara trailed off, and Lilliana's gut did a slow roll, sloshing a couple of pints of liquid around.

"What is it?" Lilliana set down her glass on the table with a shaking hand. "Cara? Tell me."

"Follow me." Cara signaled to another of their Ramreel staff. "Contact Reaver. Tell him Lilliana is here."

Heart lodged securely in her throat, she followed Cara to the nursery. She was surprised to see two cribs.

And two babies.

Cara went to one of the cribs, and when she gently picked up the sleeping newborn inside, Lilliana let out a sob. She knew. Knew with all her heart and soul that the baby was hers. She couldn't take her tear-filled eyes off the beautiful bundle as Cara walked over.

"This is Raika," Cara murmured. "Your daughter."

Lilliana's heart burst as she took the infant in her arms. "I can't believe it." Tears blurred her vision, and she had to speak around the lump in her throat, but she wouldn't have it any other way. "I didn't think I'd ever see her again."

"She's perfect," Cara said. "But let me tell you, she's got a set of lungs on her. When she cries, the fish in the ocean hear her." She smiled and wiggled a tiny sock-covered foot. "That's where the name came from."

An anxious little twinge pinched her belly. She and Azagoth hadn't decided on names, and she hated that he'd had to come up with something by himself.

"Her name means ocean?" She looked up at her friend. "Please tell me it doesn't mean fish."

"Ah…no." Cara's cheeks heated. "It means hellmouth."

"What?" Lilliana glanced down at the sweet little face and wondered what had gone through Azagoth's head. "I can't imagine what he was thinking."

"It's an elvish word or something," Cara said. "I think he just needed something to call her, and seriously, just wait until you hear her cry."

Well, Raika was a pretty name. Maybe it could be a middle name. She couldn't wait to talk to Azagoth about it.

"You asked me if I knew where Azagoth was," Lilliana said. "What did you mean?"

Unease put creases at the corners of Cara's eyes. "The last I heard, he was in Sheoul, battling Moloch."

"So he *was* there." Lilliana grinned. He'd come for her. Her elation faded, however, as Cara stood there pensively, her weight shifting from foot to foot. "What? What is it?"

"He's going to be in a lot of trouble, Lilliana. He—"

"I know. He released a bunch of demons from the Inner Sanctum, and he broke out of Sheoul-gra, but I'm sure he'll get a slap on the wrist."

Even to her own ears, that sounded like bullshit.

"No," Cara said softly. "He didn't let just a handful of demons out. He let them all out. And then he destroyed Sheoul-gra."

Lilliana froze, unable to process what her friend had just told her.

"No," she said. "That just doesn't make sense. It doesn't..." She trailed off because it absolutely did make sense.

Azagoth had always been self-destructive, and if he'd believed she was dead or that her death was imminent, he'd implode. If she knew nothing else about her mate, she knew that.

And it was what she'd feared.

"Oh my God," she whispered. Holding the baby close, she sank into the rocking chair next to the crib. "What's going to happen to him?"

Cara went down on her knee next to her. "I don't know much. Ares and Thanatos were drawn to the battle hours ago. I didn't hear anything until a few hours ago when Revenant and Blaspheme showed up. He said Sheoul-gra was destroyed." She shook her head. "We knew Azagoth was planning something big, but we didn't know what."

"How?" she asked, so numb her voice was flat. "How did you know he was planning something?"

"He sent the Memitim and Unfallen to live here with us." She stroked Raika's black, wispy hair. "And he gave us the baby to raise if you didn't return."

A sob broke free of Lilliana's chest at the finality of it. Everything she knew was gone. Sheoul-gra might have been a bit of a prison, but it had been a prison with Azagoth. She'd rather be in Hell with him than in Paradise alone.

"I'm so sorry, hon." Cara handed her a tissue.

Lilliana nodded in gratitude. "What happened with Revenant?"

"Last I heard, he was on his way to talk to some important angels to figure out what to do about Azagoth. Blaspheme went to Underworld General. I guess she's a fully haloed angel now so she can't get in. I don't quite understand how it happened, but I'm not all that well-versed in the ways of your people."

As a human, Cara was an outsider in their world, but she was more familiar with it than she gave herself credit for.

"I have to know what's happening," Lilliana said, coming to her feet. "Azagoth needs to know I'm still alive."

Something beeped, and Cara dug her phone out of her shorts' pocket. "It's Harvester. She's coming to get you."

"Why?"

Cara grinned. "They got Azagoth." Her smile faded. "They've imprisoned him, and…they need you."

Lilliana hurried over to Cara. "Can you watch Raika for a little longer?"

"Of course." Cara took the baby, and although Lilliana knew she was leaving her in the best care available, it still hurt. But it wouldn't be long before they'd be together again.

She just hoped that *together* included Azagoth, as well.

Chapter 44

Azagoth had gone from one prison to another. His freedom had lasted fewer than twenty-four hours.

And he didn't give a shit.

Without Lilliana, he had nothing. If Heaven wanted him to rot here for all eternity, he was okay with that. But he'd rather they killed him.

They didn't seem inclined to do so, though. No matter how much he insulted them, or how viciously he attacked them when they tried to enter the cell, they just laughed.

Pricks.

They'd left him in a featureless white room that expanded so, as far as he could tell, there were no boundaries. Just...space. It was a unique kind of torture that only angels could devise.

White nothingness. Like what was inside their fucking skulls.

A black doorway sort of fizzed into existence, and Azagoth snarled. The cell negated his power, but he still had teeth, claws, and—

No way. He couldn't breathe. Couldn't move. Couldn't say a damned thing.

Lilliana!

Her smile when she threw herself through the doorway was the most amazing thing he'd ever seen. His heart exploded, and he charged at her, too late remembering he was about twenty feet tall and had fangs the size of her forearm.

He should have known it wouldn't matter to her. She threw herself against his chest and didn't flinch as he curled his claws around her.

"Azagoth," she murmured against his scales. "You're okay. You're safe."

Holy shit, he couldn't believe this was happening. "You're alive. Oh, thank fuck, you're *alive*." His voice rumbled from the dark depths of his beast, but as he held her, his body began to morph. A few heartbeats later, it was his arms around her, not his claws, and he could feel her delicate heat against his skin. "How is this possible? Moloch said you were dead."

"I almost was. But I got an assist from Maleficent, and she got me to Ares' island." She stepped back to look at him. "And I saw Raika." One chestnut eyebrow arched. "Hellmouth? Really?"

He laughed. "We can change it." Assuming he wasn't executed—or worse, imprisoned for all eternity. Either of which was a real possibility despite Heaven's refusal to kill him up to this point.

"No," she sighed. "I like it." She reconsidered for a moment. "Well, maybe as a middle name."

"Whatever you want." He'd give her anything in his power, which, right now, was limited.

She folded herself into his arms again, and he rubbed his hand on her shiny black armor. "This is a new look. I like."

"Yeah?" She rubbed her palm over the worn sleeve of his coat. "Well, you've got some sort of hotness going on yourself."

Her heart beat against his, lulling him into a sense of peace he hadn't had since before all of this began.

"I'm so sorry about everything. Sheoul-gra, Journey, and Maddox—"

"Shh." He stroked her hair, too lost in the moment to want to go back to the horrible places he'd been. They'd honor Journey and his sacrifice, and he'd tell her about Maddox. But not now.

"Oh, Azagoth," she breathed. "What's going to happen now?" She looked up at him, her expression fierce, matching the awesome armor she wore. "I won't let them hurt you."

Before he knew that Lilliana was alive, he hadn't cared about the answer to that question. But now, he very much had an opinion.

"Hey, assholes," he called out. "What's the plan?"

Clearly, they were waiting for a signal. The door shimmered open again. He groaned when Uriel entered, followed by Reaver, Harvester, Metatron, Jophiel, Gabriel, and that fuckwit, Phaleg.

"Uh-oh," he said. "All the biggies are here. Guess I'm in for a stern talking to."

Metatron didn't look like he was in the mood for humor. "We lost a lot of lives in the battle, Azagoth. Between you and Hades' fallens, our ranks were decimated."

"I'd say I'm sorry, but..." Azagoth shrugged.

Uriel glared. "And I'd say you could go to Hell, but even they don't want you."

"It's true." Harvester willed a pink tropical drink into her hand. "Revenant isn't thrilled with the mess you made. I mean, he's impressed—the tornado grinder was especially creative, if I do say so myself—but he's insisting that you not come back."

Metatron, dressed in formal white and gold robes, still looked pretty damned steamed. Azagoth didn't really know the archangel all that well, had only seen him twice—and that had been several thousand years ago, but he knew this was one guy he shouldn't piss off.

"You destroyed the Inner Sanctum and razed Sheoul-gra." Metatron's deep, resonant voice boomed in the space. "You released every soul. Every single one. And you didn't just release them as souls, which have limited power in the physical world. No, you made them corporeal, so there are now billions more demons swarming the realms."

"That's not entirely accurate," Azagoth said flippantly, and so much for his earlier thought about not pissing off Metatron. "Billions were killed during the battle."

Metatron's eyes glowed silver as he hit another level of angry. "And now, because you destroyed Sheoul-gra, there's nowhere for the souls of the dead to go. You have caused immeasurable damage to the Heavenly and human realms, and you broke the terms of your contract willfully and repeatedly."

"On top of everything, you're an asshole," Phaleg added.

"Huge asshole," Uriel agreed. "You deserve to die for what you did, but you're also really damned powerful, and we need you to help fight Satan, so our hands are tied."

"You *will* pay for what you've done." Jophiel was the only one among them wearing armor, its pristine white plates made to repel evil, and Azagoth had to lean into the pressure it exerted on his body. "*Many* people will pay for what you've done."

"Not enough," Uriel snapped. "He's getting off easy. I still say we should put him down."

"The Council of Orders has spoken," Metatron said. "He's not getting away with anything. He'll still be punished."

"I will not be caged again," Azagoth growled, and Lilliana nodded in agreement.

"That's not the punishment." Reaver, dressed casually in jeans and an untucked blue button-down, gave everyone but Harvester a don't-fuck-with-me look, and Azagoth got the feeling he was a big reason that Azagoth wasn't facing execution. "You're going to have a new duty."

Phaleg muttered something under his breath, and Uriel looked like he'd sucked on a lemon, but his voice was strong as he addressed Azagoth.

"As we prepare for the End of Days," Uriel said, "we're finding that we need more angels to help. Now, we have massive damage to repair, as well. We're going to pull all angels from their duties of escorting human souls through the Nether to their final destinations. Since the Inner Sanctum is destroyed and there's no place to hold demon souls, your *griminions* are jobless. They can take over for the angels until Hades rebuilds Sheoul-gra."

Azagoth didn't let them see his relief that they weren't going to destroy Hades for helping Azagoth and killing a bunch of angels. Oh, he had no doubt Hades would be spanked hard, but at least he was alive. The bastard had probably gotten a lot of leverage out of the eternal hellfire artifact Azagoth had given him.

"What about after the *griminions* go to work for Hades? Am I supposed to collect every human soul myself? That's gonna create quite the backlog."

Reaver shook his head. "You're going to build a team of Reapers."

"Reapers?"

"Humans who aren't shitty enough for Hell but who are too shitty for Heaven." Harvester smiled around her straw as she took a sip of her frothy drink. "I came up with the Reaper idea. Anyhoo, you're going to give them a chance to either redeem themselves...or doom themselves forever. Right now, they sit in Purgatory, but this will give them one last chance to wise up. Plus, it'll save a lot of time when Judgment Day comes. Ugh. Imagine having to pore over the records of all those morons."

Everyone nodded in agreement.

"That doesn't sound too bad," Azagoth said. "Which means, there's a catch."

"Oh, there's a catch." Phaleg's smile was downright sinister, and Azagoth tensed. "By releasing all those demons from Sheoul-gra, you've thrown off the balance of good and evil between the realms. Someone needs to clean up your mess before the End of Days, and it seems fitting that the one who was born into this disaster be the one to fix it."

Lilliana went taut, her armor creaking softly in the sudden silence. "What are you talking about?"

"Your daughter," Phaleg said with relish. "Yours and Azagoth's."

Azagoth felt the air rush from his lungs as Uriel continued.

"Azagoth, your actions have cursed her to a future not of her choosing, but a noble future nonetheless. She will be a hunter, responsible for tracking down the demons you released and returning their souls to Sheoul-gra."

"Oh, hell no," Azagoth growled.

"Absolutely not." Lilliana rounded on Uriel, her eyes glowing like hot amber. "My daughter will not have her future mapped out before she's even been here a week."

"Then Azagoth should have thought about that before he went insane," Phaleg shot back. "It's already done."

That announcement dropped like a silence bomb in the chamber, and Azagoth wheeled around to Reaver, the only person he trusted to explain this bullshit. "What the fuck?"

Reaver exhaled slowly. "Remember right after Bael's death, when I warned you not to kill Moloc? I gave you a message directly from the Moirai. 'If you kill him, all that you know, all that you are, will be destroyed.' Remember that? You've changed your life and the lives of everyone you know, of those you *don't* even know." Reaver waved away Harvester's offer of her drink before rethinking it, swiping it, and taking a substantial gulp. "Look," he said, as he handed the glass back to her, "I've broken rules and affected lives, so I'm not going to blow hypocritical smoke up your ass. But no matter how much good you think you're doing, no matter how right you think you are, there are always consequences."

Rage, hot but impotent, seared Azagoth's insides. Lilliana was furious too, but dammit, Reaver was right. Azagoth had known what he was doing when he did it, and he hadn't cared. Nothing had mattered but getting Lilliana back.

And he had.

He had his mate and his daughter, and his surviving children were safe with Ares. Unfortunately, his daughter would pay the price for what he'd done, and he'd regret that for the rest of his life.

But at least she was alive.

Still, he'd been elated at the prospect of one of his children growing up without a pre-determined destiny, and Lilliana had been, as well. He'd fucked that all to shit, hadn't he? He didn't even want to look Lilliana in the eye, afraid, for just a moment, of what he'd see.

What if she couldn't forgive him for this? What if Raika couldn't?

Lilliana exhaled as if she'd been holding her breath, but her voice was strong and even as she faced the angels.

"I don't like it, but we have years to work it out." She gave him a reassuring smile before gesturing to the unending whiteness. "Are we supposed to do it from here? This...what is it, anyway?"

"It's a prison we maintain in the human realm," Phaleg said, speaking more to Azagoth than to Lilliana. "The location is secret. Especially from evil assholes like you."

Suddenly, Phaleg's head whipped back, and he stumbled a few steps as if he'd been sucker-punched.

"Don't call him an asshole again," Lilliana growled. "And maybe you should consider shielding Heavenly power here, as well as Sheoulic power."

"You bi—" Phaleg broke off as Azagoth snared the fucker by the throat. "Don't say it. Seriously. You've seen what lengths I'll go to when it comes to my female."

Harvester laughed. "Please, Phaleg. Say it. I dare you."

"Let him go," Metatron intoned, clearly not overly concerned. Azagoth released the idiot, who rubbed his throat and glared. "We have a place set aside that you're going to love."

He'd said that with a straight face, so maybe this *place* wouldn't be too bad.

And, as it turned out, it wasn't.

Chapter 45

Reaver and Revenant materialized in Underworld General's parking garage, which was packed with cars. The black ambulances were in their designated spaces, and a paramedic Reaver didn't know was hosing one out.

"You ready?" Reaver asked, and Revenant cursed.

"This is not going to be pleasant."

Apologizing for Wraith's death, and worse, the unknown status of his soul? Yeah, Reaver wouldn't want to be in Revenant's size-ginormous boots right now.

The emergency department was strangely quiet and packed with far more staff than patients. As the doors closed behind them, Eidolon turned, and a moment later, everyone was staring. Some seemed curious, like Eidolon and Con, Sin's vampire mate, and Gem and Kynan. Others, namely the rest of Wraith's siblings, Shade, Sin, and Lore, were staring daggers at Rev.

Serena, Wraith's mate, stood quietly between Tayla and Runa, watching them with red-rimmed eyes as she rubbed the bare skin on her arm where Wraith's mate-*dermoire* had been.

"Oh, good, you're *all* here." So much sarcasm dripped from Revenant's voice that the floor was slippery with it. Frowning, he glanced around at the lack of activity. "Wouldn't know a war just took place."

"We've diverted the patient load to the clinic for a few minutes." Eidolon walked toward them. "The staff wanted a celebration of Wraith's life." He glared at a couple of smiling male nurses. "Although I think some of them are here to celebrate his death."

"I'm sorry about Wraith," Revenant said, sounding genuinely remorseful. "I liked him. Better than the rest of you. But Blaspheme's life was in danger—"

"You're still a bastard," Shade snarled.

"And that's not going to change," Revenant shot back.

"Cocksucker," Sin growled, and Reaver stepped in before things devolved.

"We came to tell you about Sheoul-gra," Reaver said. "It's been destroyed."

The room went silent. Even the patient wailing in one of the exam rooms had shut up.

"Destroyed?" Eidolon finally repeated, clearly rattled.

"Hell's fucking bells," Shade muttered. "This is going to blow up in a big way."

A murmur started up in the room as everyone grabbed their phones to text, tweet, or email the news.

Eidolon scrubbed his hand over his jaw. The demon looked exhausted; like he could use a month of sleep. Everyone in the room did.

"What about Lilliana?" he asked.

"She's okay. She and the baby are both fine," Reaver said.

"And...Wraith? Did Azagoth release his soul?" Serena lost all the color in her face. "What happened to the souls in Sheoul-gra?"

Poor Serena. She and Wraith had something special. They'd sacrificed their very lives for each other during their journey together, and Reaver wished he could give her some kind of positive update, but he only had bad news.

"Azagoth released all the souls in Sheoul-gra," Revenant said, and Serena let out a sob.

"So Wraith's soul is wandering around Sheoul, alone and lost?" She buried her face in her hands as Tayla's arm came around her.

Reaver shook his head. "Azagoth gave them physical form. He was somehow able to—" Reaver broke off as what he'd just said sank in.

Azagoth had given the souls in Sheoul-gra physical form.

Wraith's soul had been in Sheoul-gra.

Holy shit. Was...was it possible?

The Harrowgate flashed.

Somehow, Reaver knew even before it opened, that Wraith would step out.

The bastard did. Just walked out like he was arriving for work. Except he still wore the clothes he'd been in when he died, stained with dried blood. He looked as if he'd gone through a sausage grinder, and the invincibility charm was gone, but yeah, it was him.

"Fuck, man," Wraith said as he blinked at everyone. "What happened? Why the fuck did I wake up in the middle of a fucking battle—*oof*!"

Serena reached him first, hitting him with a full-body embrace so enthusiastic that he fell against the wall. The others piled on, and Reaver smiled so hard, his cheeks hurt.

Hell, yeah! That demon was impossible to kill.

"*He* should be named Revenant," Reaver said, glancing over at his twin.

Rev was still staring. "The fuck, man? That's crazy. Awesome, but crazy." He grinned. "I'm off the hook for killing him." He clapped Reaver on the back. "I'm outtie. I got a mess the size of a billion-demon war to clean up. See ya, bro."

Revenant took off, and Reaver was about to do the same when Wraith broke away from the pack of giddy demons, vampires, and werewolves, and came over.

"They said you could explain what happened," he said. "Did I save the world again?"

Reaver laughed. Wraith's death had actually nearly done the opposite, but Reaver merely threw his arm around his friend's shoulders and guided him back to his family so he only had to tell the story once.

"Sure, demon, sure."

Chapter 46

It didn't take long for Lilliana and Azagoth to settle into their new home.

Metatron had been right. It was amazing, and Lilliana loved it. Flaws and all.

The secret private island in the South Pacific was even larger than Ares' Greek hideaway. Which Azagoth thought was pretty cool.

Lilliana was just happy about the sunlight and beaches, as well as the fact that she was now free to leave, which meant she could visit Cara and Cat, or she could shop, or eat out…both she and Azagoth could.

But there was a downside.

And it was a big one.

The island had been created by angels a thousand years ago, under the direction of the very people who had warned Azagoth not to kill Moloc. The Moirai, sequestered angels who existed on another plane and in all timelines at once, had commissioned the construction of the island with some very specific instructions.

The Moirai had insisted that the island be a gateway to and from the Nether, a thin veil of existence between the human world and the Heavenly one, where the souls of humans went when their bodies died. There, they either waited to cross over, or they remained in the Nether, becoming lost and angry, their existences reported as ghosts by humans capable of seeing them.

Under the direction of the Moirai, angels cloaked the island inside a spatial anomaly, creating twelve hours of daylight during which only Azagoth, Lilliana, and Raika, as well as Revenant and Reaver, could enter or exit. It was kind of a bummer, but it was certainly better than being trapped inside Sheoul-gra.

And Azagoth had discovered one of the benefits of twelve hours of privacy.

The fact that no one could visit meant that he could walk around naked as much as he wanted.

Not a bummer for Lilliana.

They'd discovered that as soon as he put on clothes, his newly permanent Grim Reaper attire would replace them. He could get away with a pair of shorts, but that was the extent of his ability to wear anything that wasn't straight out of a dystopian hellscape.

Which meant that while Azagoth could visit friends, he couldn't exactly hang out in public places. Halloween could be fun, though.

And to be honest, Lilliana loved that look. Leather pants and boots. Weapon harnesses loaded with blades. A duster that shrouded him in darkness, and a scythe that wore flame like a bodysuit. When he lifted his hood, his face disappeared and freaked people out. And beneath it all, the engraved scythe necklace she'd given him.

Hot. So damned hot that he'd taken to lounging around the new house in his Reaper uniform just to see how long it took Lilliana to climb into his lap. Because…*hot.*

So, basically, they had twelve hours of freedom. Twelve hours inside the human realm.

The other half of the day, twelve hours inside the Nether…that was going to take some getting used to.

Every night, right around eight o'clock, a fog rolled in, cloaking the entire island in an eerie, otherworldly mist that changed the character and color of everything it touched. All objects turned black and white, with all the shades of gray in between. The palm trees twisted into gnarled claws that punched out of ashen sand. Human souls wandered around, some seeking the light, others running from it. The creatures that emerged from the ocean were like nothing that lived in the human or demon realms. Even the palatial estate, an updated relic from the days of ancient Rome, took on cracks and an ashen tone—but only on the outside.

As long as Lilliana or Azagoth closed the doors and windows, the Nether remained where it was supposed to be.

It was during those twelve hours that outsiders who could access the Nether could access the island, and it was during those hours that Azagoth did his reaping.

Lilliana figured things could be worse, and she liked being here more than she'd ever liked Sheoul-gra, so she couldn't complain. She did miss having the Memitim around, especially now that she could see things from their perspective, but she visited Cara often and got to see everyone then.

Azagoth's new job was going well, although until he recruited some Reapers, he was busier than either of them liked. The *griminions* couldn't sense non-evil death, so they mostly wandered around the Nether until they stumbled upon a soul that needed an escort, which meant that death collection was falling behind. Even worse, Heaven had already pulled all angels from the duty in order to address the chaos caused by the destruction of Sheoul-gra.

With nowhere to go, the souls of dead demons and evil humans were wreaking havoc, and demonic possessions had risen to alarming levels. According to Suzanne, Declan and his Demonic Activity Response Team had a massive backlog of calls and more investigations in progress than they could handle.

"Lilliana!" Azagoth's voice rang out from inside the house, barely audible over the churning waterfall at the far end of the pool. The Moirai had been very luxurious in their vision for this place.

Apparently, on the day Lilliana had mated Azagoth, the Moirai had been confident enough of their future that they'd demanded a modern update to the housing structure and its landscaping.

"I'm in the pool," she called out.

He materialized on the deck before her voice even faded away. And he was gloriously naked. But then, so was she.

This place was *great*.

"I should have known," he said as he started down the pool steps. "Where's Raika?"

"What, you missed the giant, slobbering hellhound over there in the shade?"

He paused on the bottom step and glanced over at where Mal was sleeping, sprawled at the base of Raika's bassinet as it sat in the shade of the cabana.

They still hadn't discussed another name for her. Well, they had, but it had gone nowhere because every time they tried, Raika had cried, reminding them why Jedda had called her that in the first place.

Someday, Lilliana swore. But for now, she and Azagoth were all about just being happy.

"I saw Revenant today," Azagoth said as he moved toward her with the lazy nonchalance of a prowling shark.

She let herself drift backward, and his mouth twitched in a predatory smile. "Yeah?"

"Yeah." He came closer, the water now to the bottom of his pecs. She flutter-kicked a little, putting more distance between them. "He said Sheoul's in chaos, and he wants to kick my ass. I'm thinking we'll want to hold off inviting him and Blaspheme over for a barbecue."

She laughed, but he was probably right. "Did he say how Blaspheme is doing? I know she couldn't have been thrilled about getting her halo."

Angels didn't actually have halos, but it was a fun idea dropped right into their laps by human imagination.

Azagoth took another step closer. "Eidolon can't alter the enchantment that prevents angels from entering the hospital and clinic, but he's building an addition that'll allow her to work. They can bring patients to her, and she can also treat angels."

Since angels generally self-healed or could go to Heavenly healers, Lilliana didn't think Blaspheme would have many angel patients. But she supposed that depended on how many angels were doing sketchy things in the human realm and would rather be treated by Blaspheme than by anyone in Heaven.

"I'm happy for her," Lilliana said. Azagoth was now nipple-deep, the water lapping at them the way she wanted to. "We're supposed to have lunch in Paris next week."

She grinned simply because she'd gotten to say that. She had such amazing friends now, and for the first time, she could meet them in the outside world.

"I talked to Cara today," she added as Azagoth began to circle, the water licking at the base of his throat.

"Mm-hmm." Sunlight glinted off the water and played on the harsh angles of his tan face, and when he spoke, his fangs gleamed. "Go on."

He didn't seem to be paying attention to anything she was saying. She'd quiz him later, but right now, she'd play along. She was enjoying his game of predator versus prey.

She shivered with anticipation.

"Well," she said, making a show of utter obliviousness by lying back to float, water sluicing from her breasts as they breached the surface. "She mentioned that Asrael is safe on the island, but he might be lonely, so you should consider sending a few griminions to keep him company. She also said that Zhubaal and Vex are working with Thanatos to hunt down the third parking lot angel. Some chick named Fearr. And, apparently, Razr decided to go to work for Ares. He and Jedda are getting a flat in Greece. I guess Jedda found a lot of some sort of magical stone there or something."

Razr's Gem Elf mate had a particular talent for locating rare gems and powerful crystals, and she'd earned a fortune, even though she limited her sales to non-evil entities.

"And I know you saw Hawkyn just a couple of days ago, but he and Aurora want us to visit their new place in Switzerland."

Azagoth had been spending a lot of time with Hawkyn—and all of his children. Just yesterday, she, Azagoth, and Raika had gone to Ares' island for brunch, and while she'd hung out with Cara, he'd spent hours with the Memitim. He'd even gone out surfing with his youngest children.

The idea of the Grim Reaper surfing still made Lilliana giggle. Next time someone needed to get it on video.

"Uh-huh." Azagoth surged closer, his wake making her bounce gently in the water.

She splashed her hand playfully, doing her best imitation of a seal that had no clue a great white was almost upon it.

"Oh, and it looks like Hades and Cat are getting a place in Sydney while he works on building a new Sheoul-gra, but she said he wants to call it something else. Tartarus, I think. He's fond of Greek mythology. Wants to create some Titans, too—"

Azagoth caught her, and she squealed in faux outrage. Laughing and splashing, he lifted her against him, and she wrapped her legs around his waist, pinning his erection against her sex.

"We haven't done this in the pool yet," she murmured as he licked the water off her neck.

"That's because your favorite place for sex is in the ocean." He lifted her just enough to settle her on his cock, and she moaned as he slowly lowered her, her sensitive tissues stretching to accommodate him.

"I don't know," she breathed, her body sparking to intense life in an instant. "Pool sex might be equally as great."

He dipped his head and captured her breast. His tongue was magic as he lapped first at one nipple, and then the other.

"Equally? Nah. I know how to make pool sex your favorite water sport," he murmured against her skin.

"I don't think that's possible—"

In the blink of an eye, he had Lilliana flat on her back on the deck, her legs dangling over his shoulders as he stood between them in the pool. His wicked grin announced his intentions as he leaned forward and bit into the soft flesh of her inner thigh.

"Yes," she whispered, repeating it again, louder, when he filled her entrance with his finger.

He pumped in and out, intermittently using the tip of his finger to circle the slick outer flesh before thrusting deep inside again. His lips sucked gently at her vein, sending electric currents of ecstasy to every nerve ending. Everything felt too sensitive to touch, and yet she wanted to rub her entire body against him.

He stopped way too soon, but she couldn't complain when he licked his way inward and replaced his finger with his tongue.

"Azagoth," she cried as the first stirrings of climax coiled in her womb.

Sensation overwhelmed her as he thrust his tongue deep and curled it up against the pillow of nerves there that made her scream.

But he didn't let her come. She was right there. Right. Damned. There.

His hands tightened on her ass as he tilted her pelvis upward and dove in again, this time licking her from her core to her clit. Long, hard strokes with alternating quick flicks of the tip of his tongue. Oh, damn…oh, yes…he was so good at this…

She screamed again as her climax took her. He worked her through it, his tongue gentling as she came down. But before the last spasms stopped, he had Lilliana in the pool again, this time in the space behind the waterfall and slide, pounding into her as the water crashed down around them.

His hips rolled into her, her body sliding against the slick stone at her back. She watched him through slitted eyes as he took her, his head thrown back in glorious male ecstasy, his jaw clenched, the muscles in his neck flexing.

"See?" His guttural, sex-smoked voice flowed through her like an aphrodisiac. "This is better than fucking in the ocean."

Okay, so pool sex beat ocean sex. But she wasn't going to admit it.

"I need more convincing," she said, panting to stave off the imminent orgasm.

"Mmm...wait until you see my plans for the diving board."

Oh, yeah. Just thinking about it, yep, that did it, and the climax crashed down on her in a tidal wave of ecstasy. Azagoth went taut, jerking wildly as he came in a roar that made Mal sit up and growl.

And that woke the baby.

Raika really was well-named.

"I got her," Azagoth said as he lowered Lilliana to her unsteady legs. "I haven't seen her all night."

He flashed to Raika, and Lilliana watched from behind the waterfall as he scooped their daughter into his powerful arms. His smile was brilliant, his gaze overflowing with love as he made adorable cooing noises.

"I'll be right back," he called to Lilliana. "I'm going to change her diaper."

Lilliana sighed and fell back in the water to relax. She had it all. *They* had it all. There had been significant consequences to what Azagoth had done, and a lot of people had died along the way. They still mourned Journey, and all of Azagoth's murdered children, and Reaver wasn't sure Wraith could ever get his immunity charm back.

But Azagoth had also ensured that Satan's prison wasn't even accessible for decades, maybe centuries since there was no Inner Sanctum through which to access it.

And, best of all, Azagoth had finally allowed himself some happiness. The job change had already affected him now that he was away from the constant malevolent radiation that had contaminated Sheoul-gra. Now that he no longer had to deal with evil beings daily, their hatred and ugliness no longer weighed on him.

He was free. They both were.

What that meant remained to be seen, but with Azagoth at her side, Lilliana was ready to find out.

Consequences be damned.

* * * *

The legacy continues...

It's a gritty new world.

Nearly three decades after the events of REAPER, the Earth is a different place. The secret is out. The existence of demons, vampires, shapeshifters, and angels has been revealed, and humans are struggling to adapt. Out of the chaos, The Aegis has risen to global power on the promise of containing or exterminating all underworlders.

Standing in their way is the next generation of warriors, children of demons and angels and the Four Horsemen of the Apocalypse.

See how they become legends in their own right.

A new series from Larissa Ione is coming soon...

Check her website at www.larissaione.com and sign up for her newsletter for the latest updates and news! And be sure to stay current with 1001 Dark Nights for more novellas from the Demonica world!

Also from Larissa Ione

Cipher: A Demonica Underworld Novella
By Larissa Ione

It's been seven months since Cipher, an Unfallen angel who straddled a razor thin line between good and evil, woke up in hell with a new set of wings, a wicked pair of fangs, and a handler who's as beautiful as she is dangerous. As a laid-back cyber-specialist who once assisted guardian angels, he'd been in a prime position to earn back his halo. But now, as a True Fallen forced to use his talents for malevolence, he must fight not only his captors and his sexy handler, but the growing corruption inside him…before the friends searching for him become his enemies and he becomes his own worst nightmare.

Lyre is a fallen angel with a heart full of hate. When she's assigned to ensure that Cipher carries out their boss's orders, she sees an opportunity to take revenge on those who wronged her. All she has to do is appeal to Cipher's burgeoning dark side. But the devastatingly handsome fellow True Fallen has other ideas — sexy ideas that threaten to derail all Lyre's plans and put them in the path of an approaching hell storm.

Danger and desire explode, even as Cipher and Lyre unravel a sinister plot that will fracture the underworld and send shockwaves into Heaven itself…

* * * *

Dining with Angels: Bits & Bites from the Demonica Universe by Larissa Ione, Recipes by Suzanne M. Johnson

In a world where humans and supernatural beings coexist — not always peacefully — three things can bring everyone to the table: Love, a mutual enemy, and, of course, food.

With seven brand new stories from the Demonica universe, New York Times bestselling author Larissa Ione has the love and enemies covered, while celebrity Southern food expert Suzanne Johnson brings delicious food to the party.

And who doesn't love a party? (Harvester rolls her eyes and raises her hand, but we know she's lying.)

Join Ares and Cara as they celebrate a new addition to their family. See what Reaver and Harvester are doing to "spice" things up. Find out what trouble Reseph might have gotten himself into with Jillian. You'll love reading about the further adventures of Wraith and Serena, Declan and Suzanne, and Shade and Runa, and you're not going to want to miss the sit down with Eidolon and Tayla.

So pour a glass of the Grim Reaper's finest wine and settle in for slices of life from your favorite characters and the recipes that bring them together. Whether you're dining with angels, drinking with demons, or hanging with humans, you'll find the perfect heavenly bits and sinful bites to suit the occasion.

Happy reading and happy eating!

* * * *

Her Guardian Angel: A Demonica Underworld/Masters and Mercenaries Novella
by Larissa Ione

After a difficult childhood and a turbulent stint in the military, Declan Burke finally got his act together. Now he's a battle-hardened professional bodyguard who takes his job at McKay-Taggart seriously and his playtime – and his play*mates* – just as seriously. One thing he never does, however, is mix business with pleasure. But when the mysterious, gorgeous Suzanne D'Angelo needs his protection from a stalker, his desire for her burns out of control, tempting him to break all the rules…even as he's drawn into a dark, dangerous world he didn't know existed.

Suzanne is an earthbound angel on her critical first mission: protecting Declan from an emerging supernatural threat at all costs. To keep him close, she hires him as her bodyguard. It doesn't take long for her to realize that she's in over her head, defenseless against this devastatingly sexy human who makes her crave his forbidden touch.

Together they'll have to draw on every ounce of their collective training to resist each other as the enemy closes in, but soon it becomes apparent that nothing could have prepared them for the menace to their lives…or their hearts.

* * * *

Razr: A Demonica Underworld Novella by **Larissa Ione**

A fallen angel with a secret.
An otherworldly elf with an insatiable hunger she doesn't understand.
An enchanted gem.
Meet mortal enemies Razr and Jedda...and the priceless diamond that threatens to destroy them both even as it bonds them together with sizzling passion.

Welcome back to the Demonica Underworld, where enemies find love...if they're strong enough to survive.

* * * *

Z: A Demonica Underworld Novella by **Larissa Ione**

Zhubaal, fallen angel assistant to the Grim Reaper, has spent decades searching for the angel he loved and lost nearly a century ago. Not even her death can keep him from trying to find her, not when he knows she's been given a second chance at life in a new body. But as time passes, he's losing hope, and he wonders how much longer he can hold to the oath he swore to her so long ago...

As an *emim*, the wingless offspring of two fallen angels, Vex has always felt like a second-class citizen. But if she manages to secure a deal with the Grim Reaper — by any means necessary — she will have earned her place in the world. The only obstacle in the way of her plan is a sexy hardass called Z, who seems determined to thwart her at every turn. Soon it becomes clear that they have a powerful connection rooted in the past...but can any vow stand the test of time?

* * * *

Hades: A Demonica Underworld Novella by **Larissa Ione**

A fallen angel with a mean streak and a mohawk, Hades has spent thousands of years serving as Jailor of the Underworld. The souls he guards are as evil as they come, but few dare to cross him. All of that changes when a sexy fallen angel infiltrates his prison and unintentionally starts a riot. It's easy enough to quell an uprising, but for the first time, Hades is torn between delivering justice — or bestowing mercy — on the beautiful female who could be his salvation...or his undoing.

Thanks to her unwitting participation in another angel's plot to start Armageddon, Cataclysm was kicked out of Heaven and is now a fallen angel in service of Hades's boss, Azagoth. All she wants is to redeem herself and get back where she belongs. But when she gets trapped in Hades's prison domain with only the cocky but irresistible Hades to help her, Cat finds that where she belongs might be in the place she least expected...

* * * *

Azagoth: A Demonica Underword Novella by Larissa Ione

Even in the fathomless depths of the underworld and the bleak chambers of a damaged heart, the bonds of love can heal...or destroy.

He holds the ability to annihilate souls in the palm of his hand. He commands the respect of the most dangerous of demons and the most powerful of angels. He can seduce and dominate any female he wants with a mere look. But for all Azagoth's power, he's bound by shackles of his own making, and only an angel with a secret holds the key to his release.

She's an angel with the extraordinary ability to travel through time and space. An angel with a tormented past she can't escape. And when Lilliana is sent to Azagoth's underworld realm, she finds that her past isn't all she can't escape. For the irresistibly sexy fallen angel known as Azagoth is also known as the Grim Reaper, and when he claims a soul, it's forever...

About Larissa Ione

Air Force veteran Larissa Ione traded in a career as a meteorologist to pursue her passion of writing. She has since published dozens of books, hit several bestseller lists, including the New York Times and USA Today, and has been nominated for a RITA award. She now spends her days in pajamas with her computer, strong coffee, and fictional worlds. She believes in celebrating everything, and would never be caught without a bottle of Champagne chilling in the fridge…just in case. After a dozen moves all over the country with her now-retired U.S. Coast Guard spouse, she is now settled in Wisconsin with her husband, her teenage son, a rescue cat named Vegas, and her very own hellhounds, a King Shepherd named Hexe, and a Belgian Malinois named Duvel.

For more information about Larissa, visit www.larissaione.com.

Sign up for the 1001 Dark Nights Newsletter
and be entered to win a Tiffany Lock necklace.

There's a contest every quarter!

Go to www.1001DarkNights.com to subscribe.

As a bonus, all subscribers can download
FIVE FREE exclusive books

On behalf of 1001 Dark Nights,

Liz Berry and M.J. Rose would like to thank ~

Steve Berry
Doug Scofield
Kim Guidroz
Jillian Stein
Social Butterfly PR
Dan Slater
Asha Hossain
Chris Graham
Chelle Olson
Jessica Johns
Dylan Stockton
Richard Blake
and Simon Lipskar

Made in the
USA
Columbia, SC